Liverpool Taffy

Katie Flynn has lived for many years in the Northwest. A compulsive writer, she started with short stories and articles and many of her early stories were broadcast on Radio Mersey. She decided to write her Liverpool series after hearing the reminiscences of family members about life in the city in the early years of the twentieth century. She also writes as Judith Saxton. For several years, she has had to cope with ME but has continued to write.

Praise for Katie Flynn

'Arrow's best and biggest saga author.
She's good'
Bookseller

'If you pick up a Katie Flynn book it's going to be a wrench to put it down again'
Holyhead & Anglesey Mail

'A heartwarming story of love and loss'
Woman's Weekly

'One of the best Liverpool writers'
Liverpool Echo

'[Katie Flynn] has the gift that Catherine Cookson had of bringing the period and the characters to life'
Caernarfon & Denbigh Herald

KATIE FLYNN

Liverpool Taffy

arrow books

Published by Arrow Books in 2000

17 19 20 18 16

Copyright © Katie Flynn, 1994

Katie Flynn has asserted her right under the Copyright,
Designs and Patents Act, 1988 to be identified as the author of this work

First published in the United Kingdom in 1994
by William Heinemann Ltd

This edition first published in 1995
by Mandarin Paperbacks and reprinted 10 times

Arrow Books
The Random House Group Limited
20 Vauxhall Bridge Road, London SW1V 2SA

www.randomhouse.co.uk

Addresses for companies within The Random House Group Limited
can be found at:
www.randomhouse.co.uk/offices.htm

The Random House Group Limited Reg. No. 954009

A CIP catalogue record for this book
is available from the British Library

ISBN 9780099416098

The Random House Group Limited supports The Forest Stewardship
Council (FSC®), the leading international forest certification organisation.
Our books carrying the FSC label are printed on FSC® certified paper.
FSC is the only forest certification scheme endorsed by the leading
environmental organisations, including Greenpeace. Our
paper procurement policy can be found at
www.randomhouse.co.uk/environment

MIX
Paper from
responsible sources
FSC® C016897

Printed and bound in Great Britain by Clays Ltd, St Ives PLC

For Margaret Campbell of Eastham,
who understands better than most why I write
these books;
thanks, Margaret

Chapter One

'Poor but honest, that's wharr I always say. Oh aye, we're poor but honest, us Kettles. Well known fact, that. Pass us one of them big brown bags, chuck.'

Biddy O'Shaughnessy reached for the pile of bags on the little wooden shelf by the rear door of the shop and handed it across to her employer, who stood, stomach pressed against the small counter, grubby fingers clutching the small enamelled scoop, cracking a joke with Sister Eustacia whilst she weighed out forty tiny bags of peppermints and then put them, one by one, into the big brown bag bought specially for such customers.

'That's the last, Sister,' Ma Kettle said, scrunching the top of the fortieth bag with a deft movement of her fat fingers. 'And 'ow about a little extry one, eh, jus' for luck, now?' She slid a few peppermints into the last bag without weighing them, twisted the top and added it to the rest of the sweets in the big brown bag. 'I don't doubt you'll mek good use of it, Sister Eustacia,' she added piously. 'Poor but honest, like meself.' She turned to Biddy, hovering behind her. 'Go and put the kettle on, Bid,' she ordered. 'We'll have a nice cuppa, me an' the Sister here, now we've completed our business.'

Sister Eustacia murmured a token refusal, whilst sitting herself down on the high stool which Biddy had towed round from behind the counter in readiness. It would have hurt Ma Kettle deeply had Sister Eustacia not accepted her invitation, albeit with pretended reluctance, and both parties – all three if you included

1

Biddy – knew it. So Sister Eustacia hauled herself up onto the stool, displaying several inches of grey woollen stocking and a pair of black lace-up boots in the process, and Ma Kettle squatted down on her own creaking wooden chair, hoisting her petticoats up as she did so and revealing, in her turn, a pair of extremely fat and dirty knees.

'*Hexcuse* me takin' the chair and givin' you the stool, Sister,' she said with a chuckle as she did every month. 'But you're the right shape for leapin' aboard a stool, whereas it's all I can do to gerron me chair come tea-time, when I've 'ad a busy day in the shop an' me rheumatics start a-playin' up.'

It was true that Sister Eustacia was tall and thin, but the idea of her leaping always brought a little smile to Biddy's lips. The nun was so gaunt and serious! Still, both women were sat down so it was time she made the tea and brought it through, otherwise Ma Kettle wouldn't half give it to her when her customer had left. Others wouldn't come into the shop whilst Sister Eustacia was there out of respect, so every minute she lingered they were losing trade. Which did show that Ma Kettle wasn't such a bad old stick after all, though one of these days, Biddy thought apprehensively as she measured a tiny amount of tea into the big brown pot, one of these days she'll be struck dead for the lies she tells . . . poor but honest, indeed! Ma Kettle had been weighing her thumbs as well as her sweets for as long as she had been selling licky sticks and sherbet fizz, and that was a long, long time. Biddy's mother remembered her own mother telling her to watch Ma Kettle's fingers on the scale and that must have been at least twenty years ago.

'Get a move on wi' that tea, chuck,' Ma Kettle shouted. 'Me tongue's hangin' out like an Abrahams carpet on a windy day . . . . Sister's fair parched, she told me so a moment's gone.'

There was a murmur from Sister Eustacia, but Biddy, standing in the little back room and ladling a spoonful of conny onny into each large, chipped white cup, ignored the nun's polite disclaimer. Sister Eustacia would be on her way back to the convent with her shopping, she would have been out most of the morning and would doubtless be glad of a cup of tea.

'Comin' up, Ma,' Biddy called back, therefore, arranging the cups on a small wooden tray and hurrying through to the shop. 'Oh, drat, I forgot the biscuits.'

Ma Kettle gave her assistant an alarmed glare, but it was too late; Biddy, hurrying into the back room, chuckled to herself, but only under her breath. Sister Eustacia just loved biscuits, she could get through half a pound whilst Ma Kettle was sipping at her hot tea, and since Ma Kettle was fond of a biscuit too she usually 'forgot' to produce her tin until Sister Eustacia had finished her tea and was about to climb down off her stool. By then, of course, Sister Eustacia's conscience would be prodding her about the length of time she had taken to buy forty ounces of mints for forty sweet-starved sisters, so she would hastily crunch down one biscuit, or possibly two, but would not stay to demolish the entire tin.

In the back room again, Biddy reached down the square biscuit tin with the picture of the Coronation of George V on the lid, then took pity on Ma Kettle and shook half-a-dozen Digestives onto a white pot plate. The old girl shouldn't lie about her honesty or weigh her thumbs in with the kid's sweets, but it was scarcely Biddy's place to punish her. Biddy was fairly sure that Ma Kettle underpaid and overworked her, but at least it was a job and with an ailing mother on her hands, any money Biddy could earn was more than welcome. So she took the plate of biscuits through and was rewarded by Ma Kettle's relieved smile when she saw the tin was missing . . . though Sister Eustacia, poor thing, just looked pleased. A biscuit is probably a treat to her, Biddy thought, standing the plate on the counter top and then picking up her duster once more. Her own Mam loved a biscuit – not that she saw many of them, not since losing her job at the big department store in the city centre where she had risen to a top saleslady position because of her nice voice and manners.

'Leave that, chuck,' Ma Kettle said presently, when Biddy's duster had reached the end of the shelf. 'Get your coat . . . . Sister Eustacia would be glad of an 'and wi' all that shoppin'. I can spare you for an hour or so.'

'Thank you, Mrs Kettle,' Sister Eustacia said gratefully, climbing stiffly off her stool and standing her cup down on the counter. 'I do seem to have a heavy load today, Bridget's strong young arms will be a great help.'

And I'm the right build for a dray-horse, Biddy said sourly, but once again, only inside her head. At fourteen she had her mother's dark curls and blue Irish eyes but her body was a child's still, unformed, skinny and fragile-looking. I'm not fragile, though, Biddy reminded herself sturdily, taking her thin jersey down from the peg on the back of the door. I'm all right with my own shopping, and fetching bags of sugar and that, but Sister Eustacia buys for forty – one of these days I'll break my bloomin' back carting her shopping right across the city and then up Mount Pleasant. What's more, it doesn't do my shoes much good, and I'm just bound to dirty me blouse and I doubt I'll be able to wash it and get it dry until Sunday the way the weather's been lately.

Biddy always wore her best things to come to work, though – Mam insisted. A white blouse which she had bought in St Marks jumble sale and a navy pleated skirt, which was more darn than pleat, looked well on her, a good deal better than the quantities of skirts, petticoats, shawls and other swathings which covered Ma Kettle's bulging person. Biddy didn't wear stockings despite the fact that it had been a wet and damp September, for you had to be very rich to wear such things, but she had shoes – they had been Mam's best until the racking cough had caused her to be given her cards because her head of department, Mrs Browning, said she was turning the customers' stomachs, spitting into her handkerchief the way she did.

But Mam had not been best pleased when Biddy had first announced that she was going to work for Ma Kettle after school and on a Saturday.

'She's a mean old body,' Mam had said, tying her abundant blue-black hair up in curl-papers before going to bed. 'She'd cheat her own mother, that one. What's she paying you?'

Informed that it was one and sixpence a week, she had snorted. 'Well, it's a start, chuck. But if she treats you bad you're out – understand? We can manage on my money – we've done so ever since your Da died.'

But that had been six months ago and now that Biddy was full time she got three and sixpence, which was a lot better. Besides, so much had happened in those six months, most of it unpleasant. The cough, which was only a tiny little hacking cough, had got worse and worse. Mam went up to Brougham Terrace, to the Health Clinic there, but the doctor was in a bad mood and just gave her a linctus and told her to stop smoking – she had never smoked a cigarette in her life – and stay in nights. Mam had never gone out at night like some people's mams did, she and Biddy sat over the fire, reading, writing, talking . . . laughing.

We were great laughers, Biddy thought wistfully now, pulling her old jersey down over her head and returning

5

as slowly as she dared to the shop. We could laugh over almost everything, Mam and me. I wonder when it stopped? When blood came with the cough and frightened the pair of us into fits, she supposed, standing with her head bent whilst Ma Kettle hung the brown paper packages up her arms as though she were some exotic sort of hatstand and then proceeded to pile the rest on top. It was enough to scare anyone, that blood – so bright, so scarlet! But it hadn't got any worse and until her Mam had been sacked they had honestly thought that it would pass.

'We'll go to New Brighton for a weekend before the summer's over,' Mam had said. 'That'll set me up for the Christmas rush. I'm always grand over Christmas if I have a few days off in the summer.'

'There you go, chuck,' Ma Kettle said now, steering the laden Biddy out through the doorway. 'Sister Eustacia will see you doesn't go walkin' under no trams or trolley-buses. And don't linger comin' back, you put your best foot foremost. Understand?'

'Yes, Miz Kettle,' Biddy said from behind the parcels. Her voice was humble but her expression, had Ma Kettle been able to see it, was not. Why couldn't the old skinflint give her a penny for the tram, or a ha'penny for a bun to eat on the way back, then? But that wasn't the Kettle way, Biddy thought, scowling dreadfully. Her employer would hand over extra sweets for the nuns but she'd get the money back by giving short weight to others. There was no way she could reclaim a penny for a tram from her young assistant, so no penny would be forthcoming.

'Are you all right, love?' That was Sister Eustacia, feeling guilty, Biddy hoped, for burdening a fellow-Christian like a poor little donkey. 'Can you see your way?'

They were out of the shop now. Biddy felt pavement beneath her mother's black shoes and the keen air, smelling of tripe, paraffin and motor cars, teased at her nostrils. This was Scotland Road, the hub of the universe, the place that Biddy loved best, with its bustle, its black, brown and yellow seamen, with the very curs who trotted along the pavement intent on their own business seeming more cosmopolitan and knowing than other Liverpool dogs.

Mam, however, had always thought the Scottie common; low.

'Now there's good and bad areas in the city, same as there are in all cities,' she had told Biddy, when her daughter was just a snippet of three or so. 'The Scottie's rough, you can meet anyone down there, and it isn't the King I'm meaning, either. It's really good for shopping though, I'll grant you that. There's nowhere better than Paddy's Market if you're looking for a bargain.'

But in those far-off days, handsome Elias O'Shaughnessy had been very much alive, first mate on the *Fleetwood Chaser*, which crossed the Atlantic in one direction carrying cotton goods and came back with its holds full of raw cotton for the spinners and weavers in Lancashire. Mam had not had to work at all, but she went out, some mornings, to do fancy embroidery and special ironing for her former employer, who was a society hostess and relied, she said plaintively, on seeing her dear Kath at least three times a week. Then the O'Shaughnessys had lived in a small but comfortable house in Dombey Street in Toxteth, were pillars of the local church and well thought of by friends and neighbours. Biddy, their only child, had worn a matching coat and hat, and leggings and neat strap shoes, and fed the ducks in the park and played with other nice little children whose parents were in comfortable circumstances.

'We've only got you, and you're going to have everything we can afford to give you, because we want you to have a good life,' Daddy had said, hugging her. She had been sitting on his knee, reading to him from her primer, and she could remember it so clearly, because that had been the last time she saw him. After that had come the dreadful letter telling them he had been drowned. Then came her mother's tears, the change from their pretty house to a couple of bare rooms in a tenement block, and then the gradual slide into illness and despair which was partly alleviated by Biddy's job until the awful day when Mam was sacked.

'Biddy, take a moment's rest here, dear child.'

Sister Eustacia's voice brought Biddy abruptly back to the present, to Scotland Road and its crowded pavements, the smell of tripe changing to shoe-leather as they passed Dick's the Bootmakers, then being overtaken by the sweet smell of warm bread flooding out of Cottle's.

Biddy was still trying to get her breath and to stand steady so that the parcels didn't tumble, when Sister Eustacia seemed to make up her mind. A thin, bony hand began to take parcels from the piles in front of Biddy's eyes and when they could see each other, she gave Biddy quite a pleasant smile.

'Bridget, child, I've got a little bit of money left over from my shopping; Mother Superior won't grudge me since I go down to the markets for her goods instead of buying them nearer to the convent. There's a tram stop here, we'll ride home in comfort. You won't mind walking back?'

'Walking back without the parcels will be a piece o' cake, Sister,' Biddy said from behind her tottering grocery bags. 'Is the stop near?'

Even with the parcels removed from before her nose she still felt she must put some things down before they fell out of her increasingly weary arms.

'It's right here. Can you stand some of those packages on the paving stones, now? It'll give your arms a rest till the tram comes by.'

Oh happiness, Biddy thought as she began to stand her burdens down and rub her aching arms. It was good to be out in the bright, crisp morning suddenly, good to be about to ride on a tram, even if the company of a nun did rather damp down the excitement of the occasion. We used to ride trams all the time and I never thought twice about it, Biddy told herself, standing guard over the parcels and gazing dreamily up the road towards the Gaiety Cinema, with its pictures of the stars and the posters proclaiming what was on unfortunately not clearly visible from this distance. We used to go to the cinema and eat a meal at a restaurant . . . we had our days out, to the seaside, picnics in the country . . . but they'll come again, the good times. Mam says she's resting well now, with no job. She'll probably be fit as a flea by Christmas.

'Ah, this looks like our tram. No dear, don't try to pick up all the parcels, it's a quiet time of day, the conductor will carry them aboard for us.'

A nun, Biddy knew, was unlikely to have to carry anything much for herself in a city like Liverpool, where a religious order got the respect it deserved from the largely Catholic inhabitants, but Sister Eustacia's order being less well known than some, she occasionally had to draw attention to herself with a discreet downward jerk of the head to her flowing black habit and the beads which hung at her waist.

'All right, Sister, but there's a powerful number of parcels; I'd best give him a hand.'

Biddy began to load herself up and as the tram stopped beside her, its bell giving one last clang as it did so, she hopped aboard, leaving the conductor to get out, pick up the rest of the parcels, and give Sister Eustacia his hand.

'Mornin', Sister,' he said affably. 'Where's you goin' dis fine mornin'?'

'To the Wellington Rooms on Mount Pleasant, please,' Sister Eustacia said with all her customary politeness. 'Me and me little helper, here.' The long, chilly fingers touched Biddy's cheek. 'How much would you be wantin' from us?'

'I'll not charge for a parcel-carrier,' the conductor said, grinning at Biddy. 'Sure an' she's doin' you one favour, I'll do you another. If an inspector comes on board I'll run up and give her a ticket at once, mind.'

'That's uncommon good of you – bless you, my son,' Sister Eustacia said, making a small sign of the cross with her two fingers. 'Sit by me, Bridget, but keep an eye on me parcels.'

Isn't it an odd world, now, Biddy mused, sitting beside the nun on the wooden slatted seat and dragging the biggest parcel to rest against her skinny calves. Here's nuns at school telling us not to lie or cheat, yet Ma Kettle tells everyone who'll listen that she's poor but honest when she's neither, and Sister Eustacia lets the tram conductor give me a free ride, when if I hopped on board and then off again without paying, like the bad boys do, she'd go all po-faced and talk about sin, and the bible, and how hot the flames of hell burn.

She glanced sideways at her companion, but Sister Eustacia was examining the big brown paper bag of peppermints. She was not counting them exactly – more gloating, Biddy thought suddenly. Eh, there's not much fun for a load of holy women shut up in a convent all day; this shopping trip once a month is the poor soul's pay-ment for an awful lot of kneeling on hard floors and saying prayers for people who can't be bothered to pray for themselves. And not a peppermint would she touch until she was given leave, even though there was a free bag in there, a little extra, handed out by Ma Kettle probably in much the same spirit as that of the bus conductor when he had refused to accept a fare for Biddy. There's a lot of good in people, Biddy concluded, wriggling round so that she could look out of the window as the tram joggled along down Byrom Street and swerved left around the Technical College. What's a free ride for me and a few parcels, after all?

If the journey to Mount Pleasant was completed in record time, the journey back to the Scottie was not. To say that Biddy loitered would not have been fair, but she certainly did not hurry. It was a clean, crisp sort of day, especially welcome after so much rain and cold, and for some reason Biddy felt happy, as though the free ride was just the beginning of the good times which she was so sure would soon come back.

What was more, as the tiny little door in the great big gate creaked open to Sister Eustacia's knock, the nun turned to Biddy and pressed something into her hand.

'Here, Bridget . . . you're a good girl. Buy yourself a bun, or a ride home in another tram.' She turned unhurriedly back to the little door and to the squat, bespectacled nun peering out. 'Ah, Sister, can you send for someone to help me with my shopping?'

Biddy had thought about another tram ride, but the truth was, it would only get her back to Kettle's Confectionery sooner and when she got there it would undoubtedly be time for toffee-making, which would be enjoyable enough on a cold day but which did not appeal when the sun was out – and Biddy was on borrowed time thanks to Sister Eustacia.

If we had walked we wouldn't have reached here for

another forty or fifty minutes; perhaps not for a whole hour, Biddy reminded herself, wandering slowly along the sunny pavement. So there's no way I could be back in work yet. And I'm not wasting money on a tram fare. I'll buy myself a big currant bun and an apple; I just fancy an apple.

She had her currant bun and her apple, ambling along as she ate, and then decided to have a sit-down for ten minutes in St John's gardens. But there, belatedly, conscience pricked. She was being paid, this really was Ma Kettle's time, and though she had a cast-iron reason for not getting back exactly early, she did not feel it would do to turn up late. Sure as a clock ticks I'll be seen by some interfering old busybody who'll tell Ma Kettle I was spotted on the tram, she thought bitterly. And then I'll lose the job and Mam and me'll never get out from under.

From under precisely what she did not explain, even to herself. She just chucked her applecore into a bed of roses, still blooming as gaily as though the month was June and not September, and set off at a smart pace for the Scotland Road and Kettle's Confectionery.

'Ah, 'ere she is! I've got the toffee boilin', chuck, but it'll be ready for pourin' in ten minutes. I couldn't save you but a morsel o' bread an' jam, but there's tea in the pot. Get there awright? Sister pleased wi' you?'

Biddy sidled round the counter and headed for the back room. She felt as though there was a sign on her forehead with *big currant bun and an apple ate in your time* emblazoned upon it, but when she saw the size of the piece of bread and the thin smear of jam she was quite glad she had been deceitful. It was just about enough to fill a tooth cavity, and she'd been slogging all that way on foot with enough weight in her arms to break 'em . . . or at least, that was what old Ma Kettle thought.

'Sister was pleased,' she called back, however. Remember how hard you had to search to find this job, she commanded herself. When you're a bit older, a bit more ladyfied, when you talk in a 'shop voice' all the time an' not just sometimes, Mam says you'll get decent work in Blacklers or George Henry Lee's, but until then take what you can get and be grateful.

'Good, good. You won't let that toffee overboil, chuck?'

'I'm taking it off the stove now,' Biddy said, adding beneath her breath, 'If I've got the strength to lift the pan after having nothing to eat since tea last night.'

'What? What was that? Leave the bread 'n' jam till the toffee's coolin', there's a good girl.'

'Right,' Biddy said, thinking that in the time it would have taken her to swallow the bread and jam she would have lost less than half a second. She heaved at the blackened pan, staggering as it left the stove-top with a decided squelsh and she felt its full weight. 'Got it, Mrs Kettle. . . . Cor, it's no light weight this lot.'

'It's coconut toffee,' Mrs Kettle said, appearing in the doorway. 'Ah, you ate the bread an' jam first, I see. Well, no matter . . . pour careful, girl, I don't want toffee all over me decent scrubbed table-top.'

'I didn't . . . eat . . . it,' Biddy panted, muscles cracking as she strove to tip the pan gently into the first of the half-dozen tin cooling trays. 'It's still there, missus, on the wall-table. It's just rather little.'

'Steady, steady!' Mrs Kettle said anxiously as the flow began and the sweet brown stuff began to run steadily into the tray. 'That's right, that's right . . . not too full now, or you'll never 'ammer it up into small enough bits. My lor, that stuff cost enough . . . steady I say!'

'The pan's so heavy,' Biddy wheezed, shifting it along to the second tray. 'I'm not Samson you know, Mrs Kettle.'

'You eat like 'im,' Mrs Kettle said, not nastily but just as one stating a fact. 'All that bread an' jam gone in a coupla o' minutes! Ah no, I see you've left a tat.'

Biddy finished pouring toffee and stood the pan back on the stove top, sweat running down the sides of her face. She glanced across at the disputed piece of bread and jam.

'I haven't had time to eat anything, Mrs Kettle,' she pointed out. 'I got the toffee straight off the stove – isn't that what you left me, then?'

'No it is not,' Mrs Kettle said, sounding injured. 'You'd run an errand for me, Bid . . . is it likely I'd cut you down to that? Bread's a price, I grant you, but I declare no one's ever called me stingy.'

Not to your face, Biddy's mind said, whilst her mouth, much the more tactful member, agreed that she had never heard anyone be so rude.

'No, nor you should,' Ma Kettle said huffily. 'I left you the best part of 'alf a loaf . . . well, three decent slices,' she added. 'Now where . . . ah!'

She had opened the door leading to her own private quarters as she spoke and there, on the back of the door, hung a navy donkey jacket and a navy cap. Mrs Kettle leaned through the doorway. 'Ja-ack! Come down 'ere this minute, you bleedin' rascal! Wha' did you go an' tek the bread 'n' jam for, eh? Don't I feed you? That was for me assistant!'

A muffled roar came from beyond the doorway. It sounded like a denial, interspersed with some laughter, and an explanation, but with the doorway filled by Ma Kettle and Jack being in the flat upstairs, Biddy could not hear what he said.

'Jack says it were Maisie, then, greedy great gannet,' Ma Kettle muttered, having obviously interpreted the roar without any difficulty. 'That girl! I pays 'er to keep me place clean and she sneaks orf into me boilin' kitchen an prigs bread an' jam what's meant for me bleedin' shop assistant! I'll clack 'er bleedin' lug for er!'

Biddy, who had seen a stout, cross-looking girl poke her head round the door occasionally with a message for Ma Kettle, grinned to herself. She knew nothing about Maisie save for her appearance, but it occurred to her that anyone who worked for Ma would have to learn to look after themselves. Obviously it applied whether you cleaned her flat or sold her sweets, because Maisie must have been hungry to have taken the bread and jam.

Ma Kettle withdrew from the doorway and slammed the door. Crossly. Then she waddled across to the small cupboard to the left of the stove. Bending down she withdrew a loaf and a pot of jam, three-quarters used. 'Jack's sorry, 'e'd 'ave stopped 'er, only 'e didn't know it were yourn,' she explained, beginning to hack another slice off the loaf. 'None of me lads would tek what waren't theirs . . . poor but honest, that's us Kettles; well known fact.'

It was very late and very dark before the toffee was all made and cooled, hammered into sufficiently small pieces to please Ma Kettle, clattered into the big sweet jars and placed high on the shelves. And it was not as though the toffee was her only job. There was cleaning the sweet-making pans, which could take a couple of hours if Ma Kettle had forgotten to leave them in hot water, and scrubbing the worn lino in the back room and the boards in the little shop. The big window had to be cleaned, the display dusted and any flies which hovered must be pursued with the fly-swat, this being a much more acceptable method of fly-slaying – to the customers, at least – than hanging fly-papers or setting wasp-traps. When you were not serving customers you were always busy, so that by eight o'clock, when Kettle's Confectionery closed at last, Biddy was always so tired that she walked home in a daze, often arriving so weary that it was all she could do to cut herself and her mother bread and cheese for their supper.

But tonight, perhaps because of her little trip out and the two meals she had enjoyed, Biddy found the walk home less tiring than usual. She and her mother now had a room in a house in Virginia Street, just behind St Paul's church which, in its turn, was behind Exchange Station. It was quite near the docks, which Biddy liked, and handy for work, though you couldn't say it was the healthiest spot in the city. All day and for quite a bit of the night the racket of the trains – and the filth from their engines – befouled the air and though their landlady constantly reminded them how fortunate they were, Biddy sometimes had her doubts.

When Mam's cough got worse she had tried to move, but it wasn't easy. Mrs Edith Kilbride's rent was possible because Mam kept an eye on their landlady's four small children whilst she went off to work at the nearby station as a cleaner. Kath O'Shaughnessy and Edith had lived on the same street in Dublin, years ago, and had remained good friends, which would have made leaving difficult. Besides which, paying a normal rent, until Kath was back in work once more, was next to impossible.

Despite the lateness of the hour there were plenty of people around in the streets and quite a crowd were coming out of Exchange Station. Biddy dodged round them and dived down the subway which came out in St Paul's Square. From there it was a short walk along Earle Street and into the narrow house in Virginia Street.

Biddy was humming a tune as she ran up the stairs, for their room was on the first floor. She hoped her mother had managed to get something for their tea – for some reason she thought it might be fish – and was already anticipating a nice bit of cod with a pile of boiled potatoes and maybe even a bit of cake for a pudding. The tiny widow's pension which the O'Shaughnessys drew had been due this morning, which usually meant something substantial for tea. Biddy's own wage, though useful, was too small to provide anything hot and the savings which Kath O'Shaughnessy was carefully husbanding were used to pay the rent.

Biddy stopped outside their room to get her breath, then tapped on the door and opened it. She always tapped as though it was a real front door, though of course it was only one room, and her mother usually called out cheerfully, then came across to give her daughter a kiss. But today, as Biddy entered the room, everything was different. For one thing her mother was in bed, not up, and for another, she was not alone. A tall, worried-looking man was sitting on the edge of the bed writing something in a book and Edie Kilbride was standing by the mantel, her face very pale. She turned as Biddy entered the room, looking stricken.

'Oh, Biddy, dear . . . oh Biddy, I don't know how to tell you . . . sure an' 'tis the last t'ing either of us expected . . . oh Biddy, this is Dr Godber, who has somet'ing to say to ye.'

The man on the bed turned towards her. His face was solemn but as he turned he had glanced down at his watch and Biddy could tell that he was longing to be on his way.

'Ah, Bridget! I'm afraid I have sad news for you, my child. Very sad news.'

'She's been took bad, hasn't she?' Biddy quavered, moving towards the bed. 'Poor Mam, she's been getting better slowly, but now she's been took bad. What must I do, sir?'

17

As she spoke she glanced towards the pillows – and stopped short, a hand flying to her mouth. There lay her mother's shape, but it was covered completely by a sheet, pulled up to hide her face.

The doctor followed her glance.

'She's . . . she's gone to her reward,' he said awkwardly. 'I'm afraid, Bridget, that your mother haemorrhaged about an hour ago. She lost a great deal of blood and died soon afterwards.'

'Died?' Biddy could see the man's mouth moving, she could hear his words, but somehow they had no meaning. A great sheet of glass had been interposed between them and she felt as though someone had stuffed her mouth with cotton wool and her ears, too. Was that why the doctor's voice was so small, so insignificant? And what had they done to Mam, why had they pulled the sheet right over her face? She would have difficulty breathing, he really ought to be more careful of a patient, even if she was neither rich nor important.

She leaned forward and twitched the sheet down before anyone had divined her intention or could stop her.

There lay the mortal remains of Kathleen O'Shaughnessy, her face glassily pale, her eyes closed. The pillow on which her head lay was dark with blood, her hair, loose for once, matted with it. And horrifyingly, even as Biddy watched, her mother's jaw dropped slowly open and her head rolled a little on the blotched and bloodstained pillow.

Biddy screamed, as shrill as one of the trains drawing out of Exchange Station, and jumped back, then as swiftly moved forward, to fall on her knees by the bed.

'Mam, are you all right? You aren't dead, you aren't, you aren't! Oh, Mam, say something!'

A pair of hands caught her shoulders, pulling her

upright, then turning her so that she faced away from the carnage on the sheets.

'It's awright, Bridget, it's awright, she's gone luv, she's gone where no one can't 'urt her no more. Come on, come on, you don't want to stay 'ere, because your Mam ain't 'ere no more, she's left, that ain't your Mam, that's just an empty shell, a body what she don't want no more. She were a good soul, your Mam, a good friend and a good little fighter, but she's gone from 'ere, now, and you must be gone too. Come down wi' me an' the kids, we'll get a meal, talk about what's to be done. Come on, come downstairs wi' your Aunt Edie.'

Biddy had never called Mrs Kilbride anything but Mrs Kilbride, but now she sobbed in the woman's arms, clutching her desperately, hanging onto the only solid thing in the suddenly tippling world, Edith Kilbride's plump, motherly arms.

'Is . . . is she really dead?' she asked fearfully. 'Really gone for good? Won't there be no more laughs, no more good times?'

Mrs Kilbride did not answer at once but Biddy heard her swallow convulsively and felt the plump little hand pat her back.

'Sure there'll be laughs an' good times, chuck, but it'll be up to you to make 'em, now. Your Mam can't help you there. Ah, she were a good Mam to you an' a good pal to me. . . . Come on, come downstairs, I'll 'ave the kettle on and we'll wet our t'rottles an' 'ave a bit of a chat, like. Come on, leave the doctor to see to things here.'

Biddy heaved a deep, tremulous sigh and glanced once more towards the bed. Dimly, she realised that there was truth in what Mrs Kilbride had said. That thing lying on the pillow wasn't really her mother, it was just a cast-off shell which had been left behind when her mother's soul had fled.

Slowly, but without a backward glance, she allowed herself to be led from the room.

'It's ever so good of you, Mrs Kilbride, to suggest that I stay wi' you and keep an eye on the kids, like my Mam used to do,' Biddy said wearily, when the funeral was over and she was packing her pathetically few possessions into the old carpet bag her mother had once used for her heavy shopping. 'I'm not ungrateful, honest, but it wouldn't be fair on you, not in the long run. Mrs Kettle's said I can move in wi' them, she doesn't have a daughter, only sons, so I'll be useful. And it'll be a roof over my head and a job, for a while at least.'

She had been very surprised when Mrs Kettle had not only come to the funeral but had made the offer.

'You come along o' me and live over the shop, same as all us Kettles do,' she had urged. 'I'll feed you, dress you, see you right. What d'you say?'

She had to say she would, of course. Mrs Kilbride couldn't afford to feed another mouth unless that other mouth could bring in a wage, and since Biddy couldn't be in two places at once she could not envisage herself working for Ma Kettle and taking her money home to the Kilbrides, whilst also staying at home all day to look after the kids.

'There's a truckle bed you can use,' Ma Kettle planned busily. 'Being as 'ow I been a widder-woman these fifteen years, you can share my room. Of course I shan't pay you a wage, like, seeing as 'ow I'll be treatin' you like me own flesh an' blood, but I'll see you right, no need to worry about that.'

'Thanks,' Biddy said dully. 'Thanks very much, Mrs Kettle.'

She was too shocked still to do more than think, fleetingly, that at least the food would probably be better than she and Mam had managed out of their small resources. Often there were quite appetising smells floating down from the flat above the shop; she had sat at the counter minding the shop and eating bread and jam and her mouth had downright watered at times.

'You fetch your gear, then,' Mrs Kettle said. 'What about your Mam's things? You're welcome to bring any furniture, fittings, stuff like that. And if you want me to dispose of anything . . .' she paused delicately, her bushy little caterpillar eyebrows twitching interrogatively, '. . . we might mek a few bob, between us,' she finished.

'It's all right, thanks,' Biddy said. 'Aunt Edie was good to Mam because they were pals as girls, in Dublin. They were the same build, so she's having Mam's skirts and jumpers and that, and there wasn't much in the way of furniture. The bed was ruined . . . so I'm lettin' Aunt Edie have what's good there, to make up.'

'Aunt Edie?' It seemed to Biddy that Ma Kettle drew back a little when she said the words. 'I never knowed you'd got an aunt in the Pool. I daresay she'll want you when you're big enough to earn a decent wage. Perhaps I'm wrong to offer, and you with a relative actually on the spot.'

'She's got a lot of kids,' Biddy said tiredly. 'She can't afford to keep me. But if you've changed your mind, Mrs Kettle . . .'

'Me, change me mind? Bridget O'Shaughnessy – dear me, what a mouthful! – Bridget O'Shaughnessy, the day I withdraw a kindness may I be roast on a spit! She ain't your real aunt, I daresay?'

'No, not my real aunt. Just a friend of Mam's,' Biddy admitted. 'When shall I fetch my stuff over, Mrs Kettle?'

'Why, tomorrer, if not sooner! And just you call me Ma, same's the boys does. Want a hand wi' your gear?'

Since Biddy's gear consisted of a spare skirt and

blouse, a cloth-bodied doll called, rather unoriginally, Dolly, who was too shabby and dirty to be worth selling, the carpet bag and her mother's wedding ring, Biddy told her benefactress that she could manage, thank you. She went back to the house in Virginia Street, said good-bye to everyone – the kids cried – and picked up her bag. Then she trudged slowly round to the shop, suddenly feeling as though the world had slid away from beneath her feet, leaving her spinning uneasily in space.

Three days ago, she thought wonderingly as she walked, three days ago I was Somebody. I was daughter to Kath O'Shaughnessy, lodger to Mrs Kilbride, shop assistant at Kettle's Confectionery shop. And now what am I? I'm nobody's daughter, nobody's lodger even, certainly nobody's shop assistant, because a shop assistant is paid a wage and Mrs Kettle had made it clear that she would not be paid. Now I'm just Biddy O'Shaughnessy, an orphan who Ma Kettle is about to befriend. Or take advantage of. We'll see.

And she trudged on along the dusky pavements, heading for whatever fate had in store. As she passed the shop windows she saw her reflection, saw one small, skinny fourteen year old, with dark curls, blue eyes, and a pointed chin. Once someone said my chin was obstinate and when I wouldn't eat my greens Da called me a fuss-pot, she recalled, thinking back to those long-ago, happy days. Once I would have looked very carefully at Ma Kettle's proposal and probably turned it down. But that was when I knew where I was going and what I wanted, Biddy told herself ruefully, changing the carpet bag from her left hand to her right, for though not particularly full, it soon began to feel extremely heavy. Yes, that was before Mam went and left me. Now I've got to fend for myself and I'd rather a roof over my head than a gutter and yesterday's *Echo*.

Well, her thoughts continued, I'm down now, flat as a ha'penny on a tramline, but I'll recover myself, given time. I'll lie low for a bit and see what's best, but for now, it's Ma Kettle's and like it. Otherwise they'll slam me into an orphanage or the workhouse or something, and I wouldn't like *that* at all.

Ma Kettle was waiting for her. The shop was closed but the door hung open and there she was, boiling toffee in the back room and keeping a weather eye open, she explained, for Biddy.

'Normally, I'd tell you to finish this boilin' off for me,' she said, ushering the girl into the back room and through the doorway which, until this minute, had been forbidden territory for a mere Kettle employee. 'But seein' as you're goin' to live in, you'd best come up and meet the rest o' the fambly.'

Carpet bag in hand, Biddy followed Ma Kettle up a flight of stairs and into a large, rather dismal living-room. It should not have been dismal, for there were dark red curtains pulled across the window, a deep, comfortable-looking sofa and number of saggy arm-chairs with faded, dark red upholstery – Biddy shuddered – the colour of dried blood, and the only light came from a dim little bulb with a red shade which robbed it of any brilliance it might once have possessed. It shone down on a large table covered with a maroon chenille cloth and on four upright wooden chairs with carved backs and tight leather seats. Even the walls were dark, the paper having lost any colour it might have possessed in favour of a uniform brown years ago. In fact, the only bright part of the room was the fire which roared up the chimney and the brass fire-irons which twinkled in the grate.

There were three young men disposed about the room

in various poses and Ma Kettle introduced them to Biddy in an undertone, so as not to disturb them.

One was at the table directly beneath the red-shaded light. He was probably seventeen or eighteen and was poring over a book through a pair of small, wire-rimmed spectacles balanced on his oddly upturned nose. He was pudgy, with light brown hair, and took no notice whatsoever of either his mother or her companion. Biddy was informed in an awed whisper that this was Ma Kettle's youngest, her beloved Kenny.

Jack came next. He sat by the fire, elbows on knees, a slice of bread on a toasting fork held out to the flames. He was in his early twenties, tall, well-built, dark-haired, and wearing a seaman's brief white shirt and blue trousers. He looked round and grinned as his mother said his name, white teeth flashing in his tanned face. Jack, Biddy remembered, was a sailor and not home often. He was the one who had allowed the maid to prig her bread and jam though, so her answering smile was tepid.

The third man sat opposite Kenny at the table eating a plate of what looked like scouse. Biddy knew this must be Luke, the eldest son, but Ma Kettle told her so anyway. Luke reminded Biddy sharply of Ma Kettle for he was stout and had little grey eyes which met her own shrewdly, calculatingly. He was twenty-five, she knew that much about him from idly listening to Ma Kettle boasting in the shop, and worked at Tate's. He was, naturally, the source of the cheap sugar which Ma used in her home-made sweets.

'And this is Biddy O'Shaughnessy,' Ma Kettle said, once she had named each of her sons. 'Biddy's comin' to live 'ere for a bit, boys. She'll give an 'and in the shop, in the 'ouse. . . . You want anything doin', just 'ave a word wi' me and I'll see she sets to and does it. You 'ad your dinner yet, Biddy?'

'No, not yet,' Biddy said, thinking again that the scouse smelled good. 'I left Virginia Street before Aunt Edie got round to thinking about a meal.'

'Right. Just for tonight you might as well eat in 'ere, wi' us.'

She waddled out of the room and Biddy followed her into a tiny, dark little kitchen with a knee-high sink in one corner and a smelly, coke-burning stove in the other. There was a broken-down chair, a bare electric light bulb overhead and a large table. It was warm because of the stove, but cheerless, unfriendly. All the rooms are the same, they none of them want me, any more than Ma Kettle or her boys do, Biddy thought despairingly. Oh, how will I live in this horrible house with all these horrible people?

But it was not a question to which she could give an answer. Instead, she watched as Ma ladled a very small helping of scouse and a couple of boiled potatoes onto a plate and handed it, rather grudgingly, to her.

'There y'are; same as us,' she said, as though Biddy suspected that Kettles ate something far more glamorous than mere scouse. 'You'll be like a daughter to me, you shan't go short.'

Sitting down at the table and devouring the scouse in a couple of minutes, Biddy looked up hopefully as she scraped the spoon round the now-empty plate. And how had Ma managed to ladle out the stew without getting a single piece of meat in her spoon? There had been meat in Luke's portion, lots of meat, she had noted it specially.

'Done? Well, then, we'll go through together and see about the toffee,' Ma Kettle said, whisking the plate from under Biddy's nose. 'I won't get you to wash up yet, since Luke's still eating.'

Biddy took a deep breath. It was now or never; she sensed it.

'Mrs Kettle, I've not eaten since last night and I'm – I'm still hungry. Is there any scouse left?'

The boys had all been busy with their own affairs, but now Biddy was painfully aware of three pairs of eyes fixed on her, as well as of Ma Kettle's incredulous, beady gaze.

'You're still *hungry*? After a plateful of me good stew, what's full o' meat an' luv'ly fresh veggies? Can I believe what I'm hearin'?'

'Yes, I'm afraid you can,' Biddy said clearly, using her very best 'shop' voice. 'I'm *extremely* hungry and though I'm sure it was a mistake, there was no meat in my helping. However, if there's none left, perhaps you could give me some money to get some chips? You did say you'd feed me instead of wages, and . . .'

She shot a quick glance at Luke, opposite. His little eyes were like marbles, hard and glassy, and his small mouth was tight. Beside her, Kenny continued to ignore her, apart from giving her one incredulous glance from behind his spectacles, though whether he approved or disapproved of the stand she was taking, Biddy had no idea. Over by the fire, Jack was grinning, taking his toasted bread carefully off the fork, though he said nothing.

'Ah . . . well, if you've 'ad no brekfuss, nor nothin' else all day . . . I know, you can fill up on bread 'n' jam,' Ma Kettle said triumphantly. 'There's enough o' that stew left for the boys' dinners tomorrer, if I does extry spuds. Or rather, you can do 'em,' she added, quite unable to keep a trace of sheer malice out of her tone. 'Seein' as 'ow you're goin' to gi' me an 'and about the place.'

'I don't work so well on bread and jam,' Biddy said demurely. 'I need a decent dinner, Ma.'

It was the first time she had omitted to call her employer Mrs Kettle and the shot went home. Ma looked uneasily at her boys, now all three of them studiously avoiding her glance, then heaved a great sigh. 'Scouse it is, then,' she said heavily. 'Someone told me girls couldn't put away their food the way lads do, but I see 'twas just one of them tales folk tell. Come through to the kitchen, chuck.'

Much later that night, when she was curled up in the tiny truckle bed with Dolly clasped to her bosom and Ma Kettle snoring like an elephant in the big brass bedstead not more than a foot away, Biddy went over her day. It had been painful beyond measure to watch her mother's coffin being slowly lowered into the impersonal earth at Toxteth Park cemetery. Then it had hurt to say goodbye to Mrs Kilbride and the kids. She had never been particularly happy in the scruffy, down-at-heel little house on Virginia Street, but at least Mam had been there and they had enjoyed some pleasant times, especially when Mam felt well and they had talked about her starting work again, moving to a better neighbourhood, training Biddy up so she could be a saleslady in one of the big clothing shops.

Still, girls do leave home at fourteen and go into service, Biddy told herself. Probably, if Mam hadn't met my Da and fallen in love with him and fled over here to Liverpool, I'd have gone into service in Dublin round about now. And I'd have felt pretty lonely and lost in someone else's house, too.

But in service you had other servants. In service you were paid a wage, got time off, could go home sometimes, perhaps as often as once a week. You could save up, buy yourself the occasional treat, have a best friend to giggle with. Since her mother's illness and her own employment by Ma Kettle, even friends from school had called less often, busy with their own lives and unable to spend their time waiting for Biddy either to finish work or finish nursing her Mam.

If things were different I could get back with Kezzie and Maude and Ellen, Biddy thought hopelessly. But things aren't different, and I'll just have to put up with what I have got, for the time being. And besides, I did all right today, didn't I? Old Ma Kettle was rocked back on her heels by me asking for more scouse, just like Oliver Twist in that book me and Mam read last year, but she gave me some, she shelled out. Perhaps, if I can keep it up, she won't use me too badly, and I'll like living here. Perhaps even the boys might not be too horrible, once I get to know them.

One thing, you've got to stand up for yourself in the Kettle household, because if you don't no one will, she thought, just before she went to sleep. I've got to be tough, like them, or they'll flatten me.

And presently she slept, to dream of putting a ha'penny on the tramlines so that it might be squashed penny-sized, only to find that the ha'penny had turned into Sister Eustacia, who had reproached her for doubling her income in so sneaky a fashion. And she had stood up to Sister Eustacia and told her about Ma weighing her thumbs and doing the kids out of the odd sweetie, and Ma had come surging out of the back room, saying, 'No scouse for you, amn't I goin' to treat you like me own daughter, you serpent's tooth?'

After that, the dreams got odder and odder. Ma made her wear a pair of boy's trousers and a boy's shirt because she said clothes were always handed down in good, close, Catholic families and the trousers tripped her up when she was serving people and the shirt sleeves dangled in the toffee and got disgustingly sticky. And at intervals throughout the night the dream-Ma would shout, 'No scouse for you, madam – amn't I goin' to treat you like me own daughter, you serpent's tooth?' and poor Biddy would think up clever arguments to get herself fed properly but they never worked. Either the table would turn into an elephant, trumpeting loudly, or it would tip over and run out of the room, or the food would simply disappear whilst Ma, with a big smile on her face, advised Biddy to fill up with bread 'n' jam and whisked the bread into the fire and the jam into her apron pocket.

When Biddy woke it was still dark, and the trumpeting elephant table was standing by her truckle bed. She gave a little squeak of fright and the table turned into Ma Kettle, huge in a white petticoat, man's socks and a long grey shawl.

'Come on, child,' Ma Kettle said, not unkindly. 'Jack's off back to sea this mornin' so you must be down early to mash the tea. Then you can start off the brekfuss . . . the boys 'ave bacon, a couple of eggs each, a pile of bread wi' margarine on . . . but us wimmin, we'll mek do wi' bread 'n' scrape an' a nice pot of tea, shall us?'

Biddy was tired after a restless night and confused to find herself in Ma Kettle's frowsty little bedroom, but one thought came clear to the front of her mind as she climbed stiffly out of bed and reached for her clothes. Don't let her push you around, the thought said. Stand up for yourself!

'Bacon and egg,' she said therefore, with all the firmness she could muster. 'I work best after bacon and egg.'

'Ah,' Ma Kettle said, after a pause so long that Biddy began to wonder whether the older woman had gone back to sleep. 'Oh ah. Bacon an' egg, eh?'

'Bacon an' egg at breakfast,' Biddy said hastily. It was years since she'd tasted bacon and egg, but she did see that if Ma Kettle chose to take her literally she might well find the rest of the family eating roast chicken whilst she dined – lightly – on a tiny piece of bacon and a pullet's egg. 'Girls need something more for dinner, of course.'

'Of course,' Ma Kettle said. She sighed. 'Better get a

move on; Jack's fond of an early cuppa. And he'll want his brekfuss betimes, too. Better shift yourself, chuck.'

Biddy, throwing her clothes on, said meekly that she would do her best to hurry. She realised that, having got her own way, she must be careful not to provoke Ma Kettle by being cocky. So she did not wash and Ma Kettle did not suggest that she should, she just hurried downstairs and began to hunt out the ingredients for the boys' breakfast.

At least she isn't going to try to starve me, she told herself as she got the huge frying pan out of the cupboard and put it carefully on top of the stove. As the fat began to hiss and spit she broke the first egg into it and stood the bacon ready. A real breakfast, and as soon as the boys were fed she, too, could eat this wonderful food! It was worth getting up early, worth slaving for Ma Kettle all day in the shop and half the night in the house, if she, Biddy, ate as well as the boys!

Chapter Two

In January no beach is at its best, but Richart David Evans,
Dai to his friends, sitting on the little cliff above the beach
at Moelfre, looking down on the grey shingle, the black
fanged rocks, the slow inward saunter of the silvery
winter waves, was not seeing the scene before him. His
mind was closed to the beauty, as it was to the cry of the
gulls, and the salty, exciting, indefinable smell of the dark
green weed and the wooden fishing boats, pulled up
above the tideline.

His Mam was dead. After weeks of suffering she had
died first thing in the morning four months ago, when
Da had been out in the long garden at the back of the tall
house on Stryd Pen, hoping to find that one of the hens
had laid an egg with which he might tempt his heart's
darling, for there was no doubt in Dai's mind that Davy
had loved his Bethan true.

Davy had been devastated by her death, unmanned
by it you could say. For weeks he had been inconsolable
and Dai and his sister Siân had done their best to comfcrt
him, to see that he ate, slept, even mourned, with some
degree of self-control. But a month ago Siân, who had
been engaged to be married for over a year but had
delayed the wedding first because of her mother's illness
and then her death, had wed her Gareth and moved into
his cottage in the nearby village of Benllech. And Da, Dai
brooded darkly, had done the unforgivable.

He had brought another woman into Mam's home.

'Fond of the girls is your Da,' Mam had whispered to

her son just before she died. 'Marry again he will, love – marry again he must, for that's your Da for you. Don't resent the girl of his choice, Dai, my dear, but if you need a home while you come to terms with what's happened, don't forget my old friend, Nellie McDowell that was. She's Nellie Gallagher now and if you need help, or . . . or anything . . . the sort of thing you'd have turned to me for . . . then Nellie will do what she can. Her address is in my little bureau. We still exchange letters from time to time. If you hurt, love, you must go to her. There isn't a better woman living.'

'Mam, Da wouldn't . . . but I don't want to talk about it. And if it pleases you, I'll see this woman some time. Oh Mam, we love you so much, I don't know what we'll do without you.'

Bethan had smiled, the thin face suddenly bright with real amusement. 'I know well what your Da will do! Now give me a kiss and go about your business; I just wanted one quiet word.'

Two days later she was dead and now . . . Dai gritted his teeth and thumped his knee with a clenched fist. Now his father had brought Menna from Amlwch into the house because he said it needed a woman's touch – and it didn't take any particular effort to realise three things. First, that Davy had known Menna for some time, and known her quite well what was more. Second, that he had not brought her in to act as his housekeeper but for a far more intimate purpose. Third, that Menna, whilst delighted to be living with Davy, had no desire whatsoever to share a house with his son.

Oh Mam, Mam, how well you knew my Da and how foolish I was not to see that his weakness for a pretty face was stronger even than his love for you, Dai mourned now, staring blackly out over the sea. And what do I do now? Stay here, to keep at bay at least some of the scandal that will soon be rife? Or go? It will mean leaving the *Sweetbriar*, and the fishing, and my nice little attic room and pretty Rhona from the Post Office, but then a man has to leave his Mam's home one day and make a home for himself. My time to leave has come sooner than I expected, because I've been so content here, but I can't stay. Not when Da installs her as his wife, which he will do. It's the only way; the villagers won't have him living shamelessly in sin with a little town hussy who doesn't know our ways.

But what to do? The *Sweetbriar* was his own craft and he and his friend Meirion worked her together; they could find the fish when others searched in vain, they were a good team and made money, quite a lot of money at times when fish was short and others could not find.

There was the lifeboat, too. He had just been taken on as a deckhand and loved it, was almost looking forward to the heavy seas of winter as a chance to prove himself. If he left . . .

The village had been his life for twenty years, he knew nothing else. Every man, woman and child here was his friend, would stand by him, agree with him if he told Da . . .

But Mam had known this would happen and had warned him that it was no use resisting. She knew Davy well, his charm, the way his dark eyes warmed and softened when they fell on a loved one. She understood completely that Da couldn't go on without a woman, and had urged her son to accept Da's choice – but Menna! Brassy-haired, shrill-voiced, she was the kind of woman that Dai liked least, the sort he avoided when he took a boatful of fish round to Amlwch and popped into the pub afterwards to wet his whistle before turning for home.

So leave then. No option, no choice. Just leave. Meirion would continue to fish the boat, give Dai a share of his profit if his friend was in need. So far as Dai was concerned Meirion could have the *Sweetbriar* and welcome; better him than Davy Evans, who would probably sell it to buy Menna a gold anklet chain or a locket or whatever silly frippery such a flibbertigibbet might desire.

But go where? He did not intend to run to Liverpool, with his tail between his legs, to this woman friend of Mam's – what was her name? Gallagher, that was it. A Scottish-sounding name, or an Irish one, he wasn't sure which, he just knew it wasn't a good Welsh name. And anyway, what could a motherly woman do for him? He had lost the only mother he wanted, now he must take the man's path.

As he sat on the cliff edge and glowered, unseeing, at the sea, a man walked across the beach below him, then looked up and shouted.

'Dai, bach, what's up wi' you, mun? I'm baitin' lobster pots; goin' to give me a hand?'

It was Meirion.

Meirion stood on the shingle with the bag of fish pieces swinging from one hand and watched Dai scramble down the cliff towards him. Dai came down with his black curls bobbing on his head, his strong legs carrying him easily and swiftly over the rough going, his eyes intent on the ground at his feet. Like his Da, Dai Evans was good to look upon and the girls vied for his favours, but to Meirion, Dai was special. Fond of Dai he was, like brothers they had been all their lives, and worried he was at the way Dai had taken Bethan's death.

Darkly. That was how he had taken it. Meirion was used to his friend's eloquent eyes reflecting his moods, but of late those eyes had seldom sparkled and had looked opaque, angry. Then there was the girl Menna. No one approved, but there were those who understood, though Meirion was not one of them. How Davy Evans could take a brassy piece like her into his home, with Dai still so hurt by his loss, Meirion could not understand, and there was talk amongst the women – who knew everything – that Davy had always been a one for the girls, that having a bedridden wife for fifteen months before her death had tried him more than it would have done some men, that he had been visiting Menna in her father's public house in Amlwch for more than a twelve-month. . . .

Dai crashed down the last few feet of cliff and crunched across the shingle towards Meirion. He looked better, less haunted, Meirion decided, considerably relieved. The curly grin which revealed the white, even teeth was splitting Dai's tanned face and his eyes warmed when they met Meirion's in much their old way. 'Aye, I'll give you a hand with the pots, bach. Meirion, my mind is made up. I'll be leavin' Moelfre as soon as I can get a berth on a ship out of Amlwch. I'll ride over tomorrow – want to come?'

Dai had an old motorbike, his pride and joy after the *Sweetbriar*. He and Meirion had taken it to pieces and then put it together again half a hundred times; they knew it as they knew the palms of their own hands, and loved it, too. They both rode it, sometimes one in the driver's seat whilst the other rode pillion, sometimes the other. For years and years everything they did they had done to-gether – taking the *Sweetbriar* to sea, bringing in the catch, selling it, lowering each other down the cliffs on a rope to rob seabirds' nests, digging for cockles, chasing the giggling holidaymaking girls in the summer, flirting with them, teasing them . . . then turning back to the local girls for real companionship, to sensible Rhona and sweet Wanda . . . even their girlfriends were friends.

'Goin', Dai? What for? Why, in God's sweet name?'

Meirion's voice was shocked, he couldn't help himself. If Dai went, how on earth would he go on? His instinct would have been to go too, to set off for Amlwch the following day and never return if that was what Dai wanted, but it was impossible. His Mam needed him, he had been the man of the house since his Da had been lost at sea. They had a good garden, good crops, but times was hard, they needed him, and not on some little coaster miles from here, either. He must be here, on the Isle of Anglesey, looking out for them, guarding them.

'Why?' Dai sighed, picked up a lobster pot and began to insert the bait. 'Oh, Meirion, bach, you must know as well as I do that I can't stay here and see that woman take my Mam's place! What's more, she do hate me very heartily, and though I'm angry with him, I want my Da to be happy. He won't be happy with me disapproving of his woman and his woman searching her mind for ways to discredit me with my Da. So what better than a berth on a ship heading for anywhere but here? What better than a complete break?'

'But . . . but the *Sweetbriar*, your place on the lifeboat . . . even the old bike, damn it! Dai, you can't go, this is our place, where we belong! You can't let her push you out!'

'She's not pushing me out, I'm going before she starts,' Dai said crossly. 'She'd try, I don't deny it, but she won't have the trouble. As for the *Sweetbriar*, she's yours until I come back, or decide not to, or whatever. And yes, miss the lifeboat I will, but if I sign on aboard a coaster in Amlwch then no time would I have for the lifeboat, anyway.'

'Where'll you live when you come ashore?' Meirion asked plaintively. He brightened. 'Or will you come home, then? Back here, to us?'

'I don't know, I've not made up my mind yet,' Dai said

guardedly. 'I'd like to, but ... well, there's no gettin' away from it, mun, Menna hates me right well.'

'She won't mind you in small doses,' Meirion said with surprising shrewdness. 'It's only twenty-four hours a day, seven days a week, that she finds difficult, I guess. Right. I'll come over to the port with you. What time are you leaving?'

Biddy gradually settled down in the Kettle household. She was startled and a little upset to find that Maisie had been sacked, but as Ma quickly pointed out, with two of them at it the work of keeping the flat clean and the boys neat shouldn't be too difficult. And Ma Kettle could have been worse, for all she was tightfisted and dishonest. She had at first ordered and then tried to wheedle Biddy into giving short weight but in this Biddy proved adamant. 'I'd burn in hell if they didn't catch me and spend me life in prison if they did,' was her stoutly repeated excuse, and when Ma Kettle explained that it was not so much dishonest as good business practice, that in fact her sweets were worth a great deal more than she charged for 'em, only folk were so mean they wouldn't give her a decent price, Biddy just sniffed and began to clean down.

'Then you'd best not serve customers; you'll cost me too much,' Ma grumbled but Biddy, who believed in speaking her mind, pointed out that at least an assistant who was too honest to cheat the customers was also too honest to cheat her employer, which meant that the little wooden till with its tiny compartments for farthings, ha'pennies, pennies and so on was safe from the threat of thieving fingers.

This caused Ma Kettle to look thoughtful and afterwards Kenny told Biddy that she had taken exactly the right stand. "'Cos we 'ad a gel afore you, Trix 'er name was, an' she took from the till, nicked sweets, gave 'er mates special prices, walked off 'ome one night wi' a bag o' sugar in 'er bloomers . . . Ma prizes honesty after that.'

Oddly enough, Kenny, who looked such unlikely friendship material, was becoming a good friend to Biddy. His appearance was against him, of course, the hard little eyes behind the spectacles seeming to look accusingly out on the world, but that was just short-sightedness. Kenny was bright at his books and enjoyed being tested on his recently acquired knowledge and Biddy liked to help, and he saw his parent rather more clearly than she saw herself.

'Stand up to 'er,' he continually advised Biddy. 'She'll like you for it in the end. 'Sides, you works 'arder than most, it wouldn't do to let 'er keep you short o' grub. Think what she saves on Maisie's wages, let alone on yours. You want to see her wi' Aunt Olliphant; Aunt won't stand none o' Ma's bossin' – she's the younger sister – but Ma respecks her for it. So if you want seconds of puddin', say so.'

'I don't see why she grudges me,' Biddy had said once, in the early days. 'I swear she counts up every cabbage leaf that passes my lips to see whether she'd be better paying me a wage instead of giving me my meals.'

Kenny chuckled. The two of them were sitting on the hard bench in the shop kitchen, ostensibly studying. Kenny worked for a firm of chartered accountants and was going to take exams to better himself and he had told his mother that Biddy was a big help to him since she understood the work and could ask him the sort of questions he would get in his exams.

Mrs Kettle didn't grumble, because they only worked after the shop was closed, and with Christmas over there wasn't the call for the extra slabs of toffee, bags of fudge, candy walking sticks and sugar mice which sold so readily over the holiday season.

'Now's the lean months,' Ma Kettle had said as February came in with a cold wind and snow in bursts. 'We should tighten our belts, eat less, not more. We won't 'ave to work so 'ard because we don't sell so much. Think on, young Biddy.'

Biddy, however, decided that the cold made her hungrier than ever and several times sharp words were exchanged over her ability to look such a skinny little thing but to eat like Jack, Luke and Kenny.

'Stick to your guns; you eat wharrever you need,' Kenny urged whenever his mother was out of hearing. 'Remind the old gal that at least you doesn't nick 'er perishin' toffee. Even Mais nicked 'er toffee.'

Spring came, but despite the milder weather and longer days it was difficult to rejoice over much, since the shop kitchen was mostly too hot anyway and of course with the approach of Easter the Kettle establishment started on Easter treats – chocolate eggs, marzipan fruit and flowers – which meant that Biddy was busy from morning till night, and often too tired to sleep soundly either, what with the stuffiness of the small room and Ma Kettle's reverberating snores.

'I'll have to get out of it by the time summer comes,' Biddy told herself desperately, as she fell into her truckle bed each night. 'I remember last summer – swatting flies, chasing bees, sweating till I was hollow and dried out – I don't know as I can stand that again.'

The trouble was that Ma Kettle was determined to have her money's worth out of Biddy. I'm sure she jots down all food costs, my share of the fire – not that I ever see it – wear and tear of chairs, tables, knives and forks, and then thinks she ought to work me harder, Biddy thought desperately, as she mixed icing sugar, almond flavouring and egg yolk in a huge bowl. Other people get Sundays off, I know they do, but Sundays is housework day and all I seem to do is scrub floors, make beds, wash the linen, peg it on the line, run out and get it in if rain threatens, put it out again, fetch it back and iron it, fold huge sheets and then carry them up to make the beds up again, starch Luke's shirts, mend his frayed collars . . . the list went on and on.

'Tell the old gal you're 'titled to a day off, same as the rest of the world,' Kenny advised. 'You could come wi' me on the ferry over to Birkenhead, and then by bus out into the country. Go on, tell Ma you need a bit of a rest. She goes off to see Aunt Olliphant, we fellers go off to see a bit o' life, why shouldn't you?'

'I will,' Biddy decided. 'She can only sack me, after all.'

And in a way it worked.

'A day off? Lor, chuck, what next, I asks meself? I treat you like me own daughter an' you want a day off?'

'If you had a daughter, Ma, and made her work seven days a week, the priest would be after you,' Biddy pointed out. 'You aren't too keen on me goin' along to mass either, are you?'

'May you be forgiven,' Ma said piously, going through the shirts that Biddy has just ironed to make sure there wasn't a crease on any of them. 'As if I'd let a member of the Kettle 'ousehold miss mass! It's only that you will loiter goin' and comin', when there's a hot dinner to prepare, that's the only reason I just occasionally asks if you wouldn't rather stay at 'ome.'

'I'd rather stay at home and rest, but you wouldn't want me to do that,' Biddy said, as near to tears as she had ever come whilst under Ma's roof. 'I'm that weary, Miz Kettle, that I hardly know how to go on. It's just work, work, work, from mornin' till night, and never an hour to myself.'

'Then you go to mass, dearie,' Ma Kettle said expansively. 'Don't you worry about me, stuck 'ere at 'ome wi' a thousand and one things to do. Just you go off and enjoy yourself.'

'I will, then. Thanks very much, Ma. Kenny's going to take me on the ferry to Birkenhead, and then into the country! We'll be home for tea, though.'

'Now wait on,' Ma Kettle said anxiously, putting down the last shirt. 'I didn't say . . . what I said was you might go to mass, I didn't say . . .'

'Kenny said you weren't mean enough to try to stop all my fun,' Biddy continued as though she hadn't heard. 'I'll work all the better for the break, I'm sure of it.'

She told Kenny later and the two of them giggled over Mrs Kettle's protestations, and Biddy waited to be hauled from her bed on Sunday morning and informed that her mentor had changed her mind. But although Ma Kettle was quieter than usual, Biddy went downstairs, got breakfast, washed up and cleared away and then announced that she would see everyone later that evening.

'If I had any money of my own I'd bring you home a bit of a present, but since I've not had a penny since my Mam died you'll have to forgive me if I come home empty-handed,' she said to Mrs Kettle as she and Kenny stood by the back door. 'Tara, then.'

Ma Kettle sniffed and when they were half-way down the road she called them back. 'There,' she said, pressing a few small coins into Biddy's hand. 'Enjoy your holiday and don't bother wi' presents; them shirts was ironed a treat.'

Wide-eyed, Biddy rejoined Kenny and opened her palm, to show him a whole sixpenny piece and six farthings.

'Mean ole bag; but at least she give you summat to spend.'

'So long as she doesn't sack me when we get home,' Biddy said, though not as though it was something she feared. She gave a little skip. 'Wish I had a best dress.... Oh Kenny, it's good to be outside without an errand to run!'

'You want to say "no", more often,' Kenny grumbled. 'She can't be led, the old woman, but she can be pushed. We all found that out years ago, or we'd be nothin' but slaves, like you.'

'It's different for you,' Biddy reminded him, slowing to a saunter and sticking the money in the pocket of her tatty skirt, for even with weekly washing one skirt will not last for ever and Ma Kettle had showed no inclination to buy her a new one, or even a new-second-hand one, which would have done admirably. 'You are her own son; how you look reflects on her. And she's fond of the three of you, you know that. Besides, you're earning good money. If she chucked you out you could afford lodgings. What would I do, Kenny? Someone of my age can't earn enough for digs, I'd be chucked in the workhouse and I really am scared of that.'

'Yeah, it's 'ard for you,' Kenny agreed. They were on the sloping road which led down to the landing stage now and Biddy sighed ecstatically and felt the little coins in her pocket with something approaching bliss. A whole day off, the sun shining, and money to spend! If only today could last for ever. But it couldn't, of course. Tomorrow was Monday; she would be busy in the shop from eight in the morning until eight at night, so she must make the most of today.

It was a wonderful day out, there was no doubt about it. After serious consideration, Kenny advised Biddy to put her money away somewhere safe and forget about it. 'Keep it for emergencies, a rainy day,' he urged her. 'Today's my treat. How'd you like a bus ride? That way we can get into real country.'

They rode the bus into green fields, got off and

climbed over a mossy gate. The grass in the meadow beyond was tall and starred with wild flowers, to none of which Biddy could put a name.

'Ain't it just lovely?' Kenny said. 'I brung a picnic – me Mam said I could but she were too lazy to cut it for me, so I done it big enough for two of us. I know how you can eat, young Biddy, so there's all sorts . . . fruit, too. Even a chunk of stickjaw.'

'She never gave you her toffee?' Biddy gasped. 'I'm sure she'd cut my hands off at the wrist if I so much as licked me finger after hammering a slab in bits. Oh Kenny, you didn't prig it, did you?'

'She moaned and groaned, but she said I could 'ave some if I 'ammered it small,' Kenny said cheerfully. 'Stop worryin', young Bid, an' enjoy the day. There's a stream over there, under them trees – ever dammed a stream, 'ave you?'

When they had cleared up a slight misunderstanding over the word 'dam', they went over to the stream. It chuckled along over its pebbly bed, with trees hanging over it and little fish playing in the brown pools. It was the most beautiful thing Biddy had ever seen and she knelt on the bank, dabbling her fingers in the clear water for ages, before the serious work of damming began.

It was such fun! She had made sandcastles at New Brighton years ago, laboriously filling her bucket and then carefully upending it so that the contents stayed firm and formed the castle's battlements. She had walked down country lanes between her parents and seen the patchwork cows, the pink pigs, the rosy apples on the trees. But this – this was even better! She and Kenny scooped clay and pebbles, formed a deep ridge, shouted to one another . . . you would never have known that Kenny was a young man of seventeen, gainfully employed at the offices of Burke, Burke & Titchworth, or that

Biddy was an orphan with no real home to call her own. For the whole of that sunny day they were just a couple of kids, playing a wonderful, messy game and enjoying every minute.

'Look at me skirt,' Biddy gasped, when they had made the dam, watched a huge pool gradually form, and then broken down the dam to let the water swirl back into the main stream once again. 'The earth here is yellowy, I'm sure it's stained this skirt for ever.'

'It's clay and a good job, too,' Kenny said roundly. 'You was beginnin' to look a right mess, our Biddy. Time Mam bought you some gear, if only from Paddy's Market. One of these days you'll be a young lady, you're quite pretty already when you laugh and aren't tired out. Now shall we 'ave our picnic?'

They ate their food, then lay down on the mossy bank, though Kenny refused to let Biddy lie in the sun as she would have liked to do.

'You'll get sunburned an' you won't be able to work tomorrer, you'll be in pain, too,' he told her. 'Best lie in the shade, chuck.'

Biddy agreed, meaning to move out into the sun for a little, but as soon as she closed her eyes she slept.

Kenny's mouth descending on hers woke her in a complete state of panic so that she was struggling already as consciousness returned and began at once to try to speak, to push at his shoulders. She had been dreaming pleasantly that they were still eating their picnic, but just at the moment when he started kissing her she assumed, the dream had changed; she was a sandwich and Kenny was about to eat her, was actually sinking his teeth into her bread and lettuce! When she woke to find it was really happening, he really did seem about to devour her, panic gripped her. He was no longer Kenny Kettle but a dangerous stranger who could mean her harm. She brought her knees up and felt them sink into his stomach and as he moved back a little she screamed and hit out. He gave a pained grunt and sat back, looking guiltily down at her, one hand going defensively to his middle, the other stroking his scratched chin. 'What d'you want to do that for? Shovin' me off like that? I wouldn't 'urt you, you know that!'

'It was the shock,' Biddy said, scrambling into a kneeling position and glaring at him. 'I was asleep . . . it's horrible to be woken up by someone suffocating you.'

'Suffocatin' you?' Kenny laughed. 'By God, no wonder you 'it out! That, you silly kid, were a kiss . . . 'cos you looked so pretty, lyin' there.'

'You should kiss cheeks, not mouths,' Biddy said definitely. 'My Mam always kissed me cheek. Mouths are for eating with . . . oh Kenny, I dreamed I was a sandwich and you were eating me!'

He had been frowning down at her, clearly both perplexed and annoyed, but at her words his face cleared and he laughed out loud, throwing his head back to do so. He no longer looked threatening or different, he just looked like Kenny, who had been kind to her, who had brought her out for a picnic despite his mother's disapproval.

'There, ain't you jest like the silly kid I called you? You kiss kids on the cheek and young ladies on the mouth, you 'alf-wit.'

'If I'm a silly kid, then treat me like one,' Biddy said with some sharpness. 'Don't you go doin' that again, I didn't like it, Kenny.'

'You screamed so sudden an' whacked me so 'ard you didn't get it,' Kenny said in a grumbling tone. 'Just when I was about to do me Valentino on you, up comes you bleedin' knee an' 'its me right in the essentials . . .'

'All right, I'm sorry,' Biddy allowed. 'But no more of that sort of nonsense, eh, Kenny?'

'But I liked it,' Kenny pointed out, scrabbling their things together. 'Biddy, you never give it a chanst, honest. You'll like it awright when you put your mind to it.'

'No I shan't,' Biddy insisted. 'But you're packing up – is it time for the bus?'

'Very near,' Kenny said. 'Umm . . . Biddy?'

'Yes, Kenny?'

'Per'aps you're right, per'aps you're a bit young for that kissin' lark. What say we forgit it, for now?'

'Good idea,' said Biddy, considerably relieved. She liked Kenny and enjoyed his company but something told her, in no uncertain terms, that if she started all that kissing business it wouldn't be long before Kenny wanted other favours. Mam had said, before she died, that Biddy didn't ought to go getting involved with lads until she'd sorted out her future and that suited Biddy just fine. Besides, she had a very strong feeling that if Ma Kettle ever found out that Kenny had taken to kissing her little skivvy, she would be out on her ear without a character, regardless of who was at fault.

The bus arrived and they climbed aboard. Kenny kept shooting little sideways glances at her; he reminded Biddy strongly of a puppy who is hovering outside a butcher's shop with intent. Every time you catch the puppy's eye he thinks you can read his mind and acts ashamed.

So because she was a kind-hearted girl she reached over and gave his hand a squeeze. 'It's all right you know, Kenny,' she said hearteningly. 'We've had a really lovely day and everything's been fine. Perhaps we'll do it again one day, eh? Come over here and dam a stream and have a picnic and that. Perhaps next time we could bring your Ma, if you'd like that.'

Kenny laughed, but he squeezed her hand back and the naughty puppy look disappeared from his eyes. 'Eh, you're a nice kid, our Biddy! I wonder what Ma's got us for us teas?'

Biddy was trotting down the Scotland Road on her way to buy Ma Kettle some strawberries for frosting when she saw Ellen Bradley walking along the opposite pavement. She immediately hollered and waved. 'Hey . . . Ellen! Come over here a minute!'

Ellen glanced around to see who had called her and spotted Biddy. Despite the fact that the two girls had not met for a year she crossed the road at once. 'Bridget O'Shaughnessy, if it isn't yourself,' she gasped. 'I thought you'd gone back to Ireland wi' your Mam, cos we've not seen hide nor hair of you down our way for so long. What's been 'appenin' to you?'

'A lot,' Biddy admitted, linking her arm with Ellen's. 'Have you got a minute, Ellen? Because it's a long story and right now I'm in a bit of a pickle and I'd appreciate some advice.'

'Advice? I'm your gal for advice,' Ellen said. 'Ask away, queen.'

Biddy noticed that her old friend looked very smart and had grown beautiful since they had last met. She must be well over sixteen, Biddy calculated, since Ellen had been a class above her in school, and she looked very self-assured. Her smooth yellow hair was fashionably short, her lips looked a good deal redder than Biddy remembered them, and her brows and lashes had been darkened. Biddy glanced at the brown and cream two-piece suit and the high-heeled brown shoes on Ellen's feet, then wished fervently that she had not been sent out in her boil-ups – the sugar-stained white apron, the draggly skirt, the blouse spotted and scarred with the making of a thousand sweetmeats. But having called to her friend, she had best explain herself.

47

'Well, first off, my Mam died a year ago next September. They sacked her from her job six months before she died and we had nowhere nice to go, but we'd have managed if she'd stayed well. After she died I couldn't afford to stay on in our room so I agreed to move in with the Kettles; I was working at Kettle's Confectionery, still am, and that's all part of my problem.'

'Change your job, then,' Ellen said, without waiting for Biddy to finish speaking. She led the way to a pile of empty crates outside a butcher's shop and perched on one, patting the space beside her to indicate that Biddy should join her. Biddy did so and the two of them sat there in the morning sunshine, watching the passers-by with unheeding eyes whilst they talked. 'Don't tell me Ma Kettle pays you enough to keep yourself . . . *We're poor but honest, us Kettles; ask anyone,*' she mimicked. 'I've not been in there for years, but when we were kids we reckoned she give short weight, the old devil.'

'Well, that was a long time ago,' Biddy said tactfully. She did not intend to get involved in a discussion of her employer's morals. 'The thing is, Ellen, she gives me bed and board but she don't pay me. Well, think about it – where could I afford to live on the sort of money I could earn? I'm younger than you, too, I'm only just fifteen. So as far as I can make out, Ma Kettle's got me for another year or so.'

'Yeah . . . don't you have no relatives, though, Bid? Usually, when someone's Mam dies, relatives take you in.'

'Well, I've *got* relatives, of course, but they're all in Ireland,' Biddy said. 'I've never met them. My Mam ran away with my Da, you see, and they came to Liverpool. Her sisters and brother, and my Gran and Grandad, must be there still. Mam tried to write when she first married, but not even her sisters bothered to reply. Then she wrote again when Da was killed, and never had so much as a word of sympathy, let alone an offer of help. So I couldn't expect them to do anything for me, could I?'

'Well, I don't know; it isn't you they were annoyed with,' Ellen began, then shrugged and sighed. 'But if Ma Kettle don't pay you much – sorry, if she don't pay you anything – then you wouldn't be able to afford the ferry across the Irish sea, so that knocks that idea on the 'ead. So is that your problem? Gettin' in touch wi' your relatives?'

'Oh Ellen, of course it isn't,' Biddy said, exasperated with her friend's butterfly mind. If that was what growing beautiful did to you, she herself had better stay plain. 'I told you it had to do with the Kettles. It's Ma Kettle's son, Kenny.'

'Kenny Kettle!' Ellen giggled. 'What a name, eh?'

'He can't help his name,' Biddy said defensively. 'But last spring he took me out for a picnic . . . we crossed over to Birkenhead on the ferry and caught a bus right out into the country. We had a lovely time, I really enjoyed meself, but then, just before we got on the bus to come home . . .'

'He kissed you?' Ellen hazarded.

Biddy stared at her. Ellen looked such a fluffy little thing with that bouncy yellow hair and her big, blue eyes, but she was shrewd, for all that.

'You're a mind reader,' she said accusingly. 'How did you know, Ellen?'

'Because that's what nine boys outer ten would ha' done,' Ellen said promptly. 'You're young an' pretty – what else did you expect?'

'Oh! But I didn't want him to kiss me, Ellen.'

'Ah well, he weren't to know that, were 'e?' Ellen asked wisely. 'Not till 'e'd tried and been told to keep 'is kisses to 'isself.'

'Oh, I see. Well, if only he'd listened it would have

been all right, but now if I so much as pass him in the back kitchen he sort of grabs at me. And it isn't only that I don't like it, but if she caught us Ma Kettle would tell me to sling me hook and then what 'ud I do?'

'Ah, I see your problem. No money, a feller what's got 'ands like a octypus an' 'is Mam jealous as a cat. Hmm.'

'I don't think Ma Kettle's at all jealous,' Biddy said fairly. 'But she wouldn't want Kenny getting mixed up wi' me, it stands to reason. She wants him to pass his exams and be a credit to her.'

'Same thing; she disapproves,' Ellen said. 'What you want, queen, is out; right?'

'Oh, yes! But how, Ellen?'

'We-ell, I do 'ave an idea, but we'd best meet again, talk it over. When are you off?'

'Off?'

'Free from work, Bid,' Ellen said impatiently. 'Do you 'ave Sundays? What time do you finish? Six? 'Alf past?'

'Oh . . . well, I don't get much time off . . . oh Ellen, I don't get *any* time off, not really, because Ma Kettle has me clean the house, do the washing and so on, on a Sunday, we work all day Saturday until ten at night because people going to the cinema shows want sweets when they come out. . . . I might get away later on Friday . . . say nine?'

'Too late. What about first thing in the mornin' on a Sun . . . oh 'eck, you work then. Tell you what, make th'old bag gi' you a day free. Say you must 'ave it, chuck. This Sunday an all. An' come along to Shaw's Alley, up the back o' the King's Dock. We'll 'ave a bit of a clack an' a cuppa an' see what we can sort out.'

'Shaw's Alley? But you lived quite near us, on Paul Street,' Biddy said, about to slide off the crate but arresting herself to unhook her apron from an upstanding nail. 'How come you've moved?'

'Honest to God, Biddy, you ain't the only one what's done a bunk! Me family live at Paul Street still, it's just me what's in the Alley. Are you comin' or not?'

'Next Sunday morning? At about tennish? That'll be all right, because she'll think I'm in Mass. I'll be there. Where's it near?'

'It's on the corner o' Sparling Street . . . don't tell me, you won't know it, not down there. Well if you catch a tram . . . no, a leckie's out o' the question, no dosh . Gawd . . d'you know Park Lane, chuck?'

'Of course,' Biddy lied haughtily.

'That's awright, then. Mek your way there, keep to the right 'and side till you come to Sparly, then it's the first proper turnin' off on your right and I'm second from the corner. Me name's writ on the door, jest knock an' come up.'

She had jumped down off the crate as she spoke, smoothed a hand over her bouncy yellow bob, and was hurrying up the road again. Biddy ran after her and grabbed her elbow.

'Ellen . . . don't go yet! Where's your job? You haven't told me a thing, I did all the talking!'

'Oh! Well, no time now, queen. I'll tell you all about it Sunday mornin', tennish. Tara for now.'

Biddy, abruptly remembering her errand, stood staring after her friend for a moment, then, with a shrug, retraced her steps to the greengrocer's shop she had been about to enter when Ellen's familiar figure had crossed her vision. Mrs Ruby Hitchcot was lovingly setting out her strawberries in a glistening mound under a notice which read 'Fresh today! Straight from the Wirral!'. She turned and smiled at Biddy. 'Mornin', queen. What can I do for you this bright mornin'?'

Biddy had met Ellen on the Thursday and by Sunday she

was in a rare state of excitement. She thought about telling Kenny, which would mean he might well walk up with her at least as far as Sparly, but decided against it. The fewer people who got wind of the fact that she had met up with an old friend, and guessed that the old friend might help her to escape from the Kettle ménage, the better.

On the other hand though, Kenny always went to the same Mass as she did, because then they walked up and back together, shared a pew, sometimes shared a hymn-book, and talked softly whilst waiting for the service to start. It made the service more amusing, Biddy acknowledged that, but now it also raised a considerable problem. If she told Kenny, then he might want to accompany her, which could be awkward, or he might want to stop her seeing Ellen, which would be worse. She absolved him of being a tale bearer and wanting to tell his mother, but if she did manage to get away he would come searching for her at Ellen's . . . and might even put his Ma onto her if Mrs Kettle demanded her address from him.

Sunday dawned warm and sunny. Kenny suggested that she might get another day off and go along to Seaforth with him. 'We could bathe,' he said hopefully. 'We could paddle, anyroad. Why not, our Biddy? It's time you 'ad some fun.'

'Look, I'm going to Mass,' Biddy said patiently. 'We'll talk about it after dinner, eh?'

He scowled. 'I'm not goin' to Mass, not on a day like this. I'm not goin' to miss this sunshine even if you wanna 'ang around the 'ouse all day. I'll meet you out and I'll have a word wi' me Mam.'

'All right, if that's what you want,' Biddy said. 'See you later, then, Kenny.'

After the day out with Kenny, Ma Kettle had been prevailed upon to buy Biddy a best coat and skirt and a pair of decent shoes. The shoes had cardboard soles and were made of thin, cheap leather and the coat and skirt came from one of the stalls on Paddy's Market, but they seemed very fine indeed to Biddy. So on Sunday morning she donned the blue coat and skirt, the striped blouse and the navy shoes, perched a straw hat on her curls, and set off for Mass.

The Kettles attended St Anthony's at the top of the Scotland Road so Biddy turned in that direction, walked a hundred yards or so and then crossed over the road and retraced her steps, feeling excitingly wicked as she did so. It was risky but after all, what could old Ma Kettle do to her? Slinging her out on her ear seemed less likely now, for it had gradually been borne in upon Biddy that she was a very useful person indeed in the Kettle household. Where else would Ma Kettle get someone who could help Kenny with his studying, cook meals, clean, launder, make sweets . . . and best of all, do it without a wage and without ever dipping her fingers into the till?

So she could perfectly well have asked for at least half a day off, but in fact that would have complicated things still further. Mrs Kettle would have grudgingly acceded to her request and Kenny, ears pricking, would have stuck to her side closer than glue. All would have been spoiled, so though this way she was deceiving Ma Kettle, Biddy did not let this affect her enjoyment of the day.

If Ellen asks me I'll stay to dinner, she planned, hurrying along the pavement in the sunshine. And when we've had our talk perhaps I can walk down by the docks . . . I wonder what it costs to use the overhead railway? She could still remember how thrilled she had been as a child when her Da had taken her for a ride on it, all the way from the Pierhead to Seaforth and back, feeling like a proper princess as she peered into the docks, whilst her knowledgeable father told her all about the shipping that swung at anchor there.

But she would not part with her hard-won money on a treat, even if it was within her means. And that was not impossible, because Biddy had discovered that she could earn a little money from time to time, though if Ma Kettle had known, Biddy imagined she would have put a stop to it at once, on the grounds that Biddy's time and talents were hers, bought and paid for by the roof over her head and her meals. Because Kenny had insisted, Ma Kettle always gave Biddy at least a penny and sometimes more for the church collection each Sunday, but Biddy would not have dreamed of pocketing money meant for such a purpose. Her money, unlike Ma Kettle's, was made by fair means only.

It was Biddy's neat handwriting which was in demand. Ma Kettle had soon discovered that a notice written out in Biddy's hand was clear and legible as well as better spelt than anything she herself could produce. And then the grocer down the road, when Biddy had popped in on an errand, had asked if she could do some notices for his window.

Biddy complied and was grateful for the pence which found their way into her pocket as a result. She refused to allow herself to spend them, however, no matter how desperately she might long to buy something, and as a result she had several shillings, all in pence, ha'pence and farthings, salted away inside her pillow, a small, hard lump amongst the feathers.

She had transferred six pennies and four ha'pennies to her coat pocket earlier in the morning and now she jingled them thoughtfully as she walked. A ride on a leckie would be nice, but she grudged spending the money, especially on such a sunny day, when walking would be a pleasure. If she wasn't asked to dinner she could always buy herself fish and chips . . . her mouth watered at the prospect . . . that was, if she decided not to go home to Ma Kettle's until really late, though that would mean her deceit in not going to Mass might be discovered, which could have unpleasant consequences.

Biddy had just decided to tell a few lies for once – enough were told in the Kettle emporium each day to make her ears burn – when she realised that she had been so busy thinking and walking that she was actually on Old Haymarket, where the trams lined up when waiting for passengers.

'You want to go straight down Whitechapel, along Paradise Street and then turn left into Park Lane,' Mrs Ruby had advised her when she asked the best way to Sparling Street. 'Best tek care, though, chuck. It's rough down by the docks.'

So now Biddy crossed over the road junction with its mass of tramlines and started off along Whitechapel. She felt light and airy, pleased with herself. She was not running away, nothing so daring, but she did feel she was paving the way for a change in her circumstances.

And a change was overdue. It isn't that the work is so terribly hard, it's just hot, monotonous and constant, Biddy thought now, wondering whether it would be all right to take off her blue coat and allow the sunshine to warm her arms, for the blouse had short sleeves. Wasn't Ma Kettle ever young herself? Doesn't she remember that finishing work, having a break, is what it's all about? She does know, because look how she spoils the boys! Luke's shirts must always be immaculate, his food always on the table, she doesn't take money for his keep the way any other mother would, so he's not thinking of marriage, he's far too comfortable. And then Jack, though he's away most of the time, gets spoiled rotten when he does come home. Breakfast in bed, his favourite grub always on tap, friends home for tea, money for the cinema or the theatre slipped into his hand as he scans the pages of the *Echo* for entertainment. Even Kenny gets what he wants . . . which is why he can ask for time off for me and get it without an argument.

A tramp with his greatcoat over one arm passed her, grinning to himself in the sunshine. He had no teeth and he was filthy but he did look happy, Biddy reflected. Perhaps teeth and cleanliness weren't everything, then. She turned to watch him for a moment; he was free in a way she could never imagine herself being. He went where he fancied, begged for food or stole it, slept under hedges in good weather and in barns in bad. She supposed, vaguely, that he must sleep in workhouses in the city since barns and hedges were both rare . . . and saw that the road had changed. She was now on Paradise Street and must start keeping her eyes peeled for Sparling Street.

'Well, Ellen, you're very comfortably settled here. It's a lovely flat, it must cost you quite a bit, so you've done well for yourself.'

The two girls were seated on a comfortable blue plush sofa in Ellen's living-room. She had already shown Biddy round the flat, which was on the first floor and consisted of the living-room in which they sat, a very fancy bedroom, all pink rugs and cream curtaining, with a very large crucifix on one wall and a rather improper picture on the other, and a tiny kitchen.

Ellen, in a pink silk dress with a dropped waist and with pink plush slippers on her small feet, was sitting on the sofa beside Biddy. She was smoking a cigarette rather inexpertly, and at her friend's words she nodded and looked pleased.

'Yes, it's awright, this. It's a pity there's only the one bedroom, but I get by.'

'I don't see why anyone should want more than one

bedroom,' Biddy said frankly. 'Ellen, what is your job? It must be an awfully good one for you to live here – you don't even share!'

Ellen blushed. Biddy watched the pink creep up her friend's neck and flood across her small, fair face.

'I do share in a way, from time to time. And as for me job, I'm a saleslady in Gowns in a big department store. The feller that's got all the power, my floor manager, is a Mr Bowker. He's trainin' me to do the buyin' for Gowns so sometimes I go up to London with 'im. In fact 'e's promised to take me to Paris next spring. Yes, it's norra bad job.'

'I wish I could get a job like that,' Biddy said wistfully. 'You are so lucky, Ellen! If I could just get a little job, perhaps even a live-in job, then I might be able to save up for a room somewhere. But I'd never run to anything like this.'

Ellen got up off the sofa and went over to the window. Without looking at Biddy she spoke slowly. 'Biddy . . . what about if we shared this place, you an' me? Only you'd 'ave to – to pay in other ways, per'aps.'

'What ways?' Biddy asked, immediately suspicious. 'I'd do the housework and the cooking willingly, if that's what you mean.'

'No, though you'd 'ave to do your share. No . . . it's – it's me voice, me accent, like. They say you won't get no further in Gowns unless you learn to talk proper, and you . . . you can do it awready, like. So would you teach me? Show me 'ow it's done, like?'

'And if I do, you'll let me live here with you? What rent would you want as well? And where can I find a job, Ellen? Because you'd want rent, and anyhow, I'd have to eat.'

'I don't want no rent. To tell you the truth, Biddy, it ain't me what pays the rent, norrin the way you mean. Me – me friend pays it.'

'Your boyfriend? Does he live here with you, then? What'll he think if I move in? You'd have to ask him first, Ellen.'

'Well, that's the other side to it, chuck. If you'd just clear off out when 'e comes over, 'e need never know. 'E don't come over all that often, per'aps twice a week, an' 'e never stays the night, 'cos . . . well, 'e never does, I swear it.'

Biddy frowned. There was something funny going on here! Now that she thought about it, girls of sixteen just didn't get to be buyers for big department stores, let alone live in the style to which Ellen had obviously become accustomed. Mam and I lived comfortably enough, but we didn't have silk dresses, Biddy remembered. Mam often said that she didn't allow her soft Irish brogue to be heard by customers, but even without a scouse accent she had never risen to be a buyer! And a boyfriend who paid the rent but didn't live in the flat and never stayed over, a job which paid Ellen, at sixteen years old, well enough to wear pink silk dresses and to have a wardrobe stuffed with expensive garments . . . what *was* going on?

'Look, Ellen, what you do is your business, but I must know what's up if I'm going to share with you,' she said as firmly as she could. 'Who is this boyfriend who's so generous . . . is he – is he *married*?'

'Oh 'eck, I knew you wouldn't jest . . .' Ellen turned away from the window, crossed the room and sat down on the sofa beside her friend. Then she turned her head and looked Biddy straight in the eye. 'Awright, the whole truth, eh? 'Ere goes, then.'

The sad little story was soon told. A child of a large family, Ellen had desperately wanted what she called 'a nice life'. She got a job as a waitress in a big café not far from the pierhead and, following the example set by the prettiest, cheekiest member of staff, she began to flirt with any male customer who seemed interested.

A great many seamen were not only interested, they wanted to get on even closer terms with pretty little Ellen Bradley, who made eyes at them and agreed to meet anyone after work who would spend a few bob on her.

Then Ellen discovered that Mr Bowker, who was middle-aged, with false teeth and a thickening waistline, was watching her as he ate his chops. He was important, he rarely came into the café, and now, when he came, he liked to be served by Ellen.

'So young, so fresh,' he murmured to one of the other waitresses. 'She's wasted in this place . . . I'd like to see her in Gowns.'

'He meant out of gowns,' Mabel told her, giggling. 'A rare one for the girls is Mr Bowker, though he does his pinching in private, like.'

Ellen hadn't known what Mabel meant, not at first, but after her very first outing with Mr Bowker she understood. She could have nice things, if she would let her elderly admirer have certain privileges.

'Mr Bowker was ever so nice, 'e took me to the flicks, bought me a box o' chocolates, drove me 'ome in 'is big motor car . . .'

She made light of the clammy caresses, the persistent hand at her stocking top, though Biddy could tell from her expression that she had been shocked by his behaviour at first. The thing was, she told Biddy, that a boy's hand could be – and often was – slapped away, but she had hesitated to give a man old enough to be her father so much as a quick shove. Not exactly a shy or retiring girl, nevertheless by the time she had finished her story her face was crimson.

The upshot of those first tentative meetings had been that Mr B was very quickly enthralled by her, and terribly jealous of the fact that in her present job other men could look at her, flirt with her – might even have the success with her so far denied him. He tried hard to get her alone, to take advantage of her, but Ellen said proudly that she'd more sense than to let him carry on the way he wanted without any strings. And the depth and degree of his jealousy, when you realised that he was not himself free to marry her, carried a price.

'A good job at the store and a place of me own, that was what I wanted in exchange for – for not lookin' at other fellers no more,' she said. ''E was all for givin' me a job in Gowns – all women customers, you see – and I said if 'e coughed up a flat an' all, 'e could come round whenever 'e wanted, but 'is ole woman, she won't stand for 'im pissin' off when 'e should be at 'ome, so it's daytimes only, thank Gawd.'

'And you let him do – do *that* to you?' Biddy asked incredulously. Ill-informed as she was, she could still see that doing 'that' with a rich old man could not be to everyone's taste.

'Oh aye, whiles 'e pays me price. Now, chuck; are you on?'

'Wait a moment. Ellen, it isn't just so's I can teach you to speak properly, is it? You're lonely, aren't you? Why don't you ask one of your sisters to share?'

'Honest to God, Biddy, you want your 'ead lookin' at! If me Mam found out I were livin' tally wi' a feller old enough to be me Da she'd tear me 'air out be the roots an' t'row me body in the Mersey!'

'Yes, I suppose ... but you are lonely, aren't you, Nell?'

Surprisingly, the use of her old baby-name brought tears to Ellen's big blue eyes, though she snatched out a hanky and wiped them away as quickly and unobtrusively as she could.

'Well, aye, in a way. All the wimmin at work's years older'n me, an' the folk round 'ere turns up their snitches at me. They think I tek sailors, but I don't, I wouldn't, that's a sin . . . it's just Mr Bowker.'

'Do you call him Mr Bowker still?' Biddy asked, amused. 'After all, you're living tally with him . . . or that's what you said.'

'I call him Bunny Big Bum when we're in bed,' Ellen said, giving a snuffle of laughter. ''E's a funny feller, but 'e means well. Now will you share or won't you?'

'I'd love to share,' Biddy said recklessly. 'What'll I tell old Kettle, though? And Kenny, I suppose.'

'Tell 'em lies, real good ones,' Ellen said at once. 'After what old Ma Kettle's took from you you don't owe 'em nothin'. Say you met your Mam's sister an' she's goin' to tek you in. And 'ear the old devil wail', she added gleefully, 'when she realises she's gonna have to pay someone to skivvy for 'er in future!'

Chapter Three

Biddy walked home in a very thoughtful mood after her visit to Ellen Bradley. She had been offered an escape route though she was quite shrewd enough to realise that it was not, perhaps, going to be an ideal arrangement. She would have to keep out of Mr Bowker's way, which would mean that any personal possessions she might amass – she had few things to take with her – would have to be kept hidden away at all times, and because Ellen did not want anyone to get to know anything about the way she lived, she would almost certainly involve Biddy in her web of deceit.

But how else was she to escape from the Kettles, without becoming a vagrant in the process? Jobs in service were possible, she supposed, but when could she apply for such a job? Scarcely in what little free time she managed to scrape. And in this venture, she realised that Kenny would not stand her friend. He was always after her to better her lot, told her constantly to stand up for herself, fight back, but he would not want her to move out. He must know that if she did so, his chances of a quick kiss and a cuddle would be cut down dramatically – cut out, in fact, Biddy told herself darkly. She liked Kenny all right, but not like that.

Ellen had invited her to dinner, so she had helped to cook a meal, helped to eat it, helped to clear away afterwards. She was glad to find that Ellen was a good cook and clearly managed her little love-nest well. She commented on this and Ellen said tartly that anyone brought up as a third child in a family of a dozen had to be handy, else they'd go under.

So along Sparling Street, up Paradise Street and into Whitechapel Biddy pondered her next move. Tell a big, beautiful whopper and claim she'd met a long-lost relative who needed Biddy's help about her own home and was willing to take her in? Or tell the truth and put up with the calumny of being ungrateful and selfish – or just walk out, leaving a note behind, and spend the rest of her life hiding from vengeful Kettles?

She was still pondering when she reached the Scottie, still wondering what to do for the best. Because of something Kenny had let drop she had realised a couple of days earlier that before she moved in, Ma Kettle had not only employed Maisie, she had had another girl in on Sundays and Wednesdays to do the laundering and ironing, to mend anything that needed mending and to do any marketing which Maisie and she herself had not done.

So when I moved in a couple of girls lost their jobs, not just Maisie, Biddy told herself. The money I've saved the old skinflint! But it'll really go against the grain to have to pay out money for three girls. . . . Lord, whatever shall I do? Perhaps it really might be better to say nothing and wait my opportunity – something must turn up.

Keeping her visit to Ellen entirely dark would not be possible, she realised, because Kenny had said he would meet her out of church after Mass. But she didn't think he would split on her because he was still her friend, though less so with every time she repulsed his advances. She wished she did not have to do so, wished she found him attractive and wanted his kisses, but the truth was he was too much his mother's son. Every time she saw his bunchy face near her own she was sharply reminded of Ma Kettle – and the last person whose kisses she would welcome would have been that lady's.

Still, she had enjoyed a day out and now she had hope. The spectre of being stuck as Ma Kettle's slave until the day one of them died had actually receded . . . and it was a stupid fear anyway, Biddy told herself. She would have got out sooner or later, now it seemed it was to be sooner.

She reached the shop and went round the side as she always did when it was shut. There was a tiny yard which stank of cats and dustbins and was looped across and across with greenish washing lines, and facing her was the back door, a great block of tarry wood with a high latch. With a sigh, Biddy crossed the yard, ducking under the sagging lines as she did so and reflecting a trifle bitterly that since usually on a Sunday afternoon the lines were laden with sheets, Ma Kettle had obviously decided to save them for Biddy to do as a treat. She reached the door and lifted the latch, heaving at the weight of it. It swung outwards, creaking, and a huge bluebottle, which must have been lured in by the Saturday smell of boiling treacle, lurched drunkenly past Biddy's right ear.

'Damned old fly,' Biddy muttered. 'I hope someone covered everything last thing Saturday or I'll be scooping fly-blow off every sweet in the place.'

The back door gave onto the boiling kitchen, which one crossed to enter a tiny, dark passageway from which the linoleumed stairs ascended to the flat above. Outside, it was still a sunny afternoon but in here it was cool and quiet. Which was odd, Biddy reflected, tiptoeing up the stairs, because usually on a Sunday afternoon the house resounded with the noise of cleaning, laundering, ironing . . . only of course since she was responsible for most of those noises, it would be quiet without her.

She reached the landing and opened the kitchen door. Someone had put the sheets to soak in the upstairs sink, which was unusual and would mean she would have to carry them downstairs wet, weighing half a ton, to wash them in the little back scullery as she always did. She sniffed the air; dinner had not been cooked today – mercy, don't say the old devil had put off having dinner just because there was no Biddy to cook it for her!

Biddy left the kitchen and stood looking thoughtfully at the two remaining doors which led off this landing. One was the living-room, the other the bedroom which she shared with Ma Kettle. The boys had the attic bedrooms above, as she well knew, since as soon as Luke and Kenny were in the kitchen having their breakfast she was supposed to rush up the stairs and make their beds. Kenny had lately taken to making his own, presumably hoping to get round her, but Luke probably didn't know how, certainly he had never so much as plumped a pillow in the nine months that Biddy had been working here.

Better try the living-room first. She opened the door, and knew before it creaked back that the room would be empty. She stood back, her heart beginning to pound; this was definitely odd. She had never known Ma Kettle go out on a Sunday afternoon without very good reason and the church service she attended was long over. Jack was home, to be sure, but he went out with his mates, not with his Mam, and Luke had recently met a young lady – not that Ma referred to her as such, she was *that nasty, scheming hussy* so far as Ma was concerned – and liked to visit her home on a Sunday afternoon.

Best look in the bedroom, then. No doubt Ma was laid down on her bed for half an hour. . . . Biddy opened the door and stuck her head round it. The big brass bedstead was empty, her own small truckle bed pushed almost out of sight beneath it. Biddy could just see her rag doll's small, round head lying on the pillow.

With a frustrated sigh, Biddy closed the door and went downstairs. Was Ma Kettle in the shop, going over her accounts or checking stock? Or in the tiny scullery beyond the boiling kitchen, perhaps pouring water into the big copper so that Biddy could start on the sheets as soon as she returned? But the shop was deserted so Biddy went through into the scullery and looked rather helplessly about her.

The little room was dark and dank and at first Biddy could make out very little in the gloom, then she spotted the note. It was propped up on the copper as though Ma assumed she would go there as soon as she got back from church. The message on it was simple.

'*Do laundry,*' it said. '*Cook dinner.*'

Biddy stood looking at the note for a long time. Ma Kettle had not bothered to say where she had gone or why, nor for whom the note was intended. She had expected Biddy back after Mass, of course, so if she had left quite early she might have reasoned that Biddy would get the sheets on the line in plenty of time to get them dry. Or she might simply have thought to herself that Biddy must not begin to believe she might enjoy a few hours off without paying the penalty.

Finally, Biddy left the scullery. She went up to her room and rooted around under the bed. The old carpet bag was still there. She took off the blue coat and skirt, the cheap shoes, the little straw hat with the ribbon round the crown, and put on her working clothes and the cracked old shoes she had worn when she first came to Kettle's Confectionery. Then she checked her change of underwear, which had lived in the carpet bag ever since she moved in because Ma Kettle had never suggested she might have the use of a drawer or two. Next she picked up her pillow and thrust her hand through the hole in one end and deep into the feathers, withdrawing the lumpy little scrap of torn linen which contained all her worldly wealth.

Then she picked Dolly off the bed and put her in the

carpet bag on top of the underwear, and after that she turned and looked around the small room. She felt a little pang, but only a little one: it had been, after all, a refuge of sorts.

Downstairs, she went back into the shop and found her lettering pen and the big bottle of blackish ink. She fetched the note from the scullery and sat down at the table. She read Ma Kettle's words again, then smiled and bent her head, beginning to write.

Presently she stood up and propped the note against the ink bottle in the middle of the table, where no one coming into the room could fail to see it. It now read, in Ma Kettle's spidery hand, *Do laundary, cook dinner*, and under that, in Biddy's neat script, *Do it yourself*.

'I don't know what came over me,' she told Ellen later that day, when the two of them were settled down over a bread and cheese supper, with the windows open to let in the breeze from the river and a glass of stout beside each plate. 'It's the worm turning, I guess. And do you know where she'd gone?'

'Can't imagine,' Ellen said, sipping stout. 'How d'you find out, anyroad?'

'Well, I was going off down the road, feeling a bit scared in case she turned up and got really nasty, when someone called me. It was Maisie, the one who used to work in the flat.'

'I didn't know you knew her,' Ellen said. 'Or that she knew you, for that matter. What did she want?'

'She wanted to know if I was slingin' me 'ook, as she put it. She grinned like a Cheshire cat when I said I was, and then she told me Ma Kettle had been invited to her sister Olliphant's for tea . . . but listen to this, Ellen, she'd been invited last week but hadn't said a word to me, in case I thought I ought to go too! As if I would, as if I cared a fig for her old sister, who's probably just as horrible as her. But wasn't that mean? To go out just leaving me that message, when she could have told me before I went to Mass that she'd be out when I got back.'

'Not that you went to Mass,' Ellen said, spearing a pickled onion and popping it into her mouth. She crunched and then swallowed before she spoke. 'Still, I know what you mean; she's norra nice woman, that one. But it gave you all the excuse you wanted to scarper, didn't it?'

'Yes, it did. And all the reason I needed not to tell her where I was goin' or anything. And if Kenny gets in first, which he probably will, he'll read the note and understand that things had just got beyond bearing.' Biddy leaned back in her chair and gave a sigh of pure contentment. 'Oh Ellen, just to be able to go to bed early, for once! Just to know I shan't be heaved out to wait on those boys . . . it's heaven, honest to God.'

'Yes, I wouldn't mind if I didn't 'ave go to in to the shop tomorrer,' Ellen admitted. 'Still, it's awright when I'm there, specially if I gets a customer early. The customers like me,' she added, 'It's Miss Elsegood and Miss Nixon what don't.'

'They're just jealous because you're young and pretty, and probably they'd like Mr Bowker to spend money on them instead of you,' Biddy said generously, for the more she thought about it the less she liked the thought of an old man pulling her about. But Ellen, though she smiled, shook her head.

'Nah, it's not that because they don't know about me an' Mr B. Well, I don't think they does, anyroad. But they know a waitress shouldn't 'ave 'ad a good job in Gowns first go off, they know there's something fishy goin' on.' She hesitated. 'What you goin' to do tomorrer, Bid?'

'Dunno. Take a look around, maybe. It seems a long

time since I went into a nice shop and browsed a bit. Why?'

'We-ell, your money won't last for ever, and . . .'

'Oh, I'll look for a job first go off,' Biddy said, conscience stricken. 'Sorry, for a moment I quite forgot I needed to earn. What pays best, would you say? Waitressing, shop work, that sort of thing?'

'Factory work's best,' Ellen said authoritatively. 'You wouldn't get taken on in a shop in them clo'es – why didn't you keep them nice things you 'ad on, earlier?'

'She bought 'em,' Biddy said briefly. 'I know I earned 'em, but I didn't want her saying I'd left with property belonging to her. She could have put the scuffers on me.'

'What, the way she treated you, chuck? She wou'n't dare! There's a law in this country 'ginst slavery, you know!'

'Yes, but it's provin' it,' Biddy pointed out, ever practical. 'It would be her word against mine, because I didn't go shouting it from the rooftops, exactly. Still, I'll look for a job first thing.'

'I only said it because it's a deal more difficult to find a job than to look,' Ellen said rather gloomily. 'Tell you what, we're much the same size, how about if I lend you somethin' to wear, eh? Somethin' decent? Jest till you're in work, like.'

'Oh, Ellen, you are kind . . . but don't lend me anything too good,' Biddy urged. 'Just a plain dress and some shoes. I know what you mean, I wouldn't give me a job myself in this old gear.'

'Right. Now if you've done wi' them onions, what about a spot o' kip? We've both gorra long day tomorrer.'

Biddy very soon realised that Ellen was right; jobs were hard to come by in the city, with a good many girls chasing every one. But she did have an advantage; she was able to accept a very small wage and she was experienced at shop work.

Against that experience, however, was set the fact that jobs on the Scottie and in that general area were out, for fear of meeting a Kettle face to face and having to put up with at worst outright abuse and false accusations, and at best coldness. But the weather was fine, Biddy's little store of money meant that she could keep going for a week or two before the situation became desperate, provided she was content to eat cheaply, and for the first time since her mother had died she knew what it was to have time to herself.

Being just fifteen, there was enough of the child in Biddy to enjoy watching the trains steaming in and out of Lime Street, walking down to the pierhead to see the ferries come and go, sauntering along Sefton Street and watching the overhead railway chugging noisily along above her head whilst the masts and funnels of the big ships were easily visible in the nearby docks.

And neatly dressed in borrowed pink cotton with her curls tied in a knot on top of her head she looked sufficiently respectable to browse for hours in Lewises, George Henry Lee's and Blacklers, dreaming of the day when she would be able to shop here, to ascend to the restaurants on the top floor and eat delicious food, to buy a straw hat with a field of daisies and poppies strewn across the brim, to try on elegant ankle-length skirts and to tittup around in patent leather shoes with heels three inches high.

But of course jobs do not just materialise, so towards the end of her first week Biddy began to search for employment. She bought the *Echo* each evening and scanned the advertisements, she looked in all the shop windows as she passed to see if anyone was after a shop assistant, and she hovered outside a small factory which made leather handbags in the hope that someone might come and put a 'wanted' notice on the big wooden gates.

She had decided to leave Tate's for the time being at

least. Luke worked there, in a managerial capacity admittedly, but with my luck, Biddy concluded gloomily, he'd be the one to interview me for the job, or I'd walk slap into him in the corridor, and that 'ud be me scuppered.

The two girls were sitting in the living-room of the flat one evening, companionably sharing a fish-and-chip supper whilst Ellen soaked her feet in a bath of cold water and scanned the paper, when there was a knock on the door. It was the first time such a thing had happened since Biddy moved in and both girls panicked at once, Biddy flying across the room and trying to hide behind the sofa whilst Ellen, going very pale, whisked the paper out of sight beneath the cushions, tried to do the same with Biddy's fish and chips, with disastrous results to the upholstery, they discovered later, and adjured Biddy, in a piercing whisper, to shut up and stay still or they would both be out on their ears.

It was Biddy who came to her senses first.

She emerged from behind the sofa and grabbed Ellen's arm. 'Say I've just popped in to share your supper,' she hissed. 'He won't suspect a thing . . . act natural, for God's sake, or a babe in arms would know we were up to something!'

'Oh yes . . . oh Bid, you're a bright 'un . . . you've come to 'ave your supper wi' me, you're an ole friend from me schooldays,' Ellen muttered, mopping her brow. 'Oh bugger me backwards, 'e's ringin' agin . . . talk about impatient!'

'Your language!' Biddy said, giggling. 'Go and let him in, and act cool, will you?'

Ellen disappeared and Biddy, sitting demurely on the sofa with her plate and its damaged food on her knee, listened. She heard Ellen's high voice, a laugh, a masculine burr of speech, and then Ellen said, 'Come along in then, for a moment,' and her feet pattered back across the linoleum with a man's heavier tread sounding behind her.

The footsteps drew nearer and Biddy had picked up the newspaper and was scanning the job advertisements when the door opened. Ellen came in, and one look at her face showed Biddy that whoever had been at the door, he or she represented no threat.

'Biddy, meet me friend Mr Alton,' she said gaily. 'George, this is Biddy O'Shaughnessy, what's stayin' wi' me for a while. We was at school together . . . George was one of me pals before . . . well, we got to know one another whilst I worked at Cottle's, on Ranelagh Street. 'E's an assistant at the Sterling Boot.' She turned to her guest. 'Sit down, do, George, an' I'll get you a glass of stout.'

George was a pleasant-looking young man with short, fair hair, a tiny moustache and blue eyes. He grinned at Biddy and sat down beside her, carefully catching his trousers above the knee and pulling them up a bit as he took his place on the sofa.

''Ello, Miss O'Shaughnessy,' he said genially. 'Nice to meet you. Nice to meet any friend of Ellen's, come to that. You in Gowns?'

'Hello, Mr Alton, nice to meet you. No, I'm . . .'

'No, she worked at a confectioner's,' Ellen said, bustling out of the room in the direction of the kitchen. She came back with the jug of stout and an extra glass. 'She's not workin' right now, more's the pity.'

'A confectioner's? I seem to recall . . . but I daresay you're huntin' for somethin' different, or d'you want another job in that line?' Mr Alton asked genially. 'Can't wait on, I s'pose? There's a waitress wanted at Fuller's, next door to the old Boot.'

'No experience,' Ellen said, answering for her. 'But you could try for it, couldn't you, Bid?'

'I wouldn't mind, but most places seem to want experience,' Biddy said. 'Ranelagh Street? That's quite near Lewises, isn't it?'

'Aye, that's right. Nobbut two minutes walk away . . . well, if you walk the way I do in me dinner-break it's two minutes, anyway. Now let me see, someone was talkin' the other day . . . people do chat while they try on boots an' shoes, some customers get real friendly, but this was a feller what lodges not far from me on Chaucer Street . . . that were about a job vacancy . . . let me think.'

He thought, frowning, whilst Ellen poured the stout, then as he accepted the glass his brow cleared. 'Got it!' he said triumphantly. 'D'you know Cazneau Street, Miss O'Shaughnessy?'

'Yes, quite well, it's quite near the Scottie . . . ' Biddy was beginning when the incorrigible Ellen broke in.

'Let 'im finish, queen. George is a right good 'un for knowin' today what the rest o' the world knows tomorrer. Tell 'er, Georgie boy.'

'Well, there's a confectioner's on the corner o' Rose Place an' they're wantin' a young lady what knows a t'ing or two about confectionery. I walk past the shop of an evenin', it's a nice enough place. Cleaner than Kettle's, on the Scottie, but old Mr James meks 'is own taffy an' that.'

'Well, thank you very much, Mr Alton,' Biddy said. 'I'll try there and Fuller's, as well.'

She told herself she had no intention of applying for the job on Cazzy, it was far too close to the Scottie, but at least she knew about it; if she got desperate she could try there. And Ma Kettle didn't go out much, she was too fat to enjoy exercise, so the chances of her actually walking into another confectionery shop and spotting Biddy behind the counter were pretty remote.

Ellen seemed to guess what she was thinking.

'She wouldn't 'ave a clue you was there,' she said cheerfully. 'Nor would them Kettle boys. When you can get taffy 'alf price or free you doesn't go an' pay for it, not unless you're light in the 'ead. Nah, you'd be safe as 'ouses in another sweet-shop.' She turned back to George. 'She used to work at Kettle's but she left,' she explained. 'Would you like a cheese sarney, George? We've got pickled onions, too.'

Upon George admitting that a cheese sarney with pickled onions would go down a treat she trotted out of the room, leaving Mr Alton and Miss O'Shaughnessy eyeing one another somewhat awkwardly.

'Umm . . . so you're jest a pal, Miss O'Shaughnessy, an old school friend, like?' George said at last. 'An' you're stayin' 'ere a while?'

'That's right,' Biddy said. 'It's ever so good of Ellen to let me, especially when I've got no job, but I'll remedy that as soon as possible, of course.'

'Course you will,' George said heartily. 'Well, me an' Ellen's old friends ourselves, I enjoy comin' here from time to time. Usually I nips into Gowns to tell 'er I'm comin', but today I jest popped up on the off-chance.'

'That's nice,' Biddy said awkwardly. 'It's nice to have friends to visit.'

'Very nice,' George agreed. 'D'you get out much, Miss O'Shaughnessy?'

'Yes, quite a bit. Especially now I'm searching for work.'

'An' what about evenin's? The flickers? The the-aytre? A bit of a knees up at the local . . . ' he broke off, the ready colour rising to his cheeks. 'Oh no, you're a bit gre . . . young, I mean for public 'ouses. Still, I guess you like a good cinema show, eh?'

'I haven't been to the cinema for ages, but I used to enjoy seeing films,' Biddy was beginning, when George leaned across and pressed something into her hand. She glanced down at it; it was a round silver shilling.

'Go an' enjoy yourself,' George said earnestly. 'Get out

and about while you're young, Miss O'Shaughnessy. See a fillum, or 'ave a spot of supper . . . jest so's me an' Ellen can 'ave a couple o' hours to ourselves, eh?'

'Oh, but . . . It's awfully kind of you, Mr Alton, but I don't know whether I ought . . . Ellen never said . . .'

'She wouldn't, would she?' George said. 'Bit awkward, what? She never knew I were comin' over tonight, for starters. But she'll be pleased as punch to know you're 'avin' a good time, and . . . ' he broke off as Ellen entered the room and turned to his old friend. 'Ellen, I give your pal a bob for the flickers; what d'you say?'

'Well, George, that's very generous of you, but you don't 'ave to go, Biddy, if you don't fancy the cinema,' Ellen said, looking almost as pink-cheeked as her guest. 'Still, if you'd like a bit of an outing . . .'

Biddy stood up and crossed the room. 'I'll be back tennish,' she said, trying not to sound as shocked as she felt. She had managed to make herself accept the presence of Mr Bowker, though she knew she would always think of him as Bunny Big Bum and dreaded their eventual meeting, but she definitely did not approve of her friend living tally with one fellow and having another visit her in the first one's expensive little flat.

'Thanks, luv,' Ellen said. 'We'll talk after.'

She must have read the coolness in Biddy's eyes and the slight stiffness in her friend's attitude – and so she should, Biddy told herself furiously, clattering down the stairs. So she jolly well should, taking Mr Bowker's money the way she does and then playing fast and loose with his affections! Still, at least George Alton was a shop assistant, not a sailor. If Ellen started bringing sailors in she, Biddy, would definitely move out!

The *Jenny Bowdler* was a coaster, carrying any cargo it could get up and down and around the coast of Britain.

She was Dai's first choice simply because she was needing a deckhand the day that he and Meirion visited the port of Amlwch, simply because he had applied to the Skipper and got the job, but he was not sorry. It was a good life, though the work was hard and time ashore brief.

And right now the *Jenny* was nosing her way into a small port on the west coast of Ireland. They had a load of timber to take ashore here and they would probably pick up bricks, or dressed stone, or – or cabbages and kings, Dai thought ruefully. And once they had exchanged cargoes they would be off again, with very little opportunity to take a look around, or do more than go into the village to send a postcard home, buy some fresh fruit or vegetables, and get back on board.

It was a fine, chilly morning, and very early. Mist curled round the hills, hiding their tops from inquisitive eyes, and on the long meadow which sloped down to the right of the harbour the dew, Dai knew from his own experience, would hang heavy. He sighed again; he liked the sea, he enjoyed the comradeship and the hard work aboard the *Jenny*, but he missed his own place, his friends, the exhausting, muscle-straining work on the fishing boats and then the pleasure to be had from tending your garden, watching the crops grow, the beasts begin to thrive.

'Wharra you thinkin' about, you dozy 'aporth?' A hand, large and square, smote Dai right between the shoulder blades, making him choke like a cat with a fur-ball. 'Are ya comin' ashore, wack?'

Greasy O'Reilly was immediately identifiable by his nasal Liverpool accent. Dai swung his fist around his back and hit something softish; no part of Greasy was actually soft. He was a square, pugnacious young man of about Dai's own age but he had been reared in a far rougher school.

'Wait'll we see dem Liver bairds come into view,' he would say to Dai whenever home was mentioned. 'Eh, Taff, dere's no more beautiful sight I'm tellin' yiz.'

'Everyone's home is special, see, Greasy,' Dai assured him. 'Amlwch isn't my home, but it's near enough for me. Tell you what, bach, when we get back to Anglesey you can come an' stay wi' me for a day or two. Then when we reach Heaven – Liverpool to the uninitiated – I'll come home wi' you.'

'You're on! We lives in a real posh slum, us O'Reillys do,' Greasy said with relish. 'An' I gorra sister, she's a smart judy, what'll do anyt'ing for a mate o' mine. 'Ave you gorra sister, la?'

'Yes; she's married to a very strong man who ties seamen in knots and chucks 'em into the 'oggin at the least suspicion of a smile in my sister's direction,' Dai had said. 'Nice try though, Greasy.'

But now, holding the stern rope and waiting to jump ashore and tie it round the nearest bollard, Dai had no time for chit-chat.

'Yes, I'm coming ashore, if you haven't split my adam's apple in two, thumping me like that,' he said. 'Ah . . . she's closing!'

He crouched on the rail, then sprang over the narrowing line of dark water and onto the cobbles below and in a couple of seconds the *Jenny*'s stern was secured, whilst ahead of him Mal Stretson followed suit with the bow rope.

The fenders bumped gently and the small ship cuddled up to the jetty like a lamb to the mother sheep. Men appeared on deck, the Skipper came down from the bridge and everyone began to scurry. They all knew that the sooner the cargo went ashore the sooner they would be able to follow suit, and the port was an attractive little place.

'Irish gairls is gorgeous,' Greasy said as he heaved at

77

the first bulk of timber. 'Gorgeous an' willin'. Oh, will ye look at that little darlin'.'

Dai raised his eyes and looked. The 'little darling' was a strapping wench of no more than thirteen or so, standing on the cobbles with a small sister hanging onto her hand and a basket on one plump hip. She saw Dai looking at her and smiled.

'You'd better ask her if she's got an older sister,' Dai muttered as Greasy began to heave on the timber. 'I'm not cradle-snatching, boyo, not for you or anyone else!'

'She's older 'n she looks,' Greasy said confidently. 'See the kid wi' 'er? That'll be 'er sprog.'

Dai grinned. 'Stupid you are, mun. Them's little girls both; but never mind, we'll find ourselves something nice for a night in port – where's the pub?'

'It's in the Post Office and General Store,' another man said, overhearing. 'Haven't you been to Ireland before, Taffy? Oh ah, a bit be'ind the times is Ireland.'

Dai shrugged and came staggering out onto the cobbles with his load. 'Anglesey's the same, so I should feel at home. Come on, Greasy, move yourself, we want to get off before dark, don't we?'

They found two girls, gentle, lovely girls who laughed with them, walked with them and refused to do anything more with them, greatly to Greasy's disgust. 'But we're just poor sailors, starved of love,' he pointed out pathetically. 'We've been at sea months . . . we're only askin' for some kissin' an' cuddlin', dat's all we want. Well, all we reckon we'll get,' he added conscientiously.

'You're two lovely fellers,' Rose said, smiling at him. 'But isn't this a small community, now? And how would we face people if they t'ought we were easy? No, no, to walk and talk is fine fun, but to go wit' the pair of you to the woods would be dangerous.'

'Woods? Who said woods? But a stroll in the sand'ills now. . .'

'Sandhills are worse; sure an' sand is soft as sin,' the other girl, Iris, said. She was walking beside Dai, smiling teasingly up at him with her soft pink mouth curved delightfully and her head tilted. 'What 'ud the Father say if he t'ought we were that sort of gorl?'

'Oh, well,' Dai said, smiling back. 'We'll never know, will we? And now how about a drink before we go back to the *Jenny*?'

They slept on board, of course, and next morning Dai rolled out of his bunk early, before they were due to take on their new cargo, and went out into the misty pearl of dawn. He walked until he found a pebbly beach and then took off his shoes and socks and waded into the slow-moving sea, bending down now and again to pick out a smooth pebble and skim it over the little waves as they hissed gently inshore.

He was so homesick! Moelfre was like this in the early dawn, when the fishing boats were putting to sea. You looked inland and saw the cows up to their bellies in the milk of the mist, you looked at the rocks out to sea and saw them monstrous, rearing out of the sea half seen, half invisible, seeming to undulate slowly as the mist began to dissipate.

And the smells here were not so different either. Sea-weed, sand, the smell of wet rocks, the softer scents of grass and leaf which came to you in wafts as you left the sea and began to climb up the beach.

He found a little lane wandering between the lush meadows and followed it a short way. He leaned on a mossy gate and considered the cows beyond, a long stem of grass sweet between his teeth. Higher up the lane trees leaned, forming a green tunnel. There would be wild raspberries in the woods, he had already sampled some of the sweet, sharp little wild strawberries from the banks of the lane.

He turned to retrace his steps. They would eat, then begin to load the cargo. Best get back before he was missed.

Get back! If only he could go back home, but there had been a fierce and terrible row between him and his father before he left and there had been deep bad feeling on both sides.

'The girl is a good girl,' Davy had shouted at him. 'No word against Menna will I hear! She is a good girl and willing to be your friend, rascal that you are, boy. You will treat her with respect while you are under my roof and no more dirty talk will there be about Menna taking your Mam's place . . . she knows she can't do that, she seeks only to comfort me, to make my hard lot easier . . .'

'Then you won't marry her? There's nothing between you?'

The silence that followed went on several seconds too long. Davy and Dai were in the meadow above the house, out on the brow of the hill which nosed down, eventually, into the sea. Behind them was the monument to those who had lost their lives aboard the *Royal Charter*, when she sank within sight of land in the worst gale any man had known. Before them was the sea which had swallowed her up – her and many another vessel, all carrying good men who did not deserve such a death.

'Marry? Ah well, now . . . that's to say . . . she is a good girl, I'm telling you, Dai bach, and your Mam would think scorn on you to say otherwise . . . if my Bethan were here . . .'

'You make me sick, mun!' The words had burst from Dai even as he bit his lip to try to prevent them. 'If Mam were here she'd have your Menna out from under her roof before the cat could lick its ear! No place for two women in one house, she'd say, and Menna would be back behind the bloody bar of the Crown, where she belongs!'

Davy was not as tall as Dai, but he drew himself up to his full height and glared at his son with something very like hatred in his dark eyes. 'Faithful to your Mam I have been for thirty year, since the day we wed! A good Da to you and Siân, too. But talk like this I will not take, d'you hear me, boy? Menna is here to stay and you are out . . . d'you hear me? Out! You shall not sully Mam's memory or Menna's good sweetness to me in my hour of need with your dirty tongue. Out! Out! OUT!'

'I'll go, and willing,' Dai had said quietly. 'And never darken my doors again, Da, as they say in the old melodramas? Is that what you want? Because I tell you straight, I won't come back here whilst you and Menna are sharing a roof and neither wed to the other. That isn't how Mam brought me up to behave, and I thought better of you. Siân and Gareth don't say much, but they're of my mind. So it's no children you'll have if you . . .'

Davy screamed 'Out, I said!' and turned on his heel. He almost ran down the long meadow, leaving his son standing at the brow of the hill, with the bitter taste of defeat in his mouth.

His father was in the wrong and would never admit it; he was behaving in a way which would have Mam turning in her grave if she knew of it, which Dai prayed was not the case. Well, it was the end, then. The end of happiness, contentment, the end of his closeness with his father, his pleasure in the home they had shared for so many years.

He knew he could take a ship out of Amlwch because he and Metrion had ridden the motorbike over there a week since, and there had been jobs, then, for someone with his experience of small boats. But then he had hesitated, not wanting to burn his boats, to close the door on Moelfre, his home, his entire life.

He would hesitate no longer, however. He would go as his father bade him and never come back. Never, not even if the old man married the bitch and gave her his name. Never, not if the sweet sky rained blood and the sea turned to boiling oil.

Never. Never. Never.

But now, sauntering along the little Irish lane and reliving that terrible day, Dai told himself that never was a long time; too long. His father would marry Menna no matter how often he said he would do no such thing, because the village would not let him keep her living there as his mistress. Davy was obstinate, but once his son had gone he would do the decent thing by the brassy little bitch.

So I could go home . . . well, I could go and stay with Siân at first, I suppose, make sure of my welcome, Dai told himself, turning to blink full into the rising sun so that the tears in his eyes were, naturally, just the tears that rise to anyone's eyes when you stare straight into that red-gold brilliance. Besides, what a fool I am to feel like this after only a few months away! In a couple of years when I go back Da will kill the fatted calf for me; that's his way. He can't hold a grudge, never could. Any more than I can.

Only I'm holding out now, Dai reminded himself, slowing his pace even further as he reached the village green and began to cross it. I'm hugging my grudge against my Da and his fancy woman close to my heart and feeding it and seeing it swell and grow huge out of all proportion, and why? Because I'm desperate for the sight and sound of my own place and someone's got to be blamed for my not going back and I can't blame myself. Oh, Dai Evans, you're a poor feller if you can't forgive a man's foolish passion and a girl's weakness, he told himself. Perhaps Greasy's right; when I find someone myself and love them deep and true then I'll understand what's come over my Da and . . . and that woman.

Because Davy was very lovable – to himself Dai could admit that. Women always did like Davy, and obviously Menna was no exception, even though Davy was old enough to be her father. So Menna could no more help being attracted to Davy than the moth can deny the flame, and if she felt – rightly – that Dai was a threat to her spending the rest of her life with the man she loved . . .

Oh shut your trap, mun, you are sounding like a talking picture or a wireless play, Dai told himself gruffly. It's going to take time before you can look either of them in the eye – and them you, for that matter. Give yourself time. Stop tilting at windmills and gnawing your fingernails to the bone, let things slide a little.

He reached the end of the village green and dropped onto the quay. Greasy was sitting on the ship's rail, eating a bacon sandwich. He saw Dai and waved.

'Where you been, tatty'ead?' he said thickly. 'You'd berrer 'urry or you won't get no bacon abnabs, I've et most of 'em awready.'

The job in Fuller's would have done Biddy a treat, but as she guessed, they really wanted a girl who had had waiting on experience.

'But we'll be starting a beginner before Christmas, so you come back, dear, in a few weeks an' mebbe we'll start you on then,' the lady who interviewed her said with a friendly smile. 'You've got a good appearance and a nice, bright way with you. Don't forget, if you don't get anything else, come back.'

'I will,' Biddy said, trying to smile to hide her sinking heart as she turned away from the shop and began to walk home. Christmas! What on earth should she do if she couldn't get work well before then?

Ellen had an answer to that, of course, and had told Biddy about it the night after she had 'entertained' George for the first time.

'Look chuck, beggars can't afford to be choosers; if you can't get nothin' what pays enough then you 'ave to supplement your income, like. That's why George visits me . . . see?'

'No, I don't,' Biddy had said, after a confused pause during which she tried to sort the sentence out. 'Why should George supplement your income? I mean you're well paid and you've got Mr Bowker. What else do you need?'

'Oh, this an' that,' Ellen said airily. 'Norra lot, just a bit more dosh than I've got, now an' then. An' you're a pretty judy. George said . . .'

'I don't want to know what George said – or not until I understand you properly,' Biddy said slowly. 'George came for a couple of hours with you, he sent me off to the cinema . . .'

'Which were a kindness, 'cos 'e could 'ave just telled you to sling your 'ook,' Ellen reminded her. 'But 'e give you money for the flickers.'

'Yes. Oh, Ellen, did he – does he – give you money for – for being with you?'

'Norra lot,' Ellen said quickly. 'But yes, 'e does. Why not? Mr Bowker pays for the flat, why should George get 'arry Freemans?'

'But . . . but you said Mr Bowker was jealous, so he got you the flat and the job so's he could have you all to himself,' Biddy said, having given it some thought. 'So if you're seeing George on the side you're cheating on Mr Bowker.'

'Oh, yeah? An' what about Mrs Bowker, eh? Ain't the ole feller cheatin' on 'er with me an' on me with 'er?'

'I don't think that's quite the point. But if you're saying that I ought to go with a feller and charge him money, that's not on, Ellen. My Mam's dead so she can't kill me, like yours would, but . . . but it 'ud break her heart and I don't intend to do that. I'd sooner go to the workhouse, I tell you straight.'

'Oh!' Ellen said, clearly abashed by the vehemence in her friend's tone. 'Oh well, it were only a suggestion, like. Anyroad, you'll gerra job. Course you will.'

At that stage, Biddy had believed she would indeed get a job and probably a good one, too. But the trouble was that most people had taken on all the staff they needed at the start of the summer and did not want to take on anyone else until the Christmas rush started. Biddy tramped the streets and got kindness from some, cold indifference from others, but she did not get a job.

So now she was putting on Ellen's pink cotton dress, a white straw hat and her own black shoes. Ellen had told her she might wear her new straw hat with the daisies round the brim, her navy sailor suit and matching cotton gloves, but it seemed rather too dressy for an ordinary July day. Besides, Ellen wanted to wear it the next time Mr Bowker took her out since he had not seen it yet, and it would not be the same if Biddy had to wash it after a wearing. All I want is to get a job, and the pink dress is respectable and clean, Biddy reminded herself. It goes better with my colouring than navy, too. So I'll rub my shoes over and then . . . then I'll go round to Cazneau Street and just take a look at the confectioner's on the corner of Rose Place. The job is bound to be gone by now, it's days since George came, but there's no harm in looking.

She was in fact beginning to realise that it was pointless avoiding the Scottie for the rest of her life. If you were poor you needed shops like Ma Kettle's and Paddy's Market and it looked as though she were destined to be poor for a good long time to come.

So she cleaned the flat, prepared food for an evening meal, and then set out, grimly determined not to come back until she had a job. She would try everywhere . . . up and down the Scottie if necessary but definitely in that area since it was the only part of the city she had not tried.

Human nature being what it is, the nearer Biddy got to the Scotland Road, the more curious she became. She had heard nothing of any of the Kettles since she left and did not expect to do so, but she was absolutely longing to know who Ma Kettle had got to replace her and how the shop was being managed in her absence. In nine months she had done so much – all the notices were now written in ink, on stiff white card, the window display was changed at least once a week, she had been a demon on flies – her prowess with a swat had called forth much laughter and not a little admiration as she zoomed round, swiping vengefully.

I wonder would it hurt just to take a peep? she asked herself, as she walked demurely along Cazneau. Well, I'll visit James's Confectionery first, just see if the job's still in the window.

She reached the corner where Rose Place met Cazneau Street and suddenly got nervous. She walked straight past the corner shop without even glancing in the window, and then stopped, pretending to look at next door's display – and then looked in earnest. LAWRENCE MEEHAN, BOOKSELLER read the sign over the door, and the place was crammed with books.

Books! At school, Biddy had been a great reader, devouring everything the nuns had put within her reach. At home, her father had encouraged her love of books, though of late years she and her mother had simply not been able to afford it. But now, all her interest was aroused over again and she went slowly along, examining every title on every spine, wishing she could go inside, turn books over, touch them, read a few words . . . if she had a job, of course . . .

She turned on the thought and retraced her steps, peering in the window of the small shop next door. There was a bright display of jars full of tempting-looking sweets, an enormous stone jar packed with the paper windmills dear to little children's hearts, and a pyramid of small stone bottles of ginger beer. But no card advertising a job as a shop assistant.

There, you left it too late, Biddy scolded herself, her heart sinking down into her boots. What an idiot you were . . . what a coward! You were too afraid of the Kettles to come back here, and look how you are rewarded! A job in a confectioner's would not be particularly well paid but at least it would have meant she was earning money and now she had lost even that hope.

But having come so far it seemed downright stupid to turn meekly on her heel and go back so she continued to walk up Cazneau, and when she reached the junction with Juvenal Street she hesitated for a moment and then turned left onto it. When she reached the Scottie all she had to do was turn right, walk a couple of hundred yards, and she would be outside Kettle's Confectionery.

And when it came right down to it, what had she to lose? She might as well pretend she had never worked there, because she never would again, but it would be interesting to see what had happened since she left.

She walked on, turning the corner, walked on again. Probably Ma Kettle wouldn't even recognise her in the pink dress and white straw hat, she reminded herself. She had never worn anything half so fine at the Kettle establishment. So she continued on her way with a certain confidence in her step. The boys would be at work, Ma would be busy . . . what a fool she had been not to do this before, it would have saved her a few sleepless nights if she had resolutely returned to the Scotland Road and faced what was just a silly fear of being embarrassed.

She reached the familiar shop front and stopped dead, her heart jumping into her mouth.

The shop was closed, the window draped with what looked like white sheets, and instead of sweets, flowers crowded against the glass. There were more flowers piled against the door . . . no, not flowers as such, wreaths.

The shock held her spellbound for moments and she was still standing there, a hand to her throat, when someone bustling along the pavement stopped in front of her.

'Well, if it isn't Biddy! The funeral's in an hour or so, love . . . will you look at all them flowers!'

It was old Mrs Hackett, a regular customer at Kettle's Confectionery. She was smiling, nodding her head at the wreaths, the white-draped window, the white card edged in black, all of which were blurring before Biddy's vision.

She was dead! The old battleaxe was dead, and all Biddy could feel was the most appalling guilt. *I bobbied off and the ol' skinflint tried to manage alone and it killed her,* she thought dazedly. *Oh my Gawd, there was me telling Ellen that I'd not bring men in, when I've as good as killed an old lady who never did me any harm . . . well, not lasting harm, anyway,* she amended. *Oh poor old Ma Kettle, what'll the boys do without Ma to boss them and slip them money and look after them?*

But Mrs Hackett was still standing there, smiling up at her, only the smile was beginning to look a little fixed. 'Didn't you know, queen? Well, I'm that sorry . . . 'twas a shock to us all, a turble shock. But life must go on, as they say.'

With a great effort Biddy concentrated on Mrs Hackett and the scene before her. 'No, I didn't know, and I'm very sorry,' she murmured. 'What – what a sad loss, Mrs H.'

The old lady nodded and muttered and Biddy smiled down at her and shook her own head but her mind was in a turmoil and as soon as she could decently do so she left Mrs Hackett and turned to make her way back along the Scottie and Juvenal Street. She felt she could not possibly go in and offer condolences to the boys, particularly as Kenny would undoubtedly try to persuade her to return and Luke would blame her for his mother's sad demise. She found she had no desire to go up and down the Scottie, pop into Paddy's Market, have a clat with old customers or neighbours. Even her curiosity over the sweet shop had vanished like frost in June. With Ma Kettle gone it no longer mattered who was in charge – perhaps Luke would leave work and take over, or perhaps his young lady would be behind the counter in a week or so. Whatever happened, people must know she had left the old girl in the lurch, they would put two and two together ... oh Gawd, wherever she worked in future it wouldn't be on the Scottie, where Ma Kettle's death would be a nine days wonder for a lot longer than nine days!

At the end of Juvenal Street she turned back onto Cazneau and it was only then that something occurred to her. That bookshop had looked so nice, why not just pop in for a moment and see if the bookseller knew of any jobs going? Tradesmen and local folk often did know such things and although she had avoided this area in her previous searchings she now realised there had been no real need. Even now, though she would not work on the Scottie itself if she could avoid it, she could see how foolish she had been to ignore the busiest part of the city in her job search. And as she was here, right on the spot, she must do what she could to help herself.

She retraced her steps but instead of going into the confectionery shop she went into Meehan's. An elderly gentleman sat behind the counter reading a very large book through equally large spectacles perched on the end of his nose. When he saw her he put a finger in the book to keep his place and gave her a pleasant smile.

'Can I help you, madam?'

Madam! I am going up in the world, Biddy thought, trying to push back the thought that, if he knew she had as good as murdered Ma Kettle, he would not have spoken to her at all, let alone so kindly. She cleared her throat nervously.

'I wonder if you could tell me whether there are any shops in the area needing staff? I came up this way because I understood that the shop next door, the confectionery, needed an assistant, but the job is taken, and since I do love books I thought I'd take a look at your stock and ask you, if you don't mind, whether you know of anyone needing an employee with previous experience in the retail trade?'

The old bookseller smiled.

'I don't think you'll find a lot around just at present, and I think I can guess why. The schools are all in, there aren't any public holidays coming up . . . shopkeepers tend to wait for the children just leaving school in the summer so they can pay less, rather than having to pay for someone who's been in work for a bit. Sad, but there you are. And rich folk are saving up for their summer holidays . . . if I were you I'd leave it for a few weeks. Ah . . . wait a moment, there was something I noticed earlier, when I was having a quiet read . . .'

He reached under the counter and came up with a copy of the *Echo*.

'I contribute the odd review to the paper,' he explained, 'and one of my pieces is in tonight's issue, so the editor very kindly sent me round the first edition off the presses. I did notice something . . .'

His gnarled finger ran down the column, then he cleared his throat and looked at her over the top of his spectacles.

'Here it is; I thought I'd seen something. Shall I read it to you?'

'Oh, please,' Biddy said fervently. She was all too aware that it is usually the early bird which catches the worm and knew that buying the paper off the street vendors meant that she was seldom the first to reach a prospective employer. 'What do they want?'

'It's one of the big shops on Ranelagh Street; they're looking for a young person, it says, to do deliveries. Could you manage that, do you think? I imagine it would mean carrying heavy parcels for long distances, but you seem strong enough and often these places provide a bicycle. Ah, since it's a large clothing emporium perhaps the parcels would not be so very heavy.'

'Which . . . which shop is it?' Biddy stammered. 'I'll go round there at once – as it says "young person" they might look on a girl as favourably as on a boy, don't you think?'

'I do. You must ask for a Mrs Mottishead and the shop is called Millicent's Modes.'

'Thank you very much; I'll go round at once,' Biddy said. She glanced around her. 'And I'll spend my first wages in here,' she added spontaneously. 'It's such a lovely shop!'

'Thank you again, madam,' the man replied. 'And if you do obtain the position you can tell me all about it when you buy your first book; good afternoon . . . Ah, one small thing.'

Biddy paused in her flight.

'Yes, sir?'

He was fumbling under the counter and presently held out his hand to her. 'I wonder if you have money for a tram? Consider this a loan, if you like, but a tram would considerably speed your arrival at Ranelagh Street.'

'Oh, sir!' Biddy gasped, taking the money. 'I'll pay you back as soon as ever I can – this is so kind of you!'

'Nonsense, my dear. I know a prospective customer when I see one! Now be on your way – and good luck!'

When Ellen came home that evening, Biddy met her at the door. Her whole face was alight and a marvellous smell of cooking came from the kitchen behind her.

'Biddy! Don't tell me you've gorra job at last!' Ellen squeaked. 'Well, I'm that pleased . . . where are you workin'?'

'At Millicent's Modes, half-way up Ranelagh Street,' Biddy said proudly. 'The money is nothing compared to what you earn, but it'll do me until I can get something better. Everyone's rather standoffish but it won't make any difference to me, because I'm the delivery girl. They're going to get me a bicycle and I'm to go all over the place, mostly between the shop and the lady who does their alterations, who is a gem, a positive gem, Miss Whitney told me. Apparently this woman used to live in Renshaw Street, but she's not been well so she's gone to live with her daughter, in a back-to-back on Great Richmond Street, and Miss Whitney says she keeps having to send staff panting off up there when they could be more gainfully employed doing their proper jobs. I was lucky really, since they'd both thought of employing a boy, but having seen me, both Miss Whitney and Miss Harborough agreed that girls were, in general, more careful and that when I wasn't delivering, I could serve customers. What do you think of that? And they're going to pay me five bob to start and seven and six if I suit. That's ever so much more than Ma paid me, when she paid me anything, that is. So . . . oh, Ellen, do you know, I'd clear forgot?'

'Forgot what?' Ellen said, squeezing past her and going into the kitchen. 'Wharra you gorrin the oven, chuck? It smells that good!'

'Roast mutton with onions and potatoes cooked in the gravy,' Biddy said. 'But Ellen, I went down the Scottie, and the most awful thing has happened. When I got to Kettle's it was shut, and the window was all draped in white. Old Mrs Hackett said the funeral was in an hour and I came out of a shop and saw the hearse go past – ever so posh it was, with the huge coffin an' black horses . . . I felt ever so bad about it.'

'Oh, Bid!' Ellen gasped, genuinely shocked. 'Whatever 'appened?'

'I dunno. I suppose . . . well, she wasn't used to doing the hard work herself, I suppose she overdid it. She was always tight-fisted – I don't mean to speak ill of the dead but everyone knew she'd never spend a ha'penny if she could get away wi' spending a farthing – so I daresay she couldn't bring herself to pay someone to do all my work. I feel so guilty, Ellen, as if I'd killed her myself.'

'Aye, you would, but you shouldn't,' Ellen said after a moment's thought. 'I don't want to speak ill of the dead either, in case someone's listening, but she were a right old bitch to you, queen, and you no more killed 'er than I did. In fact you probably give 'er a new lease o' life, slavin' for 'er the way you did. If it 'adn't been for you she could 'ave popped off even earlier. I'm sorry she's snuffed it – well, fairly sorry – but she didn't do nothin' for nobody, so I shan't lose no sleep over 'er. And now just answer me this, afore I forget. Can you ride a bicycle? I don't remember ever seeing you aboard one?'

'Well, strictly speaking I can't, but I had a go on one the year before my Da died and I think I had the hang of it then. Da borrowed me one from a kid up the road and said if I could keep upright for the length of our street he'd buy me a bicycle of my own for Christmas. Only he died before he could. Does that count, d'you think?'

'Don't really marrer, I guess,' Ellen said, putting her nose up and sniffing the rich scent of cooking just like the kids in the Bisto advert. 'You'd learn quick enough when you 'ad to . . . an' now let's gerrat that grub before it overcooks on us.'

Chapter Four

Biddy soon began to enjoy working at Millie's, as the staff called it. She wobbled a good deal on the elderly bicycle at first and rammed the pavement edge several times, causing herself to suffer abrupt descents, but she soon got the hang of it, though of course with the big black iron carrier on the front piled with boxes, the balance was very different from the neat little machine she had learned to ride ten years before.

Miss Whitney and Miss Harborough were a couple of cold fishes though, and preferred to say nothing when she limped in with skinned knees, apart from a sharp 'And what 'appened to that silk gown, Miss?' before turning back to their own affairs once more.

But on the whole, Biddy decided she preferred it that way. The Kettles had taught her that, for good or bad, interference was not to be welcomed. Ma Kettle had tutted and got upset when Biddy burned her fingers by snatching hot tins out of the oven or inadvertantly pouring hot toffee too fast so that she splashed herself, but her concern had been in case Biddy was less quick next time, so it could scarcely count as genuine interest.

'It's ever such fun,' she said blissfully to Ellen after a couple of days during which she had delivered a great many boxes to various addresses, all to her employer's entire satisfaction. One of these deliveries had been a box containing a gown, a hat and some elbow-length gloves to a Mrs Isabella Purgold at No. 19 Grove Park. It was an enormous old house in Toxteth and the Purgold cook had given Biddy a cup of tea and a Welsh cake hot from the oven, and this and other kindnesses had undoubtedly coloured Biddy's view of her new job. 'You're out in the open air, cycling around, you visit posh houses which means you can have a good old squint at their lovely gardens and sometimes a close look at kitchens and hallways, too. Do you know, even in this day and age some of our customers employ butlers!'

'I'll 'ave a butler one of these days,' Ellen said. The two of them were eating buttered toast before leaving for the day's work. 'Come on, let's shift . . . at least you've got your old bike, I've gorra catch a leckie.'

'You can come on my carrier if you like,' Biddy offered, ducking to avoid the swipe her friend aimed at her. Ellen was very much the young lady in her tight skirts and frilly blouses; you wouldn't catch her riding pillion on a bicycle, particularly if another girl were steering it.

'Gerron wi' you,' Ellen said, snatching her coat off its peg and slinging it round her shoulders. She perched a small hat on her yellow hair and thundered down the stairs, shrieking over her shoulder as she went, 'don't forget to fetch me 'ome some chops, it's my turn to cook tonight!'

When Biddy got back to the flat that evening, with the chops and a nice big cabbage, Ellen was already home and in a high state of excitement. 'You know you've been teachin' me to speak posh, Bid?' was her first remark as Biddy entered the kitchen. 'Well, I been doin' it at work for weeks an' weeks . . . well, ever since you come to live, anyroad . . . an' when I'm with Mr Bowker, acourse. An' it's paid off. He's takin' me to London to look at autumn fashions, we're leavin' tomorrer mornin' fust thing!'

'Well, that's wonderful,' Biddy said rather doubtfully. 'I'll miss you ever so much, Ellen, but I'm glad for you.

Where will you stay? Not together, will you, in case it gets back?'

'Course together, an' how can it possibly get back? We're goin' as Mr and Mrs Smith,' Ellen said triumphantly. 'We're goin' to ever such a posh 'otel, we're 'avin' a suite o' rooms, an' all, wi' a proper tiled bathroom, fluffy carpets, a great big double divan bed . . . ooh, it's goin' to be ever so romantic.' She hugged herself tightly, beaming at Biddy . 'We'll see the King an' Queen, we'll go to the the-aytre, we'll 'ave us dinners at posh restaurants . . . no expense spared, Mr Bowker said.'

'I've seen the Queen back in '34 when she came to the "pool,"' Biddy said complacently. Inside her head she thought, *and without having to put up with some old man fumbling at my stocking tops, either,* but she said nothing aloud. Ellen had mentioned the fumbling at her stocking tops the first time she had told Biddy about Mr Bowker and though Biddy was quite shrewd enough to realise that the stocking tops had been but the beginning of Mr Bowker's explorations, she found that her mind refused to go beyond that, and was thankful to find it so.

'You're a poet and didn't know it – *I seen the Queen,*' Ellen giggled, obviously so excited over the prospect of the London trip that anything would have amused her. 'Oh Bid, I can't wait! We'll 'ave a chauffeur-driven car when we wanna see the sights. Mr Bowker says the bath's as big as me bed 'ere, very near . . . gold taps, 'e says, an' bathtowels what two could share they're so 'uge.'

'You make it sound like the Giant's castle in *Jack and the Beanstalk,*' Biddy said, smiling at her friend's pink, excited face. 'Oh go and start packing, I know you're longing to, I'll cook tonight.'

'Oh Bid, I love you!' Ellen squeaked, rushing out of the kitchen without delay. Her voice echoed through the doorway. 'Shall I wear me cream linen, or d'you think it'll gerrall mucky in the train?'

It had never occurred to Biddy for one moment that she might have any sort of difficulty due to Ellen being away, but she did. She waved her friend off at an early hour in the morning then cycled off to work as she did each day.

She worked hard, and it was hot, so by six o'clock she was longing for a rest and a cool drink but she still had one more parcel to deliver before she could make her way home. And that, naturally, was at Mrs Bland's, on Great Richy.

Biddy was rather looking forward to having the flat to herself, so she cycled off good-temperedly enough, weaving through the traffic and trying to avoid both the potholes – caused by motor vehicles – and the dung-piles – caused by dray-horses – so that she could keep both her person and her parcel clean and unrattled. She reached Mrs Bland's daughter's small house, delivered her box, refused an offer of a cup of tea and a cheese sarney with mixed regret, and turned once more for home and the flat on Shaw's Alley.

She arrived there late, hot and rather cross, to find George on the doorstep, looking every bit as hot, though the crossness faded when he saw her pushing her bicycle wearily along the pavement.

'Ello, Miss O'Shaughn . . . I mean Biddy; where's Ellen?' he greeted her. They had agreed that it was foolish for him to call her Miss O'Shaughnessy and that Biddy would do very well some weeks before. 'I went into Gowns in me lunch break but she weren't there, an' that sharp Nixon woman told me Ellen 'ad gone 'ome early.'

'Oh dear, how horrid of her, because she must have known perfectly well that Ellen wasn't at work today,' Biddy said, getting out her key and inserting it in the lock.

She dared not leave the bicycle out in the Alley but always took it into the tiny, square hallway which they shared with the occupants of the ground-floor flat. 'In fact she's not here at all, she's got a few days off and is staying with . . . with friends.'

She pushed the bicycle ahead of her into the hallway and propped it against the stairs. The ground-floor flat had a front entrance, she and Ellen the side, so she always left her bicycle down here, where she and Ellen – and any guests they might have – were the only people likely to go near it. Having stowed her bicycle, Biddy turned to George. He had come into the hall and was standing watching her, his expression enquiring, but as she spoke he heaved a sigh and turned towards the outside door.

'She's with 'im, you mean,' he said resignedly. 'Oh well, can't blame 'er, I suppose. No point in me waitin', then?'

'No point at all, she won't be home until the end of the week,' Biddy assured him. She hesitated. He was a close friend of Ellen's and he did look awfully hot. What was more, he would now have to turn round and walk all the way to Chaucer Street, and though the sun wasn't as hot as it had been at noon, the streets were like echoing, airless canyons and would continue to be extremely stuffy until darkness fell. 'D'you want to come up for a quick drink? There's some lemonade on the cold slab.'

'That 'ud be prime,' George said gratefully, standing aside to let her lock the outside door. 'It's a long way back to Chaucer Street in this 'eat, though I could stop off at the Eagle, on Parry, for a quick bevvy, I suppose.'

'Yes, I suppose you could,' Biddy echoed guardedly. She knew that the Eagle was one of the public houses on Paradise Street but had no idea what sort of a reputation it had. 'Come in, George.'

George followed her into the kitchen, where she hung

her jacket on the hook behind the door and then went over to the cold slab to fetch the lemonade. She had made it herself, buying and squeezing the lemons, boiling them up with sugar and pearl barley and finally putting the lot through a fine hair sieve. Now she poured some into a glass, added water, and then turned to George. 'I'd quite forgot, there's a bottle of that stuff Mr Bowker drinks – sherry wine I think it is. He gave it to Ellen. Would you like to try some?'

George said he wouldn't mind so Biddy poured him a tumblerful and pressed it into his hand.

'Go and drink it in the living-room,' she urged hospitably. 'I'll make a couple of rounds of sandwiches and then come through and join you. I really don't think I could bear a cooked meal, not with the heat being what it is.'

George carried her lemonade and his tumbler of sherry through to the living-room and Biddy followed after about ten minutes with a big plate of cheese, lettuce and cold roast pork sandwiches, garnished with various pickles. She and Ellen were very fond of pickles.

'There you go,' she said, setting the plate down on the low table between them. 'Dig in, George.'

'Ta, Biddy. It'll be a pleasure. My goodness, you cook the best bloomin' sangwidges in the 'ole of Liverpool so you do!'

They laughed together at his small joke, then set to and demolished sandwiches, pickles and yet more lemonade and sherry wine.

'That were grand,' George said at last, leaning back in his chair. His voice sounded deeper than it usually did – slower, too. 'Well, what 'ud you like to do now, chuck?'

Biddy shrugged. 'I don't have a lot of choice so I expect I'll wash my hair, iron my blouse and skirt for the morning, and go to bed. How about you, George? I suppose you'll be wanting to get back?'

She was too polite to indicate that he had been in the flat quite long enough, but she hoped, nevertheless, that he would take the hint and leave quite soon. So she was rather disappointed when he smiled and shook his head.

'No 'urry, no 'urry,' he said genially. 'What about six pennorth o' dark?'

'What's that?' Biddy asked.

'I meant would madam like to accompany me to a moving picture? There's quite a variety to choose from . . . did you get the *Echo*? If so, read 'em out and choose the one you'd most like to see.'

'Oh . . . no thanks, George. I don't think Ellen would be too pleased to find I'd gone off to the cinema with you,' Biddy said, having realised that he was asking her out. 'Anyway, it's too hot.'

'Not in the cinema it ain't,' George said at once. 'Honest, Bid, it's ever so dark and cool in the big picture 'ouses. Come on, be a sport . . . Ellen won't mind, not you an' me she won't. Why, I don't mind 'er goin' off wi' 'er old feller, do I?'

'It wouldn't make any difference if you minded like anything,' Biddy reminded him sadly. 'Still . . . what's on at the Forum? Or the Futurist?'

'That's a fair way to walk, though,' George pointed out fairly. 'What about the one on St James Street? What's it called?'

'The Picturedrome. But George, if we go up to one of the cinemas on Lime Street it's halfway back to yours and about the same for me. So that would be fairer.'

'D'you think I'm the sort o' feller what don't walk a girl 'ome after a visit to the flickers?' George said indignantly. 'No, I wouldn't dream of lettin' you go off alone after dark. We could go back to Ranny to the Regal . . . but let's make it the Picturedrome, shall us?'

Biddy frowned, but having examined the various

attractions they chose the picture showing at the Picturedrome, mainly because it starred Mae West, about whom both had heard intriguing stories.

'We can go in now, chuck, and you can still be in bed by soon after ten,' George said, helping Biddy on her with her jacket. 'Are you sure you wanna wear this? It's awful 'ot still.'

'You can't go out without a coat of some sort, not at night,' Biddy said, rather shocked. She decided not to bother with a hat, though, and put her hair up on her head with a length of pink ribbon to match Ellen's pink cotton. Good thing I was wearing it when she packed, she thought, having examined her friend's empty wardrobe, or I'd be going to the pictures in my working clothes!

She and George went down the street, joined the queue, and went into the more expensive seats. They settled themselves, George produced the humbugs he had bought on the way in, and they leaned back in their chairs just as the magic curtains parted to reveal the opening credits.

And that, Biddy thought afterwards, was just about the only enjoyable moment she spent in that cinema until the interval.

George, who had seemed so nice and sensible when Ellen was in the flat, became horribly active as soon as the main feature started and darkness fell. First he put his arm round her; then he tried to squeeze her breast. Shocked, Biddy discouraged this by elbowing him in the stomach and pinching the back of his hand, aiding her efforts by telling him to 'stop that' in no uncertain terms.

The trouble was, George did not seem to understand that she meant what she said and only desisted, in the end, when she informed him, in a furious under-voice, that if he touched her once more she was going to walk out and go straight home.

'I were only bein' friendly, like,' George muttered, shrinking down into his seat. 'Dere's no need to t'ump a feller!'

A hoarse laugh from someone in the seat behind cut him off short. 'Dat's ri', gairl, you tell 'im! The cinema's for watching de bleedin' screen, not for pushin' your luck wi' your young lady,' the hoarse voice commented. 'Give 'im pepper, the 'ard-faced get!'

This caused Biddy almost as much embarrassment as George's groping fingers and she dug him crossly in the side. 'Now see what you've done, we'll be a laughing stock. Just shut up and sit still.'

George morosely obeyed, but during the interval he bought her an ice cream and apologised. The hoarse-voiced one had either forgotten them or left the cinema, at any rate he didn't comment again, and for the rest of the programme George behaved himself pretty well, though he did hold her hand. But Biddy, faced with either holding his hot and sweaty palm or letting that palm stray where it willed, decided that hand-holding was the lesser of two evils and grasped him firmly, her grip more constabular than fond, though George seemed unaware of it.

When the film ended George apologised again as he was walking her the short distance home. 'I thought I were bein' polite, see?' he said miserably. 'Ellen, she'd be mortal offended if I didn't give 'er a cuggle an' a few squeezes in the flicks. Honest to God, I were just bein' polite, Biddy.'

'I accept your apology so long as you don't do it again,' Biddy said resignedly. 'Lor', it's quite lively round here despite it being so late – I suppose it's because it's been such a hot day and no one can sleep.'

It was true that on every doorstep men and women stood or sat, chatting, calling out in soft voices, eating fish and chips. Indeed, the smell of the vinegary fish and chips was so delicious that when George suggested he might buy them some, she was easily coerced into agreeing. With Ellen away she was too afraid of an unexpected expense to throw her own money about, but throwing George's was a different matter. Besides, she thought rebelliously, he owed her something for all that wrestling in the cinema, which had quite spoiled her enjoyment of the main feature.

'But you aren't coming up to the flat unless you swear on your mother's life that you won't start any of that nonsense again,' Biddy said severely. 'What about it, George?'

'I swear on me Mam's life that I'll be a good lickle boy,' George said, putting on a squeaky, childlike voice. 'Oh Miss O'Shaughnessy, I'll be good, I'll be good, I'll be good!'

Biddy laughed, but unlocked the door and ushered him into the flat. 'There's plenty of that sherry still . . . or there's a couple of bottles of stout left, if you'd prefer it,' she said, peering under the sink where they kept their drinks. 'Or I could make you a cup of tea if you'd rather.'

George opted for the stout so Biddy poured his drink and her own lemonade and carried the two thick, straight-sided glasses and the second bottle of stout through into the living-room. George was sitting on the couch, with the two newspaper-wrapped parcels before him on the small table. Biddy eyed him, but decided it was safe enough to sit beside him on the couch provided a good foot of cushion separated them. After all, he had sworn on his mother's life, what more could she ask of him?

All through the fish and chips and the drinks they chatted amicably, and then Biddy stood up. 'I've got to turn you out now, George,' she said half-apologetically.

'But it's work tomorrow for both of us. Good night, and thank you for a very pleasant evening.'

She held out her hand. George took it – and pulled with a fierceness and abruptness which had Biddy catapulting forward with a gasp, to find herself neatly fielded by George's arms.

'Hey! This is just what . . . '

'Every decent feller kisses a girl good night,' George said smugly. He was holding her pressed so tightly to his chest that she had no room for manoeuvre, scarcely room to breathe. 'Come on, be a – be a li'l sport.'

The little sport tried to kick and found herself suddenly sitting down hard on the couch, then being pressed back into the cushions by George's weight. Then his mouth came down on hers – and it was absolutely horrible, even worse than being kissed by Kenny. Fumes of stout and sherry mixed were bad enough, but George seemed to have some mad idea that kisses were accompanied by *licking*, and by a spirited attempt on his tongue's part to get into her . . . ugh ugh! . . . mouth!

At first Biddy fought with clenched teeth, but then she tore herself free for a moment and spoke. 'George, I said . . . '

It was enough. Before she knew it he was on her again and this time, having opened her mouth, she found it horribly full of George, who was being quite disgusting and accompanying all this tongue business with hands which did not merely explore but pillaged. She heard the buttons on her – Ellen's – pink cotton pop and scatter, felt cool air for a moment on her flesh, tried to get her hands up to drag the sides of her dress together, got them trapped somehow . . . tried to scream . . . but he was almost suffocating her, she could not breathe, she must breathe . . .

She bit. It was not easy because the weight of his jaw

was holding her mouth open, but she managed it. She bit hard, what was more, and viciously. George squawked – lovely sound – and began to pull back. But it might be just a trick to calm her fears, so Biddy brought both knees up into his crotch and had the immense satisfaction of hearing him give an almost feminine screech, at the same moment rolling off her and onto the floor with a heavy thud.

Biddy rolled off the sofa after him, got to her feet and bolted. George was moaning, trying to speak . . . she had bitten his lip, there was blood on his chin . . . but she did not wait to listen. She simply flew out of the living-room and into the kitchen, where she dragged open the cutlery drawer, fumbled for a weapon, and waited, a carving knife in one hand and the sharpening steel in the other.

Presently George's head poked round the door. His mouth had stopped bleeding but it had swollen and gone all puffy and one eye was darkening; it was already little more than a slit.

'Wharra you wanna do 'at for?' he enquired thickly. 'I worren' goin' to 'urt 'oo.'

'Well, I intend to hurt you,' Biddy said quiveringly. 'If you come one step further into this room I mean to hurt you very badly. I – I shall beat your head in with this . . .' she flourished the steel, ' . . . and cut your heart out with this,' she added poking the carving knife in his direction.

'Oh,' George said doubtfully. 'You're a bloody 'ickle vixen, d'you know 'at?'

'I may be a vixen, but you're a ravening beast, George Alton, and you shan't mess me about ever again,' Biddy said roundly. 'I mean it; I'll carve your bleeding face off your neck if you don't go home and let me go to bed.'

'I'm goin', I'm goin'.' George said sulkily. 'When she comes back I'm goin' to tell Ellen o' you.'

'You won't need to, because I shall tell her on you first,'

Biddy said triumphantly. She flourished her weapons. 'Out, George. Now!'

She followed George as he shambled across the hall and out and down the stairs, waited until she heard the front door slam, then went quickly down to lock up.

The first thing she noticed was that her bicycle was missing.

It was positively the last straw. Biddy shot out of the doorway and into the road and there, trying to pedal defiantly off, was George. Only he wasn't used to her bike with its big iron carrier, and was making heavy weather of it.

'Stop, thief!' Biddy shrieked. 'Stop that man, he's stealing my delivery bicycle!'

She did not just shriek, either. She ran, knife in one hand, sharpening steel in the other, and caught him up as he was trying, very inexpertly, to turn left into Park Lane. A number of men, lounging outside the pub on the corner, were just beginning to stir themselves, having obviously heard her shouts without altogether understanding them, when Biddy caught up with the erring George. She grabbed the bike by the back mudguard and pulled with all her strength.

As the bike shot backwards George gave a terrible howl and clutched himself, doubling over, then collapsed sideways into a heap.

'Eh, chuck, you've done 'im a mischief I wouldn't mind bettin',' an elderly man said, giving the writhing figure on the pavement a disparaging kick. 'Drunk, is 'e?'

'I don't know and I don't care. He stole my bicycle,' Biddy said. She could feel the curls on top of her head standing up like a dog's hackles with rage and indignation. 'I'm off back to my bed. Good-night, all.'

There was a chorus of good-nights from the men, some ribald remarks which Biddy completely ignored, and a moan from George. Then Biddy hopped onto her bicycle and cycled home, sore, stiff and aching, but with laughter beginning to bubble to the surface.

By golly, but George had got his comeuppance this evening! One way and another, he'd think twice before treating a young lady like a common prostitute again!

She went into the entrance hall of the flat, carefully locking the door behind her in case a vengeful George tried to burglarise her again for making him look such a fool, and propped her bicycle up in its usual spot. Then she climbed the stairs, let herself into the flat, locked up . . . and simply fell on the bed, fully dressed, and giggled weakly for a few moments, until she found that she was crying as well. Tears coursed down her face, ran into her mouth, down the sides of her neck . . . because it had been a really horrible evening and she never wanted to set eyes on George Alton again.

She boiled a kettle so that she could wash in hot water, remembering as she did so that George had sworn on his mother's life that he would leave her alone. His poor mother – I do hope I haven't condemned her to death, so to speak, Biddy thought. Oh, wouldn't it be awful if he got home and found his Mam dead? She suppressed the horrid thought that it would certainly teach him a lesson and began to wonder, instead, what she would say to George the next time she met him, because since she and Ellen shared the flat, she could scarcely hope to avoid him for the rest of her life.

But it was no use worrying; ten to one George's Mam would remain hale and hearty for another twenty years, and ten to one Ellen would sympathise with her plight and condemn George as no gentleman.

With this heartening thought, Biddy scrubbed herself clean, slipped into her nightdress and went off to bed, where she cuddled Dolly close and told her she much preferred her to a horrid young man, much. And presently slept the sleep of the righteous, despite her aches and pains, which were extensive enough to make her moan softly whenever she turned over.

'Well, so you whacked George in the gob an' locked 'im out – serve 'im right for muckin' you about,' Ellen said, when she got back and was told the saga of the cinema visit. 'Wharra puddin' 'ead! 'E needn't come round 'ere tryin' to mek up to me after that. No sir!'

'I'm glad you aren't annoyed with me, but I couldn't think what else to do,' Biddy explained. 'I didn't want to hurt George, but it was him or me. If only he'd not drunk all that stout . . .'

'It'll 'ave been the sherry; 'e ain't used to sherry,' Ellen said wisely. 'An' as for you bein' responsible if 'is Mam dropped dead then you'd best start prayin', since she died when George were three years old an' 'e's twenty-five if 'e's a day. Now stop chewin' over what's done, 'cos it can't be undone, an' let me tell you *my* news. Bid, we 'ad a great time, it all went like a dream, and Mr Bowker says when 'e goes to Paris in the spring . . .'

'Oh, the swine, no wonder he was willing to swear on her life that he'd be good! Still, I do feel relieved to know I've done no harm there. But wait on, Ellen! Tell me about the London trip first, so I can be properly envious.'

In fact, Ellen told Biddy about her London trip many times over the course of the next few days. The only part of it she had not enjoyed was the first night, when Mr Bowker had snored horribly loudly and kept her awake for hours, and just when it seemed that sleep was about to overtake her the traffic had started up and the hotel staff had begun to clatter.

'And I didn't much enjoy talkin' posh all day and night,' she admitted as the two girls made themselves a meal a few nights after her return. 'Me jaw ached and me eyes watered wi' so much squeezin' of me vocal chords. But it were worth it – we never 'ad a cross word.'

'That's lovely,' Biddy said absently. 'Ellen, do you mean you won't be seeing George again?'

Ellen shook her smooth blonde head. 'No, I don't suppose I will! 'E wouldn't dare come crawlin' round me, not after what 'e done.' she sighed. 'We've seen the last o' Master George Alton.'

'Good,' Biddy said decidedly. 'You don't need him, anyway, Ellen. Not now you've got my money coming in. I'm on six shillings a week now, you know.'

'You did mention it,' Ellen said dryly. She looked sideways at her friend, who was chopping onions at the kitchen sink. 'Biddy . . . don't you want a feller?'

'No,' Biddy said shortly. 'No time. Cor, these onions are strong, my eyes are running.'

'When I asked you to share, I thought you'd be good fun, though,' Ellen said thoughtfully, after a moment. 'I thought we could go around together, meet fellers, go dancin' . . . all you ever want to do is eat an' sleep.'

She sounded so injured that Biddy bit back the laugh which threatened.

'I'm awful sorry, Ellen, but my job's really tiring,' she said. 'But if you want to go dancing on a Saturday night I wouldn't mind going with you. It would be fun, and though I don't exactly want a feller, I wouldn't mind a very quiet one, just someone to go around with a bit. But I'm still a bit young for all that . . . that . . .'

'Oh, that! I din't mean that, exac'ly. But a girl can't go dancin' without a feller . . . that's to say you go in without 'em, then they come over to you and bob's your uncle!'

'Ye-es. Only don't you think . . . I mean if Mr Bowker got to hear of it . . .'

'That's the trouble,' Ellen said. 'Mr Bowker sometimes

don't get the chanst to see me for a week, ten days. I gets awfu' lonely then, Bid. It's different for you, what you've never 'ad you never miss, but . . . well, I gets lonely.'

It would have been rude to say, in an astonished voice, 'Do you *like* all that nasty business, then?' so Biddy wisely kept her mouth shut, and after a moment or two Ellen said, 'Then we'll go dancin' next week, eh? On Sat'day? There's quite good places to go – the Acacia, up on Everton Brow, that's good, the best one for us, I'd say. We can catch a leckie, they run 'em late on Sat'days.'

'Well, so long as you realise I can't actually dance a step,' Biddy said somewhat anxiously. 'They won't try to make me dance, will they?'

Ellen laughed. She was looking sleeker, more contented than ever since her London trip, Biddy thought. Wouldn't it be odd if Ellen really was in love with Bunny Big Bum, and eventually got him to the altar? Though divorce was dreadfully wicked, but if Mrs Bowker was quietly to pass away, and she was old and ailing, Ellen often said so . . .

'No one will make you dance, goose,' Ellen said bracingly. 'Besides, it's called the Acacia Dancing Academy, which means they do lessons, too. Only I'll teach you . . . here!' She began to shove and push at the kitchen table. 'Give me an 'and wi' this, then we'll 'ave room for a practice session.'

The port of Grimsby, on the east coast of Lincolnshire, was as good a place as any to have engine trouble, probably better than most since it was a large and thriving port. And at least, as the Skipper said, they had managed to get the old *Jenny Bowdler* safe in harbour before the engine gave one last wheezing cough and packed it in.

'It'll be the best part o' two weeks, lads, afore we sail

again,' the Skipper told his crew. 'Anyone want to sign off?'

Dai hadn't spent his wages, they were all tucked away, a nice little amount. He looked at Greasy, who was in a similar position, except that Greasy helped to support his mother and the kids, and raised his eyebrows. Greasy gave him a bit of a nod; go ahead, the nod said, if you make the move I'll back you up.

'I'd like to sign off, Skip, and Greasy O'Reilly would, too,' Dai said. 'It isn't that we're discontented, but we'd like to see more o' the world, see? And there's big sea-going vessels, fishing boats, all sorts, eager to sign experienced hands. We'd relish a change, like.'

Seamen, when they're young, go from ship to ship all the time. It's the best way to gain different experience, to fit you to take your ticket, if you've a mind to do well in the merchant service, the Skipper knew it as well as Dai and Greasy. So he just grinned at them, wished them luck and paid them off. The other men on board would probably stay for a while at any rate, then they, too, would change ships.

'Where'll we go, Taff?' Greasy asked after the two of them had arranged a cheap bed in a communal lodging house for seamen on the waterfront and were returning to the *Jenny* to pack up their gear. 'What'll we do, eh, la?'

'Shall we have a go at trawling, mun?' Dai asked innocently. 'Nothing quite as good as a fishing trip, there is. It's nearly October and up in the north the fishing boats will be making their way along the coast, following the herring shoals, and the Scottish fishergirls follow the boats. They sweep down from John o'Groats to Land's End, bringing their catches ashore at each port for the girls to clean and process. Why, those girls can gut the herring quicker than you can swallow a mouthful of ale, and they swear better than a Liverpool navvy – if we sail from here you'll have all the female company you want, come October.'

'You want to fish for herring, then? That's orright by me, la! But they shoot their roes in October, November, you say, and then what'll we catch? An' I've never caught a fish in me life, though I don't mind eatin' 'em when the chance comes.'

'Oh later, I want to go distant-water trawling,' Dai said dreamily. They reached the *Jenny* and went on board, clattering noisily down the companionway to their quarters. 'No use going home until spring, by then my Da will have had a chance to miss me, see? Sîan writes regular, bless her, and a batch of letters I've had; they caught up with me here. My Da married his little brass barmaid and is beginning to miss the homemaking he had with my Mam, see? I'll give him the winter to knock Menna into shape, then I'll go home.'

'What's this distant-water trawling?' Greasy asked, suspicion in every tone of his voice. He took an untidy and probably dirty pile of clothes and crammed them into his filthy holdall. 'I don't like the sound o' it an' that's a fac'.'

'It's catching the great Icelandic cod and the real big 'uns, right up in the north. It's seeing polar bears an' penguins, and the air so cold it's a danger to breathe in without a warm scarf round your face, mun,' Dai told him, rolling his clothing neatly and stowing it in his own bag. Working on small fishing boats teaches you tidiness the hard way. 'It's icebergs bigger than the biggest sky-scraper in New York and snow wherever you touch land and the blown spume freezing before it clatters on deck in foul weather. It's wicked hard, wicked cold . . . but exciting, dangerous, all the *interesting* things,' Dai said with deep conviction. 'You'll not be interested, I suppose?'

'Whassa money like?'

'If you survive, it's the best. They call distant-water trawlermen two-day millionaires because they make it and spend it fast. But I don't suppose . . .'

'Now you're talkin', Taffy; I'm on.' Greasy's voice was laconic, but Dai saw the sparkle in his friend's small grey eyes, the grin twitching at Greasy's long, mobile mouth. 'No need to talk like a ha'penny book, I got your drift and I'll come wit' you. Awright? Got the message?'

'Aye, you'll come distant-water trawling, but we'll start with the herring first. Well, the *Girl Sally* will be taking on at the end o' the week which gives us long enough to get geared up an' let our folks know.' Dai, standing by his stripped bunk, hesitated. His bag was packed, his only decent pair of shoes were slung by their laces round his neck . . . but was it fair to involve Greasy in something like distant-water trawling? It was the most dangerous way to go to sea, and all ways were pretty dangerous. He himself was all right, he knew what he was doing, longed for the challenge, and besides, no one was waiting for him, no one would shed more than the odd tear if he went down out there, amongst the ice-floes. But Greasy was one of a big family, they needed him – and the money he earned.

'Eh, la, you've got a face like an empty beer glass – I can see right through it,' Greasy remarked with a sigh, then leaned across and punched Dai's shoulder. 'I'm tough, remember? Eldest of 'leven kids, brung up to fight me way outa any paper bag what stands in me way, that's Greasy O'Reilly. There's only two t'ings I want from me life, Taff – wimmin an' 'ard cash. I 'aven't done too good wi' the first lately, but the second makes up for a lot. So I'm goin' distant-water trawlin' now even if you back down, me fine bucko – got it?' He pushed his unshaven face close to Dai's. ''Ave I got t'rough to you, son?'

'Yes, just about,' Dai said equably, slinging his bag up

across his shoulder and padding across their sleeping quarters. 'And don't blame me, mun, if you come back wi' frostbite in all your extremities; things can fall off in the ice an' cold you know.'

'Extremities? Does that mean wharr I think it means? Brass monkey weather, eh?' Greasy chuckled and followed Dai up on deck. 'Oh well, la, we'd best find ourselve a coupla judies before we sign on and lose our big attractions, eh?'

It was a very cold day. Biddy was cycling along, head down, nose buried in the scarf she had acquired, thanking the lord – and Ellen – both for the warm woollen scarf and her decent pair of gloves. Biddy was no hand with her needles but Ellen was not only an excellent knitter, she loved doing it. So Biddy bought her the wool and the pattern and Ellen sat there, evenings, and knitted away, and first the thick and comforting scarf and then the lovely little navy blue gloves grew like miracles on the end of her needles.

Biddy was better paid than she had been, because her wages had risen to seven shillings and sixpence a week in September and now, in early December, she was beginning to reap the reward for punctuality and her cheerful disposition.

Tips! At first Biddy had simply done as Miss Whitney or Miss Harborough told her; she had taken boxes all over the area, had handed them in and gone back for more. But gradually, as she became a familiar sight pedalling along on her old black bicycle with the laden carrier, she was hailed by customers, servants from the big houses, and even by other traders.

'Biddy love, are you goin' past the Post Office? 'Ere's a bob – get these stamped for me an' stick 'em in the box . . . keep the change.'

There was no harm in it, it did not hold her up, or if it did she pushed a little harder at her pedals, did not dismount at the foot of steep hills, coasted down at reckless speed. And after a time even Miss Whitney and Miss Harborough began to ask for favours and pay her the odd pence.

'Take this parcel to No. 3 Shawcross Road, there's a Mrs Mablethorpe waiting for it. Oh, and Biddy, on your way back would you pick up some cornplasters from Boots, on Ranelagh Place? My mother likes the ones they sell, she thinks they're bigger than the ones I got her from Banner's, on North John Street. I'll give you ten pence, though I believe they're only eightpence ha'penny. Oh . . . keep the change.'

And no sooner had she grown used to the size and type of corn plasters preferred by old Mrs Whitney than Miss Harborough would start.

'Biddy, the hem shortening and the relining should be ready by now and we've a batch of darts to be let out, take them up to Mrs Bland and tell her we want them as soon as possible. And whilst you're that way you might nip into Leigh's, on Scotland Road, and fetch me a pound of their best butter. My brother Sidney and his family are coming over on Sunday and Mother does like me to provide a good tea for them. Oh, and if you're anywhere near Chiappe, the confectioner, you might get me some Fishermen's Friend throat lozenges and a quarter of a pound of those special Italian chocolates he sells. They make a lovely present – tell him it's a present and he'll wrap the box in pretty gold paper and put a piece of ribbon round it.' Miss Harborough counted out the money slowly. 'That should be plenty; keep the change, if there is any.'

So the little hoard, this time tucked away in another pillow, though still with Dolly on guard, gradually grew and as Christmas approached, pleasant thoughts of presents, jollity and two whole days off from work began to take possession of Biddy's mind. Last Christmas had been grim, with Ma Kettle still bent on instilling the spirit of slavery into her new possession's mind and Biddy's loss too raw and recent to allow her to enjoy the festivities, but this year would be different. She and Ellen were going regularly to dances at the Acacia and meeting lots of new friends. They were much sought after and though Biddy still held back from meeting any young men apart from actually on the dance floor, she was easier with them and enjoyed their company.

But now she was cycling along in the late afternoon dusk, having been all the way out to Brompton Avenue to deliver a party dress. Today's errand was for Mr Smythe from the shoe shop, who was a keen horse rider and had ordered a new saddle for his mare from Benjamin Holland, the saddler on Mount Pleasant, and wanted to know whether Mr Benjamin would deliver the saddle by the following Friday.

Biddy had ridden energetically on the way out, but it was a long way. She had already travelled along Croxteth Road, into the Boulevarde, through Catherine Street and left into Hardman Street. Mount Pleasant was out of her way, but the tip – given in advance – had been generous so she took the necessary turnings and arrived on Mount Pleasant as dusk was definitely falling and the street lights were being lit. She hailed the lamplighter cheerfully and he directed her to Mr Holland's premises, where she found Mr Holland sitting on a tall stool mending a harness which had come unstitched.

'Afternoon,' Mr Holland said, and Biddy speedily explained her errand.

'Oh, the Smythe saddle . . . yes, I'll deliver it Friday morning,' Mr Holland said, smiling comfortably. 'Tell Mr

Smythe ten o'clock Friday.' And as Biddy was turning away he added, 'It's gettin' dark, lass. Time you was tucked up in your own 'ome, not bicycling around the icy streets, runnin' errands for young fellers what ought to do their own work.' He ferreted in his pocket and pulled out tuppence. 'Here ... Buy yourself some 'ot chestnuts, I heard the seller callin' them not ten minutes gone.'

'Thank you very much,' Biddy said sincerely, pocketing the coins – this was her lucky day! 'I'll tell Mr Smythe Friday, then.'

Once outside the shop she mounted her bicycle once more, extremely glad that a good deal of her journey would now be downhill, and set off. She skimmed along, the icy wind nipping at her nose and bringing tears to her eyes, but the thought of the warm shop and the cup of hot tea which Miss Whitney or Miss Harborough would undoubtedly make her when they saw how ice-cold she was, cheered her on.

She came past the Adelphi at a cracking pace and swerved into Ranelagh Place. A tram was thundering down on her so she steered into the side, away from the tramlines, glancing at the tram incuriously as it passed.

She had brought the bicycle almost to a halt as she did so and as she balanced there, half on the saddle, with one foot firmly on the road surface and the other on the pedal, she caught the eye of someone staring out of the window of the tram ... and for one startled moment she thought it was Ma Kettle, come back to haunt her. But only for a moment. Then she remembered Kenny's Aunt Olliphant and realised she must have seen that lady. How odd that she should have met, by proxy, a woman she had never actually clapped eyes on but had recognised just from a strong likeness to her dead sister!

For a moment, Biddy stayed where she was, then someone hooted at her and the driver of a horse and cart, which had also stopped to let the tram go past, shouted at her to 'Gerra move on, gairl!'

Biddy obediently pushed her bicycle out of the stream of traffic and over to Ranelagh Street. Normally, she would have mounted and ridden the rest of the way home, but because she had got off the bicycle she saw it would be just as easy to walk and not to try to re-enter the busy stream of traffic. And because she was on foot, she glanced, as she passed him, at the newspaper seller on the corner, and at the fly-sheet – then stopped, staring open-mouthed.

'Abdication! Prince of Wales to go!' the fly-sheet read. And now that Biddy really looked, she realised that despite the bitter weather people were actually queueing up to buy a paper and were standing about in the cold reading, instead of hurrying back to their shops, offices and homes.

Biddy joined the queue, her money in her hand. She would buy a paper and see what was happening – the last time she had thought about the monarchy was when she and Ellen had been discussing whether or not they would get a day off for the Coronation; now, it seemed, there might not *be* a Coronation! It was that woman, of course, that Mrs Simpson person, who had wanted to marry the beautiful Prince of Wales and had expected to be accepted, despite the fact that she had been married before. Oh, what a lot she and Ellen would have to talk about when she got home tonight! And what a topic of conversation it would provide with customers, too . . . I bet the royal family have a funny sort of Christmas, after this, Biddy told herself, turning into the entry beside the shop.

She wheeled the bicycle round to the back door of the shop and went in. She had not given Mrs Olliphant another thought since reading the fly-sheet and now it did not seem a particularly odd coincidence, though before she had been looking forward to telling Ellen. Now, it was the Abdication which would be on everyone's lips. Everyone would want to have a read of her paper, that was for sure. Biddy took off her gloves, scarf and tam o'shanter and hung them near the small gas fire, then went through into the front of the shop.

'I'm back, and freezing,' she told Miss Whitney, who had just finished serving a customer and was moving behind the counter looking rather pleased with herself. 'In fact I'm so cold I haven't even opened my *Echo*, yet. Can I make myself a hot drink before I go and tell Mr Smythe his saddle will be delivered on Friday?'

'I'll make us all some tea whilst you run round to the shoe shop,' Miss Whitney said brightly. 'Why on earth are you wasting money on a newspaper, Bridget? I thought your friend Ellen usually picked one up on her way home from work.'

'She does, usually. But today, what with the Abdication and everything, I thought I'd like to have an earlier look,' Biddy said with studied casualness. 'I must say I'd like to know who'll be King instead of the Prince . . . and whether there will still be a Coronation in the New Year.'

'Abdication? Then 'e's done it, has he?' Miss Whitney said eagerly, coming through into the back room and holding out a hand. 'Let's have a quick peep, there's a good girl. I'll make you a cup of tea whilst you go and see Mr Smythe and by the time you get back I'll have got the gist of what's happening to the Royals. Oh, by the way, was Mrs Shawcross pleased with the dress?'

'I don't know; a maid took the box in,' Biddy said briefly, lingering in the doorway. Not only would the short run down to the shoe shop turn her into a moving icicle all over again, it would mean a decided delay in finding out about the Coronation. Would it be the Duke of York and his Duchess who became King and Queen, she wondered hopefully? Ellen adored the Duchess and collected all the press photographs of her that she could find. 'The saddler was awfully kind, though. He said it was dangerous out on the dark streets for a girl like me.'

'Old fool,' Miss Whitney said unkindly. 'Off you go, Biddy, get it over with. The tea'll be mashed by the time you're back.'

Not daring to continue to make excuses, Biddy ran down to the shoe shop, delivered her message and ran back again. She thought it was mean of Miss Whitney simply to take over her paper, but that was typical of the older woman. I've a good mind to charge her for it, Biddy thought rebelliously, hurrying along the icy pavement. After all, she earns an awful lot more than I do, she could well afford it.

But she knew she would not, not really. Miss Whitney could be unpredictable and Biddy really did like her job. She had no desire to find herself back on the job market.

So she joined Miss Whitney and Miss Harborough in the back room, since the hour was late and few customers visited the shop after five, and they all read the paper, discussed every possibility, and decided that, on the whole, they were pleased that the Prince of Wales was going to live for love and the Duke and Duchess of York, such lovely people, would be crowned King and Queen.

By the time she got back to the flat that evening Biddy felt she knew every tiny detail of the life the royal family would be living over the next few months, and she and Ellen were able to pore over the story a second time, for Ellen, foiled of an *Echo*, since they had sold out by the time she got out of work, had picked up another paper and they were able to compare reports.

It was not until just before bedtime that Biddy remembered seeing Mrs Olliphant on the tram, and then she and

Ellen decided that Ma Kettle's long-suffering sister must have moved into the shop in Scotland Road, to keep it running for the boys.

'There you are, girl, now you don't 'ave to worry that the shop'll go to rack and ruin wi' them lads in charge,' Ellen said cheerfully. 'Now chuck us somethin' to get eggs out of a fry-pan an' we'll eat.'

They had trawled the North Sea for herring and taken a liking to a couple of the local lasses with their fresh complexions and broad Lincolnshire accents. He and Greasy had been contented enough with their fat, Grimsby landlady in her crowded boarding house on Victoria Street, within shouting distance of the Alexandra Dock. They found the Scots fishergirls rough company, but liked them, too, for the way they could drink, swear and kiss.

But Dai's intention to sign on a distant-water trawler never wavered and Greasy, though he never said much, felt the same. It was time they got away from the shores of Britain, saw other seas, experienced other climes. And the Arctic attracted them both as being sufficiently dangerous – and the work sufficiently well-paid – for a first step to their exploration of the sea.

So the beginning of January saw them aboard the trawler *Greenland Bess* as she nosed her way carefully from her berth out into the tide-race. Dai went about his work, but he could not resist a quick glance behind them as they slipped out into the open sea . . . at Grimsby, the gaslights showing as circles of gold in the blue-black, pre-dawn dark of mid-winter, at the roof tops, red and black, at the narrow, shadowy streets which, in daytime, resounded to all the noise and bustle of any busy port.

He would miss Grimsby, and Susie Lawler, and his mates off the *Girl Sally*, but he would soon make friends with his present shipmates, and anyway Greasy was aboard.

The gulls were aboard too, standing along the ship's rail with their feathers ruffling as she came head to wind. The sea was nothing much yet, they were still sheltered by land on both sides, for Grimsby lies snug against the Lincolnshire coast with the Yorkshire coast throwing a protective arm around the mouth of the Humber, with the Spurn Head lighthouse on its final extremity, winking away cheerfully in the darkness. But with a freshening wind and the *Bess* already butting her way through the increasing swell, they would soon begin to feel the motion.

Dai stared out at the sea for a while longer, then he turned and went down the companionway to the fo'c'sle. He was not on watch for another three and a half hours, he might as well get a meal and some rest. The ship's cook was an unknown quantity, he would test him out, and besides, he would be on watch quite soon enough.

Below, men lounged on the hard benches, some with plates before them laden with bacon, eggs and fried potatoes, whilst thick white mugs of strong tea waited for their attention. Others had eaten and leaned back, reading books, playing cards, talking idly about anything but the work on hand.

Dai went over to the galley and announced his presence and watched as the galley boy slapped bacon, eggs and potatoes onto a chipped plate. He took the plate and waited for his tea, then walked back to the mess table.

Greasy ducked his head as he came into the lamplit room. He grinned across at Dai; they were on the same watch, so they were both free for a bit. 'Gerrin' your grub in, Taff? Looks good! I'll 'ave some o' that.'

In his turn he went over to the galley whilst Dai sat down and reached for the sauce bottle.

This, he knew, was just the beginning. The journey out to the fishing grounds was mostly boring, rarely either particularly exciting or particularly dangerous. And it tooks days to reach Arctic waters, where the big fish could be found. But it would give him and Greasy time to sort themselves out, to get used to the different types of work they would be expected to tackle. He grinned to himself. He'd have something to put in his next letter to Sîan, that was for sure!

Chapter Five

With Christmas over and the new year celebrations only a memory, Biddy and Ellen settled down to the serious business of earning their living. Biddy, it is true, was more serious about it than Ellen, since she knew herself to be entirely alone, without the support of parents or family. Ellen, though she did not often visit her mother's home, did go there from time to time. She had spent Christmas there, taking Biddy with her despite her friend's strenuous objections, and they had a real family day, with lots to eat, a few small presents, and plenty of good company as more and more members of the Bradley family returned to spend at least part of the day with 'Mam an' the littl' uns'.

No one asked difficult questions about Ellen's flat, so Biddy surmised that, though they might not approve, they most certainly understood. And seeing the cheerful poverty of the tiny house, crammed to the eyebrows with people and very short on possessions, she could understand both Mrs Bradley's silence and Ellen's absence.

In addition to the Bradley family themselves, all eleven of them, there lived in the small house both grandmothers and a grandfather, Ellen's Auntie Edie, a cousin of five whose mother had died and whose father was mostly at sea, and a couple of well-fed cats.

'We used to 'ave rats,' Ellen said briefly, when Biddy commented on the cats' gleaming coats and well-rounded sides. 'Mam gives 'em a lick o' milk now an' then, but not much else. They keep us clear o' vermin, an' the neighbours don't 'ave no more trouble either.'

Biddy looked at the cats with more respect after that.

January, however, seemed like the longest month in the history of the world. Biddy continued with her deliveries, but tips were rarer now, in what Ma Kettle had called the hungry months. And it snowed – how it snowed! It wasn't too bad in the city centre, where traffic and the feet of those working and shopping there kept the carriageways clear and the pavements at least passable. The street sweepers did a good job too, but once you got out a bit, then Biddy soon discovered it was not always possible to use the bicycle.

'I'm scared of comin' a cropper and ruining a parcel,' she explained nervously to Miss Whitney, one morning when the snow was blowing horizontal and piling up by the roadside, as the traffic crept slowly through the white streets. 'What's more, I can't get along at any sort of speed on the old bike while the snow's so thick. I was wonderin' whether it might be better if I caught a tram?'

'You'd best walk,' Miss Whitney said crossly. She had come back to work after Christmas very sharp and critical. Miss Harborough said it was because her mother was ill again, and cranky with the cold, but Biddy, who bore the brunt of the other woman's displeasure, felt this was no excuse.

Now, she looked resignedly at Miss Whitney. 'I don't mind walking, but it's going to take me all my time just to get to Mrs Bland's place and back again. And there are three customer deliveries to be done, all in different parts of the city; shall I start by going to Richy and then come back here and see how I've got on?'

Miss Whitney pulled a sour face and rolled her eyes ceilingwards. 'As if I've not got enough to do,' she said crossly. 'I suppose you'd best catch a tram. But don't linger, if you please.'

'I never linger,' Biddy said rather sharply. She was absolutely sick of being found fault with and thought Miss Whitney was being very unfair. 'Apart from anything else I'm too cold to hang about.'

Miss Whitney pulled a disbelieving face but she got some money out of the till, counted it, and then handed it to Biddy. 'There you are, that should be sufficient for all the deliveries, if you walk between the last two. In fact there should be no need for you to come back here until you've finished, so you can do all four.'

'Oh! Well, I suppose I can eat my carry-out in the tram,' Biddy said, rather dismayed. After tramping the snowy streets all morning she would be aching for a sit-down and something hot, but she did not like to say so to an obviously bad-tempered Miss Whitney. Instead, she put her coat, scarf and gloves on, shoved her carry-out into the deep pocket of her coat, and headed for the doorway into the shop.

Miss Harborough was sitting behind the counter filling in the stock book. She was writing very slowly and carefully, with the tip of her tongue protruding from the side of her mouth, but she made a face and jerked a thumb at the back room when she saw Biddy glancing in her direction. 'Disappointed in love,' she hissed, with a quick glance over her shoulder to the back room, where the senior sales lady hovered. 'That nice Mr Mickleburgh has got tired of waiting; he took a younger lady to the Temperence meeting, I believe.'

'Oh, no wonder she's ratty; I'm sorry I didn't sympathise more,' said the soft-hearted Biddy, hurrying towards the outer door. 'But she shouldn't take it out on us, should she?'

'No, but who else is there?' Miss Harborough said simply. 'You can't altogether blame her; she can scarcely get nasty with her Mam, she's well into her eighties.'

Biddy murmured something and slid through the door into the storm. It was blowing a hurricane and snowing like fury. When she looked up, the flakes whirled down so fast that they made her dizzy, grey goose-feathers against the lowering white clouds. But you've got a good coat, Biddy, and your lovely warm scarf and gloves, she reminded herself. She was wearing rubber boots, too, and though her feet got cold, at least they were unlikely to get wet as well. The rubber boots had been Ellen's Christmas present, and she valued her friend's good sense more every time she put them on.

At first, her journeying went well. Mrs Bland asked her in for a cup of tea, and though Biddy had to gulp it down so hot that she scalded her tongue, at least it gave her courage to go out into the storm once more and battle her way back to the main road and the tram stop. She walked on top of the snow down Great Richmond Street, turned into Cazneau Street and walked down it as far as Richmond Row, where there was a tram-stop at which several damp, cross-looking people already stood.

'Have we got long to wait?' Biddy asked her neighbour, a spotty girl of about her own age carrying an armful of what looked like legal documents. The girl sighed and shrugged.

'Oo knows? I been waitin' twenty minutes . . . one should be along any time now.'

'They'll come in a bunch when they does come, like bleedin' sheep,' a fat little man with a pipe and a filthy black coat remarked. He sucked vigorously at his pipe, making horrible gurglings. 'Aw, it's gone an' died on me – anyone got a light?'

Someone had and presently, when the trams did indeed come sheepishly along in line astern, everyone in the queue joined in an ironical cheer.

'Mine's second in line,' the girl with the legal documents said. 'Which one's yours, chuck?'

'Any. I'm going to Old Haymarket, I'll change there,' Biddy said, getting aboard the same tram as the spotty girl since the one in front fairly bulged with passengers. 'If this snow goes on it'll be over my boots before evening.'

'At least you've got boots,' the spotty one said as they sat down on the nearest wooden seat. 'My boss sends me miles, knowin' full well I'm delicate, in these 'ere papery shoes. Still an' all, it's nobbut a step from the tram stop now.'

'I'm a delivery girl,' Biddy explained, indicating the increasingly soggy parcels in her arms. 'I'm off out to Brownlow Hill next, then over to Canning Street, and since the senior sales lady said I wasn't to go back to the shop I suppose I'll have to eat my carry-out as I leg it over to Hartington Road.'

'I dunno where 'alf of them are,' the spotty one said gloomily. 'Still, you've got the boots for it.'

'That's true,' Biddy agreed, and they both lapsed into silence until the Haymarket was reached, when Biddy jumped down, waved to her new acquaintance and set off, crossly it must be admitted, to find the tram which would take her to the bottom of Brownlow Hill.

Despite the weather, though, she did well enough, doing the delivery in Brownlow Hill in good time and apologising in such heartfelt tones for the soggy state of the parcel that a kind-hearted housekeeper gave her a sixpence and sent her on her way with a screw of blue paper containing sultanas. 'The scones ain't ready yet, queen, but you mi' as well suck on these,' she said, handing them over. 'What a day, eh? Real brass monkey weather.'

Biddy smiled and agreed, then set off to walk through to Canning Street.

It was a long, wet trek and by the time she delivered the third parcel the fourth was looking very poorly indeed and in her pocket her carry-out was oozing all over the place, bread and jam having become almost a part of the paper they were wrapped in.

'Well I declare!' Biddy said aloud, almost in tears as she contemplated the ruin of the only meal she would get until six or seven that evening. 'I can't eat this, and I'm freezing cold and terribly hungry. Shall I spend that sixpence on chips? Oh no, I've a *much* better idea!'

For it had occurred to her that she was not all that far from the flat in Shaw's Alley, and no one would blame her – indeed, no one would know – if she nipped back there now, changed out of her wet things, dried them out before the gas fire and got herself a cup of tea and a bun.

As well as that, she could dry out the brown paper of her final parcel, which might mean that at least the garment within would arrive at its destination not actually soaked.

So Biddy trudged past St James's cemetery and the new cathedral, along Upper Duke Street, and turned down Cornwallis Street. Once there, it was straight onto St James's until she reached Sparling Street. And then it was no time at all before she was fumbling for her key, inserting it in the lock, and letting herself into the flat, almost sobbing from cold and looking like a snowman, for she was caked in the stuff from head to foot.

She went up the stairs wearily, leaving a mixture of mud and snow on every step, and unlocked the door to the flat itself. No fire had been lit but even so it felt gloriously warm to Biddy.

I'll put on the gas fire and hang my wet things in front of it, and then I'll boil a kettle and have a hot wash, she promised herself gleefully. It would serve Miss Whitney right if I didn't go out at all any more today, but just stayed here, in the warm. She would get really worried around five and serve her right, miserable old slave-driver.

But she would not do it, of course, because she liked her job, though she could not wait for spring to arrive.

Biddy bustled round the kitchen, preparing herself some dry sandwiches – she threw the soggy ones out of the window for the birds, poor things – and getting a drink of hot cocoa, a real luxury in the middle of the day. She spooned conny onny into her cup, added cocoa powder from the tin, and when the kettle boiled she poured the water carefully on top of the milk and powder, stirring fast as she did so to prevent lumps forming.

She had taken her coat, scarf and gloves off, and her boots, too, and now, whilst she waited for the cocoa to be cool enough to drink, she examined the rest of her garments. Her brown cardigan was soaked – she slipped it off – and so was her skirt. Best change that, too. She thought stockings a waste of money but was wearing an old lisle pair of Ellen's, much darned, and some thick fishermen's socks over them, to try to combat the cold from the rubber boots. The stockings were soaked from boot-top to welt, but the socks were dry.

She was sitting on the kitchen stool, sipping her drink and taking ravenous bites from her jam sandwich, when she heard a noise in the hallway below, or thought she did. Gracious, suppose someone came visiting and there was she, sitting on the stool in her knickers and patched, shrunken vest and nothing much else! I'd best get some dry things out, Biddy told herself, conscience-stricken, though she heard no more sounds from the hallway. Better safe than sorry, anyroad.

She slid off the stool and padded barefoot across the kitchen. She stopped for a moment on the tiny landing, then opened the bedroom door. She had a clean grey skirt in her half of the wardrobe. . . .

But something was happening amongst the pink blankets and crisp white sheets of the big double bed. There was a heaving and a grunting, much movement, little cries. . . .

Was Ellen ill? Had she not gone to work after all this morning, or had she been sent home? Biddy took an incautious step into the room and suddenly realised that there was a face she didn't know staring, round-eyed and incredulously, up at her. Hair stood up, thick and grey, streaked with white, on the stranger's head and just under his chin was a yellow thatch topping a small, cheeky face which she knew well. Ellen was in bed with . . . oh God, it was Mr Bowker, Bunny Big Bum himself!

To say that Biddy was dumbstruck was putting it mildly, but at least she acted in the best way possible. She simply turned on her heel, closing the door gently behind her, and fled. Back in the kitchen, she rearranged her coat, scarf, tammy and gloves so that the side which was dry was turned away from the heat and the side which was still wet towards it, and then she got herself hastily into her still-damp skirt and blouse. She left her cardigan to drip, but she put on the fishermen's socks. Then she sat down on the stool again, her heart thumping and her cheeks burning, and waited for retribution.

It was not long in coming. Presently the door opened cautiously and Ellen came into the room, closing the door gently behind her. Her face was scarlet.

'Oh, Bid . . . I told 'im you was a sister, just popped in to see me, like, an' 'e said what about the lock, 'e'd locked it 'isself an' 'e wasn't about to believe you was able to get through a locked door. 'E's ever so angry wi' me, 'e went on at me ever so. Can you think of anythin' to calm 'im down?'

'I think the only thing to do is tell . . .' Biddy was beginning, when the door opened again and Mr Bowker came, with calm and deliberate steps, fully into the room.

He looked steadily at Biddy and it occurred to her that he had quite a strong face, and was not at all the foolish old man she had imagined. He had flattened his thick grey-and-white-streaked hair and his roundish, pinkish face no longer looked flustered or embarrassed, but rather accusing instead. He addressed her at once, without preamble.

'Were you about to say the only thing to do was to tell the truth? Because I do commend that attitude most earnestly.'

'Yes, I was,' Biddy said. She could feel Ellen's anxiety and her own bright colour had fled, she knew, leaving her white as milk. She was so happy here and through her own foolish forgetfulness she had mucked the whole thing up. Mr Bowker would send Ellen away and naturally that would mean that she, Biddy, would be homeless once more. Why oh why had she not remembered that Mr Bowker often came back with Ellen in their dinner break? Why oh why was she such a selfish idiot?

'Good. Truth may avail you something, though I've no idea what. Fire ahead then.'

There was a pause whilst Biddy collected her thoughts, then she began to speak. She spoke slowly and clearly and did not once look at Ellen but kept her eyes fixed on Mr Bowker's chilly grey gaze.

'Ellen and I are old friends. We were at school together and we lived near, too. When my mother died, though, I had nowhere to go, and Ellen offered to take me in.'

Ellen gave a low moan. She obviously thought that Biddy had not really intended to tell the truth, but what else could I do, Biddy thought miserably. Lies were far too complex – too late, as well.

'She offered to let you live here?'

'Yes, she did. On condition that I understood it was

not her property and behaved myself properly, and was never here when you wanted to call. She – she was lonely when you weren't able to be with her, and with me here as well there could be no – no misunderstandings over – over her position.' Beside her, Biddy felt Ellen relax a little. 'She thought it was better, safer, all round, if there were two of us, rather than her living here alone,' she finished.

Mr Bowker frowned. 'Two of you would be safer than one?'

Ellen clearly thought it was time she took a hand. 'Mr Bowker, you know I'd 'ad fellers before I met you. Well, some of 'em were . . . were persistent, like. They saw me with a neat 'ome – home – of my own and I couldn't tell 'em about you, could I? It were – was – difficult for me to keep 'em at bay until Biddy here moved in.'

Mr Bowker nodded slowly, but his eyes never left Biddy's. 'And you are a good girl? I'm afraid I don't know your name, apart from Biddy, that is.'

'I'm Bridget O'Shaughnessy, sir,' Biddy said breathlessly. 'And I'm a good girl . . . well, I'm not yet sixteen, so young gentlemen don't consider me old enough to be interesting, I don't think.'

Mr Bowker gave a short bark of amusement. 'No? Are the young men of Liverpool blind, Miss O'Shaughnessy? However, I take your word for it because I can see you're not a liar. And I do believe you've got a point. You can keep little Ellie here on the straight and narrow far more easily than I can, because I have – commitments – which make it difficult for me to visit her as often as I should wish. Do you pay rent?'

'Not very much. Two shillings a month.'

Mr Bowker's eyebrows rose. 'Ellen is very generous with my property, two shillings a month is a small rent indeed! Very well then, Miss O'Shaughnessy! I am prepared to let you remain here, paying your present rent, whilst you can tell me with your hand on your heart that Ellen doesn't bring gentlemen back to the flat. I don't believe she does, but I'd like to be certain.'

Biddy, guiltily remembering the late-lamented George, nodded her head vehemently.

'Indeed I'm sure Ellen wouldn't bring gentlemen back here, Mr Bowker, but you have my word that if she did such a thing, I would move out at once. I can't say fairer than that, can I?'

He nodded curtly, then glanced across at Ellen, his eyes softening. He's mad for her, Biddy thought, he really adores her and believes every word she tells him! And he's rather nice, she must settle for what she's got, though to do Ellen justice since George had disappeared she had never once brought anyone back to the flat, and though she enjoyed flirting with her dancing partners she was as reluctant as Biddy to meet them outside the Acacia dance hall.

'Agreed, Ellen darling? You wouldn't deceive me?'

Scarlet-faced, Ellen threw herself across the kitchen and into Mr Bowker's arms, causing him to stagger and go almost as red as she.

'As if I would, Mr Bowker!' she said rapturously. 'Oh, I hated deceiving you over Biddy, now everything will be so nice and straightforward. But Bid, whatever are you doing here in the middle of the day?'

'I got soaked through doin' my deliveries,' Biddy admitted. 'My carry-out was all soggy as well, so I came back for a warm and some dry clothes. Only I never thought . . .'

'We must go,' Mr Bowker said, cutting across Biddy's explanation. 'Come along, my dear, we'll leave Miss O'Shaughnessy in peace to finish her meal and dress in dry clothing.' He turned to Biddy, starting to smile.

'Good afternoon, Miss O'Shaughnessy, it's been a pleasure meeting you.'

They reached their fishing ground on the eighth day out and began their search. Already ice was building up everywhere, so that very soon the *Bess* would not look like a ship at all, but just a roughly made chunk of ice. Dai and Greasy were old hands now, this was their third trip and they knew exactly what they were doing. They fought the encroaching ice without being told to do so because they knew that if the ice built up too much then the sheer weight of it could force the vessel to turn turtle, and if that happened there would be no survivors. In the extreme cold, men would be dead moments after touching the water.

Everything was different out here, even the compass could lie as it swung wildly, searching for magnetic north. The sea seemed always rough, the breakers coming at you from all angles, and because of their nearness to the pole the earth's rotation deflected their little cockleshell craft from their planned path.

But below decks it was as warm and pleasant as the crew and the officers could make it. Above, it was a white hell of ice, with everything hidden a few yards from the ship's side by the persistent, drifting fog.

Dai knew better than to lean on the rail because anything you touched out here would freeze you into position like a fly in amber, but he stood near it, staring. He wore a woollen hat beneath his sou'wester, a scarf wrapped around his nose and mouth, two thick jerseys under the waterproof smock, but he was still cold. His breath had frozen on the scarf and when he breathed out it semi-melted, then froze again. The only thing that thrived in these conditions were the fish, and there were fish down there, big 'uns, but you didn't shoot your trawl until you were right on top of them, and the skipper would choose the right moment.

Presently the bell for watch change sounded and Dai turned and made his way to the bridge; he was on bridge watch for the next four hours and that meant spending an awful lot of time keeping your eyes peeled . . . not for other shipping but for icebergs.

They were beautiful, there was no doubt about that, but deadly, too. They swung along as though they knew where they were going, performing their cumbersome dance of curtsies and dips as they went, great mountains of azure and emerald ice, carved by the rough seas into peaks and turrets, castles and canyons. The bit you saw seemed vast, but you soon learned that beneath the 'berg on the surface wallowed ice seven times as large again. If you went too close – or if she veered in your direction before you could take evasive action – you could be sucked under by the currents she caused, or holed on her hidden ice.

Dai entered the bridge and the warmth enfolded him like a blessing. Behind the wheel the Mate turned and grinned at him.

'Taking over from me? Keep her on slow ahead . . . there's pack-ice around as well as the 'bergs. But we'll see Bear Island soon, and that's where the best fish lie. No use trawling until you've sounded the sea-bed, ask anyone. Well, ask the old man, he's the one who'll give the order to shoot the trawl. All right?'

'Fine,' Dai said, slipping into the place the Mate had just vacated and putting his hands to the smooth wood of the wheel. 'Col will be along quite soon, he'll see I don't do nothing stupid.'

'I'm staying until Col gets here,' the Mate said with a dry chuckle. 'One stupid move by you, boy, and we could all be dead. Look at that one, on your port bow!'

The iceberg was another castle in the air, fretted turrets reaching up towards the sky, delicate sea-green ribs flanked by misty blue shadows which deepened to indigo. And against it the sea sucked and swirled, now green, now grey, now whiter than snow as a big wave crested and crashed against the ice. It gives you something to remember, the strangeness, the beauty, Dai told himself, glancing at the 'berg and then back to the *Bess*'s intended path. But it didn't do to forget what you were doing and let yourself marvel at it; you wouldn't last long if you did that.

They had found bottom, which meant they had found fish, or thought they had, and were about to shoot the trawl. All hands were on deck, except firemen and the chief engineer of course. The firemen never stopped stoking their boilers, the engineer watched his dials and corrected them, tuning the engine's note until it sounded just right. It was important not to lose power in these tricky, unpredictable seas.

It was near midnight, the sky clear for once and streaked and coloured by the Northern Lights, which would have illumined every face aboard, only the oil lamps were lit for shooting the trawl. The men lined the rail, watching the sea's surface but with one eye on the old man, standing on the bridge, watching them, the sea, the sky . . . his eyes everywhere.

Two men went to the winch, two more manned the door. The others took up their appointed places, Dai and Greasy amidships on the port side. Everyone poised, waiting.

The Skipper had his hands on the wheel; they called him the old man when he wasn't listening but he was no more than twenty-eight or nine. You needed to be young and strong out here. Slowly, the Skipper brought the *Greenland Bess* broadside to the wind. The sea surged inboard as the engines slowed to a mutter, holding the little ship steady.

The Cod End was swinging out now, the Skipper leaning out of the bridge window, staring about him, judging, waiting. The trawl was unlashed and Dai found he was tense as a bow-string, eager for the command which must come any moment now.

'Cod End outboard! Let go!'

There was a flurry of activity as the trawl shot into the sea. The Skipper had withdrawn into the bridge again and was once more giving orders down the voice pipe to the engine room. Dai watched as the trawl began to float free, the floats pulling against the swell. The order for 'Slow Ahead' had been given but the Chief knew his job; the *Bess* wallowed and went astern for a few seconds to allow the trawl to spread across the water before it sank.

The deck hummed with activity now. The winchmen released the brakes, the fore door and after door were released and crashed into the sea with a tremendous roar.

The deck hands cleared the deck; they were not wanted now, but as soon as the *Bess* stopped again the hands rushed out into the cold once more to do their appointed tasks and presently the Mate leaned over the rail and examined the trawl, now held in position, sunk to the right depth, and trawling everything which came within its maw.

'All square, and level aft!'

Up on the bridge the Skipper nodded, spoke to the crew member on the bridge with him, and turned away from the window.

On the deck, Greasy and Dick nodded to each other and headed for the companionway. Below, they lit cigarettes with freezing, trembling hands and took deep, nerve-calming drags.

'In three hours she'll be bulgin' an' we'll haul,' Abe Brown said, squeezing past them. 'Better get some rest as you aren't on watch.'

They nodded, every muscle aching from the recent strain. Three hours and it would all happen again, only this time the trawl, with luck, would be full . . . considerably heavier. But they had a vested interest in the catch . . . every man aboard would be watching eagerly, praying for a good haul. Bonuses were paid on fish caught.

'C'mon, let's see if anyone's got a card game going; it's scarcely worth going to bed for three hours.'

Greasy nodded. The two of them walked along to the mess deck.

'I'm gonna write to me Mam,' Greasy said, as they settled on the wooden bench. 'I'll post it soon's we git ashore. You join the card school if you like, Taff.'

'Can't be bothered,' Dai said lazily. 'I'll write to my sister.'

But they had both drifted into an uneasy sleep by the time the bell sounded for the haul to commence.

Spring came at last, a long, sweet spring to make up, Ellen said, for the worst winter for years and years.

'I don't think it was a particularly bad winter,' Biddy protested, but Ellen said waspishly that she had thought it was pretty bad when she was trying to bicycle up Mount Pleasant in a blizzard and since that was true, Biddy stopped arguing.

The two girls were getting on as well as ever, but Biddy had noticed that Ellen was nervy, edgy. Her friend had made no attempt to bring anyone back to the flat since the awful day when Biddy had met Mr Bowker for the first time, but though they still went dancing and enjoyed young men's company, it was gradually borne in upon

Biddy that Ellen, who had so loved to flirt, seemed to have lost all interest in such frivolous pastimes.

Instead, she spent a great deal of time doing things to her hair, trying new cosmetics and buying pretty clothes. She even began to do a little dressmaking, and one day she came home with a pad of thick, interesting looking paper and a box of colours and announced that she wanted to go on the ferry over to Woodside and paint the scenery.

'Can you paint?' Biddy asked tactlessly.

Ellen narrowed her eyes at her friend. 'Anyone can paint,' she said firmly. 'Are you comin' or not?'

'Well, what'll I do while you paint?' Biddy said. 'What if it rains?'

'If it rains we shan't go,' Ellen said firmly. 'Don't be stupid, Bid, no one paints in the rain.'

'Well, I'll see what it's like next Sunday,' Biddy said cautiously. 'One day a week off isn't much. I don't want to waste it sittin' on a river bank watching you dabble.'

'Well, I'm sick o' hangin' round the flat all day Sunday, waitin' for somethin' to 'appen,' Ellen said pettishly. 'If only Mr Bowker wasn't so scared of 'is wife 'e could take me trips on a Sunday. I'm goin' to tell 'im if 'e don't watch out I'll get meself a seven-day-a-week feller.'

'Then you'd lose your nice flat – and so would I,' Biddy said, trying to jolly Ellen out of her glooms. 'We'd neither of us like that much, would we?'

Ellen shrugged. 'Oh, I dunno. Mebbe I wouldn't an' mebbe I would. I'm fed up wi' t'ings the way they are an' that's the truth. Straight up!'

'It's the spring,' Biddy said wisely. 'Everything's all new and flowery and that, but life goes on just the same, only duller. But things will brighten up; Mr Bowker will take you to Paris, like he said, and . . .'

'Yeah, there's that,' Ellen said, brightening. 'I'll ask 'im when we're goin' tomorrer, first thing.'

Mr Bowker told Ellen that they would leave in a fortnight and stay in Paris five days, and though she pouted at him and said it wasn't long enough and what was wrong with a week, she came home much more contented with her lot and drove Biddy mad for days and days by insisting that they talk nothing but French in the flat.

'But we can't speak French, we weren't taught,' Biddy protested, only to have a penny primer shoved into her hand.

'I bought us books, one each,' Ellen said triumphantly. 'Parlez-vous Français, mademoiselle? An' now you say you can speak a little . . . it's on the next page, I think.'

Biddy had interesting plans for her friend's absence. She intended to spring-clean the flat, colour wash the walls in all three rooms and get some new curtains. Instead of dancing on a Saturday night she would go to the cinema – alone – which would be a rare treat and she would also look seriously in the Echo for another job. She was extremely fond of Ellen, loved her in fact, but more and more lately she got the feeling that, if it was possible, Ellen would like to move in with Mr Bowker on a full-time basis. I must be prepared, she told herself desperately, I must try for a better paid job so that if we ever lose the flat I can support myself.

She had one other plan which she intended to put into practice during Ellen's absence. She intended to make toffee.

Biddy hated waste and it had occurred to her some time before that all the knowledge that she had amassed of the sweet-making industry was being totally wasted. It wasn't difficult to make really delicious sweets and people liked them – why should she not spend some of her savings on sugar, margarine and milk, on flavourings and cocoa powder, on peppermint essence and icing sugar, and see if she could sell what she made? Of course

142

she realised that to turn Ellen's little flat into a sweet factory would be very unfair, but whilst Ellen was away she could see no harm in a little experiment. If the sweets did not sell, or if they came out wrong, then she would have lost some money and gained some knowledge – the knowledge that she was not cut out to run her own business. But if, on the other hand, the sweets were delicious and sold well . . . it was at the very least another string to her rather meagre bow.

On the day that Ellen and Mr Bowker departed, Biddy did her work as usual, but she took the opportunity of nipping into one of the cheap grocery shops on the Scottie and buying up a large quantity of loose sugar. Ellen had left on a Wednesday and would return quite early the following Monday morning, so on Thursday Biddy completed her purchasing and then waited, in an agony of impatience, for Friday. She had told her employer, firmly though with an inward quake, that she needed an afternoon off to decorate the flat whilst her friend was away. Christmas was over, Easter had not yet arrived, and Miss Whitney seemed to have got over her wintry temper; at any rate she said that it would be all right so Biddy hurried home at noon, parked her bicycle at the foot of the stairs, and went into the kitchen. She had actually decorated the flat already, working during the evenings until past midnight, and now she looked round with considerable satisfaction. She had the whole afternoon to make her sweets; she had better start right away!

Biddy's experiment was successful. The sweets were delicous and she really enjoyed using her skills in this direction after so long away from sweet-making, and on the Saturday she got her delivery bicycle out and crammed the sweets, neatly packed in conical paper bags, inside the carrier. She arrived at Millie's and picked up her deliveries and then began her rounds. But at every house she visited she mentioned that she had made a few sweets . . . and at almost every door she sold at least one bag and usually more.

'They're real tasty,' a gardener said, with a mint humbug in one cheek. He looked at her list and pointed to chocolate fudge. 'That sounds good; give me a pennyworth, would you?'

Well, Biddy told herself that evening, sitting by the fire in the kitchen and sewing the last hem on the living-room curtains, if I am ever homeless, there is one thing I can do.

But happily, Ellen's gloomy mood seemed to have left her in Paris, never, Biddy hoped, to return. She came home bubbling with enthusiasm for all things French and vowing undying love for Mr Bowker who, she said, had been a good 'un from start to finish.

'We seen the Eiffel Tower, the Madeline or whatever it's called, we took a cab out to that Versailles place . . . it were grand, Bid, grand! Oh, I'll never moan at 'im again, even if 'e can't come to the flat as often as I'd like 'im to. We never mentioned 'is wife once, oh Bid, we were so very 'appy!'

'That's wonderful,' Biddy said. 'What d'you think of the flat?'

Ellen glanced round her, then hugged her friend exuberantly. 'It looks prime,' she declared. 'Ted will be so pleased, 'e likes to think we're tekin' good care o' the place. Oh Biddy, you are good to spend time on our little 'ouse. I love you better'n I love any of me sisters!'

'Ted! When did you decide to call him by his first name?'

'He told me to use it,' Ellen said almost shyly. 'Oh Biddy, I've always liked 'im, but after those five days I love 'im, I really do. I – I want to please 'im, not just because of the things 'e gives me, I want to please 'im all through, if you know what I mean.'

'I know what you mean,' Biddy said, but she was secretly surprised. She had liked Mr Bowker, thought him pleasant – but for pretty, frivolous Ellen to say she loved him like that – well, it was a surprise.

'You don't know, not really,' Ellen sighed. 'I didn't know meself . . . but I do now. I don't mind any more that 'e can't be with me all the time; if 'e could, 'e would. I'll be 'appy wi' what I can get.'

This was so unlike Ellen that she reduced Biddy to staring dumbly, but then Ellen started to unpack and to show Biddy all the wonderful things she had bought in Paris and Biddy exclaimed and admired and went and made a supper for them both and finally the two girls went to bed, only to chatter half the night as Biddy told Ellen about the sweets and Ellen told Biddy all the things she had forgotten to tell her already about Paris.

They were about to haul and Greasy and Dai had been roused from their berths, to tumble out of them, half-asleep still, and struggle into their foul-weather gear.

If this catch was good they would head for home, so everyone wanted to see the trawl bulging with fish, even though that meant more work as the fish were gutted and packed into the holds and ice, cut from the deck each day, was thrown down to keep them fresh.

Dai glanced around him as he took up his position. The familiar sight of the other crew members was reassuring, though it had been a devil of a voyage this far. They'd found three times at the start of the fishing, only to haul an empty trawl aboard. Then they'd snagged the trawl, the winch had stuck, and Bobby had fallen on the ice and broken his wrist.

But now all seemed well. Dai was gently swinging the

enormous hammer with which he would strike the pin out of the towing block to release the trawl. He waited, poised, ready. He heard the Skipper faintly from the bridge, giving the order which would bring the *Bess* broadside to the wind. They all felt the engines slow, shudder and the Skipper shouted out through the window, 'Let her go, Taff!'

Immediately Dai swung the hammer and smote the towing block. The warps left the block, the bridge telegraph rang for stop . . . and the winch began to heave in the trawl.

Dai's hands were frozen, his jaw ached with the cold, but he moved forward to take up his position as the winch continued to turn and the doors came up, then the trawl, the floats breaking surface first.

The men leaned over to the side to heave the net aboard and suddenly everyone was dodging out of the way, as the Cod End was jerked aloft. If something went wrong now a man could be killed by the weight of fish in the net, for it was bulging, heaving, wriggling with the size of their catch.

The Mate gripped the knot of the Cod End with both hands and tore it undone. The fish crashed onto the deck and slithered and slipped and slid into the pounds. A huge haul, the faces looking down on the fish beamed. A couple of tons? Dai couldn't judge, wasn't sufficiently experienced, but beside him Col was grinning, the Mate smiled, up on the bridge he could see the Skipper's satisfied face.

That was it, then; the last haul had been worth all the sweat. They were homeward bound!

It was a bright April day with a sweet breeze blowing off the Mersey and the spring flowers in the gardens and squares in full bloom. Biddy worked hard all morning, delivering summer dresses all over the city and now she was cycling slowly back to Ranelagh Street, hoping that Miss Whitney and Miss Harborough would have some more deliveries for her, or at least some alterations which she could take round to Mrs Bland. During the winter she was quite pleased when she was asked to work in the shop but on a day like today she wanted to be outside.

Turning into Ranelagh Street, she got down off her bike and wheeled it across the pavement down the entry. Because the weather was fine she left it outside the back door and popped into the shop. She had cheese and beetroot sarnies today, her mouth watered at the thought of them. And if Miss Whitney would let her, she would take her food down to the pierhead and sit on the wooden seat along with all the old sailors and watch the shipping and think about the coming weekend, when she and Ellen had quite made up their minds to catch the ferry over to Woodside and have a picnic and paint and mess about all Sunday.

We'll go to Mass first, both of us, she was thinking, for Ellen was not by any means a regular churchgoer. Then we'll go off on the spree . . . it'll be fun to have a day out for a change. Ellen was right, the winter was a long one, now spring's here we should make the most of it.

She was in the shop, waiting for Miss Whitney to finish serving a customer, when the door burst open and a figure flew in. Miss Whitney glared, the customer swung round and stared, and Biddy was about to step forward and say, in the approved fashion, 'Can I help you, modom?' when she recognised the intruder.

'Ellen! What's wrong?'

Ellen looked ghastly. White as a sheet, her striped blouse was done up on the wrong buttons and bunched up under one ear and her coat was cock-eyed. She wore no hat and her yellow hair was wildly windswept, and to Biddy's horror she saw her friend was wearing slippers; slippers, in the city centre and on a weekday! But Ellen was plainly in a terrible state.

'Biddy! Oh thank God . . . can you come? The most awful thing . . . I can't explain here . . . Biddy . . . can you come – now this minute?'

Miss Whitney's eyes were like saucers and her mouth had dropped open. She did not speak as Biddy ran out from behind the counter and took her friend in her arms.

'Calm down, Ellen, just calm down. I'll come with you, everything will be all right, now we'll walk quietly down to the river, it's my dinner-break now anyway . . . come with me, we'll sort it all out.'

'I'm so sorry, madam,' Miss Whitney was saying to her customer. 'I don't know what all that was about but my assistant is a sensible young thing, she'll calm the gel down. And now, if you would like to try . . .'

The glass door shut behind them and Ellen began to moan. Tears welled up in her eyes and ran down her ashen cheeks.

'Ellen, what *is* it? Can't you tell me? How can I help you? Is Mr Bowker ill?'

'I'm not sure. But I think he is. When I run out 'e was mekin' the most awful snorin' noise, 'e didn't seem to hear me when I asked what were wrong . . . Bid, you must come back to the flat, if 'e's ill then I'm in terrible trouble.'

'All right, though it isn't your fault if he's ill,' Biddy said, submitting to the urgent tugging on her arm. 'How did you get here?'

'By taxi. It's waiting. Do come on!'

'I'm coming as fast as I can,' Biddy said patiently. 'Ah, I can see the taxi . . . what a good job he waited. We'll be back there in no time now.' The girls climbed into the back of the taxi and Ellen said, 'Shaw's Alley!' so briskly and with such decision that Biddy began to hope her friend was coming out of her terrified state, but Ellen would only shake her head and look nervously at the back of the driver's head when asked questions, so Biddy sat back and waited. They would be at the flat soon enough.

'Oh, don't ask questions, Bid, just come an' tek a look! Tell me 'e's awright an' I'll stop cryin', you can be sure o' that. Come on, tek a look.'

Mr Bowker was in the bedroom. He was lying on his back, his grey head on the pillow, his naked body half-covered by the sheet. He looked almost well, almost ordinary, though his expression was stern.

Biddy touched him gently. His flesh was cool, but what else should she expect? He was naked and it was a chilly day. She leaned over him. He did not move and she realised, with a chill, that his chest was not moving either. He did not appear to be breathing.

Beside her, Ellen put a quivering hand on her lover's shoulder. 'Ted? Ted, love, it's Ellie. Are you all right? Oh Ted, I do love you so much, but you mustn't be ill, you really mustn't. Tell me you're all right really . . . just sleepin'!'

'Get me the round mirror off your dressing-table,' Biddy said suddenly. 'Hurry, Ellen.'

Uncomprehending, Ellen fetched the mirror and handed it to her friend. Biddy took it and held it to Mr Bowker's lips. After a couple of minutes she looked hard at the mirror. Its bright surface was undimmed.

'What did you do that for?' Ellen said, her voice shaking. 'Oh, Bid, I'm bleedin' terrified!'

'You must pull yourself together, dear,' Biddy said. Her own voice was none too steady. 'I'm afraid Mr Bowker . . . oh Ellie, I'm almost certain he's dead!'

The two girls stared at each other in consternation. What on earth were they going to do? Mr Bowker and

Ellen should both have been back at work by now and wherever he had died, he must not be discovered in the flat of one of his employees. Biddy was quite calm enough to realise it, but Ellen suddenly began to weep, tears pouring down her face. She threw herself on the bed, clasping Mr Bowker's dead body in her arms, smothering his face with kisses.

'Oh Ted, Ted, don't leave me, I can't face it,' she sobbed. 'You know 'ow I loved you . . . you was all I wanted, the money an' the trips away an' the pretty clothes didn't marrer a damn. Come back to your Ellie, don't leave me!'

'Darling Ellen, he's gone and he can't come back,' Biddy said, her own eyes filling with tears. 'But we must be sensible – you must be more than sensible, you must be very brave. Go and get dressed properly, dress slowly and carefully, Ellen, brush your hair, wash your face, and put some make-up on. Don't you see, we can't let him be found here, and you've got to go back to work and act absolutely normally or we're lost.'

'Act normally? *Normally*? When Ted's dead, when he won't come 'ome to me no more . . .'

'Yes, normally. Unless you want the police, and the most dreadful scandal – why, you might even find yourself in the dock! We don't know why he died yet, though I'd guess it was a stroke or a heart attack, but whatever it was, love, we can't let him be found here. Particularly not like this.'

'Oh, Bid, I'll do me best but I'm not meself,' Ellen said helplessly, the tears still raining down her face. 'What must I do? Say it agin.'

'You must go into the kitchen, boil some water, have a good wash and get dressed slowly,' Biddy said clearly. 'Dear Ellen, I'm going to dress Mr Bowker whilst you do that, and then you must go to work. No, don't shake your head at me, I said you'd have to be awfully brave and I meant it. But think of poor Mr Bowker, the scandal, Ellie dear. You wouldn't want that for him, would you?'

'There'll be a scandal when 'is wife finds out 'e owns the flat what I live in,' Ellen said mournfully, but she wiped her eyes with the heels of her hands and gave Biddy a watery smile. 'I'm ashamed that I can't 'elp you wi' Ted, but I'd only break down. I'll go an' wash now.'

She left the room. Biddy collected Mr Bowker's clothes from the chair on which he had laid them and began to dress him. It was unbelievably difficult and several times she was tempted to call Ellen through to help, but each time she resisted the temptation. Hard though it was to push the inanimate limbs into sleeves and trousers, it was better to struggle on alone, and get the job done before Mr Bowker's limbs began to stiffen, rather than have a hysterical Ellen on her hands.

It was tempting to tell oneself that it would be all right to leave off the underpants, or the front buttoning vest, but Biddy knew they must get everything right so that no one suspected. His sock suspenders and armbands, both objects which Biddy had never come across before, baffled her completely until it occurred to her to ask Ellen what they were. They were diligently put in their right places and then Biddy, who had done most of the task without once fully opening her eyes, looked down at Mr Bowker as he lay, neatly on his back once more, on the bed.

Poor chap! He had been a good husband to a very difficult woman, a good lover and provider to Ellen . . . he had even been good to Biddy in his way, since he had not turned her out and had always spoken nicely to her. And now he had been mauled about by her inexpert hands – the sock suspenders had been tried, doubtfully, in some unusual spots before it occurred to her to get

Ellen's advice – and would, she supposed vaguely, presently be transported somewhere distant at the dead of night, where he could be respectably discovered in the morning.

'You 'aven't 'alf made a mess of 'is 'air,' an accusing voice behind her said, causing Biddy to jump almost out of her skin. 'Gimme a comb, for God's sake.'

It was Ellen, washed, dressed and tidy. Even her eyes looked less swollen, though there was a tell-tale redness about them if anyone had looked closely. Ellen snatched a comb off the dressing-table and tidied Mr Bowker's hair, then smoothed a small hand down his cheek and round his chin. It was, Biddy thought, the sweetest and gentlest of farewells and it carried with it all the meaning and the love which had been missing when Ellen had cast herself so tempestuously upon her lover's body earlier.

'There, my darlin',' Ellen said softly. 'Thank you, dear Father, for the good times, an' take good care o' my Ted, 'oo never 'urt nobody.' She turned away from the bed. Tears glittered in her eyes once more but she smiled resolutely at Biddy. 'All over now, Bid. What's to do next, then?'

'Oh, Ellie, you're wonderful,' Biddy said warmly. 'Go off to work and forget everything. We can't do much else anyway until . . . until much later. I'll finish tidying up here and then I'll go back to work as well. We'll come home at the usual time – I'll tell Miss Whitney and Miss Harborough that you'd gone home and found – found someone had picked the lock and got into the flat. You'd come to get me so's I could see if anything of mine was missing.'

'Will that do?' Ellen asked fearfully. 'They won't send for the scuffers or nothin', will they?'

'No, because I'll say that when I got back I realised I must have left the door on the latch and no one had been in at all,' Biddy said, improvising rapidly and quite astounded by her own capacity to lie at a moment's notice. 'I'll say I flew out in a great rush and left things in a mess, having overslept. Don't worry, Ellen, that side of it's easy. Now just you go back to work, there's a dear.'

'All right, if you're sure you can manage,' Ellen said. 'I'll be a bit late, but all they can do is dock me pay. What'll I say when Mr Bowker doesn't come back, though?'

'No one will ask you to say anything, not if he's been as careful as you say he has,' Biddy said shrewdly. 'If they ask you, just shrug and say something a bit cheeky . . . you know the sort of thing.'

'Right.' Ellen was still very pale, but Biddy saw, with considerable relief, that her friend was calm and collected. 'I'll go now, then. An' . . . thanks, Bid. I'll never forget what you done for me today.'

Alone in the flat, Biddy tidied up. She was loth to move Mr Bowker but she had said Ellen was to tell people she thought they'd had a break-in. Suppose the lie came true? Suppose someone really did break in, or suppose the window-cleaner came? And looked through the window and saw a fully-dressed corpse lying on the bed?

'I'm sorry, Mr Bowker, but it's for the best,' Biddy said apologetically, pulling him into what looked like a comfortable sleeping position, on his side. She thought about curling him up which would look more natural, but when she tried there was resistance and she realised he was already stiffening. Best not, then. He would be easier to move straight up than curled over like a dried-up railway sandwich.

Presently, having done everything she felt she should, she locked the flat and hurried back to work. She told Miss Whitney and Miss Harborough the story she had concocted for Ellen and was gratified at the ease with which they swallowed it, Miss Whitney even going so far as to tell her to buy a Yale lock for the door, so that it would automatically lock when shut.

'It would be worth the money for the peace of mind, Biddy,' she said rather severely. 'You lost a good hour's pay, running off like that.'

'Sorry, Miss Whitney,' Biddy said meekly. 'I'll mebbe do that – buy a Yale.'

And with the words, the enormity of it all hit her like a blow to the stomach. She had no idea how long it would take, but soon enough the flat would be closed to them and she and Ellen would be homeless. All the months of saving and scheming, all their sweet-making, for she had shown Ellen how to make sweets too, and they had produced quite a lot, was going to be needed at last. Total independance, which she had dreaded, was just around the corner.

'Come along, Biddy, don't stand there dreaming; Miss Ryder came in this morning and bought a tea-gown, only it's a little long in the skirt; she wants four inches off it. And Mrs Bland will have let out those darts for Miss Hetherington of Randolph Street, so if you take the skirt and pick up Miss Hetherington's dress . . . you can kill two birds with one stone.'

Shuddering slightly at the thought of killing birds, Biddy took the proffered parcel and set off. It took her most of the afternoon to complete her errands, for Mrs Bland had a gown finished for another customer on the Boulevarde, so one way and another Biddy was kept busy until it was finally time to go home.

She arrived back as dusk was falling and the lamplighter was doing his rounds. She climbed the stairs and entered the flat, feeling her heart sink as she did so. She went into the kitchen, put the kettle on, crossed the hall and opened the bedroom door. For some reason she was deeply disappointed to find that Mr Bowker's body was still there, though since only she and Ellen knew what had happened, and since Mr Bowker was in no state to walk out on them, heaven knew what she had expected to find.

So. There was to be no miracle, neither had it been a dream or a nightmare and no one had come along and stolen Mr Bowker, or seen him through the window and caused an outcry. Now he was once again her problem. Biddy stood staring down at the bed for a long time, then went back into the kitchen, made the tea, and was drinking her first cup when Ellen clattered up the stairs and into the room. She looked almost her usual self and smiled quite brightly at Biddy.

'Tea? Lovely. Bid, is 'e . . . is it . . .'

'I haven't moved him, so he's still there,' Biddy said, trying not to sound impatient. After all, Ellen had as much right as she to pray for a miracle. 'Hush a moment though, Ellen; I'm trying to think of a plan.'

Moments passed. Ellen poured herself a cup of tea and stared into it like a fortune teller into a crystal ball. Biddy continued to think.

At last she heaved a sigh and sat back in her chair. 'Look, Ellen, they're going to start wondering as soon as Mr Bowker doesn't turn up at home tonight; right?'

'Yeah, I reckon so.'

'But they won't start searching, because all men stay out late sometimes, or have appointments, or work over. Would you say that was right too?'

'I dunno,' Ellen said doubtfully. 'I think 'e usually went 'ome straight after work. 'Is wife weren't a well woman, and she 'ad a bitter tongue.'

'Well, there you are, then. If he doesn't turn up at his usual time everyone will think to themselves, *the poor feller's got his leg loose and isn't likely to come running back with his tail down for a few hours*, and they won't give the matter another thought. Right?'

'Mebbe,' Ellen said, still cautiously. 'It's difficult to know, 'cos I don't know 'oo she'd tell.'

'It doesn't matter,' Biddy said patiently. 'What does matter is that we've probably got twelve hours' grace before the police and so on start searching. Because someone must know he owns this flat and I suppose it's an obvious place to look. Only not at once.'

'My Gawd, d'you think the scuffers will come 'ere?' Ellen said fearfully, standing her cup back on its saucer with a clatter. 'Oh Bid, we've gorra gerrim out of 'ere by then!'

'Yes. And we can't take him far because it'll be a carrying job and we're neither of us that strong, but if we use my bicycle . . .'

'Your *bike*? Biddy, 'ow are you goin' to get 'im to stay on?'

'We're going to have to pretend he's drunk and sort of lie him across the seat and the handlebars,' Biddy said, having made up her mind. 'Then we can push him into the Wapping Goods station which is only a stone's throw away, and somehow get him aboard a goods waggon. Then when he's found he'll be miles from here and it'll probably take them ages to identify him. What about that, eh?'

'It sounds all right,' Ellen said, cheering up. 'Oh Bid, it sounds foolproof! When do we start?'

'When the pubs have closed,' Biddy said. 'Once the pubs close the streets are quiet and then is the sort of time a couple of girls might be pushing their drunken feller back to his own home. Yes, we'll leave it until the pubs close.'

It had sounded easy enough in the well-lit kitchen, but the fact proved to be very much more difficult. Just getting Mr Bowker out of bed was awful and took their combined efforts, and getting him downstairs was worse.

'Don't bump him on the bannisters,' Biddy implored her friend in a hissing whisper as they strove to line Mr

Bowker up with the staircase. 'If he's bruised they'll suspect foul play.'

'Oh God . . . look, Biddy, let's wrap 'im in somethin', 'is poor fingers keep stickin' out.'

They wrapped him in a blanket and this considerably eased their descent, though Biddy pointed out that there was no way they could push him through the streets disguised as an extremely large papoose.

'Wharron earth's a papoose?' Ellen asked, pushing her hair off her hot, damp forehead.

'It's a Red Indian baby. They swaddle them up in blankets. Here, prop the bike up against the wall whilst I . . .'

They struggled silently for five minutes, sweat running down their faces, then Ellen leaned Mr Bowker against the banisters and scowled across at her friend.

'He's too stiff,' she whispered. 'He won't bend, not natural, like.'

'Don't moan, get him on the bleedin' bike,' Biddy hissed back in a furious undertone. 'It's late, and dark, and there's not likely to be many about, put your arms round him and hold him up whilst I move the bike.'

It took them twenty minutes to get Mr Bowker aboard and then they discovered other snags; his feet, for one. They would not stay on the pedals, but they kept getting thumped by them as the pedals revolved, and Biddy was deathly afraid of bruising. In the end they took the chain off – a black and messy business – and with Mr Bowker balanced stiffly and awkwardly between saddle and handlebars they unlocked the door and pushed the bicycle and its grisly burden into Shaw's Alley and round the corner into Sparling Street.

There was, as Biddy had predicted, no one about, but to their dismay a considerable amount of sound was still coming from the direction of the goods station.

'They must work all bloomin' night,' Ellen moaned. 'What'll we do now, our Biddy?'

She was clutching the corpse whilst Biddy handled the bicycle, which was acting rather like a horse would in similar circumstances, except, of course, that the bicycle had no excuse since it could not sense the nature of its burden the way a horse would. But perhaps because of Mr Bowker's unnatural stiffness, or the height of him, or the weight, the bicycle veered from left to right and from right to left, looking far more drunk than either the girls or its passenger.

'The dock . . . I'll turn in a big circle and we'll go over to Wapping Dock,' Biddy gasped breathlessly. 'Hang on, both of you.'

She managed to turn the bicycle rather neatly and then headed grimly down Sparling Road towards the brightly lit dock area. A quick glance at Mr Bowker did not exactly convince her that he looked like a live drunk, but she had often stepped over a man lying comatose in the gutter, drunk as a lord, and knew that drunkenness had many faces.

'What'll we do? Tip 'im in the 'oggin?' Ellen wheezed. Being a shop assistant was not a good training for lugging corpses, Biddy realised. She herself, used to hefting heavy parcels and riding an elderly bicycle for hours at a time, was taking it far more in her stride.

'No. We'll prop him in a corner, a dark corner, and leave him,' Biddy whispered. 'Look, under the docker's umbrella, that will be fine. Come on, not far now.'

It was not far. As they emerged from Sparling Street, however, they saw that they were not the only people abroad at this hour. A figure was huddled on the steps of the public house on the corner, singing softly in a cracked old voice.

'Another bleedin' drunk,' Ellen hissed, as venomously

as though poor Mr Bowker was indeed a drunken friend. 'Just let's 'ope 'e isn't noticin' us, that's all.'

'He's not noticing anyone,' Biddy said, as they passed the blackened, tramplike figure. 'He's too busy feeling sorry for himself.'

It was true that the tramp kept moaning beneath his breath whenever he stopped singing and as they passed, keeping well clear, it was obvious why.

'Filthy ole bugger's been sick as a dawg,' Ellen said. 'Ah, nearly there, queen.'

They pushed the bike the last couple of yards and collapsed against one of the pillars which supported the overhead railway. Biddy looked around, selected an appropriate spot, and pointed. Together, they heaved their passenger off the bicycle – which fell over with a clatter so loud that both girls froze where they stood, convinced that it would bring the Law down upon them – and somehow managed to drag him to the spot they had chosen against the pillar but out of the light of the gas lamps.

'Prop him up,' Biddy hissed. 'That's it . . . now scarper!'

She nearly forgot the bicycle, but remembered it in time and jumped aboard, forgetting they had disconnected the chain until her foot, on the pedal, went crashing to the ground.

'Doesn't matter, I can push it,' she said, but she was speaking to empty air. Ellen was already across the road and turning into Sparling Street.

Pushing the bicycle, bruised and aching all over after that short but terrible journey, Biddy limped home.

To face, she thought grimly, whatever the morrow might bring.

Chapter Six

For two whole days Biddy and Ellen waited to hear what would happen to them. At work, Ellen said there were grumbles about Mr Bowker not putting in an appearance but nothing more interesting was said. No one made any bones about assuming that his wife was ill again, and one or two said he was a 'poor feller, wi' a woman like that holdin' the purse strings', though so far as Ellen knew Mrs Bowker was not a rich woman. And if his wife telephoned to speak to other heads of department about her missing husband the information was not passed on to the staff.

By dinner-time on the second day, when Ellen had nipped out in her break to tell Biddy, just with a look, that nothing had happened, Biddy became secretly convinced that no one had noticed Mr Bowker and that, if she should chance to pass along Wapping later that day, she would see him, still propped against the pillar, gazing sightlessly ahead of him.

She voiced the thought to Ellen, who said she was a fool, and then said that she herself had wondered about body snatchers . . .

'We've got to keep our nerve and wait it out,' Biddy said that evening, as they prepared their meal. 'Remember, there are heaps of drunks in Liverpool. Until they find out, he's just another one.'

'I keep tellin' meself that,' Ellen said miserably. 'But if we don't 'ear somethin' soon I won't 'ave any nerve to keep. I'm a nervous wreck, honest to God.'

'Yes, I'm not what I was,' Biddy agreed gloomily. 'Did you bring the *Echo* in? Let's have a read whilst the potatoes cook.'

She skimmed through the paper – then stopped, a finger marking her place. 'Ellen,' she said slowly. 'It's in here! I don't know why I didn't think of it, but it is in here, in the stop press. Shall I read it to you?'

'No . . . let me look.' Ellen grabbed the paper and the two heads, the fair and the dark, bent over it.

'Man collapsed on Wapping Dock. A man aged between fifty and sixty was found dead on Wapping Dock earlier in the day by a docker on his way to work. He is believed to be Edward Alexander Bowker of Upper Hope Place. Mr Bowker is believed to have suffered a heart attack; foul play is not suspected. Mr Bowker leaves a wife but the couple were childless.'

'We-ell!' Biddy laid the paper down and blew out her cheeks in a long whistle. 'It's all right, Ellen, we're going to be all right!'

'We're off the bleedin' 'ook,' Ellen said joyfully. 'Oh Bid, I'm that glad, 'cos it were none of it nothin' to do wi' you. You were a real brick to me and I won't ever forget. Gawd, let's get our suppers on the go, I'm that starvin'!'

The next day at work there was a certain amount of oohing and aahing, but the fact that Mr Bowker had been well-liked actually cut down the discussion. Though the senior staff were all interested in who would take over his job, the junior staff had their own lives to lead.

'It isn't even a nine days wonder,' Ellen said rather sadly to Biddy when she got home that night. 'Most of 'em haven't even mentioned it. 'Eads of Department don't interest 'em unless the feller's a real stinker, then they'd put the flags out. As it is, they're just carryin' on as usual.'

'I wonder how long it'll be before they twig that the rent isn't being paid for this place? Or did he own it?' Biddy said. She was making peppermint creams and the rather sickly smell pervaded every corner of the flat. 'Either way, we'll be kicked out soon enough.'

'At least it's summer; we can kip down in St John's gardens or catch the over'ead railway out to Seaforth an' sleep on the sands,' Ellen said with a giggle. 'We ought to start huntin' for a place, though, Bid. Somewhere we can share.'

They knew they should search, but somehow they did not. Instead they continued to live in the flat and to go to the Acacia each Saturday night. Ellen flirted desultorily with the young men she danced with, but it seemed to Biddy that all the pleasure had gone out of it with Mr Bowker's death. It was not that Ellen was sad any more, because she had got over that stage. She was just idly going through the days, seemingly content enough but not wanting another friendship to take the place of the first.

'We're marking time,' Biddy said one fine evening in July, when they had walked down to the pierhead to watch the big ships steaming up the Mersey whilst they enjoyed the breeze and the sunshine. 'It's as though we can't really get on with our lives until we know what's going to happen about the flat. Still, it can't be long now.'

It was not. They got back to the flat with fish and chips which they had bought from a shop on Park Lane and found a thin-faced gentleman waiting on the doorstep.

'Mr Bowker? Is 'e in? Rent was due a fortnight since. 'E's always been a regular payer, but . . .'

'He had a heart-attack some while ago,' Biddy said

when Ellen seemed disinclined to answer. 'Who paid the rent last month?'

'Quarterly; it's due quarterly,' the man said. 'Dead, you say?'

'Yes, he's dead. But in the past we paid our rent to him each week,' Biddy said, thinking on her feet so to speak. 'Will it be in order if we pay you direct in future?'

The man had been looking annoyed and aggressive, but he nodded quite pleasantly at her words, visibly relaxing.

'Aye, that'll suit. Can you pay me now?'

'How much do you want?' Ellen asked, speaking for the first time. 'We don't keep cash in the house, but I'm sure we can withdraw some money tomorrow.'

She was using her 'posh' voice, to Biddy's amusement, but it seemed to do the trick.

'I'll want six pun' ten shillin',' the man said in a businesslike voice. 'It's a good flat – self-contained.'

'Right,' Ellen said, as though pound notes grew on trees and she had a flourishing orchard. 'What's your address, Mr er . . .? I don't think I caught the name?'

'Mr Alderson. And your name, Miss? For me books, like.'

'Oh . . . I'm . . . I'm Miss Sandwich and this is Miss . . . Miss Fisher,' Ellen gabbled, clearly unprepared for the question. 'Where's your office, Mr Alderson? We'll pop in tomorrow, if we may.'

'I lives at Barter Street, not far from Prince's Park,' Mr Alderson said. He gave them a sharp look. 'If me rent's not paid by midday tomorrer, mind, I'll re-let and you're out.'

Ellen drew herself up and gave him a glare of well-simulated fury. 'Mr Alderson, I've said we'll see you tomorrow. Come, Miss Fish.'

She unlocked the door and pushed Biddy inside, then

slammed and locked the door behind them. Biddy, gig-gling wildly, sank down upon the bottom stair.

'Oh Ellen, you said I was Miss Fisher, not Miss Fish,' she gasped out at last. 'And . . . and why did you call yourself Miss Sandwich, for heaven's sake? I don't think it is a name at all!'

'It is! Anyway, it don't matter 'cos we'll never see 'im again. Oh Biddy, gerroff them stairs an' let's go up and eat us chips! I'm always 'ungry these days.'

'It's because you're still unhappy,' Biddy said wisely, getting to her feet. 'All right, we'll go and eat.'

Later however, when the fish and chips had been washed down by a cup of good, hot tea, she returned to the subject. 'Ellen, I know we couldn't possibly afford six pounds a quarter, but there are other flats. Your sister Polly's in work, if she came in with us, and one or two more, wouldn't we be able to afford something? You don't want to live at home with your Mam again, do you?'

'No, I don't. But . . . oh, Biddy, I may 'ave to! I 'aven't said nothin' before, but I think . . . I think . . .'

'You think what? Don't say they're going to sack you from your lovely job!'

It was the worst disaster Biddy could imagine, since it would mean that Ellen would not be earning, but it turned out that there was another disaster which had not even crossed her mind.

'No, they've said nothin' at work, but they soon will; Biddy, I think I'm in the family way!'

'The f-*family* way?' Biddy stammered. 'What do you mean? You don't mean you're going to have a baby? But how can you, when Mr Bowker's been dead almost three months?'

'I reckon I'm more'n four months gone,' Ellen said miserably. 'You said yourself I ate a lot; I'm eatin' for two,

I guess. So it's either go in one of them places for bad girls or go 'ome, and if me Mam'll tek me in . . .'

'Oh, Ellen, of course she will, your Mam's ever so kind,' Biddy said, hugging her friend. 'But I thought you were careful, or Mr Bowker was, anyway. I thought you said . . .'

'It were a mistake,' Ellen said drearily. 'Anyone can mek a mistake. And now I've told you I've gorra admit it's real, see? Before, I told meself it weren't goin' to 'appen, even though I knew it were.'

'And you've not told your Mam yet, nor your sisters?'

'I've not even told meself I said,' Ellen pointed out rather sharply. 'So much 'as 'appened, chuck, that it were easy to push it to the back of me mind. But now I've gorra face up to it. I'll tek a day off work – can you tell 'em I'm sick? – an' go down an' see me Mam.'

'Right,' Biddy said. 'I'll see if I can get a place some-where . . . there must be somewhere . . .'

'Come wi' me, back to me Mam's,' Ellen suggested, but though Biddy thanked her and hugged her once more, she refused.

'Your Mam will have enough on her plate with you and a new baby,' she said shrewdly. 'Your house bulges at the seams already. But I'll manage, never you fear. Us O'Shaughnessys are a tough lot, my Mam told me so.'

It was easy to talk about lodgings but not so easy to get something even half-way decent, as Biddy discovered next day. She carried her trusty carpet bag in to work with her, stowing it away in the back room, and told Miss Whitney that the rent of the flat which she and Ellen shared had been put beyond their means by a new land-lord and asked for a couple of hours off to search for new accommodation.

After two hours she returned to the shop. 'It'll have to

be the day off, or I'll be sleeping in Millie's doorway,' she told Miss Harborough despairingly. 'I never thought a place would be so hard to find, never! And some of 'em's not rooms, they're just a bit partitioned off, and the bugs . . . well, it's not what I'm used to.'

But desperation began to set in as six o'clock got nearer. She returned to the shop and reclaimed her carpet bag, then trudged off again. And before night fell she found a room, of sorts.

The house itself was situated in a court off the Scotland Road, too far from Millicent's Modes to be truly practical. The room on offer, to a single young lady or gentleman, had been the property of a daughter of the house, and she bitterly resented being pushed out and incarcerated with half a dozen smaller sisters, particularly by a girl of her own age. She said quite audibly, whilst Mrs Tebbit, the landlady, showed Biddy the room, that 'Mam really wanted a feller – we all does', which did little to reassure Biddy as to her welcome here.

But it was a roof, somewhere to put her carpet bag and Dolly. Biddy had brought her own pillow, complete with the little lump of savings buried deep in the feathers, and the woollen blanket which Ellen had knitted out of bits and bobs of leftover wool.

'You'll bring your own beddin', o' course,' Mrs Tebbit snapped, when she saw Biddy staring, appalled, at the dirty, stained mattress with the stuffing oozing out from one end. 'I never provide no beddin'.'

Biddy was grateful she had brought her own bedding. The house was terribly overcrowded with a couple of seedy-looking middle-aged females whom Mrs Tebbit had referred to, collectively, as 'Auntie,' an ancient grandfather who had glared at Biddy with pointless senile fury as she was taken through the back kitchen, and an old grandmother with a flourishing beard and moustache who reeked of liniment. And of course there were eight or nine assorted children and presumably a Mr Tebbit somewhere in the offing, since the youngest child was still a babe in arms.

But at least I've got a room of my own, Biddy thought thankfully. At least I shan't have to share anything but the stairs and hallway.

Something of this may have shown in her expression, however, for Miss Jane Tebbit, the injured daughter, who appeared to be about Biddy's age and was already beginning to look and sound like her mother, put her oar in as Biddy stood silently surveying the small room.

'We don't carry up your washin' water, neither,' she said aggressively. 'There's a tap in the yard, you 'elps yourself.'

Biddy thanked them both, tongue in cheek, and proffered the first week's rent, which was received with a sniff.

'My ladies usually pay a month ahead,' Mrs Tebbit said, taking the money with assumed reluctance. 'Or two weeks?'

'A week is what I'm used to paying,' Biddy said calmly, but with a deep shake of fear inside her in case the woman called her bluff. She was afraid of sleeping rough, and equally afraid of having to go to a boarding house or small hotel and pay their exorbitant prices if this place fell through.

However, despite the sniff, Mrs Tebbit obviously felt that half a crown in the hand was a good deal better than waiting for another desperate person to appear, and she and her daughter disappeared down the rickety stairs, leaving Biddy to 'make yourself at 'ome,' as Mrs Tebbit put it.

Alone, Biddy sat down on the bed, then sprang up again and examined the surface of the mattress uneasily.

Bed bugs! She might have known, and they were dreadfully difficult to get rid of. What was more, the bites the disgusting insects made on their victims were easily identifiable; employers did not like those who worked for them to show the marks of poverty and deprivation too clearly. They found it easier to say that Miss so-and-so was dirty and didn't wash, though God knew if washing cured bed-bugs there wouldn't be one alive in most of the houses along the Scottie Road.

Paraffin? Was it that which killed them? You could catch them on a wet bar of soap and put them out of the window, or set fire to them with a lighted match, or squash them . . .

Biddy shook the mattress vigorously, then propped it up against the wall and pulled the rickety iron bedstead into the middle of the room. She put her pillow on it, then laid her blanket out and put Dolly down on the bed. She would rather sleep on bare springs than share her bed with the fat grey bugs which needed her blood to live.

The next few weeks were miserable ones for Biddy. She and Ellen had planned to go up to London to watch the Coronation but Ellen was in no condition to travel and Biddy didn't have the heart to go alone. She went to the cinema and watched it there, and fell in love with the whole family – the pretty little Duchess who was now Queen Elizabeth, her handsome husband and their two beautiful, curly-headed little daughters. But somehow it all fell a bit flat after the lovely plans she and Ellen had made together. No one, as yet, had taken the place of her friend.

So Biddy continued to work as hard as ever, handed over the rent to Mrs Tebbit each Friday, and searched for decent accommodation which she could afford whenever she got the opportunity. But when she found a nice little room the price was beyond her, and often to her horror she found even worse conditions than those under which the Tebbits lived.

Once she went round and visited Ellen, to find her friend almost as miserable as she.

'They sacked me from Gowns when they saw me stomach sideways,' Ellen said. 'I spent me savin's on a sewin' machine, though, so I'm takin' in curtains, alterations, stuff like that. It makes me a bob or two.' She smiled at Biddy. 'Makin' sweets, are you? To 'elp out, like?'

'If you could see where I live you wouldn't ask,' Biddy said, pulling a face. 'It's not a nice place, Ellie, and they aren't nice people. I try to eat away from the house because it's so dirty, so I couldn't possibly make sweets there. Still, as soon as I find somewhere decent I'll be out, you may be sure.'

'I'm thinkin' of havin' the kid adopted,' Ellen put in. 'What do you think, Biddy? There's no Da for it, so I might as well, hey?'

'What does your Mam think?' Biddy asked guardedly. She could quite see the advantages of adoption, but parents could be funny about such things she had heard.

'She says it's my life and my soul that'll be at risk if the Lord don't approve,' Ellen said rather uneasily. 'I'll wait till its born . . . but I might let someone 'ave it who can give it a chance. I can't, God knows. But in a way, I want the kid.'

'You'll marry, though, Ellie, one of these days,' Biddy said. 'Then you're bound to have other children.'

'Oh aye? Oo'll marry a judy what's got another feller's kid?' She flapped a hand at Biddy as her friend began to answer. 'Ne'er mind, lerrit rest, time will tell.'

Summer turned to autumn, and with the colder weather, Biddy was forced to spend money she could ill afford on an extra blanket. She went up to Paddy's Market though, and bought second hand, which was a help, and could not resist taking a quick look at Ma Kettle's emporium as she went past; even her life there seemed bearable when she was lying in her narrow bed at the Tebbits', listening to them quarrelling and swearing at one another downstairs, or hitting the kids or each other when tempers really rose.

Not that I'd go back, she reminded herself sometimes. At least here I'm all right during the daytime. I've got a nice job which I enjoy and I'm earning my independance slowly but surely.

As the weather got steadily colder, living with the Tebbits became easier in some ways and more difficult in others. The bed-bugs disappeared, and since the fleas could be kept at bay with liberal doses of Keatings powder, Biddy felt she could stand them. But the paraffin stove in her room, on which she was supposed to cook her meals leaked, which meant fumes forced her to open the window whilst using it. So any warmth from the little stove was lost through the open window, and anyway she was becoming increasingly suspicious over her can of paraffin, which seemed to become empty, in some mysterious fashion, whether Biddy lit her stove or not.

Someone's nicking my paraffin, Biddy told herself, and decided to save up for a lock. She did mention the strange way her paraffin disappeared to her landlady, but Mrs Tebbit drew herself up, sucking in her stomach and pushing out her very large chest, and announced that there were no thieves in her house, a remark so reminiscent of Ma Kettle that Biddy had hard work not to laugh.

She did not laugh a week or so later, though, when December brought the first snow-storm of the season. Biddy had had a hard day bicycling through the newly laid snow, and though it was pretty and she enjoyed the freshness and sparkle which it added to the dingy, early-morning streets, she remembered all too clearly the difficulties it had made for her the previous winter and dreaded a repetition. What was more, Ellen's baby had been born a fortnight earlier and she had gone round to the Bradley home and taken some clothing for the child, only to realise that, though Ellen adored her son, things were going to be hard for her. The baby seemed to drain her of energy and even her sewing did not bring in enough money to support them both. Biddy had willingly handed over a bob as well as the clothes, but she could see that her friend would have her work cut out to manage and intended to do her best to help out. Cold weather, therefore, was very unwelcome on several counts.

However, she cycled up the Scottie Road and turned off into John Comrade Court, known locally simply as Commie, actually anticipating her return to the Tebbit household with something akin to pleasure. She had a couple of eggs up in her room and half a loaf of bread, so she had splashed out on a pint of fresh milk when she had seen a milkman earlier, and intended to make herself French toast, a delicacy of which her mother had been inordinately fond.

The milk was in a ginger-beer bottle, nestling in the pocket of her warm duffle-coat and she had some bull's-eyes which a customer had given her. Quite a feast – and best of all, a new book!

Living so near to the shop now, she often popped in on Mr Meehan, the bookseller on Cazneau Street, and picked something to read out of his tuppenny tray, for Mr Meehan did not just sell smart new books, but some older ones as well.

Biddy had gone in there earlier, having a delivery in the area, and Mr Meehan, who had always been a good friend, had suggested to Biddy that she might like to put her name down for a place with Mrs Freddy, at Accrington Court, just down the road from her present abode.

'Mrs Freddy's clean, a good cook, and a pleasant sort of person,' Mr Meehan had said, smiling at her. 'But her rooms are very popular, which is why she has a waiting list. Costs nothing to add your name, madam, and she charges three and six a week with evening meal.'

'I'll go at once and put my name down,' Biddy said. 'Thank you very much Mr Meehan, you are good to me. Can I have this one, please?'

Mr Meehan took the book and glanced at it, then flipped it open. '*Lorna Doone*,' he said. 'You've not read it, madam?'

'No, not this one,' Biddy assured him. Often she bought books she had read and enjoyed when her parents had been alive, but occasionally she took a chance and bought something she had never even seen before. She had been attracted to *Lorna Doone* both by the first few pages and by the illustration in the front, which was a brown and white photograph of the most beautiful river she had ever seen. She took the book from him and opened it at the photograph. 'Where's that, Mr Meehan? It's so beautiful!'

'It's Watersmeet, in Devonshire,' Mr Meehan said. 'The story takes place in Devonshire, on Dartmoor, if I recall. You'll enjoy it, madam.'

He took Biddy's money and they smiled at one another. He always called her madam, it was his little joke. 'Go round to Mrs Freddy's and say I sent you,' he advised as she turned towards the door. 'You deserve better than that Mrs Tebbit, and you would fit in very well at No. 3 Accrington Court.'

So Biddy had cycled round there and added her

name to what looked like a rather lengthy list.

'You're at Mrs Tebbit's?' Mrs Freddy had said, however. She shook her head sadly. 'Oh dear me! Well, even if I don't have a vacancy I'll see whether I can find you somewhere else. Those Tebbits!'

She left it at that but Biddy, cycling back to the shop, had felt a warm glow. She would escape from the Tebbits, either with or without Mrs Freddy, but it would be pleasant to feel she had an ally, someone else who wanted to help her.

But now, however, she had come down to earth. She would light her paraffin stove, make her French toast and a nice cup of tea, and then get into bed to keep warm and read her new book. The Tebbit household did not run to oil lamps upstairs, but Biddy had a supply of candles hidden away and one of them would last her until she grew too tired to read and wanted only to sleep.

She turned her bicycle into the entry down which she could reach the Tebbits' back yard. She kept her bicycle there, chained and with a strong padlock on the back wheel, but so far no one had ventured to interfere with it. As she secured the bicycle the snow, which had stopped for a while, started up again. Slow, lazy flakes at first, gradually growing thicker. Good weather to be out of, Biddy concluded, legging it for the back door. She burst into the kitchen to find the family assembled there, seemingly in accord for once. They were chattering and laughing, the fire blazed up and for once a reasonable smell of cooking came from the oven let into the wall beside the fire.

'Oh . . . sorry, I didn't realise you were in here,' Biddy said above the din. 'I'd have come through the front door if I'd known.'

'S'orlright, chuck,' Ray Tebbit said. He was a seaman, not home often, and Biddy always felt sorry for him because it seemed hard to come home from the sort of life she believed sailors lived, not to family comfort and good cheer but to the noisy quarrelling and frequent fights of the rest of the Tebbit clan.

Still, they all seemed happy enough tonight. There were chestnuts roasting on a coal shovel and the miserable Jane was toasting a crumpet, actually smiling as she shielded her face from the flames.

They must be celebrating Ray's return, Biddy thought, climbing quickly up the stairs. What a pity they aren't a pleasant crowd – how nice it would be to be part of a family again. Still, Ellen's Mam had asked her to spend Christmas Day with them, that was something to look forward to, and because of a general feeling of goodwill to all men at this time of year, her tips were building up once more. The lump in the pillow was quite uncomfortable some nights, when she turned over without care.

In her own room, Biddy tipped a good supply of paraffin into her stove and lit it. She left the door a little ajar, hoping that it would clear the fumes and make it unnecessary to open the window, then she took off her coat, hat, scarf and gloves and laid her groceries out on the edge of the bed. She was hanging her coat on the hook of the door when she remembered her tips; best put them in the lump at once, before she forgot them. She did not intend to leave them in her coat pocket all night, though really they would be pretty safe. No one ever came into her room when she was in residence.

She slid the money out of her pocket, counted it, then went over to the bed. She pulled her pillow out from under Dolly and her fingers found the neat slit in the seam. She pushed her hand in amongst the feathers, feeling for the lump. It wasn't there, but she always pushed it right down, well out of view and feel.

It took her all of five minutes to acknowledge the awful truth.

Her savings had disappeared.

The ship was iced up worse than Dai had ever known it and a heavy swell was running, so when the black frost began to rise from the water everyone had been too busy to notice it. You can't see black frost, but you can feel it; it is black frost which causes each breath you take to include tiny particles of ice, and ice in the lungs can kill a man.

But Dai kept his muffler round his mouth and nose, and he kept his great heavy gauntlets on, too. Because he – and every other man aboard who could be spared – was chopping ice. Desperately, with all their strength, they were chopping at the ice which had already all but immobilised the ship.

The trouble was, Dai knew, that a heavy sea which came inboard time after time, froze solid between each wave, so that the ship was becoming layered in ice which weighed her down in the water until her usual buoyant forward movement became little more than an uneasy wallow.

Clear the ice or die. Get her free of it or see her turn turtle . . . it's the last thing you'll see as you gasp the iced air into your lungs for the last time.

They all knew the truth of it, all dreaded it. So they used picks and shovels and they battered and beat at the ice. Even the laziest man on board was galvanised into action. Greasy raised his pick and brought it down and diamonds flew across the deck, first small, then impossibly huge, koh-i-noors, every one.

'You're doin' fine, Grease,' Dai said through his muffler. 'We'll clear the whaleback in ten minutes – look at the masts!'

The masts were beautiful, slender candy sticks, blue-white and elegant. Dai felt he could have snapped one off and eaten it . . . but the masts, too, must be cleared before any man aboard could go off watch.

'Aye. Like a woman, beautiful but deadly,' Greasy said thickly. 'Hey up, look 'oo's 'ere!'

It was the Skipper. He was of little use on the bridge; you cannot con a motionless vessel, so he had come to lend his strength to the ice-clearing party. Side by side with them, strength for strength, he worked all that long afternoon, until the *Bess* began to answer to the helm, to take on the seas at their own game, to respond.

'She'll live,' the Mate said at last. He stood back to let the crew go below first, then had to hack at his boot with his pick-axe because it had frozen to the deck in those few seconds. The crew began to shuffle down the companion-way, too tired to push and shove, to joke and blaspheme as they usually did, and the Mate followed them, talking as he came. 'She's a grand little ship, the *Bess*.'

'Obstinate little bitch, she wouldn't let the ice turtle her,' Colin said with affectionate pride. 'Eh, put the wind up us, didn't she though? Just like a bloody woman!'

'Gives you an appetite, mun, ice-clearing do,' Dai said with relish as they filed onto the mess deck. 'That's why the Skipper joined in, 'tweren't to give us a hand like, 'twas to get himself ready for Bandy's beef stew and dumplings.'

They all laughed. Bandy, the cook, was popular with everyone because he could cook in a raging arctic storm, his bread always rose and filled the small ship with its delicate, delicious smell and he made pancakes which a master chef would have envied – made them, what was more, with a heavy swell running and his stove moving up and down in rhythm whilst pans and pots flew through the air and thumped anyone standing in the galley.

'Never known the ice as bad as that,' Greasy remarked as he sat down at the table and plonked his plate of stew down in front of him. 'We've done a year on distant water, but we've never known ice that bad, have we, Taff?'

'Nor me,' Colin said. 'And this is my third year.'

There were murmurs of assent all round the room. 'Aye, it were pretty bad.' 'You don't often get it that thick on the masts.' 'It's always bad wi' a black frost, but that 'un beggars description.'

Dai nodded and attacked his stew. He ate it with relish, enjoying the new bread which accompanied it almost as much as the meal itself. Afterwards there was stewed apples and custard, after that coffee, hot and strong, in thick white cups.

'On watch, we are, in three hours,' he said to Greasy presently, as they sat back, replete. 'Let's get some shut-eye.'

They went to their bunks, took off their sea-boots and rolled into their blankets. Dai usually slept like a log the moment his head touched the pillow, but not tonight. Tonight his thoughts refused to let him sleep. They played round and round the scene out on the deck, with the old man giving the ice hell and every one of the crew working like devils, no one slacking, stopping for a rest, complaining. They had all known it was a race against time and they worked as a team until the sweat froze on them and their hands were covered in bleeding blisters.

He was never bored on the *Bess*, though he was often frightened, nearly always tired. But that had been a narrow escape, that icing up, he knew it by Colin's face, by the Mate's relief as he watched them go down the companionway, by the Skipper's mere presence on deck. I wish Mam were alive, she'd understand why I love it, why I'll keep coming back, he told himself wistfully. Da would have understood once, but not any more. All he can see, now, is Menna's white young body and the brassy yellow hair of her, all he can see is Davy Evans having his way with a woman young enough to be his daughter. He won't be interested in his son, not yet awhile.

But Bethan would have loved to hear about the *Bess*, would have understood. And suddenly, he wanted to talk to a woman, not a girl who would smile and kiss him and be willing or unwilling to go to bed with him but a woman, a motherly woman.

In the bunk beside his, Greasy sighed, then spoke. 'Taffy? I t'ink I'd like to go 'ome when we get back this time. Not to Victoria Street but 'ome. To me Mam. To Liverpool.'

There was a wealth of longing in his voice and Dai could have hugged him because it wasn't just he who had wanted a bit of mothering, Greasy did too.

'Yeah, mun,' Dai said, from under the blankets. 'My Mam said to go and see her friend in Liverpool, her name's Nellie Gallagher. If you go home, I'll come with you and find Mrs Gallagher. She may not even know my Mam's dead, yet. I should have visited, should have gone before. It was my Mam's last wish, you could say.'

'We'll both go,' Greasy said. His voice had deepened with exhaustion and the rapid approach of sleep. 'We'll both go, our Taff. Together.'

Biddy couldn't believe it at first. All that money, just gone, and she always so careful to push the small cloth bag deep into the feathers before she left for work each morning. She searched the bedding, the surrounding floor, she even looked in the pockets of every garment she possessed, just in case she had sleepwalked around the room and stowed her precious savings somewhere different.

But it was not a big room; the most diligent of searches could take her no longer than half an hour and at the end of the time Biddy descended the stairs, cold fury in her heart. She stalked into the kitchen and when the family went on squabbling and laughing she banged her hand hard on the half-open kitchen door.

It had the desired effect. Voices broke off in mid-sentence and every head in the room swung towards her.

When she saw she had everyone's attention, Biddy spoke, her voice hard. 'Where's my money?'

There was a short, uneasy silence. Mrs Tebbit was the first to break it. 'Gone, chuck . . . you'll owe again from tomorrer.'

'Not my rent,' Biddy said coldly. 'My savings. I kept my savings in a little white cloth bag inside my pillow. I went to it just now and my money had gone, bag and all. Someone from here must have taken it and I want it back, smartish, or I'll call the police.'

'None of my family would touch your money,' Mrs Tebbit said. Deep scarlet colour rose in her fat, lard-like cheeks. 'Ow dare you say such a thing, you baggage!'

'Who else would take it? Who else *could*?' Biddy asked. 'Strangers don't wander in off the streets and go up to my room and fiddle around in there. But someone does, I've known someone goes in and picks over my things when I'm at work, someone uses my paraffin, but this is going too far.' She stared at each one of them in turn, even giving the tatty, down-at-heel kids a long, chilly look. 'I'm going upstairs, now. If my money isn't handed back in the next ten minutes, I'm going down to the police station. I hope that's clear?'

No one answered. Eyes darted about, but no one spoke. Biddy threw them one last look and left the room. She went upstairs slowly, hoping against hope that someone would follow her upstairs, slip that familiar little cloth bag into her palm. But no one did.

In her room again, Dolly lay in an abandoned attitude on top of the ravaged pillowcase. A few feathers, dumb witnesses to Biddy's frantic search, floated lazily into the air as Biddy had opened the door, then settled slowly on floor and bed as the closing door cut off the draught once more.

Biddy waited for a good deal longer than ten minutes, but no one came clattering up the stairs, no one called her name, knocked, admitted the theft. Slowly, reluctantly, Biddy let the moments drift by, then she descended the stairs once more. At the foot she hesitated, then put her head round the kitchen door.

'I'm off for the police,' she said. 'Shan't be very long I don't suppose. Are you sure you wouldn't like to give me my savings back?'

She could tell by the looks on the faces that they knew who had robbed her, guessed that there had been harsh words exchanged, but they had obviously come to some sort of decision and it was clearly not to hand her money back.

'No one 'ere's got your filthy money,' Mrs Tebbit said at last, her tone as surly and aggressive as the expression on her face. 'Fancy you saltin' away all that money – or tellin' folk you 'ad, anyroad. Well, you're gonna get your comeuppance now, milady, an' no mistake, 'cos you've been pipped at the post. You say you'll tell the scuffers – well, tell away. Two can play at that game and we'll 'ave something to say an' all. What about the money missin' from me downstairs dresser, eh? Someone took it – oo's to say it weren't you, Miss 'Igh-an'-Mighty? Anyroad, our Jane went down to the cop-shop soon's you left, and reported it, said it were possible our lodger 'ad been sticky-fingerin' it. So chances is you'll be the one the scuffers wanna see!'

Biddy turned and left the room. She would go to the police, she would! As if they would believe a crowd of tatty, dirty Tebbits against Biddy O'Shaughnessy, who had never been wrong-sides of the law in her life! Though there was the flat . . . but that had been a long while ago and there had been no trouble. And there was poor Mr Bowker . . . he had been given a grand funeral and was buried in Ford cemetery, she and Ellen had taken flowers not all that long ago. Could any of this rebound on her? Of course it couldn't, she would go to the police and she just hoped they threw all the Tebbits into prison, or sold their miserable possessions to force them to pay her back!

But she found that instead of making her way to the police station she had climbed the stairs again so she went into her room, sat down on the bed, and began, very quietly, to weep. She could do nothing! The Tebbits had already made their complaint, what would any policeman think if she went along to the station now? They would think she was trying to cover up her own theft by reporting another . . . oh God, what should she do? She could not stay here and wait for the law to pounce though, she would have to leave.

'I'll change my name', Biddy thought frantically, chucking things into her trusty carpet bag. She tied her blanket round her pillow, stuffed Dolly into the bedroll, and headed for the door. She looked around the bare little room and gave a big sniff, then wiped her eyes with her fingers and went back to pick up the tin of paraffin. It was half full – should she leave it? But she did not want the Tebbits to get anything else of hers. Where would she take it, though? She had no money and no hope of any until the end of the week, and it was Christmas in ten days.

She would probably get tips next day and could buy chips and a tin of conny onny to see her though until pay-day. But what then? She had spent enough hours tramping the streets earlier in the year to know that good lodgings, even poor lodgings, were rare as hen's teeth in the city. Could she possibly go to the Bradleys and beg them to take her in, just until she found somewhere else? Mrs Bradley was ever so nice, a big, fat, friendly woman, tolerant of others, fond of all her sprawling brood. She had taken the erring Ellen back, surely she would let Biddy doss down on a floor somewhere for a couple of nights?

Biddy knew she would, and perhaps that was the trouble. Poor Mrs Bradley had worries of her own without Biddy adding to them. Ellen's baby, Robert, was much loved, but naturally his presence added to the Bradleys' difficulties, and if Biddy did beg the family to take her in then yet another person, in a house already bursting at the seams, might be the straw which broke the camel's back.

Until now, indeed, Biddy, as Ellen's best friend, had tried to pass on any bits and pieces which might make life easier for the new mother and her little son, but now . . . it's all I can do to keep body and soul together for meself, Biddy thought mournfully. I can't do a thing for Ellen or Bobby.

But it would only be for a few days, until I found somewhere else, Biddy reminded herself, closing her bedroom door slowly behind her and beginning to descend the stairs. I'll find somewhere else in a day or so, somewhere I can afford. Somewhere which doesn't want rent in advance . . . oh, I could kill that beastly Jane Tebbit, it took me years to save up that money and I might as well not have bothered, I would have done better to buy pretty clothes and nice shoes, or to give Ellen more of a hand, at least I'd have something to show for the money.

Half-way down the stairs, with her face set in hard,

defiant lines, Biddy saw the kitchen door below her open a crack. She continued to descend the stairs, ignoring the door. It would be a small Tebbit, spying on her so that he or she could turn and shrill 'She's gone!' to the others, so they would know themselves safe from her.

It was not a small Tebbit. It was Ray, the seaman son of whom Mrs Tebbit was so proud, looking very red-faced.

'Ang on a mo, Miss O'Shaughnessy, where's you off to?' he said. 'Don't you let them scare you off . . . I'm ashamed of me Mam, that I am. She knows very well we ain't lost no money, she's just trying to shield the person what took your savin's.'

'I'm going,' Biddy said with controlled violence. 'There's nothing for me here now, and nothing for a Tebbit to steal any more, so you might as well let me go without any fuss.'

'Ere, 'ang on queen, you've paid till the week's end, I'll see me Mam don't ask any rent off of you for a week or two. Where'll you go if you march out now, eh? What'll you do?'

'I've got friends,' Biddy said stiffly. 'Don't worry about me, I'll survive. I always have.' She jerked open the big old front door and almost tumbled onto the pavement. 'It's no use asking you to get my money back, Ray, because I daresay she's spent it by now, so if you'll just leave me alone to get on with my life . . . '

'Let me carry your bag,' Ray said, trying to tug it out of her grip. 'Then I can see with me own eyes that you're goin' to friends. 'Ow would I feel if they found you dead in a gutter tomorrer, eh? How'd me Mam feel?'

'Delighted, I should think,' Biddy said sourly, retaining her hold on the carpet bag. 'Just you let go of me, Ray Tebbit, or I'll scream for a policeman no matter what your Jane has told them. Go on, bog off!'

'I don't suppose Jane told 'em much,' Ray said, but

he stopped tugging at her bag. 'She's an awful little liar, our Jane. 'Ang on, le' me give you your tram fare, any-road.'

'I don't need a tram fare, I've got me delivery bicycle,' Biddy said, walking round the front of the house to the entry which led to the back yard. 'Unless some member of your family's swiped that as well, of course.'

'It's only Jane, the rest of us wouldn't,' Ray muttered uneasily. 'Look, 'ere's a bob, it's all I've got on me. Go on, take it, you never know when you may need it. What about your dinner tonight, eh?'

For the first time, Biddy remembered her plans for the evening; the two eggs, the ginger-beer bottle full of milk, the half loaf of bread. She had brought the food in her carpet bag because she was determined to leave the Tebbits nothing, but where could she cook it, what would she do with it? It was far too late to cast herself upon the Bradleys tonight, she would have to find somewhere to lay her head in the next couple of hours or she would be taken up as a vagrant and thrown either into gaol or the workhouse, she did not know which she dreaded more.

They had reached the back yard and Biddy unlocked her bicycle with trembling hands and then took the shilling Ray was offering.

'I shouldn't thank you, because your bloody family owe it me – but thanks,' she said rather unsteadily, putting the carpet bag into the carrier and beginning to push the bicycle out of the yard. 'You're all right, Ray. Good-bye.'

Ray might have followed her as he had threatened had she gone on foot, but on the bicycle she was far too fast for him. She leaned hard on the pedals and fairly tore up the Court and into the Scotland Road, and then she turned left and pedalled equally fast for the city centre, because though she still had no idea where she was going she felt she wanted to be on well-lit streets, with people about.

There were hotels, lodging houses, surely she could get a bed somewhere just for one night? But with a bob? And if she spent her bob on a bed then she wouldn't have any money to buy herself chips.

She cycled along the gaslit streets until she reached Ranelagh Place, then she turned into Ranelagh Street, her eyes seeking out Millicent's Modes. Was there somewhere here where she could doss down for the night? Some little nook or cranny where the scuffers wouldn't come poking around looking for drunks and tramps?

But apart from the shop doorway, which seemed suddenly extremely exposed, there was nowhere.

What about a station, though? Stations were busy places, she remembered trying to dispose of Mr Bowker in Wapping Goods station and being unable to do so for people, noise and traffic. So if she went up to Lime Street and pretended she was waiting for a train, then she might be able to snooze undisturbed and safe on a seat until morning. If I can just get through this night, she told herself, if I can survive until morning, then I can go to the shop, explain what's happened, see if Miss Whitney or Miss Harborough can tell me what to do or help me in some way. Come to that, I can go round to Ellen's once its daylight. Yes, that's what I'll do. All I want is somewhere to stay safe until day comes again.

The *Greenland Bess* was homeward bound with her fish-pounds heaving with cod, codling, sea bass and the smooth-bodied halibut. When the men were not hauling the trawl, shooting it, conning the ship, breaking ice, they were gutting the fish. Greasy, who seemed to take to the life of a fisherman with considerable verve, didn't like the gutting.

'A feller could lose a leg,' he remarked to Dai when a huge, eel-like fish, apparently dead as a dodo, suddenly came to life in the pound and attacked his sea-boot, ripping the strong rubber as if it were paper with its hundreds of exceedingly sharp teeth. 'No one ever told me a bleedin' fish would turn round an' try to gut *me*, for a change!'

'Happens all the time,' Dai said laconically, making a private vow to watch the big fish in future and to keep all his most precious parts well out of the reach of those needle-sharp teeth. 'Still, can't be too careful, mun. Don't turn your back on 'em.'

But that was all a thing of the past now; going-home time was clean-up time, the time you scrubbed every inch of deck, polished all the brasswork on the bridge, mopped down seating, tables, floors.

'I feel like a bleedin' 'ousewife,' Greasy grumbled as he and Dai scrubbed endlessly across the deck, removing the last traces of fish. 'I'm surprised the Skipper 'asn't give us a duster to tie round us 'air, like one o' them black mammies you see in Yankee fillums.'

'You would look good in blue and white check,' Dai nodded. 'I'm more for pink gingham, me. Come on, get scrubbing, mun, there's beer on the mess deck and Bandy's makin' chips.'

'Not fish, for Gawd's sake? Tell me we're not eatin' fish again?'

Dai laughed. Contrary to popular belief trawlermen going to distant waters do not live on fish, but they do eat an awful lot of it, especially towards the end of a voyage.

'No, not fish, honest. Corned-beef fritters.'

'Oh.' There was a short pause whilst Greasy stared into space and thought about his next meal, then he sighed and nodded his head. 'Corned-beef fritters, eh? Do I like 'em?'

'You love 'em,' Dai said solemnly. 'We all love 'em. But unless we get this deck clean as a new pin – cleaner – we won't be havin' 'em. We'll still be scrubbing.'

'Aye; that's what the Mate said, I seem to remember. Taff?'

'What's up now?' Dai said resignedly, attacking a new stretch of deck. 'Do you scrub as you talk, Greasy, or we'll still be cleaning this deck come midnight.'

'You meant it, didn't you? You will come 'ome wi' me after this trip, to Liverpool?'

'Why not? The Mate says we've two weeks this time, because of the damage to the trawl and the lifting gear, so we've plenty of time to get there an' back by the next trip. If we sign on, that is.'

'I'm signin' off after this trip,' Mal said, behind them. He was polishing the rail. 'Money's good, but by 'eck, the work's not. Reckon there's easier ways to earn a livin'.'

'Come up to Liverpool with us, sign on a coaster,' Dai suggested, very tongue in cheek. Trawlermen were a breed apart, they rarely went back to ordinary merchant shipping once the fishing had got them. 'Have yourself a rest, Mal bach.'

'Mebbe I will Taff, one day, but for now I'll save me wages and me bonus instead of spendin' it all in the pubs on Freeman Street. I may sign on again in a few weeks though. Not on a distant-water ship, but on a drifter, or somethin' trawlin' the North Sea. Somethin' a bit easier, not quite so . . . aw hell, you know.'

'That's done, then.' Dai and Greasy rose simultaneously. 'Let's go to the mess deck, see if the chips are cooked.'

As they passed Mal, still diligently polishing, another deck-hand overtook them and paused to speak.

'I heard Mal just now; says it every trip 'e does. Always signs off . . . then signs on again when we sail. It's in the bloomin' blood, this lark is. You can't just walk away.'

'Try me!' Greasy said. 'Once I'm 'ome in the 'Pool – jest try me!'

Biddy slept jerkily on a bench in Lime Street station and woke, stiff and aching. She went to work, did her best to do all that she should, and asked Miss Whitney and Miss Harborough if they could suggest anything. Miss Whitney rolled her eyes.

'Christmas only nine days away and you're wanting time off to search for a room?' she said coldly. 'It won't do, Bridget. Look in the *Echo*, ask your friends, but don't keep taking time off.'

Biddy did her best to get somewhere, but with Christmas rapidly approaching and with her penniless state, she could find no one willing to take her on without even a week's rent in advance.

On Biddy's second night of sleeping rough the really bad cold weather suddenly set in. She reached Lime Street station late, too late to secure a bench, so cycled off again, this time to the cathedral. She found a shelter for the workmen and crawled inside, but had a disturbed night, largely due to her own nightmares, which woke her at hourly intervals, convinced she was about to be discovered and charged with trespass by some very large, very unfriendly police constable.

On the third night she left work on time and went straight to the railway station, staking her claim to a good bench which was against a wall and therefore warmer than those in the middle of the forecourt. She had just fallen asleep, or so it seemed, when she was rudely awoken by a hand on her shoulder and a voice in her ear, both appearing more dreadful to her sleep-fuddled mind than they proved to be once she was properly awake. A very dirty old tramp was shouting at her, telling her that he always slept here and who did she think she was, stealing an old man's favourite kip? If she was catching a train, he told her querulously, she should use the waiting room, not his bench, and if she was not catching a train then she should leg it before he told the scuffers on her.

Biddy dared not leave her bicycle on the station; even with the chain on the back wheel and the padlock securing it, anyone could lift the machine onto a train and then tackle her security system at their leisure, so she did not take the old man's advice about the waiting room, nor did she try to argue with him over his right to the seat, though she did mutter something about possession being nine-tenths of the law. But he gaped uncomprehendingly and gave her a shove, so she and her bicycle left the station in the coldest and most depressing hour of the day, just before dawn, and she began to cycle slowly down Lime Street, wondering drearily whether she could continue to keep on the move until the shop opened, or whether she would presently fall asleep, bicycle or no bicycle, and be killed in a spectacular crash.

When she reached Ranelagh Street she turned into it and got off the machine. She began to push it along the pavement, without any clear objective in view, trying to wipe her nose on her sleeve as she did so, for the night was perishingly cold and she thought she was catching a chill. When she reached Millicent's Modes she turned into the doorway, and was pleasantly surprised at how warm it felt after the draughts on Lime Street Station and the cold of the streets.

This was not so bad after all! She glanced cautiously around but the road appeared to be empty, so she propped her bicycle across the entrance so that she was shut in by it, and with numb fingers chained the rear wheel and fastened the padlock. Then she undid her bedroll and hung one thin blanket over the bicycle. This was marvellous, her own little room! With even that slight shelter, things improved considerably, so she wrapped the remaining blanket round her shoulders, put her pillow in the corner where the shop window and the door met, and lay down.

Three nights earlier she would have found it impossible to sleep, on a frosty night, in a shop doorway wrapped only in a blanket, but after the worry and sleeplessness which had already been her lot, she could scarcely keep her eyes open. She felt safe here, far safer than on the station, and it was wonderfully private and, after the open streets, wonderfully warm. Biddy lay awake for about two minutes reminding herself that she must not be found here in the morning and then she simply fell asleep and knew no more.

She awoke, once again, to find someone shaking her and a voice complaining bitterly about something.

'You wicked, ungrateful . . . what do you mean by it, sleeping in the doorway of the very shop which employs you! Get up at once and be off and don't bother to come back! Yes, I'm giving you the sack, my lady, and richly you deserve it, too! Bridget O'Shaughnessy, will you wake up!'

Biddy opened dazed, sleep-filled eyes. Immediately she realised that her worst nightmares had come true. Miss Whitney and Miss Harborough stood over her, identical expressions of amazement on their well-bred faces, whilst she struggled to her feet, almost overcome with fear and humiliation.

'I'm – I'm truly sorry,' Biddy stammered, trying to roll up her bedding with fingers that were all thumbs. 'I c-couldn't find l-lodgings, everyone wanted a w-week's rent in advance . . . I did explain . . . '

There was quite an audience now; staff from other shops stared, their expressions amazed, as Miss Whitney and Miss Harborough heaped scorn on Biddy's head and explained to anyone – and everyone listening – that they had no idea the girl was sleeping rough, they paid her a good wage, she was frequently tipped . . . ah, the young these days, no sense of responsibility, no pride in themselves . . .

Biddy finished off her bedroll and took the padlock off the rear wheel of the bicycle. Miss Whitney could not mean to dismiss her just because she had had her money stolen, lost her possessions, was in dire straits! But it soon became apparent that Miss Whitney meant to do exactly that.

'Take yourself off, Bridget, and be thankful that I did not send for a policeman and give you over to him for trespass,' she said coldly, once the crowd had dispersed and the three of them and the bicycle had gone down the entry and in at the back entrance of the shop. 'I'm not saying you've not done a good job of the delivering, but we really cannot put up with this. The shame of it!'

'Where did you think I was sleeping, Miss Whitney?' Biddy asked tearfully, standing beside the bicycle and patting its saddle as though it were in truth her trusty steed. 'I told you a girl at my lodgings had stolen my savings and I'd been forced to leave, I told you I hadn't managed to find anywhere else . . . I even asked you for advice, asked if you could help! I had no choice but to sleep somewhere!'

'There are cheap places for young people to stay in the city, I know there are,' Miss Whitney said forbiddingly. 'But you did not intend to search in your own time, oh no! You preferred to trespass on both our good nature and our premises . . . it won't do, Bridget. You may leave at once . . . and do stop patting the bicycle in that absurd way!'

Biddy took her hand off the bicycle as if she had been stung. She stared at Miss Whitney for a long moment, then swung round to stare at Miss Harborough. That lady had the grace to look very embarrassed and uncomfortable.

'Miss Whitney . . . I understand how you feel, with Christmas coming up and everything, but although we rarely see Captain or Mrs Goring they do own Millicent's Modes and they might be highly displeased to find you had dismissed Miss O'Shaughnessy . . . deep though her fault has been there are mitigating circumstances . . .'

'Nonsense, Miss Harborough,' Miss Whitney said coldly. 'Take your things, Bridget, and please don't return here.'

'But Miss Whitney, who'll do the deliveries for you? And . . . and you owe me four days' wages,' Biddy said wildly. 'I am in desperate circumstances, you know that. If you really mean to turn me out, then I must have my wages for the past four days.'

For one truly dreadful moment she thought that Miss Whitney was just going to refuse to hand over a penny of the money owing, but the older woman hesitated, then shrugged sharply and moved out into the shop itself.

'Very well,' she said over her shoulder. 'I'll pay you the money owing, though in view of your behaviour I feel I should be justified . . .'

'It's her nephew,' Miss Harborough suddenly hissed. She was pink-faced and plainly agitated. 'Her nephew's been sacked from Lewises for prigging two pair o' gloves an' a silver gauze purse. He wants a job in time for Christmas. Oh Biddy, I do feel bad, she's been hoping to get rid of you for days, but she's no right . . . oh, my dear child . . .'

'Here you are,' Miss Whitney said. She gave Biddy a handful of small silver and copper. 'I think you'll find that's right. Goodbye, Bridget, and I hope that when you get employment again you give more . . .'

But Biddy, with her carpet bag weighing her down on the left side, the can of paraffin on her right and her bedroll under her arm, was trudging wearily across to the shop door, her head down and despair in her heart. What on earth was she to do? She could scarcely go to Mrs Bradley's place now, with no job to bring a little money in and no savings. If she went to the police station and explained her plight she would be kindly but firmly put in the workhouse . . . what on earth was she to do?

'Well I never did! Not a word of gratitude for my giving her money when I could just as well have said she was being sacked without a character and had no right to a penny-piece!'

That was Miss Whitney, her annoyance at Biddy walking away whilst she was in mid-telling-off clear. Biddy heard Miss Harborough murmur what might have been an expostulation, but she took no notice and did not so much as turn her head.

Things are bad, they could scarcely be worse, Biddy told herself as the cold air outside the shop made her nose start to run again and brought tears to her eyes. But at least, now she's sacked me, I don't have to listen to that sanctimonious old bitch going on and on. At least I can just walk away from her!

The *Greenland Bess* docked in Number One fish dock at noon. The previous night everyone aboard slept the sleep of the just, whilst bunks scarcely moved, beer bottles stayed where you stood them down and dreams were of shore-going, not of the monstrous dangers of the deep.

'We're ahead of the others,' the Mate said as they chugged gently up the Humber towards the dock. 'We'll get a good price.'

Seagulls had screamed out to welcome her in as she came up past Flamborough Head and Spurn Point. Now they held their positions on rail and mast and superstructure, swaying as the small ship swayed, heads turning, bright eyes questing for the fish that they could smell but could not, as yet, see.

Men looked different in their shore-going clothes; smaller, less aggressive and sure of themselves. Bright ties, suits with over-bold stripes, shoes with lift heels. The clothes themselves seemed ill-at-ease on the tanned toughness of the distant-water trawlermen. But Dai and Greasy joined the others to queue at the office to be paid off, with their bonuses all worked out plus their wages for the month's voyage.

'Signing on in a fortnight?' The clerk asked each man. 'All being well she'll sail then; she'll be in dry-dock ten, maybe twelve days.'

'Yeah, might as well,' Greasy replied. 'If we're back in time, of course. We're goin' 'ome to Liverpool for Christmas.'

It was only then that Dai realised their fortnight would include the holiday and felt a sharp stab of homesickness. Oh to be going back to Moelfre and to his home in the street which would up from the harbour to the top of the cliff! To see Bethan's loving smile, to boast of his adventures, to tell tall stories . . .

Still. Not much joy to be got out of home right now, not with Davy set against him and Sîan married and gone. Make the best of it, mun, he urged himself, signing the book. And see this Gallagher woman while you're about it. No harm. And it was Mam's last wish, after all.

They wasted no time but went straight to the railway station, which was close to the docks so that the fish spent as little time as possible in transit.

'We can't warn 'em we're comin', but that won't

marrer,' Greasy said confidently as he and Dai boarded the train and dived into an empty carriage. 'Me Mam'll 'ang the flags out whatever.'

'What about an uninvited guest, though?' Dai said rather uneasily. It seemed hard on Mrs O'Reilly to be descended upon by not one, but two. 'You're always saying the house is crammed with O'Reillys, how'll she cope with an Evans, and all?'

'We'll stop off at Great Homer Street an' buy some grub an' some bottled beer, mebbe some sweets for the littl'uns; nothin' fancy, mind. An' you've got your bedroll so she won't need more blankets,' Greasy pointed out blithely. 'She won't worry none; me Mam's norra worrier.'

'Right. And of course I'll go round to Mrs Gallagher's as soon as I can, and then I'll probably be staying there,' Dai agreed.

He did not, in fact, anticipate that an old friend of his mother's would ask him to sleep over, but he did not intend to embarrass the O'Reillys by his presence over Christmas. I'll get a bed in one of the Seamen's Missions, he told himself. Or even in a boarding house, heaven knows I could afford it. But I'll not spend more than two nights with Greasy's folk, it wouldn't be fair, no matter what Greasy may say.

It made him feel better to have made a decision and for the rest of the journey he slept. One thing about distant-water trawling, he told himself drowsily, waking once when the train clattered into a tiny station and heaved itself to a stop. One thing about it is that it stretches you fully, mind and body, so that you're grateful, at the end of a voyage, just for time to yourself to sleep and relax.

Cross-country travel is never easy, but they managed somehow to complete their journey only an hour or so after darkness had fallen. Dai tumbled out of the train, rubbing his eyes and coughing as the freezing, coal-scented air clutched at lungs which had been breathing the stuffy, smelly air of the overcrowded train for most of the day. But a trawler is all warmth and tobacco fumes below and the iced wine of an Arctic winter on deck, so he speedily recovered himself and stood, with his bedroll under one arm and his bag at his feet, staring about him.

Because he was so tired and had slept so deeply it felt like the middle of the night to Dai, but glancing above his head, he saw from the face of the clock which hung above the concourse that it still lacked five minutes to seven o'clock. Good, they would be able to get to those shops Greasy had talked about, do their buying and still be back at Horatio Street before the O'Reillys settled down for the night. He turned to Greasy, who was standing there with a silly smirk on his face, just looking around him.

'Well, then? Do we walk, get a bus, or what?'

'Hey, less o' that, you iggerant bloody Taff,' Greasy said with great good humour. 'Ain't you never 'eard of Green Goddesses? Them's trams,' he added. 'Leckies. We'll get one 'ere what'll tek us straight where we wants to go. Eh, I can't wait to see me Mam again,' he added, then shot a conscience-stricken glance at his friend. 'Sorry, Taff, I forgot.'

'It's all right, it doesn't worry me,' Dai said gently. 'You've no cause to fret on my account.' He squared his shoulders and hefted his bedroll. 'Now where do we go to catch this "leckie" of yours?'

Chapter Seven

The two young men caught a tram which would take
them to Great Homer Street where they would do their
shopping. As the tram buzzed along through the gas-lit
streets, Greasy entertained Dai with stories of Paddy's
Market, where you could buy anything in the world you
wanted, probably for less than a bob. He also pointed out
local landmarks, including St George's Hall, which was
almost opposite Lime Street station, and the Free Library
and Museum, which looked like a palace to Dai. In fact
by the time the tram deposited them on Great Homer
Street, Dai was really looking forward to exploring the
city.

'It's a far cry from Holyhead,' he said ruefully, looking
out at the streets, still bustling with shoppers at eight
o'clock at night. 'I bet even London's no bigger or busier
than this.'

'I bet you're right, wack,' Greasy said contentedly,
steering his friend round a group of revellers outside a
pub and then accompanying him into a large provisions
shop, where it seemed to Dai's dazzled eyes that every
possible eatable was on sale. 'Now 'ave a look around,
then we'll decide what to buy.'

They were well-laden by the time they left the shop.
They had decided on a bag of oranges and another of
nuts, a slab of sultana cake and another of marble cake, a
big square of margarine and a slightly smaller one of
butter, a very large and smelly cartwheel of cheese and a
bag of mixed sweets, including the famous Everton mints.

'This'll keep 'em quiet for a week,' Greasy remarked, one cheek bulging with an Everton mint. 'It's 'ard for me Mam to manage, even wi' our Pete an' me both givin' her the allotment from our wages – no marrer 'ow she tries, the money don't stretch to feedin' eight kids, norrin winter, anyroad.'

'We didn't buy meat,' Dai said suddenly. 'Where's a butcher? I'll get a joint of some description, or a bird. Would they like a bird?'

'Best wait afore we buy a bird, in case Mam's got somethin', but you're right, they'll enjoy some meat. Now lemme think . . . I gorrit . . . sausages! There's a pork butcher on the corner up 'ere . . .'

They were heading for the pork butcher when, ahead of them, a fight started on the pavement. At least, it sounded like a fight; sharp cries, a woman's shriek and then the thud and slap of flesh on flesh had Dai and Greasy, already heavily laden, in two minds whether to turn aside or go and take a look.

'We'd best get back,' Dai said. 'No point in us sticking our noses in; one look at a seaman's jersey and some people . . .'

'We've gorra go that way, that's where the butcher is,' Greasy pointed out. 'Besides, wharrever it is'll be over by the time we get there.'

They pushed their way through the crowd thronging the pavement and discovered the most extraordinary scene. A big, burly man and a very much smaller person seemed to be disputing the ownership of a tattered carpet bag. The burly man was shouting that he was being robbed whilst the other said nothing, being too busy simply hanging on whilst the burly man hit out wildly and shook the bag – and the young person who held it – as a terrier shakes a rat.

Dai stepped forward. 'Stow that,' he said sharply,

grabbing the big man by the shoulder. 'No need to hit him, you're twice his size. Anyroad, it's easy to settle this particular argument. What's in the bag, mister?'

The man stopped slapping but he continued to try to tug the bag out of the other's hands. Dai glanced at his opponent and realised all in a moment that it wasn't a lad, as he had assumed, but a young girl. He caught a glimpse of tangled dark curls, large, furiously flashing blue eyes, and a mouth shut as tightly and as determinedly as a trap, before the burly man made another attempt to take the bag and, when the girl hung on, he swung his fist at her, catching her a glancing blow on the side of the head.

The girl winced, but hung on – actually came back to the attack. She kicked out, hard, and the man kicked right back so that she had to dodge, which she managed to do without once releasing her hold on the bag.

Dai, however, was having no more of this; other by-standers might think it amusing, but he did not intend to stand by whilst a very large man beat a very small girl.

'One more move from you and I'll flatten you, boyo,' he growled, grabbing the man's wrists in an iron grip. 'Where was you dragged up, eh? Hitting a lady!'

'Some lady – thievin' bitch, more like,' the burly one growled. His big, beefy hands were still clamped round the handles of the carpet bag. 'Mind your own business, you bloody nosy taff.'

All Dai's chivalrous instincts were aroused by this piece of nastiness. He gave a growl and transferred one hand to the burly one's nose whilst still retaining his hold on the other man's thick wrists. He tweaked it savagely so that the man shouted. The small girl, still hanging onto the carpet bag, gave a tiny, breathless giggle.

'Manners,' Dai said breathlessly. 'Now tell the lady you're sorry for using language before her.'

The man, mindful of Dai's grip on his nose, muttered something which could have been an apology and Greasy, who was standing guard over the shopping and personal possessions which Dai had dropped when he grabbed the man, leaned forward at this point and put his oar in.

'You wanna pick on someone your own size, matie! 'Sides, it's simple to solve the problem, as me bezzie said – what's in the bag, eh? You say first, 'ardclock, an' the lady says next.'

The big man began to bluster, but the two young seamen were determined and Dai's grip on his wrists was not to be denied. Dai had not spent a year hauling a trawl to stand any nonsense from a blubbery, cowardly sneak-thief, which, he had decided after one glance from the girl's blue eyes, was an accurate description of the burly one.

'Why should I say, eh? Wha' business is it of yourn?'

The girl, still clinging unto the bag, spoke out then. She had a clear, unaccented voice and she spoke with confidence, though her face was grimed with dirt and streaked with tears. 'I can tell you what's in it, since I packed it this morning! There's a change of underwear, a pillow, a blanket, six pennies and three ha'pence, a heel of bread, a bit of cheese, and a rag doll. That's all.'

'Them's . . . them's me old woman's clothes . . . me little daughter's stuff,' the man began, but as he did so he loosed his hold on the carpet bag for an instant.

It was sufficient. The small girl wrenched her property out of the man's hands, turned like lightning, and wiggled away through the crowd. Dai tried to follow her and tripped over his bedroll and Greasy thrust the shopping into his arms and told him, crisply, that he'd done his bit and now they'd best stop being unpaid scuffers and get into the butcher's before they closed.

'Yes, but we got to find that girl, mun,' Dai protested, pushing his way through the dispersing crowd. 'She's no guttersnipe, no sneak-thief – why did she run away from us? We were trying to help her!'

Greasy shook his head pityingly. 'She din't look like a thief, but she run away, so she may 'ave been,' he said sagely. 'She'll be awright, Taff – look at the way she 'ammered that feller's shins wit' 'er boots. Anyone what can kick like that can tek care o' theirselves.'

'But she only had a few pennies, I was going to give her enough for a hot meal . . . it's a cold night, she must be sleeping rough or she wouldn't carry a pillow and blanket round with her. Look, I feel responsible. Find her I must and will!'

'Taff, you don't know this area an' I do,' Greasy said positively. 'There's a million sidestreets, two million courts, there's the docks, the railway stations, the ware'ouses . . . she could be in any one of 'em. If she don't wanna be found, an' she don't, or she wouldn't ha' legged it, she won't be found. So we'll buy them sossies an' get back to 'Oratio Street; right?'

Dai heaved a sigh and looked desperately about him. There were faces all around, but none of them were crowned by tumbled black curls or owned a pair of big, scared blue eyes. 'Yeah, all right,' he agreed reluctantly. 'But 'ave a look round first thing in the morning I will though; might catch her in a doorway or something.'

'An' you might not,' Greasy pointed out. ''Ere's me Mam's favourite butcher's . . . shall we say two pounds o' best pork?'

Dai, following his friend into the sawdust-strewn shop, agreed that two pounds of best pork sausages sounded just about right, but he spoke absently; his mind was still fretting at his problem. He really must find that girl, it was his duty to find her.

All the way back to Horatio Street, all the time he was meeting the family, eating fried sausages with doorsteps of bread, laying out his bedroll on the back-bedroom floor, he thought about her. Quite a small girl, with a dark coat and a dirty face, stout boots and a great deal of determination. He did not know her name or her age or anything about her, save that she owned an old carpet bag with all her worldly possessions neatly packed away in it. He knew she would pack neatly; even in her present miserable circumstances she would be as neat as possible, he was sure of it.

When he was wrapped up in his blanket and preparing for sleep, the picture of her as she had looked up at him popped back into his mind. She was pretty, but he had seen prettier. She had courage, but girls who had grit and determination abounded. His Mam must have looked like that when she, too, had been just a girl. But in Wales, small, Celtic-looking girls with black hair and blue eyes abound. So what was it, then? Why did he have this conviction that she was special to him, that he must not lose her?

But though he fretted away at the problem for several moments it refused to be solved. Something in him had reached out to something in her, and from that moment on he had known he must find her again. Fate? Fellow-feeling? He had no idea.

But what did it matter, after all? I will find her, he told himself, settling down. I'll find her again if it takes me the rest of my life.

And on the thought, he slept.

Biddy, with her carpet bag firmly clutched to her bosom and her heart pumping like a traction engine in her chest, flew along the pavement, not having to push or shove since she was small and slim enough to get between the people fairly easily.

That awful, frightening old man! He had almost got her bag, the only thing left now between her and destitution! She wished she could have stayed to thank the seaman who had rescued her . . . she had heard him calling after her and had felt she was acting shabbily in running away from him as well as from the burly one, but she had little choice. She dared not risk losing anything more.

Her beautiful, hand-knitted woollen blanket had gone two nights previously, prigged whilst actually cuddled round her person. A young man with a wolfish face and a foreign accent had snatched it and gone . . . she had been happy to see him go, even with her blanket tucked under his arm. He had a really evil face, and he was flourishing a long, narrow-bladed knife which she was convinced he would have used without compunction had she tried to resist the theft.

The streets were a dangerous place indeed – now she knew the truth of the oft-repeated warning. She could have had her throat slit just for the possession of her blanket – that man just now had been prepared to beat her in front of a great many people and to lie boldly, just to get his hands on a bag containing he knew not what.

So Biddy, still clutching her bag, made her way rapidly along Great Homer Street and did not look back. She had found a safe place and she intended to go there and stay there until morning.

The 'safe place' was a shed in which a market trader kept his barrow, his awning and some of his unsold goods. Biddy had found the shed earlier in the day – found, too, the boards at the back which were loose and could be wriggled aside to let a small person slip in. She had spent the previous night here very cosily, bedding down on the gaily striped awning, and had only left the shed, in fact, to go and get herself some food.

Now, Biddy let herself into the shed, put the boards up again, and glanced contentedly around her. Some wrinkled apples would help out the bread and the cheese, and she had filled her ginger-beer bottle with water earlier, so she would have a drink as well. It was scarcely stealing, she told herself, biting into a small and wrinkled apple, to take market fades, especially such poor ones. And she had to live. Besides, the man who had stolen her blanket had not done so to fill his stomach but probably so that he could sell it. She, at least, stole from an urgent desire to keep body and soul together.

Kneeling on the awning, she opened her bag, got out her remaining blanket, her pillow and Dolly. She made up the bed, then sat back on her heels and fished bread and cheese out of the bag. The bottle full of water had been left under a fold in the awning – it was still there, she got it out and stood it handy – so now her evening meal was complete.

She ate quickly, for she was hungry, and as she ate she allowed her mind to go back to the incident on Great Homer Street earlier in the evening.

He had been awfully kind, that young seaman. Nice looking, too. She could see his face in her mind's eye clear as clear – the bunched up dark curls, the square-jawed, determined face, the dark and peaceful eyes. Yes, he was very nice looking, and she had hated running away from him – I felt more like running towards him, she remembered ruefully, more like just throwing myself into his arms and saying 'Look after me, because I'm so tired out with trying to look after myself!'

But you couldn't do things like that, of course, or only in your dreams. A young man would scarcely respect a girl who did that, the very first time they laid eyes on each other.

And yet . . . there had been something in those liquid dark eyes when they met her own, some message of familiarity and affection, as though they had known one another long ago and far away.

Bridget O'Shaughnessy, you are a sentimental little fool and you read too many of those stories in Peg's Paper, Biddy told herself. Love at first sight is just one of those silly, romantic stories which never happen in real life – I mean how could it? How could you just to look at a man and know he's the one for you? He could be married and a wife-beater, he could be an active white-slaver, he could be the sort of sailor who has a wife in every port! Forget him, she advised herself as she finished her food and began to pull her blanket about her. Forget him and start thinking how you will spend tomorrow. The young man is nothing to you and never will be, so put him right out of your head.

If it had been left to her sensible, practical mind, she would probably have obeyed and forgotten him, but her far from sensible and very susceptible heart had been touched, and refused to allow Biddy to forget that strong, calm face, the tanned hands which had rescued her, the logic which had proved who owned the carpet bag beyond doubt. He would always be special to her, it would be a long time before she stopped hoping to glimpse him again as she roamed the Liverpool Streets.

But only so I can thank him, of course, she told herself primly just before she fell asleep. I owe him my thanks, at least.

Oh, what a little liar, her heart remarked conversationally, when she was on the very edge of slumber. *You don't*

*want to thank him and walk away, you want to be with him,
get to know him . . . love him.*

And since Biddy's sensible mind had already fallen
asleep, her heart continued to insert the seaman's sturdy
figure and beautiful, dark-eyed face into her dreams all
the night long.

It was strange, because when she woke next morning
Biddy could not remember any of her dreams, though the
face of her rescuer was indelibly printed on her mind, but
something had definitely come over her. The sense of
worthlessness, the conviction that she would never get a
job, was a nuisance to friend and foe alike and might
just as well be dead, had completely disappeared. Instead, she woke feeling positive, energetic and
determined. She would stop being so foolish this very
day! She would go to the Bradley house in Samson Court,
off Paul Street, and explain that things had gone very
wrong for her. She would ask permission to have a good
wash, would borrow a clean skirt and jumper off Ellen,
and would then go out, job-hunting. And, she told herself
firmly, you will find a job and a good one too, because
you're worthy of work. Everyone who has employed you
in the past has been pleased with you, even horrible Miss
Whitney had only sacked her because she slept in the
shop doorway and Miss Whitney had a nephew who
needed a job.

This sudden rush of self-confidence did not leave her
either, when she crawled carefully out of the back of the
shed, towing her bag behind her. It did not even falter
when she remembered she had left her ginger-beer bottle
behind . . . if she had done such a thing yesterday she
would have burst into floods of tears and wished herself
dead once more. What a difference that young man's
championing of me has made, Biddy thought, raking her

fingers through her hair and then setting off at a brisk trot. If she kept up a good pace she could be in Paul Street in no time.

Biddy arrived at the Bradley house just as the eldest son, Henry, was going off to work. He grinned at her, self-conscious in a jacket, with a tie round his neck. ''Ello, Biddy, you're around early! Wanna see our Ellie? She's still in bed, lazy trollop!'

'Hello, Henry,' Biddy said. 'Yes, I'd like to see Ellen. Can I go in?'

'Sure. Mam's gerrin' brekky for them as 'as time to eat it.'

He grinned again, then hurried out of the court and into Paul Street.

Biddy knocked gently on the door, then opened it. 'Cooee! It's me, Biddy,' she called. 'Can I come in, Mrs Bradley?'

Mrs Bradley's round and cheerful face appeared in the kitchen doorway. 'Oh, hello, Biddy,' she said at once. 'Don't 'over out on the doorstep, come right inside, queen. Our Ellie's been rare worried about you. She's in bed now though . . . want a spot o' brekky?'

'I wouldn't mind,' Biddy said, her mouth watering at the smell of tea and porridge which was wafting through into the front room. 'Mrs Bradley, I've come to ask a favour. Can I have a wash and borrow a skirt and jumper off Ellen? You see . . .'

The sad little story was soon told. Mrs Bradley, bustling round the kitchen with the porridge pot, tutted. 'You should ha' come 'ere at once, queen, we don't 'ave much, but what we do 'ave we share. 'Ere, get that down you.'

Hot tea tasted marvellous, the porridge better. Biddy tried to eat and drink slowly but somehow it was all gone in no time and she was eyeing the loaf.

'There's margarine in the cupboard and a scrape o' jam,' Mrs Bradley said, cutting a hefty slice off the loaf. 'Go on, fill up. You're a growin' girl . . .' she laughed, '. . . like our Ellen,' she added. 'She's still fat, is our Ellen. You go up an' 'ave a word when you've ate.'

'I will,' Biddy said thickly through bread and marge. It had never tasted so good . . . and the tea was sheer heaven after so long on water. 'I'm going to ask her if I can borrow a skirt and jumper. I – I've not been able to wash my things and I didn't bring much away with me anyway. I left in such a rush.'

But before she could go upstairs, there was a heavy thumping and Ellen came down. She was, as her mother had said, still large, but she beamed with delight to see Biddy and came running across the room to give her a kiss. 'Oh, Bid, I've been so worried about you! I went into Millie's an' that sour-faced lemon wouldn't tell me where you was, only that you didn't work there no more.'

'She sacked me,' Biddy said briefly. 'I've been sleepin' rough.'

Ellen squeaked and put a hand to her mouth. 'Sleeping rough? Oh, Biddy, why didn't you come 'ere?'

'I don't know. I think I was a bit mad,' Biddy admitted. 'But I'm here now, Ellen. I'm going to borrow a skirt and jumper off you, if you don't mind, and have a wash, and then I'm going to apply for some jobs. I think I could ask Miss Harborough to give me a reference, because she was cross with Miss Whitney for sacking me, said it wasn't right.'

'Course you can borrow some clo'es; I can't wear any o' me nice stuff,' Ellen said regretfully. 'Want a squint at the *Echo*?'

'Oh, please! I've missed seeing the paper terribly,'

Biddy admitted. 'Not that there'll be anything for me, I don't suppose,' she added rather gloomily, 'with Christmas only a couple of days away they won't want shop staff.'

Ellen fetched the *Echo* and sat down opposite Biddy at the kitchen table. She handed the paper to her friend and took the bowl of porridge her mother was holding out. 'Ta, Mam. I know what you mean about shop work, but there's other jobs. . .'

Biddy's eye scanned the pages keenly, then she put the paper down, shaking her head. 'No shop work, or not the sort I could do, anyway. But I do wonder about one of the Register Offices? There's several of them about, that I do know.'

'One I can't forget is Bradley's, on Bold Street,' Ellen said with a giggle. 'Not that I ever tried there, because it's Domestic Servants, of course. But Mrs Aspinall's Registry, at No. 35 Bold Street, is well thought of, so I've heard. There wouldn't be any harm in trying there . . . but don't go until after Christmas, dear Biddy! Spend Christmas here!'

'I'd love to, but I can't risk missing out on a job,' Biddy told her. 'Someone may have been let down, or need a servant badly, I can't risk waiting and then finding everyone is suited. Look, I'll walk round there this morning, see what the situation is, then come back here tonight, if you're sure you don't mind.'

'Mind? We'll be real upset if you don't come back to us,' Ellen said vigorously. 'Wharra friends for, eh? I shan't forget what you did for me when I were in trouble.'

'You'll be in trouble right now, my lady, if you don't get your breakfas' ate and yourself and the baby down to the clinic,' Mrs Bradley said. 'Go on Biddy, you run upstairs an' 'ave a wash, then get into our Ellie's skirt an' jumper. An' don't go toting that bag off, call back later.

A job's easier to find if you're not cartin' your 'ome on your back, so to speak. There's a grey pleated skirt wi' a blue jumper . . . you'd look a treat in that. Ah, don't forget the jug o' water, I hotted you some special.'

Biddy went up the stairs and washed and changed, reappearing presently in the blue jumper and grey skirt. She had washed her hair and dried it, then tied it into a neat tail at the back of her head, using a length of Ellen's blue ribbon, secure in the knowledge that her friend would not mind. Now she stood anxiously at the foot of the stairs, watching her friend's expression. 'Do I look all right? Good enough to get a job?'

'Good enough to eat,' Ellen said exuberantly. 'Come on, we'll put each other on the leckie, an' we'll see you tonight. Don't be late, 'cos I made some curtains for Mrs Gregory last week an' tonight we're 'avin' mutton scouse to celebrate. You don' wanna miss that!'

'I'll be back,' Biddy said thankfully. 'Don't worry, Ellen, I'll be back.'

Bold Street was in a smart area of the city, but Biddy, thanks to her job as a delivery girl, knew most of it by heart. She had never actually visited any of the Employment Registers – there were three on Bold Street alone – but she always lingered when passing the Lyceum, the Liverpool Library, and Liberty's wonderful window displays.

Now, however, she ignored the lures of theatre, books and fabulous dresses and materials and went straight to the Employment Register run by Mrs Jane Aspinall. She lingered outside for a moment or two, adjusting her little hat – well, Ellen's little hat – and smoothing away a stray wisp of hair, but then she went inside.

It was a pleasant, bright little room with a long

counter, behind which sat two ladies. They looked up and smiled as Biddy entered, then looked down again. There were telephones before them, and large ledgers. It all looked very businesslike. Biddy wondered doubtfully whether she had been right to come.

Walking over to the counter she cleared her throat. The lady nearest her looked up again and smiled encouragingly.

'Yes, madam?'

It reminded Biddy sharply and poignantly of her friend Mr Meehan. Just as soon as she had a job she would go round and see him again and he would probably tell her that she had been silly not to come before. Why on earth had she panicked the way she had and kept away from all her friends? But the woman was looking at her enquiringly, so she gathered her wits and spoke.

'Good morning. I'm looking for a position in someone's house, as – as a domestic servant. I would like to live in, if that's possible.'

The woman was grey-haired with a pair of rather small but very shrewd brown eyes. 'Ah, yes. Parlour maid? Kitchen work? What previous experience have you, Miss ... er ...? My name is Mrs Edmonds, incidentally.'

'O'Shaughnessy; Bridget O'Shaughnessy. Experience? Well, I ran the home for my mother whilst she was ill,' Biddy said a little uncertainly. 'I've worked at a small sweetshop where the owner expected me to do the laundry, clean the house and cook the meals when she was otherwise occupied, but lately I've worked for a gown shop – Millicent's Modes. I'm sure they'll give me a reference, if you would like one.'

'Hmm. Let me see what's wanted at present. Cook general? Do you think you could do that sort of thing?'

Honesty forbade Biddy to agree completely. 'I'm not sure,' she said cautiously. 'If it was very simple cooking ... but I can make confectionery, of course.'

'Wages?'

'Oh yes, I'd like to be paid,' Biddy said thoughtlessly, remembering Ma Kettle. The grey-haired lady gave her the sort of look idiots all over the world are probably used to receiving and Biddy, blushing, realised she had not given the expected reply. Trying to turn it into a joke, she added hastily, 'as much as possible, I suppose.'

A frosty look stole into the eyes of the woman behind the counter. 'Miss O'Shaughnessy, that is not the attitude you will be expected to display in domestic service, I suppose you realise that? We could not recommend anyone who . . .'

'I'm sorry, I wasn't really being impudent, it was because the lady I worked for at first didn't pay me any wages, just my keep,' Biddy said, her voice trembling a little. 'It – it wasn't a happy situation, so when you said "Wages?" I thought you meant . . .'

'Quite. A scandalous way to behave,' the grey-haired one said, appearing to relax a bit. 'However, perhaps you should discuss wages with your prospective employer rather than with myself. Now tell me, Miss O'Shaughnessy, why have you decided to apply for a job in domestic service? I don't hesitate to tell you that it is not as well paid as shop work and carries with it a certain . . . well, almost a stigma with some young people. They would prefer to work in a factory or shop, where at least their evenings and days off are entirely their own. In service, the mistress's wishes must always come first, even if it means you are working very much later than you had expected, or doing things which are not, strictly speaking, your job.'

Biddy took a deep breath. 'I was living with a family who were not honest,' she said. 'They stole my savings and when I gave them an hour to return my money or I would go to the sc . . . police . . . they went to the police at once and said that it was I who was the thief. So I left there; I had little choice. Now, I'm staying with friends in Paul Street, but it's a very overcrowded house already and I can't continue to live with them. So I thought . . . domestic service would mean I could live in, and I'd be paid a wage . . . it just seemed best.'

'Yes, by and large I agree with you. And why did you leave your last employer, Miss O'Shaughnessy?'

'Because a relative of Miss Whitney's came to the city and couldn't find work, and Miss Whitney decided to employ her relative in my place,' Biddy said promptly. 'But she was not dissatisfied with my work . . . I'm a hard and conscientious worker, Mrs Edmonds.'

The older woman stared at her very hard for a moment and then gave a little nod, as though she had read something she liked in Biddy's frank countenance. 'I shall give you a chance, Miss O'Shaughnessy. There's a lady who has a nice house just off the Boulevarde, in Ducie Street. Do you know it?'

'Yes, I know it,' Biddy said at once. 'It's close by Granby Street, isn't it?'

Mrs Edmonds looked surprised. 'Yes, that's right . . . you certainly do know the city, Miss O'Shaughnessy.'

Biddy smiled demurely. She did not intend to admit she'd been a delivery girl if she could avoid so doing. A shop assistant in a smart gown shop was much more acceptable to this sharp-eyed lady, she felt sure.

'Mrs Gallagher – that's the lady's name – needs a general servant, which usually means cooking, cleaning, answering the door etcetera. She has a woman in to do the rough scrubbing and so on. It's live-in, with all day Sunday and Thursday afternoons off, uniform provided, no other servant. Mrs Gallagher wants someone before Christmas, if possible, because her previous girl left some

213

while ago and they haven't bothered to replace her since they've been away a lot. Oh, there are three in the family, Mr and Mrs Gallagher and a daughter of about fifteen, I believe.' She drew a pad of paper towards her. 'Would you like to go along for an interview? They are on the telephone, so I can ring her right now and we can arrange a suitable time.'

'Yes, that would be very nice,' Biddy said, hoping this was the expected response. Apparently it was, for Mrs Edmonds nodded and took the telephone receiver off its hook, though she kept her finger pressed down on the rest.

'Would you mind waiting over there, Miss O'Shaughnessy?' She indicated a chair set well back against the wall on the opposite side of the room.

Biddy went and sat in the chair. It was too far away for her to hear any of the ensuing conversation and in any case Mrs Edmonds deliberately pitched her voice low, but she could not help wondering what this Mrs Gallagher would be like – and Miss Gallagher, too. Miss Gallagher was only a year younger than herself, they might even become friends!

Presently Mrs Edmonds hung her receiver back on its hook and beckoned Biddy over. She folded the sheet of paper upon which she had been writing and slid it into an envelope which she then sealed and pushed across the counter. 'There you are, Miss O'Shaughnessy; a letter of introduction. Mrs Gallagher says if you catch the tram you can be with her quite soon, so she'll expect you when she sees you.' She paused delicately. 'I take it you have the tram fare, Miss O'Shaughnessy?'

Not for worlds would Biddy have admitted that her tram fare was also her dinner money. She nodded and smiled brightly, taking the envelope and slipping it into her coat pocket. 'Thank you, Mrs Edmonds. If – if I get the job do I come back?'

Mrs Edmonds shook her head. She was all smiles suddenly, as though simply seeing the last of Biddy was enough to cheer her up. 'No, Miss O'Shaughnessy. The rest of the business will be transacted entirely between Mrs Gallagher and myself. Good morning.'

It was a long walk out to Ducie Street, but Biddy was a good, fast walker when she set her mind to it. She was passed by two trams, but told herself that since Mrs Gallagher had said she would expect her when she saw her, she was unlikely to take against her just because she was perhaps a little later than she expected. Also, Biddy was quite shrewd enough to realise that someone who wanted a live-in servant by Christmas could probably not afford to be too fussy – everyone would prefer to spend the holiday at home or amongst friends rather than waiting on total strangers.

She reached Ducie Street at last and pulled the envelope out of her pocket. She glanced at the nearest house . . . not too far away, then. She walked on, found the right number and went up the short path to the door. For a moment she just stood there, suddenly sure she was making an awful mistake; she would be no good at this sort of thing, she had the wrong attitude. She had been nothing but a slave at Ma Kettle's, now she would find herself equally powerless, equally put-upon.

She very nearly turned and fled – but then she remembered the man who had stolen her blanket and the one who had tried to steal her carpet bag. She remembered the little house in Paul Street bulging with sixteen souls whilst poor Mrs Bradley scratted round to find everyone food and clothing.

She even remembered the baby Ellen had just had which would make life even harder for the Bradleys.

It would not be fair to run back to Samson Court and put upon her friends.

So she stood her ground and knocked, disciplining herself not to flee when she heard, from within the house, someone approaching the front door.

It was a pretty, slim woman with light brown hair and steady grey eyes. She had very pale skin and looked calm and self-assured – very different from me, Biddy thought; I'm a bundle of nerves. But when the woman smiled at her she smiled back, because it was a friendly and attractive smile.

'Good afternoon. Would you be Miss O'Shaughnessy? I'm Mrs Gallagher – do come in.'

Once in the hallway she held out her hand. 'How do you do? I'm afraid I'm not very good at this, Miss O'Shaughnessy, but if you'll come through to the kitchen perhaps you can watch whilst I prepare my husband's tea and we'll have a chat. It will give both of us some sort of idea . . .' her voice trailed away. 'This is the kitchen.'

The kitchen was nice and overlooked the back garden. It was modern by most standards, as modern as the house, with kitchen units all round the walls, bright linoleum on the floor, and a modern gas cooker as well as a blackened stove which probably heated the hot water as well as warming the kitchen itself.

'This is where most of the work's done, so I've tried to make it as up to date and pleasant as possible,' Mrs Gallagher said. 'As I'm sure Mrs Edmonds told you, there are only three of us, but we do entertain from time to time and we have quite a large dining-room.' She smiled at Biddy. 'Sit down, Miss O'Shaughnessy. Do you have a letter for me?'

Feeling her face go hot, Biddy guiltily produced the

envelope, looking a little the worse for wear, from her pocket. 'I'm sorry,' she said apologetically. 'This is the first time I've applied for a job in domestic service and I'm really rather nervous.' She had decided, on the spur of the moment, that she would much rather Mrs Gallagher knew the truth. That way, at least she was less likely to be disappointed if Biddy did not come up to expectations.

'Yes, so Mrs Edmonds says in the letter,' Mrs Gallagher said, having read the short note. 'I'll take you round the house, Miss O'Shaughnessy, show you the room you would have if you decided to take the position, and give you some idea of the work involved. I'm sure Mrs Edmonds told you that we have a woman in three times a week to do the rough work and a man who does the garden, cleans the boots and shoes and so on. But all the rest of the work will, I'm afraid, fall on your shoulders.'

'I don't mind hard work,' Biddy said. 'But I'm not sure my cooking is good enough . . . Mrs Edmonds said you needed a cook general . . .'

'I do most of the cooking myself,' Mrs Gallagher said gently. 'I enjoy cooking. But such things as peeling vegetables, preparing meat, making strawberry and raspberry preserve in the summer . . . things like that are easier with the work shared.'

'So long as I'm told what to do,' Biddy murmured. 'I don't want you to think I'm being difficult, but . . .'

'I think you're being sensible,' Mrs Gallagher assured her. 'Now just follow me and we'll do the rounds. . . . You can see the garden through the kitchen window, though there isn't much to see at this time of year, and only cabbages in the kitchen garden, which is right down the end, furthest away from the house.'

As she talked she was leading Biddy across a square

hall and she paused outside the first door she reached. 'The dining-room.'

It was a large room with an enormous table and a very grand mahogany sideboard. There were a dozen dining chairs upholstered in red leather, some pictures on the walls, a display of silver dishes on the sideboard and a large mirror behind them.

'You'd dust and clean generally in here, and help to serve food when we've guests,' Mrs Gallagher said, leading the way to the next room. 'Sitting-room.'

Another pleasant, large room, cluttered with chintz-covered chairs, occasional tables, several lamps, a wireless set and a quantity of strange objects plus a mass of coloured paper, whilst three young ladies, all aged about fourteen or fifteen, sprawled around a low central table on which was set out a large bowl of fruit, another of nuts, a jar of sticky paste and several pairs of scissors.

'My daughter, Elizabeth, the one with the plait, and a couple of her friends.' Mrs Gallagher raised her voice. 'Liz, you said making Christmas decorations, not eating all the nuts I've bought! Mind you clear up the shells.'

Liz of the long, light brown plait turned and grinned at Biddy. She was a pretty girl, lively and bright, wearing a deep pink woollen dress with a rather scruffy white apron over it.

'Sorry, Mam,' she said. 'We will clear up – and we *are* making Christmas decorations . . . see those beautiful chains and silver fir cones? . . . only it's hungry work, so we have raided the nuts rather, I'm afraid.'

'Well, never mind, there's still another couple of days before *the* day, so I suppose I can buy some more.' Mrs Gallagher withdrew, shutting the door gently behind her, and crossed the hall once more. She opened another door. 'My husband's study . . . not too large, and he's pretty tidy. He works for the newspaper, so he needs a telephone in here and we have another in the hall. Also we have one by our bed, because sometimes the newspaper needs him at night. He's a tidy type, my dear old Stuart, but he does hate things being moved, so since we don't want him having an apoplexy I always advise anyone cleaning in here to avoid so much as touching the papers all over the desk and if there is a pile of papers on the floor, just to leave them. He's very sweet tempered really, and extremely patient, but now and then he does *roar*, which frightens my charlady, Mrs Wrexham, dreadfully. At first she used to cower in the kitchen biting her nails and trembling, but she's grown accustomed now and takes no more notice than I do. Now that's all that need worry you down here; that room,' she gestured to her left, 'is a small downstairs cloakroom and the other door is just a glory hole for tennis racquets, boots, sleds and so on. Now we'll go upstairs and take a look at the bedrooms.'

There were five bedrooms on the first floor and two attic rooms. The bedrooms seemed the height of luxury to Biddy, especially Elizabeth's. It was all decorated in pink and white, with the prettiest curtains and a lovely, thick white rug, and Elizabeth had her own gas fire and a gas-ring, too, so that she could make herself a hot drink whilst she was up here studying.

'We want her to be comfortable and to consider study a pleasure,' Mrs Gallagher said simply. 'She's a clever girl, but she gets lonely, sometimes. And I must admit she makes a lot of work and does throw her things around rather, besides filling the house with young people and coming in for meals at odd hours . . . dashing upstairs and traipsing mud all through the place. However! This is our room, the dressing room's next door. I always do our rooms so you won't have to come in here unless I need a hand with something. The other rooms on this floor are just spare bedrooms, though they'll be in use this Christmas. I have a – a younger sister, Mrs Lilac Prescott she is now; she and her husband and their small children will be coming to stay over Christmas which is why I really am rather keen to get someone before then.' She looked ruefully over at Biddy, her eyes smiling though her mouth was serious. 'My sister is a dear girl and will do all she can to help, but her twins . . . well, they're really the naughtiest little boys you could imagine . . . does this put you off, Miss O'Shaughnessy?'

For the first time since she had entered the house, Biddy laughed. She liked Mrs Gallagher, she liked the sound of the sister, the awful twins, Liz and her friends thundering through the house scattering mud, Mr Gallagher *roaring* if his papers were touched. Even Mrs Wrexham the charlady, cowering in a corner and biting her nails because 'the master' was cross, sounded nice somehow. There was a cheerful informality about the Gallagher household which appealed to Biddy.

'No, Mrs Gallagher, it doesn't put me off, it makes me think I could be very happy here,' she said therefore. 'May I see the attic rooms, please?'

'Oh mercy, I always said honesty was the best policy,' Mrs Gallagher exclaimed. 'The rooms are both yours . . . I mean they go with the job, since you might yet turn me down! Follow me.'

They scampered up the attic stairs like a couple of kids, Biddy thought afterwards, and there were two small white doors, one to the left, one to the right, with a square landing in between. Intriguing doors, Biddy decided, staring at them. What was behind them?

'Bedroom,' Mrs Gallagher said, flinging open the left-hand door. 'Gas fire, in case it's cold, which it jolly well is right now. Single bed, plenty of blankets, a chair, a rug and of course wardrobe, chest of drawers . . . all the usual offices.'

'Very nice,' Biddy murmured. It was a delightful room, truly delightful, with every evidence of thoughtfulness and welcome.

'Yes, it is nice, isn't it? Liz said she wouldn't mind moving up here, so we guessed a girl could be happy, here. And the living-room.' She opened the right-hand door and gestured Biddy past her. 'What do you think?'

It was charming. The low window was curtained in warm red velvet and the rug was red with garlands of flowers. A small dining-table and two upright chairs stood in an alcove whilst in the main body of the room two easy chairs were set out before the little gas fire, a gas-ring just like the one in Elizabeth's room stood beside it and three pictures hung on the walls, all of them cheerful country scenes.

'It – it's perfect . . . absolutely perfect,' Biddy stammered. 'And this is all for your . . . your servant?'

'For you, if you would like to work for us,' Mrs Gallagher said gently. 'You see, Miss O'Shaughnessy, when I was your age I – I didn't have very much and I did work hard. To have a room like this would have been very precious to me, it would have made me very happy. So now I hope this room will make some young woman very happy too.'

'Oh, it will! And . . . and I can come and work for you, and have these two rooms?'

'Yes . . . but we haven't talked about money, yet,' Mrs Gallagher said, smiling and pink-cheeked. Biddy's rapture had obviously thrilled her. 'Would ten shillings a week suit you? It doesn't seem much, but it's all found, and it's what Mrs Edmonds recommended. If you can't manage . . .'

'On ten shilling a *week*, and not having to buy food? Oh, I'll manage just fine, Mrs Gallagher,' Biddy said, her tongue tripping over the words in her excitement. 'Can I start tomorrow? Can I move my things in then?'

'Tomorrow would suit me admirably, especially if you could manage quite early in the morning, since we're meeting the Prescotts off the London train at noon,' Mrs Gallagher said, her eyes sparkling. 'Oh, how wonderful to have help in the house again, with the evil twins on their way and Christmas almost upon us. You will not regret coming to work for us, Miss O'Shau . . . my dear, what is your first name?'

'Oh, I'm Bridget, but everyone calls me Biddy,' Biddy said joyfully. 'I'll be here by nine, Mrs Gallagher, if that will suit?'

'Admirably,' Mrs Gallagher said. She led the way down the attic stairs. 'I feel sure, Biddy, that you and I are going to get along famously!'

'I'd like working here even without the rooms,' Biddy said, following close. 'But with those rooms for my own – it'll be heaven, Mrs Gallagher!'

After Biddy O'Shaughnessy had left, positively bubbling with happiness, Nellie Gallagher sat in her kitchen, looking a little ruefully around her.

She liked Biddy, had liked her on sight, so that was good. She thought they would work well together, which was better. Because the last girl, Peggy Pound, had been a right little monkey. Idle, none too clean, an inventive liar . . . a bad influence all round who had made a deal of trouble before Nellie had managed to admit to herself that Peggy would have to leave.

The trouble was, Peggy was an orphan, as Nellie had been – still was, Nellie supposed ruefully now, sitting at her own kitchen table and pouring herself another cup of tea, since marriage and a daughter of her own did not endow her with parents. So because Peggy was an orphan, from the very same orphanage in which Nellie and her adopted sister, Lilac, had first met, Nellie had felt it incumbent upon her to try extra hard with Peggy.

But it had been trying wasted, because all Peggy ever thought about was having fun and doing as little work as possible. She had decided that carting water up two flights of stairs in order to wash her person was too much trouble, so she stopped washing. She seldom made the family a meal and when she did she burned more than she cooked. She had disliked Mrs Wrexham and told lies about her to Nellie, and she was jealous of Liz and frequently tried to get her into trouble with either parent, she was not fussy which.

The final straw had come when she started bringing young men in. Not even decent young men, Nellie thought indignantly now, pouring herself another cup of tea and leaving it to get cold whilst she remembered the many sins and wickednesses of Peggy Pound. She picked up the most dreadful young men on the streets, thieves, lay-abouts, the worst sort of scoundrels, and brought them back to Ducie Street, to the two attic rooms which Nellie had furnished so lovingly for some poor girl.

And I didn't even have the courage to sack her myself, Nellie remembered sorrowfully now. But darling Stuart, bless him, who had been an orphan in Liverpool, as well, darling Stuart had dealt with Peggy. Kindly but firmly, he had given her an ultimatum; stop bringing men into my house, stop thieving money from my wife's purse and my daughter's money-box, or out you will go. I mean it.

She couldn't stop, that was the trouble, and Stuart, even as he gave her the ultimatum, had known she couldn't stop. She was used to having a man in her bed and money in her purse; she could not just stop for the sake of a job she did not even value, let alone enjoy.

'She'll end up a sailors' whore on the waterfront,' Nellie had wept, lying next to Stuart in their big double bed the night after the ultimatum had been delivered. 'She'll die young, of some horrible disease. Oh Stu, my darling, what did we do wrong?'

'Nothing, sweetheart, nothing! She's a bad lot, we should never have taken her in; matron, if you remember, was very doubtful. Now go to sleep, and in a couple of days . . .'

And of course Peggy went, not even unwillingly. She had found a better way to make a living, she told Mrs Wrexham, whilst Elizabeth listened, wide-eyed. There were fellers around who just wanted to see a girl comfortable . . . all she had to do was crook her little finger . . .

'There's one other little thing she has to do,' Stuart said wickedly, when Nellie repeated the conversation that night. 'I bet she didn't put that into words, though.'

And ever since then, for months and months, Nellie had managed without a maid. Only it was beginning to get her down, because it was a big house and she had responsibilities. As a newspaper editor-in-chief, Stuart entertained quite often, and although Nellie rather enjoyed the cooking, she had to keep having temporary staff in to serve and wait on and help out generally.

'Employ someone else, only this time, go through one of the Employment Registers,' Stuart had insisted. 'Don't worry, my pet, they interview everyone they send to see you first; you won't get a long line of little Peggys knocking at the door.'

And the very first girl had been Biddy . . . Bridget O'Shaughnessy, who would do her best – Nellie just knew it – and was young enough to be a companion for Elizabeth yet old enough to be relied upon.

Oh Lor, Nellie said to herself now, sitting up straight and pushing the cold tea away. Oh Lor, I never asked her age! Oh goodness, and it'll be the first thing Stu asks me when he comes home tonight – he'll think I'm a real nitwit not to have asked!

Getting to her feet, she began to organise dinner. She and Elizabeth would have a makeshift luncheon when Elizabeth's friends had left, but tonight, with Stuart home, they would have a proper meal. Tonight they would have soup first, then pork chops and apple sauce, then apricot pudding. Stu was extremely fond of his Nell's apricot pudding. And she would be able to tell him that Biddy was starting next day, at nine o'clock, which would please him.

The day passed pleasantly, with Nellie doing the housework, reminding herself at frequent intervals that from the very next day she would have help and would not have to struggle on alone. At around five o'clock she began to prepare their meal, taking pleasure in it. The phone rang when she was opening the tinned apricots and she had to abandon the tin and run through into the hall, taking down the receiver with distinctly syrupy hands.

'Hello?'

It was Stuart. He was awfully sorry, but he would be late this evening; something had come up, something important. 'Have you cooked my dinner?' he asked anxiously. 'What was it?'

'Leek soup first, then pork chops, and apricot pudding to finish,' Nellie said, trying to sound cheerful and not resigned. 'But all I've done so far is start to make the apricot pudding.'

Stuart groaned. 'It's my favourite . . . tell you what,

make it and save me a piece. A big piece. Could you warm it up when I get in? I shan't be much after ten.'

'Of course I could,' Nellie said happily. 'Oh, Stu . . . the Register sent a girl, like you said they would.'

'They did? Oh sweetheart, I'm so glad for you. What was she like?'

'Lovely. A dear little girl. Her name's Biddy O'Shaughnessy.'

He laughed. 'Crumbs, what a mouthful! When does she start?'

'Tomorrow, nine o'clock. But how d'you know she wanted the job? I only said the Register had sent her round.'

'She'd have been mad not to take the job if you liked her,' Stuart said simply. 'See you later, sweetheart; don't forget, a big piece of apricot pudding.'

They rang off and Nellie wandered back into the kitchen. Despite the news that Stuart would miss his meal she felt happy, because just to hear his voice, so full of understanding and affection, made her feel warm and comfortable, loved, precious.

It had been like that from the start, of course. Nellie began to make her pudding mixture, gazing out at the damp back garden without seeing it, remembering the first time she and Stuart had met.

She had been nursing wounded soldiers in France and Stuart had been convalescing from a splintered kneecap though, as a War Correspondent, he wasn't actually engaged in the fighting. She and a friend had been off duty, walking through the snowy countryside of Northern France, when he had heard her familiar Scouse accent and called out to her, offering, as one Liverpudlian to another, to take her tobogganing down the snowy slopes.

The toboggan had turned out to be a battered tin

hospital tray – it was a good deal more battered by the end of the afternoon – but despite this, Nellie had had the time of her life, and she had known from that moment that Stuart was the man for her. Of course it had not been that simple, nothing ever was, but after the war they had met up again and married, and since then Nellie's life had quite simply revolved round Stuart and their only child.

Reminiscing about those early years always filled her with wonder at her own immense good fortune. She had been a skinny little orphan with no particular skills, yet she had ended up married to the best man in the world, and had given birth to his beautiful daughter. Little Nellie McDowell, who had never expected much from life, was married to an important newspaper executive and happy as the day was long, though she would have been equally happy had Stuart been a tram driver or indeed a factory worker or a street sweeper. When two people are still deeply in love after – heavens, after getting on for two decades – then, Nellie knew, they were much blessed.

But gazing into space and counting her blessings would not get the meal cooked. She began to roll out her suety crust.

Nellie had finished the apricot pudding and was half-heartedly preparing vegetables and setting out two chops on the grill when the kitchen door burst open and Elizabeth came in. She smiled beguilingly at her mother and poured herself a glass of home-made lemonade, then sat down at the table with a thump. Her friends had gone to their own homes for luncheon, returned afterwards to take Elizabeth to the park for an impromptu game of three-a-side hockey, then they had accompanied her home again for tea and Nell's rich fruit-cake and butter shortbread.

'The girls have gone, Mam. They said to thank you very much for the tea. Can I help with dinner? When's me Da gettin' home?'

'Talk properly,' Nellie said reprovingly. 'Dad's going to be late, it was him on the phone just now. And you could get the soup out of the larder and put enough for two into a pan and put the pan on the stove if you like.'

'If it's just us, don't let's bother with soup,' Elizabeth said as her mother hoped she would. She drained her glass and burped, then patted her mouth with her hand. 'Pardon me! Are you mashing the spuds?'

'Are you creaming the potatoes?' Nellie corrected; it never ceased to amaze her that Elizabeth, who went to a private school and was getting a good education, still spoke, half the time, with a Liverpool accent. But then all the girls did, so she was only conforming, in the way children did. And she only talked like that when she was being a bit daft, and with either her close friends or family. On other occasions, nothing could have been purer than her small, clear voice.

'Well, are you? Mashing the . . . I mean creaming the potatoes,' Elizabeth said, laughing. She reached across and picked up the cabbage which Nell had got out ready. 'Can I cut the this up very finely, like you showed me, and do it with a little butter and an onion, in the French way?'

'If you like. Liz, did you like the girl I brought into the sitting-room this morning?'

'She looked nice,' Elizabeth acknowledged, beginning to slice the cabbage with great care. 'Is she going to take the job?'

'She is. I confirmed the arrangements with Mrs Edmonds of the Register an hour ago. I liked her so much. She'll be good for all of us.'

'Good for us? I don't see . . .'

The doorbell cut across her sentence. Nellie sighed and flapped a hand at Elizabeth, who had half risen to her feet, cabbage in one hand, knife in the other. 'You get on with that cabbage; I'll go to the door. I expect it's someone selling something.'

Dai had come up the road with some trepidation. Now that it had actually come to the point, he wondered whether he had been wise to come, or whether it was best to let sleeping dogs lie. His Mam, God bless her, was dead and gone. Her friend Mrs Gallagher had probably never been told that Bethan had died. Was it wise or sensible to open the wound, go round to the woman's house, talk about his Mam to someone who was, when all was said and done, a complete stranger?

He had spent quite a lot of the day fruitlessly searching for the girl with the blue eyes, though he had pretended to Greasy that he was buying Christmas presents. But he had had no luck. He had asked for her all over, describing her in some detail, but had met with no response. People had either not seen the blue-eyed girl or not noticed her. And when the day began to grow dusky it had occurred to him that he had best go round to this Ducie Street, if he intended to call on Nellie Gallagher, or go back to Greasy's place.

He liked the O'Reillys, they were a nice bunch, but he had promised himself that he would not impose on them over Christmas. And he only had a day and then it would *be* Christmas, so he should find Mrs Gallagher, introduce himself, and then book in at the Seamen's Mission, down on the waterfront. That way he would salve his conscience without hurting anyone's feelings, because the O'Reillys would think he was staying with his Mam's old friend, and his Mam's old friend would assume he was still with the O'Reillys.

It was quite a big house, though. Much grander than he had expected. Nice, he would grant you that, but grand.

He walked up and down the road a couple of times, looking curiously at the houses, and in particular the one which belonged to the Gallaghers. Nice front garden, brightly painted front door, clean, colourful curtains at the windows. . . . Damn it, he was going to knock; what was the point in coming all this way by tram only to turn tail and go back again without calling? Mam would be disgusted with him.

He walked up the short path and reached for the bell. He pressed his finger on the central button and rang it for several seconds. Then he stood back and waited.

He heard the quick, soft footsteps, the fingers fumbling with the door handle, then the door swung open. Golden light flooded out, temporarily blinding him, for he had been wandering the quiet, gaslit streets for the best part of an hour. He smiled in the direction of the person who had opened the door, however, and tugged off his seaman's cap. The maid who had answered the door – he caught a glimpse of a very large white apron and a small, delicate face with a dab of flour on the nose – gave a sort of strangled gasp as he did so. 'Davy? My God, it is you, isn't it? What in heaven's name are you doing here?'

'I . . . I wonder if I might see Mrs Gallagher,' Dai said, unable to make head or tail of the woman's words. She had obviously confused him with someone else – odd that it should have been his father's name that she had used, but then Davy was not an uncommon name.

'Oh, I can see now . . . I'm so sorry.' the woman's voice was soft. 'Just for a moment I thought you were someone else . . . can I help you? I am Mrs Gallagher.'

'I'm Dai Evans . . . Richart, I suppose I should say.

Mrs Gallagher, my Mam told me that if ever I was in Liverpool I should come to see you . . . my God!'

For Mrs Gallagher had given a sharp gasp, a small moan, and collapsed in a heap on her hall floor.

Dai didn't know what on earth to do. He went inside and bent over her and even as he did so her eyes flickered and opened, staring up into his face for a moment with cloudy puzzlement. Quickly, Dai put his arms around her and pulled her to a sitting position. He said, 'I'll fetch help – is there anyone else in the house?'

She gave a huge, shuddering sigh, then struggled to her feet. She gave him a watery smile.

'You're Bethan's boy,' she said slowly. 'My dear friend Bethan's boy. I had a note a while back . . .'

'My Mam died fifteen months ago,' Dai said wryly. 'I'm sorry not to have come to you before, Mrs Gallagher, but I'm at sea, distant-water trawling I've been this past year, and only now have I come to Liverpool.'

'I'm so glad you came . . . but my dear boy, you must come in . . . do you mind if we go into the kitchen? My daughter, Elizabeth, is in there . . . we're making dinner . . . you'll stay, of course.'

'But I don't think I should trouble you any more,' Dai said slowly. 'You aren't well.'

Nellie smiled and shook her head. 'I'm fine now; it was the shock, Dai. You are – you are so like your Mam, see, and I'd been thinking about her . . . your Mam wrote to me, she must have given the letter to a solicitor to be sent in the event of her death . . . I'm so sorry, Dai, Bethan was a marvellous woman. She had so much love and charity in her. She was – she was very kind to me, once.'

'She always said you were very kind to her,' Dai countered, smiling. He looked curiously at this little friend of his Mam's. She was quite a bit younger than

Bethan and she had gentler looks with the golden brown hair and the steady grey eyes. What foils they must have been to one another when they were friends as girls, he thought now, the one so fair and delicate, the other so dark haired, pink cheeked, sturdy! 'Look, let me come back another day, when you've got over the shock of meeting someone out of your past, so to speak. Better it would be, perhaps.'

But she was shaking her head at him reprovingly, taking him by the hand, drawing him into a pleasant kitchen, all firelight and the good smell of cooking, whilst a young girl, chopping cabbage at the big scrubbed wooden table, turned and smiled at him.

'Sit down, Dai, sit down,' Nellie said, beginning to bustle about. 'A cup of tea now, and some of my rich fruit-cake. Pass the tin over Elizabeth, there's a good girl. Oh, Dai, I'm forgetting my manners! Elizabeth, dear, this is Richart, usually called Dai, the son of – of my good friend Bethan Evans. Richart, this is my daughter, Elizabeth.'

The two young people eyed one another cautiously, then shook hands.

'Hello, Elizabeth; nice to meet you. Please call me Dai, when someone calls me Richart I always feel I'm either back at school or in disgrace.'

'Hello, Dai, it's nice to meet you, too. My Mam talks a lot about your Mam but I don't think she's mentioned you much.'

'No. Well, when they were friends, you and I, Elizabeth, had not even been thought of. Oh, tea . . . that's wonderful!' He took the cup from Nellie and turned back to the younger girl. 'I've been working on a trawler in the Arctic ocean, and I tell you, Liz, it's hot tea that keeps us going!'

Elizabeth, who had been eyeing him warily, laughed and seemed to relax. She was very like her mother but with her hair a shade deeper, an almost reddy gold, and her skin flushed with health. 'The Arctic ocean? Oh, Dai, will you tell us about it? Have you seen whales, polar bears, penguins?'

'I've seen 'em all,' Dai said, laughing back at her. 'Why, you should see the fish we catch! My mate, Greasy, had his boot torn off him by a dead conger eel once . . .'

'A *dead* conger eel? That's one of those tall stories they talk about – Dad calls them fishermen's tales, come to think of it! Now come on, the truth now!'

'No, honest! The eel had been in the fish pounds for the best part of a day . . .'

He ate with them, of course. Nellie took him up to the spare room and showed him how comfortable he could be over Christmas, though she understood that he must go back to his friends tonight and tell them that he would be moving in with the Gallaghers the following day.

'We're having a real family Christmas and there's no one in the world I'd sooner have to share it with us than – than Bethan's boy,' Nellie said, her eyes shining with affection. 'Stu knows how close Bethan and I were, it was sad that we never met after we married, but we wrote often. Friends can stay close that way – we could read between the lines, even, so that a cheerful letter that hid pain was quickly responded to in the right way.'

'Mam never showed no one the letters, but they were always by her side,' Dai acknowledged. 'Nellie . . . are you sure you don't mind my calling you that? Nellie, she said if I ever wanted mothering . . .'

Nellie patted his arm. Elizabeth had gone to bed and Stuart had not yet arrived home so the two of them were sitting, side by side, on the sofa in the living-room whilst, as Nellie put it, they got to know one another.

'You're a good lad, Dai,' she said softly. 'And it's my

belief that you – your Da has disappointed you some-how. Can you tell me about it?'

Dai found that he could tell her, found, even, that it eased him to tell her. 'They say, in the village, that Davy knew Menna even before my Mam passed on,' he said bitterly, as the story ended. 'Hate her I do, Nellie. A brassy, hard little bitch after what she can get, and my Da sniffing after what he can get . . . and my Mam . . .'

His voice broke and he stopped speaking. Nellie put her arms round his broad young shoulders and hugged him hard.

'Don't waste energy hating her, she's not worth it,' she said, surprisingly. 'You love your Da, but he's a weak man; he always was, from what Bethan told me. I do remember her saying he was – was always after the girls. Just love the side of him that loves you, and try to remember that he needs a woman to look after him. It's a shame that he couldn't pick on a decent girl, but Menna was around when he needed her. And don't let her stop you going home, Dai, bach. It's . . . it's your heritage, it's what your Mam wanted for you. . . . I remember her saying that you would inherit it all, the cows on the headland, the sheep in the meadow beyond, the fishing boat, the beautiful old house and garden. . . . And it isn't only that, Dai, it's all the rest – the beach, the hills . . . the Island of Anglesey, where you were born and raised. That's your heritage, too.'

'Aye, you're right,' Dai said. He was astonished at the depth of feeling he already had for this pale, slight woman who seemed to understand his feelings almost without speech. His Mam had been right, Nellie Gallagher was a friend worth having. 'I will go back, Nellie. But not right now; not yet. It's a small village and I can only live at my Da's house, and whilst she's there . . . I'm not strong enough to go back there.'

'Right. But don't leave it too long. And write to your Da, tell him that you're missing him and Moelfre. You'll have to come to terms with Menna one of these days or lose your Da, Dai, and you don't have to tell me you love him because I know you do, even if you aren't yet willing to admit it.' She sighed and got to her feet. 'Any relationship based on love is a good relationship, Dai. Davy was always very lovable, or – or so I understood from Bethan.'

Dai stood up as well. 'good you are for me, Nellie,' he said, smiling down at her. 'Better I do feel than I've felt for many a month. You're right, I may dislike Menna, but I do love my Da, and I'll be writing to him. And now you're sure I can come to you? I won't be in your way, won't spoil your family Christmas?'

'You'll make my Christmas,' Nellie assured him. 'And Stuart will be delighted to have another man about the place. Lilac's husband, Joey, is at sea most of the year so when he's home he spoils the twins disgracefully. Stuart will be glad to entertain someone who talks of something other than kindergartens, potty training and read-and-learn. Come back in time for lunch tomorrow, and bring your traps.'

'I will. I'm more thankful than I can say, Nellie, for your kindness,' Dai said sincerely. He had not felt so relieved about his father since his mother's death, but now Nellie had made him look at their relationship he realised that it was, as she said, based on a very deep love. He must not let that love dissipate just because his Da had taken a silly, fluffy little creature to comfort him for his dear Bethan's loss. Each to his own comfort, Dai reminded himself. Each to his own. 'And I'll post a card and a letter to my Da first thing in the morning, to reach him before Christmas,' he added as he stood on the doorstep. 'See you tomorrow, and thanks again!'

Chapter Eight

Nellie waved Dai off and then turned back indoors again. Stuart was later than he had hoped, but the large slice of apricot pudding was between two plates, waiting to be steam-heated through, and she had a jug of coffee keeping warm on the back of the stove.

She wondered how Stuart would take the news that he would be entertaining an extra guest for Christmas. She smiled to herself, pottering contentedly round her kitchen, setting out the breakfast for the morning. He would be pleased because she was pleased; he had heard her talking about her friend Bethan for years and had often suggested that the two of them should arrange to meet.

He knew nothing, of course, about Dai. Oh, he knew that Bethan had a son named Dai just as he knew Davy was Bethan's husband. What he did not know and need never know was that Davy had once been Nellie's lover – and that Dai was Nellie's own little son, the son she had born in Moelfre more than twenty-two years ago and left with Bethan, who had reared him as her own.

Unless he guessed, of course. Stuart and she were so close that keeping secrets from one another was next to impossible. She had often been aware, in the early days of their marriage, that Stuart, who knew she had born an illegitimate child, was deeply jealous of her first lover. No amount of telling him that she had never really loved the man who had fathered that child could entirely convince him.

But time had done the trick. With every year that passed, her quiet but deep devotion to him and to their daughter had soothed his jealousy, calmed his fears. She doubted that Stuart had given a thought, either to the illegitimate child he assumed she had had adopted (and in a sense, of course, he was right) or to her first lover, for a dozen years, so he was unlikely to start agonising over it now.

He was a nice young man was Dai. Frighteningly like Davy at first glance, the same clustering black curls, the dark blue eyes, the quirky, teasing smile. But when you looked closer you saw a steadiness, a seriousness even, which Davy had lacked. Dai was responsible, sensible, reliable, and he was only twenty-two years old, whereas Davy, who had been considerably older than that when he had fathered Dai, had always been a lightweight . . . and far too fond of women.

Nellie had never regretted losing Davy because by the time she had born Dai and left him with Bethan she had fallen totally out of love with the handsome young Welshman. Perhaps knowing what their love-affair could have done to Bethan had something to do with it, perhaps even his deceiving them both – for he had not told her he was married just as Bethan had never known he had a mistress – had taken that first fine gloss off their affair. But whatever the reason, by the time Dai was a year old she had recovered from her temporary madness and was growing up, mentally as well as physically.

Stuart had been her only true love. He was her strength, her rock. He was patient with her, explaining current affairs -- the horrors of the Spanish civil war, the frightening way the Germans were behaving, as though they had forgotten the 'fourteen-'eighteen war – even the pecularities of the British legal system and the difficulties faced by their new young King and Queen, became simple when Stuart explained them. Yet he managed never to make her feel foolish or ill-educated, sharing his knowledge easily, matter-of-factly.

And Elizabeth was her darling daughter and a companion second only to Stuart so far as Nellie was concerned. I'm a family person, she told herself now, a simple woman content with simple things. And though Davy and I made a baby together, it was just . . . just youth and silliness. There wasn't so much as a scrap of real love between us two, just friendship and a natural physical need for closeness, and a bit of flattery because I'd not had a boyfriend before him.

But it was so good to see Dai again! Last time he had been a bonny, dark-haired baby, crowing with delight when she had held him up to see the lambs playing in the field, gripping her hair with incredible baby-strength, smiling at her with that wide, totally trusting toothlessness which only the very young can show.

He's a man now, and a handsome one, yet he's still that baby, too, she told herself as she laid the table for breakfast and began to close the fire down for the night. It was almost midnight, and even if Stuart came in the next few minutes it was unlikely he would want to eat this late. I'm glad Dai's got in touch with me, and grateful for dear Bethan's generosity in putting us in touch. Sweet, selfless Bethan, giving Nellie back the son she had lost all claim to so long ago.

But there was little point in hanging around the kitchen; best make her way to bed now. Stuart would come in quietly, so as not to wake her. She made herself a cup of cocoa and had left the kitchen and was closing the door behind her when a key rattled in the front door lock. Nellie's heart bounded joyfully; Stuart! She ran across the hallway and pulled the door impatiently inwards so that Stuart, still trying to disengage his key from the lock, followed it and almost trod on her.

'Darling Stu, how late you are! I don't suppose you feel like apricot pudding, but I'll make you some cocoa, or hot milk with a tot of rum in it if you'd rather.'

Stuart's dark eyes were heavy with tiredness but his thin face creased into a grin at her words and he bent and kissed her, first teasingly on the nose, then seriously, on the mouth. Nellie put her arms round him and hugged, then exclaimed. 'You're soaking wet! Is it raining?'

'Raining? It's snowing, my love. We're in for a white Christmas! Ah, but it's good to be home. I've been trying to get a piece done for the paper tomorrow . . . did you listen to the six o'clock news?'

'On and off,' Nellie said. 'Come through into the kitchen, it's nice and warm in there still. Why do you ask if I listened to the news?'

'I wondered whether you'd heard; reports have been coming through saying that the Japs have attacked a British ship in the Yangtse River – HMS *Ladybird*. They killed a rating and injured several others. Apparently it was mistaken for a Chinese vessel, or that's what the Japs say, anyway.'

'They're as bad as the Huns,' Nellie said grimly. 'Horrible, cruel little men. I don't remember the *Ladybird*, but wasn't there something about an American ship?'

'Yes, that's right. The *Pansy*. She was sunk with the loss of several lives.'

'Oh Stu, where will it all end? I do hate it so. Why must nations fight?'

'It seems to be human nature,' Stuart said gloomily. 'It just seems worse at Christmas. But there's no point in discussing the news, it's bad enough to be working late all evening on such a dismal story, I just wondered if the BBC had reported it. Can I have hot milk, please?'

'Darling, of course. Here, give me that wet coat, I'll

hang it on the clothes rack whilst the milk heats, it'll be dry in time for you to wear it for work tomorrow.'

'Thanks, sweetheart,' Stuart said, watching affectionately as his wife measured milk into a pan. 'What would I do without you?'

'Go thirsty,' Nellie said, smiling at him. She put the pan on the heat, then walked across the kitchen and pulled the curtains a little apart. 'Oh Stu, look at that snow!'

Stuart followed her gaze; looking past her he could see the whirling flakes as they multiplied against the dark night sky. 'I said we'd have a white Christmas,' he said smugly. The milk began to hiss up the sides of the pan and he grabbed it off the heat just as Nellie abandoned the window and came across to him. 'What do you think of that, eh?'

'A white Christmas is a wonderful thing for us . . . but not so good for others,' Nellie said thoughtfully. She began to pour his milk into a blue-and-white mug.

'Oh, the Societies will be doing the rounds,' Stuart said quickly. He went over to the pantry and got down the big red cake tin with the picture of Queen Victoria on the lid. 'Any cake left?'

'Oh Stu, if you eat rich fruit-cake this late you'll get the most terrible indigestion and be up half the night! That's why I didn't offer you apricot pudding.'

'Cake won't hurt me; I'm starving, I had sandwiches for my dinner and a cup of weak coffee.' Stuart cut himself a large wedge and then sat on the edge of the table, watching as Nellie finished pouring the milk and then bustled over to the Welsh dresser and produced a bottle of rum from its depths. 'That isn't cooking rum, is it? I want the real McCoy!'

'It's the same sort you buy for the dining-room,' Nellie said. 'How big is a tot?'

'About tot-sized. Here, let me do it.'

Stuart poured the rum into the cup and Nellie made herself another cocoa with the small amount of milk remaining in the pan.

'That stuff smells horrid,' Nellie remarked as her husband, with the wedge of cake in one hand and the rum and hot milk in the other, walked with her across the kitchen. 'I wonder what it's like in cocoa?'

'You'd hate it, you always fuss when I breathe it on you in bed,' Stuart said. He sipped at the milk as Nell opened the kitchen door and ushered him through. 'Never mind, eh? Only one more day of producing a newspaper and then it's Christmas!'

Biddy arrived at the house in Ducie Street at nine o'clock on the dot next morning and Mrs Gallagher answered the door herself, just as she had the previous day. 'Good morning, Biddy; you are prompt,' she said. 'Is that all your luggage?'

'Yes,' Biddy said baldly. It was no use trying to explain how she came to possess almost nothing. 'Shall I leave it in the kitchen until later?'

Words could not have expressed her joy when Mrs Gallagher told her to take it up to her room, settle in, and then come down to the kitchen, where she, Mrs Gallagher, would be waiting.

'You'll find your uniforms hanging in the cupboard; I think they'll fit you, you're slimmer than Peggy but about the same height,' she said. 'Put one of them on and come down and I'll see if you need tucks or lettings-out.'

'Yes ma'am. And then what will I do?' Biddy asked.

'We'll start off by preparing luncheon together,' Mrs Gallagher said with her lovely smile. 'And then we'll go over the house, both of us, just dusting and so on. Mrs Wrexham and Mr Hedges come three times a week, so the place is pretty clean and tidy. Except for Elizabeth's bedroom, of course. And then later, we'll prepare the spare rooms. . . . Oh, I quite forgot, we have another guest, a young man, who will be arriving at about noon. We'd best do the small room out for him first, perhaps. Now off you go, Biddy.'

Biddy ran up the curving staircase and then up the narrower attic stairs, her heart almost bursting with pleasure and excitement. She had two whole rooms of her own now, and a place in this pleasant household, and she did not intend to spoil this wonderful opportunity. She would work extremely hard, get really good at the job, and stay here until she was too old to work any more.

She went into her bedroom, closed the door, and looked around her contentedly. In fact she kept looking round, to make sure she was not dreaming. Any roof over her head would have been welcome, but such a home as this was beyond her wildest dreams! And Mrs Gallagher was so understanding, so warm and friendly. And this room . . . she had never owned such a room in her life, nor expected to do so. She unpacked her carpet bag slowly, putting her pillow on top of the far nicer one on the bed, only her pillow was her friend, she could not imagine going to sleep without it. Then she laid her blanket on the chair, where it looked rather grand, and put Dolly on guard by the pillow.

Spare shoes in the cupboard, spare underwear in the chest of drawers . . . it looks pretty lonely now but once I get paid I'll begin to pick up some more clothes, Biddy told herself, turning regretfully towards the door. Oh . . . uniform!

She opened the cupboard and there were two grey gingham dresses, a black woollen dress, two big white aprons and one little, frilly one. She guessed that the pieces of shiny white linen were to wear on her head, but doubted that she could put it on correctly herself. Never mind, she would do her best and let Mrs Gallagher show her how to manage if she got it wrong.

The dress fitted more or less, and fitted better when she put the big white apron over it. I look really nice, she thought, standing on tiptoe to look at herself in the mirror on the chest of drawers. But all she could see was her head and shoulders, so she lifted the mirror off the top and gradually lowered it to get an over-all view, even if it was in small bits and pieces.

She looked all right. Smart, really. These clothes are the ones I'll be wearing most of the time, so my other things won't get worn out nearly as quickly as they used to do, she told herself. I'll be all right here, I just know it. Safe. And happy, too. It's the sort of house that welcomes you – I felt it soon as I came in the door.

She put the glass back on top of the chest of drawers again and tucked a stray curl behind her ear. Then she set off down the stairs.

The morning flew. Biddy found the work easy when it was done with Mrs Gallagher watchful at her side. At ten o'clock she met the charlady, Mrs Wrexham, who proved to be a wispy little woman of fifty or so with greying hair, a squint and a slight but definite moustache. Despite appearances, Mrs Wrexham had an enormous, booming voice and a laugh which echoed round the house, but she was quite timid and Biddy could well imagine her hiding in a corner if someone roared. She was much stronger than she looked, though, and seemed quite prepared to scrub acres of linoleum, brush acres of carpet, clean and lay a dozen fires and then tackle what she called 'small jobs', which meant cleaning windows and blacking grates and the stove.

At elevenses time Mr Hedges came in, removing his

boots on the doorstep and shuffling indoors in his socks. He was fiftyish, too, and not a talkative man, though he did have a few quiet words with Mrs Wrexham, and acknowledged Mrs Gallagher's introduction of Biddy with a smile and a mutter of, 'Ow d'you do, missus?'

'Now let's see how you can cook a meal for one young gentleman, one young lady – that's Elizabeth – yourself and me,' Mrs Gallagher said when Mr Hedges and Mrs Wrexham had both departed. 'Mr Gallagher doesn't come home for luncheon, you'll meet him this evening, at dinnertime. Or at least I hope you will – he sometimes works very late.'

The two women set about the task of making a light luncheon for four people.

'We'll do a thick vegetable soup, I think, since the baker will call in half an hour or so; I must remember to order some of those delicious milk rolls which go so well with soup,' Mrs Gallagher said. 'Can you prepare these vegetables, Biddy, whilst I make a rhubarb tart?'

Biddy was at the sink, peeling and chopping vegetables, when the front doorbell rang. She knew it was the front one because there was an object on the wall above the kitchen door which actually contained the bells, all clearly labelled, and the bell labelled 'front' was jangling.

'I'll go,' she said, her hands going up behind her to untie her apron, but Mrs Gallagher was before her.

'It's all right, Biddy, I'll go. It will be the young gentleman who's coming to stay with us for Christmas, Mr Evans. You go on with the vegetables.'

Biddy was rather disappointed not to have had the chance to answer the front door – she had her opening remark all ready, having been coached in it by Mrs Gallagher earlier. 'Good morning madam, (or sir, of course, if it was a feller) I'm afraid Mrs Gallagher is not here at present but if you will leave your name . . .'

Still, there would be other opportunities. The black dress, Mrs Gallagher had told her, was for evenings, when they had company and Biddy would be needed to serve the meal.

'But that is for business guests,' Mrs Gallagher had added hastily. 'At Christmas it's very much jollier. We'll all help, just wait and see.'

Now, Biddy could hear voices in the hallway, then footsteps. They mounted the stairs.

Mrs Gallagher is taking Mr Evans up to the blue room, Biddy thought, proud that she had got the hang of it all so quickly. The blue room was real smart, with a blue rug on the floor and blue cretonne curtains, and the dressing-table had marvellous mirrors which you could arrange, Mrs Gallagher told her, so that you could see the back of your own head. But the yellow room was even better with its Chinese wallpaper and the picture, over the mantel, of a willowy young lady with droopy hair and a very exciting red and black dress, apparently dancing all by herself in a wood.

Tomorrow, Mr and Mrs Prescott will have the yellow room and their twin sons will sleep in the little room off it, the one Mrs Gallagher said was a dressing room, Biddy reminded herself, working happily away at the sink. We'll be a houseful then all right!

Presently, the footsteps came downstairs again. Biddy had finished the vegetables and was hesitating by the big pan. When she and her mother had made soup they had chopped the vegetables just as Mrs Gallagher had told her, and then they had melted a little dripping in a big pan and added the vegetables, cooking them until they were bright and glowing, but still quite hard. Only then had they added the stock.

Mrs Gallagher came into the room, or rather she poked her head round the door. 'Biddy, I'm just taking Mr Evans to find Elizabeth – do you know how to make vegetable soup?'

'Yes, ma'am,' Biddy said after a slight hesitation. 'That is, if you make it like my Mam did; she sweated the veg in a spoonful of melted dripping first, then added her stock.'

'Yes, that's it. Not too much stock, since this is thick vegetable soup. Oh, and can you find me a bottle of rhubarb please, and strain it through a wire sieve?'

'Yes, ma'am,' Biddy said. 'I'll do that.'

She did not have the faintest idea where the bottled fruit was kept but she was an observant girl and thought she would soon run it to earth. First, furthermore, she must make the soup.

The soup was simmering when someone knocked on the back door. Biddy flew across and opened it and it was a boy of about her own age pushing a box-cart laden with bread of varying sorts, though mostly they were large, two-pound loaves, partly covered by a checked cloth. The boy whipped the cloth off in a very professional manner and the most glorious scent of bread rose to Biddy's nostrils.

'Mornin', chuck; she wan' any bread?' the boy said, jerking his head vaguely in the direction of the rest of the house. 'You're new.'

It was a statement but Biddy answered it as though it had been a question. 'Yes, that's right. I started this morning. Mrs Gallagher wants some milk rolls but she didn't mention how much bread.'

'She'll 'ave a large brown, a small white an' 'alf a dozen milk,' the boy said confidently, but Biddy knew delivery boys; they were all trying to make a living and this one wouldn't think twice about persuading her to give a large order just to have the money in his pocket.

'I'd best ask,' she said uncertainly. 'It's my first day, I don't want to get into trouble.'

The boy widened his eyes, which were very round and dark. 'I wouldn't tell you wrong . . . wha's your name, chuck?'

'Biddy O'Shaughnessy. What's yours?'

'Albert Brett.'

'Hello, Mr Brett. Have you worked for the baker long?'

'I work for Lunt's, I've been doin' their deliveries two years. Look, me name's Bert to you, Biddy, an' you'd best go an' ask Mrs Wozzit wharrit is she's after, seein' as Christmas is comin' an' I won't be callin' for a couple o' days. 'Sides, she'll want a word wi' me today, I reckon.'

'Right, I'll see if I can find her . . .' Biddy was beginning when the kitchen door opened and Mrs Gallagher came into the room.

'Ah, Albert's here already, I see,' she said cheerfully. 'I'll take a large brown and a small white, Bertie, and I'd better have eight milk rolls, I think.'

'I told 'er that was what you usually 'ad, missus,' Bertie said in an injured tone. 'But there, you can't trust folk these days an' that's a fact.' He handed the bread over and Mrs Gallagher paid him, then pressed a small envelope into his hand. 'Christmas box, Bertie,' she said, smiling. 'I hope you have a happy day.'

'Cor, thanks, missus,' Bertie said, giving Biddy a told-you-so look. 'See you when it's all over.'

He disappeared down the path, whistling jauntily.

'Now, how are we getting along?' Mrs Gallagher said, taking her purchases and putting them in a large enamelled box with the word 'Bread' painted on the lid. 'You've got the soup started, I see – well done. Now I'll show you where the bottled fruit is kept and you can see if your wrists are strong enough to break the seal on the Kilner jar. . . . I usually have to get Mr Gallagher to open bottles for me, but Mr Evans may feel equal to the task if you and I find ourselves unable to do it.' She walked over to the large, airy pantry and pointed. 'There, on the top shelf . . . I think rhubarb is quite near the front but you must use the steps to get it down.'

'Mrs Gallagher, may I watch you make the pastry so that I can do it next time?' Biddy said shyly presently, when the rhubarb had been fetched down off its shelf, opened, strained and stood ready.

'Certainly you may. And then you may thicken and sweeten the rhubarb juice for me – we sweeten it with sugar, of course, and thicken it with arrowroot, which gives it a lovely shine. I usually squeeze an orange into the juice to add that special touch of flavour, and sometimes I grate the peel very finely and toast it under the grill and then scatter it on the tart. But Elizabeth doesn't like it much, it's Mr Gallagher who does, so we won't bother with that today.'

The two women worked on, chatting as they did so. Mrs Gallagher was so easy and approachable that Biddy soon found herself talking freely, telling her employer all about her parents, her sojourn with Ma Kettle and her time as a delivery girl, though she said nothing about her flight from the Tebbits or the reason she was dismissed from Millicent's. Already she loved her job and was desperate to keep it; she would do nothing which might make Mrs Gallagher think she had been mistaken in taking Biddy in.

When the meal was ready Biddy's was set out on the kitchen table and Mrs Gallagher and Elizabeth carried the rest through into the living-room on trays.

'It's not a real meal, it's just a snack,' Mrs Gallagher explained. 'But tonight we'll eat in the dining-room, because Mr and Mrs Prescott will have arrived – we'll be quite a party, so if you don't think you can cope just tell me, and Liz and myself will help you out.'

A snack! Biddy thought, spooning thick vegetable

soup into her mouth and following it with a bit of milk roll – so light and fluffy, so delicious. You couldn't call this a snack, a snack's a handful of potato crisps or an apple or a raw carrot. This is a wonderful meal, that's what it is.

There was a great deal of bustle and chatter when the Prescotts arrived. Biddy, helping them to take their traps upstairs, was very surprised to find that they were not rich or anything like that but quite ordinary people. Mrs Prescott – Mrs Gallagher called her 'My dearest Lilac', which Biddy thought a very unusual name – had glorious, red-gold hair and a pretty, lively face, but she wore an ordinary dark blue coat with a matching skirt which just brushed the tops of her smart little suede boots and she talked about the trials of housekeeping so that Biddy knew at once the Prescotts did not keep a maid. And Mr Prescott talked with a London accent and was a great joker, picked Mrs Gallagher up and kissed her on the nose, made a great fuss of his wife and the little boys, who were very alike but not, Biddy was relieved to see, identical, winked at Biddy when his wife began scolding the children for dragging at her coat and trying to examine the contents of her handbag and generally behaved, Biddy thought wistfully, just like her own father had, when he came home from sea.

'You must come into the living-room and meet my friend Bethan's son, from Anglesey,' Mrs Gallagher said at one point. 'Bethan died some time ago, and Dai came calling since he was in Liverpool, so we've invited him for the holiday – he's at sea, too, so he and Joey will have a lot in common.'

'You and your lame dogs,' Mrs Prescott said to Mrs Gallagher; but she said it so softly that Biddy thought no one else had overheard. 'I hope he's the only one.'

Biddy did not understand this, but anyway, Mr Prescott was speaking.

'The boys need some air,' he said. 'Wouldn't it be nice if Biddy here were to take the twins out for a walk? They will be good, won't you, boys? And it's no distance to Prince's Park.' He winked at Biddy again. 'She could buy them ice creams.'

Johnny and Fred Prescott leaped and bounced at the idea, clutching Biddy's hands and promising to be good.

'They slept in the train, the little demons,' Mrs Prescott said, 'So now they're bounding with energy. But are you sure, Biddy ? Only they do need to run off some of their energy.'

'I'd like it,' Biddy said shyly. 'I'd like to run in the park too – we could have a race, boys.'

'She'll be their idol from now on,' Mrs Prescott said, laughing, as Johnny and Fred squeaked that they would certainly race with her and beat her hollow, that boys were best, that ice creams were their favourite thing . . . 'I wish I had your energy, Biddy! But I'm afraid after a train journey with those demons, all I want is a nice cup of tea and a sit-down.'

'The kettle's on the hob, ma'am,' Biddy said, enjoying her new role. 'Shall I mash the tea before I go?'

But Mrs Gallagher, laughing, said that she and Lilac were not quite helpless and bade her get her coat down from her room and go off for her walk.

'The snow's not deep, but you should wear boots,' she instructed, then looked guilty. 'You haven't got boots, of course . . . I shall lend you an old pair of mine, our feet are about the same size. In fact, you may keep them, Biddy, if you find them comfortable. Go and fetch your coat and I'll get my wellingtons out.'

'Where did you find that pretty little creature?' Lilac asked Nellie, when introductions had been effected and Joey Prescott and Dai were talking about the sea and ships in front of the living-room fire, whilst the two adopted sisters sat on the comfortable velvet-covered *chaise-longue*, catching up on each other's news. 'You said you'd never have another maid, after Peggy.'

'She came through an Employment Register,' Nellie confessed. 'She was the very first girl they sent me and I liked her at once. I didn't even take up her references or anything like that. I do believe I've found a gem this time.'

'Or a very pretty lame dog,' Lilac said, dimpling at the older woman. 'No, don't get cross, Nell darling, I'm only teasing. When did she start work for you?'

'This morning. She made an excellent thick vegetable soup for our luncheon . . . Dai enjoyed it and so did Elizabeth . . . and she did several other jobs around the kitchen. She's neat, quick to learn, good with her hands. And a hard worker, to boot. I do hate it, our Lilac, when you pretend I do things for the wrong reasons. I needed help in the house, she applied for the job. . . . There's no question of her being a lame dog, truly.'

'No, of course not.' Lilac lowered her voice. 'But Dai . . . Nell, darling, who does he remind me of? He's most awfully like someone I used to know . . .'

'You never met Bethan, but he's rather like her.' Nellie looked into the fire, her cheeks flushing. 'Actually, he's a bit like Stuart was at that age . . . can you still remember?'

'Yes, that's it, of course. He's dark, he's got twinkly eyes and a curly mouth . . . yes, it'll be Stuart.' She pulled a face at her sister. 'Not a by-blow, I trust?'

'Lilac, you haven't changed at all, you're just as dreadful as ever! And do stop talking about someone who's in the same room . . . . Tell me about your horrid little boys, queen, and stop tryin' to shock me. I got them both clockwork train sets for Christmas, I do hope they like them.'

'Dai and my dear Joe are far too busy swopping tall stories to worry about us, Nell. And the twins will be absolutely delighted with everything they receive because . . . well, we have quite a struggle now that I'm not working. But clockwork train sets will give Joey and me as much pleasure as they will the twins, I'm sure.'

'Good. And I thought the twins could have a high tea with Biddy, in the kitchen, and then we can put them to bed whilst she gets on with the dinner. Elizabeth's gone to a party the other side of the park; she wanted to refuse when she heard you were arriving today but I insisted that she went. She'll eat with us, of course, but she'll enjoy helping with the twins. She doesn't say much, but she would have loved a brother or sister.'

'It just wasn't to be,' Lilac said, squeezing Nellie's hand. 'Let's have another cup of tea, shall we? I'm spittin' feathers.'

Nellie laughed. 'Whatever do they think of you down London way, you scouser, you?' she said. 'Spittin' feathers, indeed! I brung you up better'n that, our Lilac!'

Laughing together, the two women returned to the kitchen.

It had been a hectic first day for anyone to take on board and by the time she was to serve the dinner, Biddy was so tired she could have sat down on the floor and gone straight off to sleep.

The twins were dears, but little terrors, too. They had walked across the park and half-way Elizabeth, coming home from her party, had come bouncing up to them.

'Twins dear, it's your own Lizzie!' she said. 'Are you being good for Biddy, then?'

To Biddy she added, sotto voce, that the boys were spoilt rotten, but she said it indulgently. You couldn't say much else when they were only three years old and so lovable. Johnny was the bolder and naughtier of the two; it had been Fred who had put his little arms round Biddy's neck and asked to be carried home and then, with his mouth an inch from her ear, he had murmured, 'I love you, Biddy. Will you marry me when I's a big boy?'

'I will, Fred, if you're still of the same mind when you're big,' Biddy assured him. 'Now where's that ice cream gone?'

She was grateful for Elizabeth's company when they got home, though, and she realised where most of the ice cream had gone. Down the twins' little checked tweed coats, over their small hands, even up the sleeves of their red woollen jumpers.

'How did they get ice cream in their hair?' she asked Elizabeth, as the two of them tackled the sticky little boys with soap and flannel. 'No one gets ice cream in their *hair*!'

'We does,' Johnny said, as the flannel moved away from his mouth. 'We gets it all over; our Mam says so.'

And then there was the twins' high tea . . . boiled eggs with bread-and-butter soldier boys, warm milk in bunny mugs, a banana mashed up with brown sugar sprinkled over it. Their mother swathed them in voluminous bibs but even so the floor somehow managed to receive more than its fair share of their tea.

'We ought to have a dog,' Mrs Gallagher said, surveying the linoleum with despair. 'A dog would *enjoy* cleaning up after them.'

'I wanna dog,' Johnny said immediately. 'Do you wanna dog, our Fred?'

'Not our Fred, darling, just Fred,' Mrs Prescott put in. 'Oh dear, but I say it meself, I know I do!'

The men kept well out of the kitchen, but Biddy didn't mind. It was wonderful in here in the firelight, with the twins sitting up to the table banging with their spoons and slurping at their bunny mugs, whilst the women attended to their every want and Biddy ate a plateful of honey sandwiches, drank several cups of tea, and assured her employer that this would see her through until dinner was over.

'Bathtime now,' Mrs Prescott said briskly as the boys clambered off their chairs and began to tug at their bibs as though quite willing to behead themselves if only they could remove the hated sign of a meal sloppily eaten. 'You love a bath don't you, darlings?'

The darlings roared that they loved a bath and charged out of the kitchen, across the hall and up the stairs, making as much noise as a football team and, as Biddy discovered when she went upstairs herself that night, liberally smearing sugar, banana and egg yolk over everything they touched.

'Go and help, Liz,' Mrs Gallagher told her daughter indulgently. 'Biddy and I will cope down here won't we, Biddy?'

'I'm sure we shall, ma'am,' Biddy said. In the course of the afternoon she had made, under Mrs Gallagher's instructions, a pan of leek and potato soup, a wonderful concoction made with oranges, lemons, cream and sugar which Mrs Gallagher said was a citrus syllabub, and a savoury, which was liver, onions, bread and beef dripping all mashed and mixed together and then spread on little square biscuits.

'You'll put the biscuits on the sideboard, beside the drinks,' Mrs Gallagher had told her. 'Then I'll come and tip you the wink when to serve the soup. Liz will help. When you think we've had long enough to drink the soup you can bring the beef through – the roast potatoes, sprouts and so on will be in the tureens, keeping hot in the cupboard by the oven, so they must be taken out and brought through with the beef – the trolley's over there, just watch it on the edges of carpet. I'll see to the Yorkshire pudding . . . that isn't as easy as it looks. Oh . . . gravy . . .'

But at last all the instructions were given and understood and Mrs Gallagher had gone off to change.

'We don't bother, usually, but tonight, as it's our guests' first night with us, we shall,' she said. 'Poor Biddy, what a day you've had! Look, my dear, are you sure you can cope? I really should have got someone in to help you . . . but Elizabeth is awfully good, she'll be through like a shot if you need a hand.'

'I'll be all right; soup first, when you say,' Biddy said, white-faced but determined. Thank heaven for Mrs Gallagher, she thought. If she'd been some hardnosed old woman who gave orders and walked away I'd never have got through it. As it is, I've a fair chance.

She put the little biscuits out by the drinks tray, checked that the fire was made up, the table laid properly and the soft lamps round the room lit. Mrs Gallagher said the big central light was too bright and daunting for a family party. Then she went back to the kitchen.

The soup would be served from a huge china tureen, with a matching china ladle. Mrs Gallagher would serve the soup. It looked very good, just simmering on the stove, as Biddy hovered above it with a handful of chopped parsley. Add it at the last minute, Mrs Gallagher had said. And the vegetables in their tureens – silver ones this time – were in the oven along with the beef . . . the Yorkshire pudding had been made by Mrs Gallagher and put in the top of the wall oven, where it was cooking at a high heat, her mistress had said.

'Psst, Biddy! Soup!' Having nearly given her a heart attack, Elizabeth beamed at her. 'Want a hand?'

'No, I'm fine, thanks.' Biddy scooped the hot soup dishes out of the cupboard by the oven – heavens, they really were hot – and clattered them onto the trolley, then slid the tureen onto it as well. It was really heavy, she must be careful not to drop it!

She wheeled the trolley slowly across the kitchen, across the hall and through the dining-room door. There was a carpet in here, but she should not have to cross it; a gleaming parquet path led from the door to the head of the table, where she was bound. She kept her head down and her eyes lowered, intent on her task. Just get it there, that was all she had to do, then lift the tureen and put it down in front of Mrs Gallagher, hand the soup plates round, and she could go back to the kitchen.

She lifted the tureen and managed, just, to give it a safe landing right in front of her mistress. She gave a little sigh and stepped back, taking the soup plates off the trolley, and felt someone staring at her. She glanced uneasily down at herself. She was wearing the black dress, the little white pinny, the celluloid hair-tidy, only it was a cap whichever way you looked at it. Everything looked all right from up here; and the plates, though hot, were . . .

She looked across the table, straight into a pair of dark, intense eyes which were fixed on hers. Black, curly hair, a broad brow, a quirky, amused mouth . . . it was her rescuer, her hero!

She nearly dropped the plates. God knew, she thought afterwards, how she had managed to hold onto them, but she did. And not only that, she proceeded to hand them round as she had been taught, with a murmur of apology if someone had to move to accommodate her.

The seaman who had saved her was wearing the same clothes, probably, but he had a tie under his blue shirt collar. He was looking at her . . . well, it made her blush, the way he was looking. Someone would notice, say something . . . but everyone's attention was on Mrs Gallagher, ladling soup, telling everyone that Biddy had made it, that she was bidding fair to become a good little cook . . .

'Biddy.' The seaman said it under his breath, still watching her, making her name sound like a love-word, almost a caress. 'Biddy.'

'She's settling in very nicely, aren't you, love?'

With a start, Biddy realised that Mrs Gallagher was talking to her. 'Yes, ma'am,' she whispered. 'Very nicely.'

The seaman nodded, then glanced round the table and opened his mouth. He was about to speak, to tell everyone where he had seen her before and in what circumstances! Biddy shook her head at him, her eyes pleading for his understanding, his silence. If he said – if he told how he'd found her in the street, fighting over a carpet bag with an old tramp . . . If he told Mrs Gallagher how she had run away afterwards without a word of thanks . . . she would lose her lovely job, they would think her a street urchin, perhaps even a thief!

But he had read the message. He smiled, a slow, lazy, somehow very loving smile, and casually put a finger against his lips for a second, then held out his hand to take the bowl of soup Mrs Gallagher was offering.

'Thank you, Nellie,' he said. 'Good it looks, my favourite is leek and potato.'

He had such a lovely voice! She could not place his accent but his soft cadences warmed her heart. And he was not going to give her away, he would tell no one that he knew her! Relief made Biddy feel quite light-headed. Oh he was so kind! She did so love her job, she would do almost anything to keep it.

'Thank you, Biddy.' Everyone had been served and Mrs Gallagher was handing back the half-empty tureen.

'Thank you, ma'am,' Biddy said solemnly. She put the tureen back on the trolley and almost danced out of the room. Suddenly it struck her that he was the young man who was staying in the house over Christmas – Dai something-or-other, that was his name. She had longed to see him again but had not believed it to be possible. Seamen from all over the world come into port at Liverpool a couple of times a year, then perhaps they don't dock here again for years. And now she had not only set eyes on him but they were actually going to be living, over Christmas, under the same roof!

But she must not moon about thinking of her hero; there was too much to do. She gave them five minutes by the kitchen clock, then she began to unload the hot tureens from the oven onto the trolley. The beef was in a roasting tin; she transferred that, with the help of a couple of forks, onto its dish, rushed back to the gas cooker and picked up the pan with the gravy in it, tipped the contents into the shallow gravy boat, checked the trolley over . . . tiptoed out of the room to listen outside the dining-room door.

She was still hovering when the door opened; Elizabeth stood there, with a pile of soup plates in her hands.

'Serve up, Bid,' she hissed like a stage-conspirator. 'I want a glass of lemonade, they're all drinking wine and beer and stuff.'

'Oh . . . right!' Biddy scuttled back to the kitchen, seized the trolley, then slowed down as she had been told.

'Don't ever try to rush,' Mrs Gallagher had advised. 'If you take your time you won't trip or spill or have any other disasters of a similar nature. We shan't mind waiting, we've got so much to talk about.'

So Biddy pushed slowly and arrived safely. But this time she dared not glance across at her seaman; she kept her eyes down even whilst she was transferring the contents of her trolley to the table. She knew he was watching her, though. She could feel his eyes on her, it was almost like being stroked.

'Beef . . . potatoes, roast and boiled . . . sprouts, tinned peas . . . carrot sticks . . . that's lovely, Biddy. We can manage now.'

Biddy left the room, pushing the trolley ahead of her. Elizabeth, with a very large glass of lemonade in one hand, smiled and went to go past her as she entered the kitchen.

'All serene? Jolly good. I wonder if me Da will let me have the first slice of the beef? But they're all guests, and I'm family, so I'll have to take what I'm given . . . oh do have the soup, Biddy, it really is good.'

But Biddy was too keyed up to eat. She got the pudding dishes out of the dresser and put them on the trolley, fetched the wonderful citrus syllabub in its huge glass bowl and put that on the trolley too, and was about to bring the cream out of the vegetable scullery, where it had been put to keep cool, when like a flash of lightning she remembered.

The Yorkshire pudding! It was still in the little top oven, cooking away!

She threw open the oven door and snatched at the tin. It was far too hot for such treatment and tipped, spilling hot fat onto the floor before she managed to shove it back into the oven. She raced across the room for a cloth, rushed back and slid in the fat and landed on all fours, got up again, limping, and grabbed the cloth and went back, this time getting the pudding out successfully. She looked round for a dish, found a big brown pottery one, and turned the pudding out onto it, grabbed it and raced back across the kitchen. She burst into the dining-room, still limping, and held the pudding aloft.

'Oh, Mrs Gallagher, I forgot the Yorkshire! I gorrit out all right but I tipped some fat and slid in it, that's why I were a minute or two longer than I should've been. It's done to a turn, though . . . who's going to serve it?'

Everyone laughed. She had no idea why, but they did.

Even her seaman was smiling, his eyes sparkling with amusement.

Mr Gallagher stood up. He had dark hair with a touch of white at the temples, a thin, dark face and a long line which creased his right cheek when he smiled. 'Over here, Biddy,' he said. 'Nice to know you're not *too* perfect, chuck. But I can hear a genuine scouser under that nice little voice. How are you likin' your first dinner party, eh?'

'It's hard work, but it's exciting,' Biddy said. At that moment she loved them all. They had noticed her, had been hoping she would get on all right . . . oh, she was a lucky girl to work here, she really was!

Dai woke early and lay there, lazily smiling to himself. She was here, in this very house, his little blue-eyed girl! Her name was Biddy and she was Nellie's maidservant, she was new to the job but they were very pleased with her . . . she would stay here, he need never worry about losing touch with her again!

Not that they had exchanged so much as a word all evening. She had served the entire meal, including coffee and little chocolate biscuits – he had drunk three cups of coffee and eaten six biscuits, all absently, whilst watching the door, waiting for her to reappear.

Only she had not. In fact he, Stuart and Joey had remained in the dining-room, drinking port, whilst the women went and, he suspected, helped Biddy with the washing up. At any rate when they rejoined the ladies in the sitting-room presently, Stuart looked across at his wife, one eyebrow raised and she said at once, as though he had asked her a silent but perfectly understood question, 'I've sent her to bed, poor scrap. Didn't she do well? She's a lovely girl, Stu, she'll suit us admirably.'

'Clever girl to find her,' Stuart said, with such a wealth

of love and understanding in his voice that, unaccountably, Dai felt tears sting behind his eyes.

Oh, he could remember times when his Mam and Da had been like that; had spoken across a room without either of them opening their mouths! How could Davy have done it to her, slept with Menna whilst she was dying, in pain? How could he have brought Menna blatantly to live in the house, called her his housekeeper, when she was just a brassy little barmaid who was only at home behind a counter with the beer-pull in her hand?

But . . . was it really as bad as that? Rumour, in a small village, can be vicious. He did not know whether his father had gone courting Menna whilst Bethan was still alive, though he had suspected it. But surely all those long absences . . .

Give your Da a chance, Dai, love, his mother's gentle, amused voice said inside his head. *Give him a chance to explain for himself, to tell you where he went and why, when I lay dying. He won't lie to you about that, I promise you.*

But around him conversations buzzed; the young girl, Elizabeth, came and perched on the arm of his chair. He smiled lazily up at her. A pretty child, probably not much younger than Biddy, but life had dealt with them very differently, had conspired to keep Elizabeth young whilst Biddy had matured because she had no choice.

'Dai, tell me about your home. Tell me about when you were a little boy. Do you live in a city, like Liverpool? I've never been to the Isle of Anglesey you know.'

Joey was talking to Stuart and Nellie was listening. But Lilac, the girl whom Nellie called her adopted sister, was staring at the two of them. She looked both slightly puzzled and extremely thoughtful. Dai found that he was uneasy over her scrutiny and did not much want to talk about his childhood with those very large, violet-blue eyes fixed on his.

'Well you know that Anglesey's an island, luv, quite a small island off the coast of Wales. There's no city on the island. But isn't it time you went to bed? You've had a long day – we all have – and you'll want to be up early tomorrow, to see what Santa's brought.'

Nellie must have been listening despite looking as though she was concentrating entirely upon her husband and Joey. Without turning round she said, 'Yes, Dai's right, Liz darling. Go up now . . . and you might pop in on the twins, just make sure they're sleeping soundly.'

'If they weren't we'd all know,' Lilac said ruefully. 'They'd be shouting and yelling, or charging downstairs naked as the day they were born . . .'

'But they've got dear little sleeping suits on,' Elizabeth protested. 'I saw you put them on, Auntie Li!'

'And the first thing they do when they wake up is to take those dear little sleeping suits off,' Lilac assured her. 'Why we've produced two would-be nudists I've no idea, but we have.' She smiled wickedly at her husband. 'I suppose it's you, Joey. I suppose when you were a little boy you kept taking your clothes off and now your sons do it.'

'Me! When you were a child, my girl, you were the naughtiest, most self-willed . . .'

'Well, maybe, but I didn't take my clothes . . .'

'We've only your word for that, young Lilac!' Stuart said. 'When I think of the things Nellie told me about you . . . running away, leapin' about in Mersey-mud wi' your pals, nickin' fades from the market . . .'

'There!' Joey declared triumphantly. 'If there's bad blood in these lads we all know where it came from!'

Lilac jumped on Joey and a royal battle ensued, with Elizabeth taking now one side, now the other and Nellie and Stuart laughing and applauding. But again, Dai had got the feeling that, if Nell had not interrupted the conversation, someone might have said something . . .

You're being daft, he told himself now, lying on his back and looking across lazily at the window curtains. I wonder if it's snowing out there? I wonder if I'll get a chance of a word with Biddy at breakfast? I could offer to wash up . . . Nellie's awful kind, if I were to explain . . .

But Biddy didn't want him to explain, he'd known at once, and you could understand why. This was a happy household and Biddy did not want to put anyone off, to make her position here difficult. Well, nor do I want such a thing, Dai reminded himself hastily, because I like to know where she is. And this way I can get to know her properly, really get to know her. There are bound to be opportunities – there's her day off, for a start. She must have a day off, everyone does, and from what Nellie said at dinner last night she doesn't have parents to go home to. Only friends.

Yes, that's right, I'll see her on her day off. And I'll give a hand in the kitchen; it's the sort of house where people wander in and out of the kitchen. I'll offer to make a cup of tea, I'll peel the potatoes, I'll . . .

Bless me, it's Christmas Day! A present – that's it, I'll give her a present! He had explained to Nellie that he only had little things for everyone, and he knew that the Prescotts, for instance, had not known he was going to be here and so had not dreamed of buying anything. But he had a tiny bone carving of a dog for Elizabeth, a large cigar for Stuart, a small box of very good chocolates for Nellie . . . he racked his brain, trying to think what he might give Biddy, then remembered the chunk of amber.

It was a curiosity more than a present, really, except that it could probably be made into a piece of jewellery, he supposed. He had found it on a beach in Norfolk when the *Jenny Bowdler* had docked at a little place called Wells-next-the-Sea. He and Greasy had walked along the beach at low tide and he'd found it, just lying on the tide-line, gleaming with a red-gold gleam through the detritus the surf had left behind.

Thinking about it made him sit up and glance towards his ditty bag. It was within reach if he made a long arm . . .

He towed the ditty bag in and opened it, delving down the side of it until his fingers touched the hard, smooth sides of the amber. It was large, the size of a bantam's egg and would, he supposed vaguely, cut down into several pieces which could be worn. He brought it out and held it up to the light; you had to do that, otherwise it didn't look all that remarkable. He might never have bothered with it at all had he not been curious about its shape and, having dipped it in the sea, held it up against the pale wintry sun and realised it was translucent. A local gentleman exercising his spaniel on the beach and seeing Dai examining his find, had told him he was a lucky man.

'It's a very fine piece of Succinite, which is what mineralogists call the substance known as amber,' he had said impressively, having subjected the egg-like object to a long scrutiny through a pair of pince-nez spectacles which he produced from an inner pocket and perched on the end of his longish nose. 'Amber is the fossilised resin from the extinct pine forests which flourished millions of years ago along the Baltic coast. For many years the currents have deposited it on our northern shores, but few have been fortunate enough to find such a magnificent example. The Ancient Greeks and Romans used it as a cure for a great many disorders, rheumatism amongst others, and Roman women wore amulets made of amber as a protection against witchcraft.'

'Well I never,' Dai said, astonished at such an outpouring of information. 'But what use is it today? I don't suppose there's much belief in it as a charm, not these days!'

'Nowadays we prize it for its translucence and beautiful colour and make earrings, pendants and the like from it. This is a very fine example; you must have it polished and give it to the woman in your life.'

Dai had smiled and put the amber in his pocket, thanking the man politely, but the remark about the woman in his life had stung. He had no woman in his life any more, not since Bethan's death.

Now, though, Dai knew just what to do with his amber egg. He would give it to Biddy for a Christmas box, and tell her that, next Christmas, he would have it broken up and made into something pretty for her to wear. That would show her better than anything else could that he was serious. That this was not just a casual, here-today-gone-tomorrow friendship but a loving, lasting relationship. But right now he might just as well get up. He glanced at his watch, but it was still dark so he fumbled for matches, lit one, and read the time by its light.

Six o'clock, quite early still. But he was awake and he guessed that a maidservant would be expected to rise betimes, before anyone else. He would go downstairs now and put the kettle on – she would find a cup of tea waiting for her in the kitchen as well as Dai Evans! He could dress in two seconds flat; life on a trawler meant that no one ever undressed, though seaboots, jerseys and trousers were usually shed.

He dressed, dragged a comb through his curls and set off, in his socks so as not to disturb anyone, down the stairs. The house seemed wrapped in slumber still; Dai guessed that the twins, who would normally have been awake and investigating the stockings their parents had hung on the bedposts of their shared bed, were still suffering from the effects of their journey of the day before.

I'll riddle the fire through and put the kettle on, pull back the curtains, find the tea and the pot, Dai was planning as he opened the kitchen door with infinite softness and care. What a surprise young Biddy will get, to find me down before her!

Chapter Nine

The shrilling of the alarm clock gave Biddy the most dreadful fright, though she and Ellen had owned one in the flat and set it each night. But Biddy had been worn out by the time she got to bed and then, cuddling down and waiting for sleep to overcome her at once, as it usually did, she was sadly disappointed.

All she could do was think about him, the young man who had rescued her, Dai Evans! How he looked when he was serious, how he looked when he smiled. How he had not once taken his eyes off her all the while she had been in the dining-room last night. How he had been the subject of conversation, for a few brief moments, when Mrs Gallagher and her sister had returned to the kitchen to help Biddy to wash up and clear away.

That had been quite mysterious, now she came to think about it. Mrs Prescott had kept starting sentences and not finishing them, and Mrs Gallagher had spoken, not sharply, but with a kind of definite finality, which seemed to have been sufficient to make Mrs Prescott change the subject at least.

Mrs Gallagher had explained about the relationship between her and Mrs Prescott, though – how she had been a maid of all work at Culler's Orphan Asylum when a new-born baby had been left on the doorstep. The baby had been Lilac, which was Mrs Prescott's first name, and Mrs Gallagher had told Biddy that for years the two of them had clung together, leaving the orphanage together as well . . . how they were closer than sisters, sharing everything, even secrets.

It must be lovely to have a sister, Biddy thought wistfully, staring up at the dark ceiling above her head. And then, when she had given up on sleep and was lying there indulging in a beautiful fantasy in which Dai Evans came into the kitchen and said, deeply, 'It's you! I've searched the city for you, you lovely creature!', she fell annoyingly asleep and dreamed, not of Dai Evans's dark eyes, exciting smile and strong hands, but of Ma Kettle demanding that she return to Kettle's Confectionery at once.

'You're bound to me; your dear mother wished it,' Ma Kettle said, trying to persuade her to take a bath in a huge vat of cooling toffee for some obscure, dream-like reason. 'In you 'ops love, an' soon you'll be twice the woman you was! One lickle dip in this 'ere mixture an' you won't ever want to run away from me agin . . . poor but honest, that's us Kettles, from the best of us – that's me – to the worst, what'll be you when you wed our Kenny.'

'But I'm not going to wed your Kenny, I'm going to wed Dai Evans,' Biddy protested. 'And I've got a good job now, Ma, a job where they value me. I aren't leaving there for anyone!'

'Ho, an' 'oo might this wonderful employer be?' Ma Kettle sneered, struggling, now, to pour the vat of toffee over the recalcitrant Biddy. 'Per'aps she won't want you to stay when she sees you're jest a lickle toffee-girl!'

She tipped the vat, Biddy screamed . . . and woke.

The alarm was shrilling beside her ear, fairly hopping on the small bedside table, and the hands, when she lit her candle, pointed to six o'clock.

'Drat, I set it wrong,' Biddy muttered, standing the alarm back on the table again, for she had picked it up and peered, the better to make sure of the hour. 'Mrs

Gallagher said seven this morning, because they would all be late up. Still, no point in lying here, I might easily dream about Ma Kettle again. I'd rather get up and take my time preparing for the day ahead in the kitchen.'

She lit her candle, then got slowly out of bed, because it was Christmas Day, after all, and she had no need to hurry. Then she padded across the icy linoleum to her fire, turned on the gas, lit it, and went over to the window to draw the curtains back a tiny bit.

It was snowing! Lazily, the flakes floated down, each one big as a florin.

That's not the sort of snow which lies, Biddy told herself wisely. Not usually, anyway. It's the small, fast-falling flakes which build up. Still, it'll look like a picture-book out there by breakfast I reckon. I wonder if they'll go sledging? Wish I could, I used to love it so much.

But sledging was a pastime for the rich or for kids, she knew, not for maidservants, so she pulled the curtains back across again and went over to her gas ring. A panful of water boiled quite quickly so she had a hot wash, then dressed proudly in her new uniform. It was really pretty, especially now that Mrs Gallagher had taken the dress from her and put deeper darts around the waist and bust, so that it fitted well.

'It's hard-wearing stuff, unfortunately,' Mrs Gallagher had said as she pinned the new darts in place. 'I'm not keen on grey, but it doesn't need washing as often as prettier colours. In fact if you put it down for the laundry on a Friday morning and wear the other one the following week, you should do quite well.'

'The laundry?' Biddy had echoed. 'Don't I do your washing, Mrs Gallagher?'

'Bless you, no! You'll have quite enough to do without laundering, Biddy. Mind you, small things, underwear, stockings, things like that, are washed at home, but not big things, like sheets and dresses. Now, how does that feel?'

'Fine, thank you ma'am,' Biddy said. She would have said the same had a pin been driven an inch into her side, but it happened to be the truth. 'Shall I go and change so you can alter the other one?'

'No need, it's a simple job. I'll have both dresses done before you go to bed tonight and of course you'll wear your black to serve dinner.'

So here she was, putting on her pretty, pearl-grey dress and adjusting the big white apron over it. The cap was tricky, but she perched it on her head, clipped it in place with the white kirby grips her mistress had provided, and then turned and made her bed.

'I'll leave you in the warm today, Dolly,' she told her rag doll, sliding it under the covers until only its face showed. 'There, isn't that snug? Because it's snowing, and I'm going to turn the gas fire off before I go downstairs.'

She suited action to words, then doused the candle, went over and drew back the curtains, thought about opening a window to air the room but decided against it, and set off down the stairs, her slop-bucket swinging gently from one hand.

It was a modern house, which meant that the guests would use the bathroom and the upstairs toilet – no slop buckets for them, thank goodness. But she had to riddle the stove through and get it blazing, fetch more coke in so that it could be made up as soon as it caught hold, and then start on the other fires.

Bedrooms, again, had gas fires, which meant no work because when she asked Nellie if she should bring a tray of tea upstairs Nellie said at once that it wouldn't be necessary.

'Normally I would ask you to bring us a tray, but not over the holiday,' she said. 'And there's a gas-ring and a kettle in the Prescotts' room if they want a hot drink. As for Mr Evans, young men aren't used to being waited on, particularly seamen.'

Biddy thought of Luke, impatiently banging on his bedroom floor with the heel of a shoe if he thought she was late bringing his tea, and even of Kenny, who would put his head out into the hallway and holler, 'Bid? Have you dropped dead, our Biddy? Where's me cuppa?' No wonder it had killed poor old Ma Kettle, having to do all that herself after I left, she thought now, reaching the front hallway and crossing it, to push open the baize door which separated it from the kitchen regions. Glad this set-up is so different – oh, I'm so lucky!

She was still smiling at the thought of her own luck when she pushed the kitchen door open . . . then stopped in the doorway, staring.

The fire glowed through the bars, the gaslights hissed, illuminating the room which looked homely and warm, not at all quiet and deserted, as a kitchen should look to the first person down in the morning. The curtains were drawn back too and someone, who had been standing in front of the sink looking out at the lazily falling flakes, turned round and smiled at her.

'The compliments of the season to you, Biddy! Awake I was, so I thought you'd mebbe like a bit of company on Christmas Day.' Dai came across the kitchen and took the slop-bucket from her nerveless hand. 'Let me empty that now whilst you pour us both a cup of tea. It's made and mashed, all ready for you.'

'Oh . . . no, it's all right, I can manage quite . . .' Biddy began, pink-cheeked, trying to snatch the slop bucket from him, but he warded her off, laughing. 'Look, it's me job to . . .'

He ignored her, taking the bucket over to the sink and emptying it whilst Biddy continued to stammer helplessly. He was here, perhaps not uttering quite the words of her fantasy, but it was enough, suddenly, that they were in the same room. And alone, for a while anyway. A quick glance at the kitchen clock showed it still lacked five minutes to half past six. Yes, she was in good time.

But how did one behave when a young man you thought the world of appeared in your place of employment as the guest of your employer? As Dai turned away from the sink and stood the bucket on the draining board Biddy gave a little half-bob of a curtsy, looking down at her shoes as she did so. Immediately Dai crossed the room in a couple of strides and took both her hands in his.

'Biddy, this sounds daft, but I recognised you the moment I set eyes on you the other night. You – you were special to me, I could tell, my heart could tell. We're two of a kind, Biddy, and don't you go behaving with me as you would with other people – I don't think maids curtsy to anyone now, in any event – but you and I, we – we belong together.'

Biddy pulled half-heartedly at her hands but Dai just gripped them tighter, looking down into her face with eyes which blazed with sincerity.

'Isn't it all . . . oh, Mr Evans, you're here as a guest and I'm . . .'

'I'll leave,' Dai said promptly. 'I'll leave right now, I'll walk out through that back door and then knock and walk in again. Just Dai Evans I'll be, wanting to pay court to Bridget . . . what's your last name?'

'I'm Bridget O'Shaughnessy,' Biddy murmured tremulously. The feel of his hands on hers was doing very odd things to her stomach and there seemed to be a bird held captive in her rib-cage from the way her heart was fluttering 'You are daft, aren't you?'

She had not meant to say it and gasped at herself, but he just smiled more lovingly than ever and let go of her hands for a moment to tilt her chin with one strong, tanned hand.

'Course I'm daft, people in love do always act daft. Biddy, I never believed in love at first sight until I saw you struggling with that great bully in the market, and then I knew it was true because it had happened to me. Biddy? Do you like me a little bit, too?'

Ellen would have tossed her head and said it was all very well to talk about love ... she would have given Dai sly glances through her lashes and flirted outrageously, her mouth saying 'No, no!' whilst all the rest of her said, 'Yes!' And men were good at conversations like that, they could make the sort of remark which had Ellen bubbling with laughter, saying, 'Oh, you are awful ... what a tease you are, sir, I don't believe a word you say!' whilst the man pressed closer to her, tracing shapes with a forefinger in the palm of her hand, an arm brushing against her breast, the quick, double-meaning remarks tripping off his tongue whilst his eyes made bolder remarks still, just for her to see.

But Biddy was not Ellen, had never really understood the complex games of come and go, do and don't, which her friend had played with such consummate ease. She was just Biddy, who said what she thought, what she meant.

'I was the same,' she whispered now, staring fixedly at a point about half-way down Dai's broad chest. 'As soon as I saw you I felt that you were the – the person I'd waited for, only I never even knew I was waiting! Yesterday, when I walked into the dining room ... oh, I was so happy, I could scarcely believe I wasn't dreaming!'

He nodded. 'Me, too. They'd talked about a new maid, Biddy, but you were the last person I expected to see. You came in with your head bent, and that cap-thing on your pretty curls, clutching the soup tureen as though it were your first-born . . . I knew it were you at once, though I couldn't see your face. Oh Biddy, a miracle it is that we've met up again! A bloody miracle!'

And Biddy, who disapproved of strong language, who would normally have winced at anyone describing a miracle in such terms, just nodded and looked up into his face once more. 'It is,' she said earnestly. 'It really is a bloody miracle – I prayed for it hard enough!'

And because she had raised her face at last and because he could read the worshipping expression in those big, blue eyes, Dai Evans bent his head and kissed her lips.

It should have been a light little kiss, a friendly kiss, but somehow it was not. Their lips clung, as though they had a will of their own and wished to remain close, and Biddy's body gradually relaxed until she was leaning against Dai's broad chest.

They might have remained there for ever, she thought afterwards, only they both heard a distant shout and then the patter of small feet, thumpety-thumping down the stairs.

'It's them little buggers,' Dai said, very reprehensively, Biddy thought. 'Come out wi' me after dinner . . . luncheon, I mean? I'll meet you outside the Baptist church on the corner . . . better that way, eh?'

'Much better. I'll come if I can, but . . . oh Dai, you'd better go!'

'Can't, they'll be here in two shakes. Look, gi's my cup an' I'll sit by the fire . . .'

He was innocently in position when the twins, closely followed by their father, burst into the room.

'Biddy, Biddy, look what farver Chrissmus give us!'

'Biddy, Biddy, what a go, eh? See our clockwork choo-choos!'

Peace, Biddy could see, was over for the day. The twins had been partially dressed but lacked shoes and socks and their fair curls stood on end as though they had wrenched themselves free half-way through a hair brushing.

'Come on aht of it,' their father said wrathfully, grabbing one twin by his left arm and the other by his right. 'Your mummy said dress first and she meant it. Leave Biddy alone, she's gettin' your breakfast and if you pester you won't get no grub. What about that for a threat, eh?'

But the twins were unimpressed.

'Biddy, there was choccy in our stockin's, an' a tangerine! Whistles too . . . see?' Johnny blew a long blast just to prove the truth of his words. 'Red for me, blue for Fred,' he added.

'An' we had a rag story book what you can't tear,' Fred shouted over his shoulder as he was towed out of the room. 'An' a b'loon in the top, red for me, blue for Johnny. An' . . . an' . . .'

Dai had slipped unobtrusively out of the room and was half-way up the stairs, his cup of tea in one hand. Biddy closed the kitchen door on them all and hurried back to get on with her work – to start her work, rather. But the kitchen clock only said twenty minutes to seven, so she was still early and could take her time.

Nevertheless, the breakfast today was to be a big one. Eggs, bacon, kidneys, sausages, bottled tomatoes, fried bread . . . and that was just what you might call the main course. The twins would have milky porridge and a poached egg each, the adults would have grapefruit first, then their main course and then lots of hot buttered toast and coffee.

It's a bloomin' wonder the rich can roll up the stairs to bed each night with all they eat, Biddy told herself, beginning to collect the ingredients for this mammoth meal which would last a poor person two days, if not a week. Kedgeree tomorrow, and I've no more idea how to make a kedgeree than fly to the moon. But Mrs Gallagher will show me; she says it's really easy. And this afternoon I'm going to meet Dai ... oh, how ever shall I wait!

But in fact Biddy was so busy that the morning positively flew, and that was with all the women mucking in to get everything ready and on the table in time.

'We have our main hot meal at noon on Christmas Day, then a cold supper,' Mrs Gallagher explained. 'Then on Boxing Day we have cold meals all day, except for breakfast, which is kedgeree, and the evening dinner is usually served with a hot pudding of some sort. But Christmas dinner is always a bit daunting. Never mind, many hands make light work as they say.'

And with Elizabeth and Biddy doing the vegetables, Mrs Gallagher making bread sauce and stuffing and Mrs Prescott garlanding the half-cooked turkey with pork sausages and keeping an eye on the pudding, making the brandy sauce and laying the table, everything got done in the end, though there were several moments when Biddy was sure they would not eat until teatime.

And the Christmas dinner! Her own plate was brought through from the dining-room by Mrs Gallagher, piled high with good things. Great slices of creamy-white turkey breast, chestnut stuffing steaming on the side, golden-brown roast potatoes, red currant jelly, dark purple broccoli, pale green sprouts, emerald peas ... and the gravy, golden-bubbled, over all.

'Don't worry about us, we'll take ages to get through this lot,' Mrs Gallagher said. 'Just eat it at your own pace. We'll come through when it's time to serve the pudding anyway, because we flame it in brandy, which the twins will love, and that takes practice.'

So Biddy took her time – and then could not eat half what was on her plate. She was terribly tempted to fetch a paper bag and put the dinner inside it and go out with it later, to find some poor tramp or half-starved child, but Mrs Gallagher, seeing her look guiltily at the food still piled on her plate, told her that it would not be wasted.

'It goes in the pig-bin, just outside the back door,' she explained. 'Then it's given to people who have a pig . . . Stuart doesn't believe in wasting food.' She smiled at Biddy. 'We've all been through bad times, just like you have,' she said softly. 'People don't forget.'

But Biddy, presently tucking into a very tiny slice of Christmas pudding, for she had assured Mrs Gallagher that she would burst if she was given a full helping, thought that her employer was wrong. People did forget, over and over. They fought their way up from poverty to bearable circumstances, from bearable circumstances to riches, and then their early experiences became transformed.

They began to believe they had fought their way up because they were, in some way, better and more worthy people than those who were still either struggling, or fixed at the bottom of the heap. They could no longer remember the ache of hunger, the pain of constant worry over where the next meal was to come from or the worse pain of seeing one you loved in miserable circumstances.

Now, the rich looked back and saw themselves as having been the deserving poor who had struggled out of the poverty pit by sheer hard work. Those who were still poor were condemned as idle and feckless, they drank too much, never saved money for a rainy day, frittered what they earned, when they earned anything at all, that was. Poverty had become, in their twisted minds, a punishment for failure – a deserved punishment what was more – and of course you didn't give to people like that, or pity them, or try to help. You despised them, pushed them away, preached at them ... they were less human than your fat lap-dog, less regarded than the set of your jacket, the way your skirt hung at the back.

But the Gallaghers were not like that. They were caring people who knew all about poverty and remembered their own circumstances still. Mrs Gallagher belonged to the League of Welldoers and worked tirelessly to raise money for them, and Mr Gallagher was a Goodfellow – Biddy remembered how the Goodfellows had helped her Mam when she had first lost her job, and the wonderful food parcel which had been brought round after dark that first, terrible Christmas.

Biddy finished her Christmas pudding and jumped to her feet. Time to start the washing up, if she was to be ready to go out and meet Dai by the Baptist chapel this afternoon.

'I'll just make up the fire, ma'am, and then I'll go out for a bit of a blow, I'm thinking,' Biddy said, as the last dish was put away and the kitchen was as clean and tidy as though no one had worked in it for days. 'I'll fetch some more coke in from the shed.'

'Thank you, Biddy,' Mrs Gallagher said. 'The twins have been put down for a nap, though I think they're too excited to sleep for long, and the men are snoozing with their feet up in the study, so my sister and I will have a cosy chat in the living-room and tell each other what marvellous husbands we have and how lucky we are with our children.'

'You mean you'll have a moan about me Da eating too much and then snoring the afternoon away, and Auntie Lilac will have a moan about Uncle Joe having one too many at the dockyard pub when his ship comes in and reeling down the road shaking hands with lampposts,'

Elizabeth said, coming into the kitchen and heading for the scrap bag. 'Can I take some bits of bread and stuff out to the birds, Mam? I took some out earlier and it's all gone, they've scoffed the lot, poor little chaps. And I'll give them clean water at the same time because it keeps icing over and that isn't much fun for them.'

Biddy could dimly remember that when her father had been alive they had lived in a tiny house with a tiny garden, but she could not remember her mother feeding the birds. It was, however, a way of life with Elizabeth and Mrs Gallagher, who had told her that not only did they feed the birds three or four times a day, on three very fancy bird tables erected in different parts of the garden, but they had notebooks in which they noted down the species of birds which visited them, and they drew tiny pictures of each visitor to the tables with information concerning the length of their stay in the garden, what food they preferred, and whether they were what Mrs Gallagher called 'storm-tossed', which meant that they were not normally found in Britain, or simply a summer visitor.

'You want to feed the birds?' Mrs Gallagher looked at her little wristwatch. 'Yes, no reason why not. Try them with some warm water, it won't freeze so easily, and see if there's any dripping still soft in the larder. If so, pour it over the bread because it makes it more nourishing than bread alone. Then what will you do, dear? I'm afraid Christmas afternoon is usually rather flat.'

It had not occurred to Biddy before, but now she realised that despite her beautiful home, her friends and her wonderful family, Elizabeth was probably quite a lonely girl. She was encouraged to bring friends home, to go round to their houses when invited, to socialise in any way she chose, but her parents were very content with one another's company and there must be times when, with the best will in the world, Elizabeth felt a little bit left out.

'After feeding the birds? Oh, I dunno, mooch around I suppose.' Elizabeth glanced across at Biddy. 'What are you going to do, Bid? Can I do it with you?'

'Yes, of course,' Biddy said after only the very slightest hesitation. 'I'm, going out for some fresh air, we can go together.'

She could have done nothing else, but she felt a real stab of disappointment. She had worked so hard and was so looking forward to seeing Dai alone. . . . Elizabeth was a very nice girl, but . . .

But fate, for once, was on her side. She and Elizabeth had fed the birds together, laughing over the antics of a very cheeky robin, who actually flew to the bird-table whilst the two girls were still spreading out the feast and began pecking at the food. The snow was still falling, desultorily, but it was laying too, and Elizabeth had just remarked wistfully that she hoped it would be nice and deep by the time Christmas was over so that she and her friends might go sledging, snowballing and ice-skating, when Joey Prescott wandered out to them.

'Hello, girls,' he said. 'I've ate too much, my stomach's tight as a perishin' drum. Stuart and I thought we'd walk across to the lake in Prince's Park, see if the ice is holdin'. Fancy some exercise?'

'That would be lovely, wouldn't it, Biddy?' Elizabeth said at once. 'We were only going for a walk ourselves. . . . We'll go and put our coats and boots on – is Dai coming?'

'No, the lazy beggar won't. Well, he says he's goin' to pop over to his shipmate's place so he may not be back for tea, but he'll be in for supper. What about you, Biddy? Don't let Elizabeth answer for you, luv, or you'll never open your mouth again!'

Biddy laughed but seized the opportunity gratefully. 'I'd really like to go round to my friend Ellen and wish her a merry Christmas,' she admitted. 'Umm . . . will it be all right if I don't come back for tea, though? She lives on Paul Street, a good walk from here. The trams won't be running on Christmas Day, will they?'

'No, not a chanst,' Joey said. 'I'll make it right with Nellie, though I'm sure she won't expect you back for tea; it'll only be a cuppa and a bit of cake, seein' as 'ow we guzzled fit to bust earlier.'

So Biddy hurried up to her room and put her trusty duffle-coat on over her uniform, though she did remove her white apron first. Then she donned Mrs Gallagher's wellingtons, tied Ellen's Christmas-present scarf round her head, put on the matching gloves and trundled down the stairs, feeling as hot and excited as though she were going to a party and not just walking down to the Baptist chapel on the corner.

Mrs Gallagher and her husband were in the hallway, both dressed up for going out. Mrs Gallagher was trying to make her husband wear the most enormous, stripy scarf and he was resisting fiercely. They swayed around the hall, laughing and knocking into the furniture, and never even noticed Biddy as she slipped out of the front door.

Out here it was a different world; a white world, with a keen little breeze blowing which ruffled the smooth surface of the snow and sent it up into the air in small, swirling eddies. But Biddy didn't mind what the weather did; she was off to meet Dai!

They met as arranged. Biddy came round the corner and there was Dai, hunched into a duffle-coat rather similar to hers, with his cap pulled well down over his brow and big boots on his feet. She could see almost nothing of him, yet already she would have known him anywhere, in any disguise. He did not hear her approach and was earnestly staring in the wrong direction through the whirling flakes when she touched his arm.

'Dai, I'm sorry I'm late.'

He turned and put his arms round her as naturally as though they had done it a thousand times before, instead of just the once. 'Biddy! You aren't late, it's me who's early. Where shall we go? I'd like to find a shelter of some sort so that we could sit down for a moment, but the place I've got in mind's a long walk, and I don't even know whether we'll be able to get in. Only Mrs Gallagher was talking about it at dinner, and . . .'

'Where?' Biddy asked. 'They're going to the lake in Prince's Park, so we'd better not go there.'

'No, I thought we'd walk across to Sefton Park. It's a long way but there's an aviary there, and a palm house. Mrs Gallagher said the palm house was often open . . . we could try both. There will surely be a seat in an alcove or something like that, wouldn't you think?'

'Oh, sure, to be,' Biddy murmured, falling into step beside him and feeling his arm slide round her waist with a delicious shiver. She did not care whether they found somewhere to sit down or not, so long as they were together. 'Which way will we go, though, to keep away from the lake?'

'We won't go into Prince's Park at all, we'll walk round it, along Croxteth Road and Lodge Lane. I bought a *Geographia of Liverpool* when I was searchin' for you, see, an' it's really good, gives lovely little maps of the whole city. Mind, I'm not the world's best map reader, but I've a fair bump of direction. Are you game to try and find this place?'

'Of course,' Biddy said. 'Even if I don't quite see . . . but I shall enjoy the walk.'

Her confidence was not exactly bolstered when Dai, having stared around him for a couple of minutes, announced, 'This way!' and led her boldly towards Prince's Gate West, then realised his mistake, muttered, 'Oh sugar!' beneath his breath and turned her round to face in the opposite direction.

'I do admire a man with a bump of direction,' Biddy said sweetly, smiling up at him. 'I'm sure you'll get us there, Dai, but going via the Mersey tunnel may take a while!'

'No sarcasm,' Dai growled, squeezing her waist. 'I'm on the right road now, feel it in my bones, I do. Quick march!'

They marched. The Croxteth Road was a long road, and on a snowy afternoon in December, a lonely road. But the two of them were soon so wrapped up in one another that they never noticed how far they had walked and in fact completely bypassed Lodge Lane, staying on the Croxteth Road until they reached the circus which heralded the Croxteth Gate. Here they walked between two wonderful mansions, only dimly seen through their surrounding trees despite the fact that the trees were leafless, and into the park at last.

'Not far now,' Dai said bracingly. 'Soon we can sit down and I can show you . . . well, what I want to show you.'

'How far's not far?' Biddy asked suspiciously. It was wonderful walking through the snow with Dai, but her feet were aching and she guessed that supper, albeit cold, would still tax her abilities to the utmost. Besides, they had not thought to bring an umbrella and since the snow had not held off for a moment the shoulders of her coat and the top of her scarf were already very wet indeed. 'About another five or six miles, would you say?'

Dai snorted and turned her to face him. He bent down,

for he was quite a lot taller than her, and rubbed her nose with his, Eskimo fashion. 'Poor little love, shall we give up and see if we can find a telephone booth? Then we could ring for a taxi and go home in comfort.'

'No, indeed,' Biddy said. She could no longer even feel her feet in the wellington boots, which was probably an advantage, since they must be freezing cold, she thought rather illogically. 'Come on . . . shall we run?'

They ran, slowing to a walk quite soon though, because even cutting straight across the snow-covered grass and between the trees, it was a good distance. As they went they glanced at the ornamental lake on which a number of ducks and seagulls were crossly huddled, tails to wind.

'The ice looks like it's holding,' Dai said with satisfaction. He squeezed her again. 'Got any skates, Biddy?'

'No. But I could put my stockings over my shoes,' Biddy suggested. 'I could slide great then, I bet.'

'I bet!' Dai turned her slightly and jerked his chin ahead of them. 'See that?'

It was not the aviary, not the palm house either, but it was what looked like a small workmen's hut beneath the trees. It also looked sturdy and firmly shut.

'That isn't the aviary,' Biddy objected. 'It's all shut up, we can't go in there.'

'Well, we'll take a look,' Dai decided. 'It's where they keep the deckchairs in the summer, I daresay. Come on.'

Since his arm was firmly looped around Biddy's waist she had little choice but to 'come on', so the two of them crossed the intervening snowy grass, leaving an arrow-straight path of double footprints, and went over to the hut.

Dai tried the door and to Biddy's astonishment, after a bit of creaking, it opened inwards, revealing a small, dusty but dry room in which, now that she looked about her, a caretaker or ticket-seller of some description must sit in summer, taking money or keeping an eye open through a small window whose shutters, however, were now firmly shut.

'This isn't bad,' Dai said. He pulled a canvas chair forward and Biddy collapsed into it, then he got one out and set it up for himself.

'Phew, that was a long walk,' he said, leaning back and closing his eyes for a moment. 'I wonder, was it worth it?'

Biddy giggled. 'See how you feel when we get back to Ducie Street,' she suggested. 'How does frostbite start?'

Dai's eyes shot open and he grinned provocatively across at her. 'I should know – it's one of the hazards of distant-water trawling. Tell you about it sometime I will, but right now . . . here, take it and tell me what you think, will you?'

He held a clenched fist out to her. Biddy could see by the way his fingers were curled that there was something quite large in his hand but she had no idea what it was. She wrinkled her nose doubtfully.

'I'm not touching something I can't see – for all I know it might be a toad or a lizard or – or a big, hairy spider.'

Dai shivered. 'It's not a spider; you wouldn't catch me grabbing up a spider, not even for the pleasure of having you jump into my arms,' he told her. 'It's nothing alive, honest.'

'Ugh! Not . . . not a *dead* spider?'

'Oh Biddy, how your mind do run on spiders,' Dai said impatiently. 'Can't you think of nothing else?'

'Well, no, because this strikes me as an awfully spidery sort of place,' Biddy admitted, glancing uneasily round. 'There are probably lots in here, under all the chairs, simply longing for a leg to run up . . . aaagh!'

She kicked out violently and Dai gave a shout of laughter.

'Mad you are, girl – tilting at windmills next you'll be! A large chunk of snow that was, melting and running down your knee and into your boot. And it's not a creature in my hand, I promise you that, it's something I'd like you to see. Be a brave girl, now.'

'It won't hurt or bite or make me jump?' Biddy said nervously. The little hut, which had seemed such a refuge when they were out in the snow, was shadowy and smelt of dust – and spiders. 'Do you promise, Dai?'

'See this wet, see this dry, cross my heart and hope to die,' Dai said, drawing a wetted finger across his throat. 'Don't you trust me, love?'

'Yes I do,' Biddy said. She held out her hand and gently took the object from his fingers as he released it. 'Oh, Dai, what is it? I can't see much in here, but it's warm and smooth . . . is it marble?'

'No, it's amber. It's what you females wear round your necks when it's made into beads, or on a chain when it's a pendant. It's quite a big bit, make all sorts with it you could. It's the most glorious colour, but you can't see it in this light, you need strong sunshine. Drat, never thought of that, I didn't, when I asked you to come out with me this afternoon.'

'It doesn't matter; it's still beautiful,' Biddy murmured. She tried to hand the amber back but Dai shook his head.

'No. It's for you, Biddy, a Christmas Box. And if you like it, I thought next Christmas I'd have it cut into beads, or a pendant and earrings for you.'

'A Christmas Box? For me? Oh, but Dai, it's much too beautiful! When would I wear amber, that's what proper ladies wear! Oh, isn't it a lovely thing, though? I just like the feel of it, all warm in my palm.'

'You'll wear it when you're a married lady, living in your own home with your man coming back to you from sea,' Dai said softly. 'You'll wear a blue dress with pleats, an amber necklace and a narrow velvet ribbon round your throat. You'll have your hair piled up on your head so you look like a little queen, only when I come home I'll put my hands into it and take out the pins and ribbons and it will tumble down over my hands, down to your shoulders, and it will hide your blushes when I kiss you.'

There was a long silence. In the dusk, Dai could see her small face, downturned, her eyes lowered, fixed on the amber egg in her lap. Then, just when he as thinking he must have been mad to talk to her like that, she got to her feet and came over to him. She put her hands on his shoulders and lowered her face until it was only inches from his.

'Dai, that was the loveliest thing anyone's ever said to me. I know I shouldn't, but I would love to keep the amber egg ... at least until you find someone you'd rather give it to. We – we haven't known each other long, it was just that we met in such strange circumstances ...'

'We've known one another long enough to share this seat,' Dai said. He pulled her down onto his knee and she did not resist. 'Biddy, you're very young – how old are you, by the way? - but I'm going on for twenty-three and I know my own mind. No one but you will there be for me. Not ever. Make up your mind to that.'

'I'm sixteen. I'll be seventeen next June,' Biddy murmured, her head resting comfortably in the hollow of his shoulder. 'And though I'm not as old as you, my mind is every bit as made up. I knew it as soon as I looked at you. Only we'll have to get to know one another better – I'm not earning very much, just ten shillings a week, but I can save, I'm an awful good saver.'

'I'm an awful good spender,' Dai said ruefully, against her hair. He had pulled off the wet scarf and cast it onto the spare chair as soon as she subsided onto his lap. 'But

I'll start to save from this moment on. We'll have a nice little home . . .'

'Two children, a boy and a girl . . .'

'A dog to take care of you whilst I'm at sea and a cow to give you milk . . .'

'A cow? In the city? Dai, I wouldn't know what to do to get the milk out!'

Dai laughed and kissed the side of her cold, snow-smelling face. 'No, you daft girl! We shan't live in the city, live on the Isle of Anglesey we will, near my people. Happy as the day is long you'll be, honest you will.'

'Oh! But they'll speak Welsh, and I only speak English.'

'And very nicely you speak it, too. Teach you Welsh in six months, I will – less, probably. And you'll pick up milking the cow easy as easy.'

'Oh, Dai, I'm a Catholic and I 'spect you're a Proddy.'

'Worse, I'm a Welsh Methodist; terrible old-fashioned and narrow-minded, to say nothing of bigoted, us Welsh Methodists. I go to chapel at home because my Mam did, but my religion don't weigh too heavy on me. I'm not a religious man, cariad.'

'Nor me, not when it comes to choosing a husband,' Biddy said drowsily. The cold outside and the warmth of Dai's arms were threatening to send her straight off to sleep. 'Besides, the Father at St Anthony's is a good man; I don't think he'd mind so long as we loved one another. And even if he does mind, if we aren't going to live in the 'Pool I don't suppose it matters much. Oh, Dai, am I dreaming? I keep thinking I should pinch myself. Are we really talking about marrying each other?'

'That's it. I wish I could say we'd marry tomorrow, cariad, but of course that's impossible. There's things we'll need to arrange first. But when summer comes we'll tie the knot, eh?'

'Oh yes please, Dai,' Biddy said fervently. 'Only we'd best not tell anyone else, not yet. Dear Mrs Gallagher is so pleased to have a maid she can trust, and I am very happy with her. I've never been so happy since I was a kid, nor known anyone kinder. I was desperate when she took me in, I couldn't hurt her in any way.'

'Aye, a good soul is Nellie Gallagher; you can stay with her for a while, anyway, because I've my way to make,' Dai told her. 'And sooner or later I'll have to go back to Moelfre and talk things through with my Da. We have quarrelled, cariad, but now I've a mind to go back, make things up. It'll be easier for me, knowing you're waiting in Liverpool.' He laid her back against his arm and bent over her, starting to kiss her soft but willing lips. 'Oh Biddy, I love you, I love you so much!'

'Mm . . . mm,' Biddy said, buzzing like a happy bee which finds itself deep in the scented heart of a rose. 'Mm . . . mmm.'

They reached home late, to find the women busy in the kitchen preparing the cold supper. Dai went round the front door and waited until his love was settled before he rang the bell. She came rapidly across the hall, he could hear her small feet clicking along, and opened the door to him. She smiled sweetly, wickedly, her eyes glowing with amusement.

'Oh, good evening, Mr Evans. Have you had a pleasant afternoon? If you'll just give me your coat and cap I'll take them through to the kitchen and put them on the airer; I can see you're very wet. Mr Gallagher and Mr Prescott and the children came in some time ago, so if you want to go up and have an early bath . . .'

There was no one else in the hall but the baize door was ajar and through it drifted the sounds of women talking and laughing in the kitchen. Dai grabbed Biddy and kissed her soundly, then put her back from him.

'Thank you, Biddy,' he said solemnly. 'I think I will have a bath . . . here's my coat and cap . . . and my scarf. What time is supper?'

'Supper's in half an hour, Mr Evans, but Mrs Gallagher said to tell you that if you fancy a snack before then there are biscuits and hot toddy in the study, where Mr Gallagher and Mr Prescott are sitting.'

'I'll bath first, Biddy,' Dai declared. He lowered his voice. 'What did you do with the amber egg?'

Biddy lowered her voice, too. 'It's in my pillow, amongst all the feathers, with my rag doll standing guard,' she whispered. 'I looked at it against the candle – oh Dai, I shouldn't let you give it to me, it must be immensely valuable! It's the most beautiful thing I've ever touched.'

'Then take care of it for me, cariad. And now go back to the kitchen; we don't want anyone becoming suspicious.'

On Boxing Night Dai lay in his bed and thought about Biddy, in her little attic room above him. They had known each other a little over two days, and yet he knew himself totally in love, thinking of no one else, dreaming of her, longing for her.

Christmas Day had been wonderful, even to the awful, cold walk to the park, the talk and cuddling in the cold little hut, with Biddy keeping an anxious eye out for invading spiders at first and so unable to give him her full attention – until he took her mind off spiders completely, that was, when she responded to his kisses and hugs in a most satisfying manner. And because they had found each other they had even enjoyed the walk home, both soaked to the skin, Biddy's teeth chattering like castanets, stopping now and then to hug, then running, then slowing to a walk . . laughing at each other, hugging again, almost enjoying the discomfort of damp clothes and icy extremities, because whatever they suffered they suffered together.

And afterwards they had all gathered in the big living-room and played charades and silly word games; Biddy as well. In charades, he, Elizabeth and Biddy had taken on the Gallaghers and the Prescotts and had beaten them in three games out of five. It had been great fun and, because of Biddy's presence, exciting.

Then came Boxing Day. The Gallaghers, armed with a quantity of envelopes and some very large cardboard boxes, had gone off in their motor car to deliver things. The Prescotts had taken the little boys off to visit friends. Which left Elizabeth, Biddy and Dai himself.

They got the sledge out of the loft above the garage and took it up to Everton Heights, found themselves a nice steep hill and spent most of the afternoon tipping it over, rescuing each other, laughing and pelting each other with snowballs.

They made a snowman, lent him Biddy's scarf, much to her indignation, then moved on . . . and had to come racing back over the snow to rescue the scarf before it was taken by a passer-by.

In the evening they had all piled into the motor car, Biddy as well, and Stuart drove them into Liverpool, to the Playhouse Theatre on Williamson Square, to see *The Story of Puss and his Amazing Boots*. Dai managed to get himself seated with Biddy on one side of him and Elizabeth on the other and though the two girls exclaimed and talked across him, he managed to hold Biddy's hand most of the evening and no one the wiser.

There were ices in the interval, and coffee or tall glasses of lemonade to drink. Dai would have liked a beer – Joey Prescott went out and got himself one – but he followed Stuart's lead and stuck to coffee. The pantomime was a good one, with two transformation scenes and a trapeze artist who might have seemed a little out of place in the Giant's palace to some people, but whose daring antics between the Giant's kitchen dresser and the hook on the back of his door seemed wonderful indeed to Biddy.

It was Biddy's first theatre trip and her wide-eyed wonder and tremulous enjoyment made the evening special for Dai. She sat with him on one side and the twins on the other and the three of them accepted everything which took place on stage as entirely natural. Together they marvelled over the magician who came on whilst the scenery was changed and drew rabbits from hats, miles of silk scarves from his own mouth, and sawed a beautiful lady in half, afterwards producing her all in one piece just to show you. Biddy bounced in her seat like a child of five, cheered Puss in Boots, booed the Giant, clapped the lady who came on and sang two beautiful songs and shouted 'Look behind you!' whenever cajoled by the cast to do so.

'Biddy made the performance special for all of us, especially the twins,' Stuart was heard to remark to Joey Prescott. 'She simply lost all her inhibitions and behaved like the child she is. And of course the twins – and even Elizabeth to an extent – followed her lead and enjoyed themselves twice as much as they would otherwise have done.'

Dai had managed to get one small kiss as they milled around outside the theatre, waiting for the car to pick them up. Just a little one, but all the sweeter for that. And now here he was, lying wakeful in his bed because tomorrow he would have to go round to the O'Reillys and talk to Greasy about the journey back to Grimsby. And on the floor above, his darling Biddy would be lying in her bed, no doubt soundly sleeping.

If I were to steal softly out of my room this minute, closing the door very gently behind me, if I were to climb the attic stairs very, very carefully, if I were to open her door, inch by inch, fraction by fraction, without so much as one tiny creak . . . I would see her, lying there in the cold moonlight, Dai told himself.

Her curls would be tumbled about her face and her long lashes would lie on her cheeks, and beneath the blankets the slim, strong body which he so loved to touch would be relaxed in sleep. And if I sat down on her bed and woke her with a kiss and then climbed into bed with her and cuddled down, put my arms round her . . . she would welcome me with a swiftly beating heart, a shy glance . . . but she would most definitely welcome me, Dai told himself.

But he would not do it, would not dream of it, just because she was such a sweet and trusting creature, his little Biddy O'Shaughnessy. She was too young for marriage, he should never have mentioned it to her, it was not fair because he was the only man she knew, the only man who had ever paid her the slightest attention. She should be allowed a year in which to get to know other men so that when she did make up her mind on marriage it would not be the leap in the dark which it would be if she made up her mind now.

However. She said she loved him and he loved her, so why shouldn't they plan to marry, plan happiness? Perhaps in six months he could mention the matter to Nellie as he would have mentioned it to his mother had she been alive – with a sort of shy pride, so that she would ask the right questions, become fond of Biddy, rejoice with him at his good fortune.

I'll do everything right, Dai vowed to himself, watching the moon mount the sky through a gap in his bedroom curtains. I'll mention it to Nellie, casual-like, before I go; I won't say anything's definite, I won't even say I've talked about it to Biddy, I'll just sort of hint that we're fond.

And on my next leave I'll have to go home to Moelfre and sort my Da out, he reminded himself. Got to do that I have, before I know what I've got to offer Biddy . . . not that she cares a fig, I'm sure. But I'll explain to her that it must be done, and I'll go home, talk to Davy. Who knows, maybe I'll take to Menna when I see her with an apron round her waist and a wooden spoon in her hand, maybe, if she's taking good care of my Da . . .

It would go against the grain to return to the island and not to see his darling, though. But it would be for everyone's good in the long run, he reminded himself sternly. Besides, what was one little shore-leave? Not much, compared to a lifetime's happiness. And on that thought he turned his head into his pillow and slept soundly till morning.

Dai was not the only person to lie awake in the Gallagher house that night. In her large double bed the lady of the house drank her cocoa, kissed her husband, settled down . . . and lay awake.

She had enjoyed Christmas even more than usual and that was because of Biddy. Such a good little girl, such a help . . . a treasure, no less. And Elizabeth was really fond of her, sang her praises, talked about her . . . but she talked about Dai, too.

Wouldn't it be lovely if I could tell Elizabeth that he's her brother, Nellie thought. She would be so thrilled, she's always longed for a brother or sister, that's why she's so good with the twins, so eager for Biddy's companionship. But it's impossible, I couldn't hurt my dear Stuart so.

And matters were complicated enough as it was. Lilac

had guessed. She had been a small girl of nine when Nellie had run away to Anglesey to have the baby, but even then she had been shrewd enough. Nellie had kept it from her for a good while but when she judged the moment was right she told Lilac about the baby she had been forced to leave behind.

She had never said where, or with whom, but Lilac had known Davy for a couple of years and father and son were so alike! Well, maybe not very alike now – Nellie had not seen Davy for more than twenty years – but the young man Davy had been then and the young man Dai now was were almost interchangeable. It was just the expression that was different; you only had to look at Dai to know he was a giver whereas Davy, with the best will in the world, had always been a taker.

Stuart had never met Davy, had no idea what the other man looked like, had never connected Nellie's friend Bethan with his wife's first lover. Unless someone said something – and it could not be Dai, who did not know his true parentage, and certainly would not be Nellie – Stuart need never know. He would take her fondness and friendship for the boy entirely at its face value and indeed, Nellie told herself, even had Dai not been her little boy grown to a man, she would have loved him for himself.

So Lilac was the only person who might inadvertently give her away, and Lilac never would. She loved and respected Stuart and she would never knowingly harm either of us, Nellie thought now, staring at the lighter patch at the end of her bed. So what are you lying here worrying over, for goodness sake? Just be thankful he's turned out so well, that he got in touch with you, that he's a son to be proud of, and forget that he ever lay in your arms and smiled up at you and tugged your hair. Love him as Bethan's dear son and you won't go far wrong.

She turned on her side and was soon on the edge of slumber, but even then a cautious little voice at the very back of her mind was warning her that there was something she had not thought of, had not allowed for, something that could still ruin everything. For a moment longer she lay there, trying to rationalise what must be a foolish, needless fear. But then sheer weariness overcame her and she slept at last.

Chapter Ten

Snow in August is nothing new; not in the Arctic, anyway. Dai battled his way across the deck, head tortoised deep into the collar of his coat, sou'wester pulled right down over his eyes so he could only see a small section of the deck beneath his feet.

Damned snow! They were seven days out of port and knew they were approaching the fishing grounds, but though they'd taken soundings earlier in the day they had not reached bottom yet. And when they did the Skipper would have to examine the mud or sand or whatever the lead brought up to see whether he thought they'd reached the feeding grounds, because you didn't shoot the trawl in weather like this in the wrong spot – no sir! Not only was it time-wasting, it could be worse. You could putter around searching and then find you only had coal enough for a couple of days' fishing before you had to run for home. Running out of coal in these seas was something no one dared contemplate – it was certain death.

Still, we've got a good Skipper, Dai reminded himself as he swung the lead and saw it plummet over the side and into the sea; at least he assumed it had gone into the sea since he couldn't actually see the water, what with the snow and the heaving of the swell. But he began to pay out the line, whilst beside him, Greasy moved his feet restlessly and kept shifting his weight along the rail as he narrowed his eyes against the whirling snow and tried to watch the line – when it slackened they would know they had reached bottom. Then the Skipper would want it held steady for long enough to bring up some mud, and with luck they might prepare to shoot the trawl.

Dai, also shuffling his feet, thought he felt a slight drag on the lead line; he stared downwards just as Greasy, beside him, lifted a gloved hand, one thumb erect. Dai nodded to show he understood and held on for a count of twenty, then began to bring the lead up once more. It broke surface, immediately becoming a great deal heavier, and the two men brought it inboard. Dai stared down at the sludge which had gathered round the lump of tallow wedged into the lead. It was blackish and full of tiny shell fragments, little specks of red and green which might be weed . . . he wondered if he would ever be sufficiently experienced to look at the mud, sniff it, stir it with a finger and announce that they would – or would not – shoot the trawl within the hour.

Lately, it had been suggested by the Mate that Dai might like to go for promotion. 'I started as a deckie, so did the Skipper,' he had said gruffly. 'You're young, intelligent . . . what about it, Taff?'

'I'll see what my young lady says,' Dai said warily, but he could not help feeling gratified. 'It 'ud mean moving across the country . . . but thanks, Harry.'

The Mate, a man of few words, grunted and moved away, and Dai had been thinking about it ever since, on and off. It was not everyone's game, distant-water trawling, but there was money to be made out here, by God there was! Whilst the British housewife went on buying cod, whilst the thousands of little fish-and-chip shops all over the country went on frying it, then there was profit to be made out here. If tastes ever changed, or if Arctic waters ever became overcrowded, then that was a different matter, but as things stood . . .

'Found bottom, sir.'

He had arrived on the bridge almost without noticing, and held out the lead. The Skipper took it, sniffed, touched, nodded.

'Aye; they'll be feedin' hereabouts. We'll be shootin' fairly soon so best get yourselves a meal.'

'Aye aye, sir.'

Dai ducked out of the bridge and folded his thigh boots down to calf height, then clattered below to tell anyone handy that they'd found bottom and would shoot shortly. Greasy was already sitting at the long table on the mess deck, eating what looked like a bacon sandwich. He waved it at Dai as he came in.

'Is 'e gonna shoot the trawl, Taff?' he said thickly, through a mouthful of bread and bacon. 'I thought it would be soon.'

'Yup. He'll send Harry round, get him to collect all hands. He wants us to eat first, then shoot. I'll give Bandy the word.'

The cook must have been listening because he leaned through his hatch, head and shoulders on the serving table. On their last voyage an unexpected surge had brought the hatch crashing down and Bandy had been trapped, swearing and blinding, until someone came below and released him, but it did not appear to have made him more careful.

'So we're shootin', eh? Not before time. There's steak an' kidney puddin' and two veg comin' up in ten, fifteen minutes.'

'Luverly grub,' Greasy said. 'Double helps for me, Bandy . . . an' for me young friend 'ere.'

'We'll need it when we haul,' Dai said, going over to the hatch and addressing the galley boy through it as Bandy withdrew to tend his stoves once more. 'Got a biscuit or something? Hungry I am.'

The galley boy was fourteen and a gannet; he ate everything that wasn't chained down but he could always conjure you up something between meals. Silently, he produced a bacon sandwich from somewhere and shoved it through the hatch. Dai thanked him and retreated to the mess table once more, where he sat shoulder to shoulder with Greasy and ate solidly until the sandwich was no more than a pleasant memory.

'I should be headin' for me kip now,' Greasy grumbled, eating the last of his own substantial snack. 'It's allus the bleedin' same, Taff, we allus shoots when you an' me's off watch.'

'I reckon every man aboard feels like that,' Dai said. 'Chuck us the pad, Grease; I'll write home, I think.'

'Oh, you an' your letters! Writin' to Biddy, are you? Or that other piece, on Anglesey?'

'My sister Sîan is not a "piece", she's a married lady. And yes, I'm writin' to Biddy. Just a few lines. I write a few lines most days, then when we get back to port I send off a big, fat letter. Besides, almost as good as seein' her, it is, to write.'

'But you said on your last leave you had a word with Stuart Gallagher an' he said she were too young an' you might 'old back a trifle,' Greasy said. 'If writin' every day's holdin' back a trifle then I'm the Pope!'

'He only meant not to get too serious with her,' Dai said. 'Oh shut up, Greasy, and let me write.'

He reached for the well-sharpened pencil and the pad of lined paper, brought Biddy up to date with what had happened on board the *Bess* in the last day or two and then sat back and sighed. Beside him, Greasy closed his eyes and, presently, began to snore.

Dai thought back to his last, longish shore leave, when he had managed to get back to Liverpool. Because they had had good catches and good trips from January to June he'd not gone back to Moelfre either – no time between sailings. But the money was mounting up nicely, and since the Mate had suggested he might get promotion he had borrowed books on navigation and seamanship and studied when he had time.

He telephoned Biddy though, whenever he was in port. He would ring through, let the phone bell sound three times, and ring off, then ring again immediately. That way Biddy would know it was him ringing and would run to the telephone. Sometimes the calls were more pain than pleasure, hearing her little voice so faint and far off, but at least they kept in touch that way.

Then he decided he would go up during a four-day shore leave and talk to Biddy once again about marrying, see how she felt about him staying in distant-water trawlers, but as an officer, eventually.

He got into Liverpool late one evening and knew he would have a bare forty-eight hours in the city before he had to leave again if he was not to miss his sailing. He went straight to the Gallagher house and was warmly welcomed by Nellie, Stuart and Elizabeth, Biddy hovering in the background, all smiles though her eyes sparkled with excitement and tears.

He ate with the family, talked about his recent voyages, explained that he had not been back since Christmas because catches had been excellent and the *Bess* had come through unscathed, so it was not necessary to put her into dry dock which always gave the crew a decent bit of time to themselves. But now he was here for a short spell . . . it was nice to see Liverpool in bright summer weather, to have the long evenings, to be able to admire the gardens and the parks, to tell the Gallaghers they had done wonders with their roses.

He insisted on helping with the washing up. Biddy washed, he and Elizabeth dried. Later that evening, he and the two girls went for a walk and talked a little about themselves. Biddy did not say much but Elizabeth prattled on – she was going to university, not many girls did but she would, her teachers thought she was clever enough and her Mam and Da saw no reason why not . . .

Dai told them about his hopes of promotion, the studying that he was doing when he had time both aboard the *Bess* and ashore. 'Not even been home to see my Da I haven't,' he said, addressing the words to Biddy, though he continued to look at Elizabeth. 'Came straight here as soon as I could.'

'Why don't you miss a voyage, just one? You said some of the fellows do,' Elizabeth asked him. 'Then you could see your Da and come here for longer; oh do, Dai, we could have such a good time!'

'I'm savin' up, I can't afford a voyage out,' Dai told her. 'We're well paid, but only so long as we stay with our ship.'

'What do you want to save for?' Elizabeth asked, with the disdain of one who has had everything she wants instantly provided all her life long. 'Is money so import-ant to you, Dai?'

'Indeed it is, Lizzie. Savin' up to get married I am, one of these fine days,' Dai said, and saw his love blush delightfully, though Elizabeth just sniffed and said it seemed a pretty poor excuse to her.

That evening, very late, Dai and Biddy met in the kitchen. Dai had known she would come to him as he sat in the dying firelight, the *Manual of Seamanship Vol. I* open on his knee, his eyes fixed on the door.

She slid into the room, a small wraith in her white cotton nightgown with bare toes peeping out from under it. She went straight into his arms and they hugged with desperation, kissed hungrily, wrapped up in each other, each feeling the thunder of the other's heartbeat, each knowing the giddying joy of being together.

Presently, he sat down and pulled her onto his knee. She was so soft and pliant without all the fuss and botheration of her clothing, with only the thin cotton nightdress between them. Dai groaned and kissed her neck, then began to squeeze and fondle her, to smooth his hand over her breasts . . .

The kitchen door opening nearly caused both of them to die of shock. Biddy sprang off his lap and stood, trembling like an aspen, on the hearth. Dai stood up. 'Stuart! I'm doing some studying and . . .'

'It looked like it,' Stuart said with laughter behind his voice. He jerked his head at Biddy. 'Go off to bed, love, you've done nothing wrong either of you, but perhaps you've been a bit unwise. Don't worry, Biddy, I'll have a word with this young man and that's the last either of you will hear about it. I'm no tell-tale, it goes no further.'

Biddy went over to the doorway, then paused, staring at Stuart. 'Mr Gallagher, Mr Evans wasn't . . . wasn't taking advantage of me or anything like that. We – we are good f-friends, I came down to see if – if he needed anything, and . . . and . . .'

'I know, I was young myself, once. Off with you, Biddy, you'll catch your death standing around in that thin nightgown.'

Dai went over to the doorway and watched his love up the stairs, treading so softly that not a stair creaked, then he went back into the kitchen and closed the door. 'Stuart, I want to marry Biddy and I believe she wants to marry me. I've never done anything to her – with her – that either of us could be ashamed of, though we do kiss

303

and cuddle. If I'd had evil in mind I'd have gone to her room or persuaded her to mine . . . but we do have to talk sometimes, and it's very difficult to be with her without the whole household knowing about it.'

'And what's wrong with that? Us knowing, I mean?'

'Nellie said something to me the first time I stayed with you; she said she was glad she hadn't married the first man who took her around and paid her compliments, and she hoped both Biddy and Elizabeth would take their time, meet people, before they took the plunge into matrimony. Apparently she's known several girls who've married the first man who asked them and lived to regret it. She wasn't meaning me and Biddy, I knew that, but I could tell – thought I could tell – that she would say we ought to wait. Besides we can't afford to marry yet and Biddy's so happy here, she was terrified that if Nellie or you found out that we liked each other, she might be asked to go.'

'Never! But you know, Dai, Biddy really is rather young and very innocent. I doubt very much if anyone other than yourself has kissed her, certainly she doesn't go out with young men. I won't ask you to do anything foolish, like not seeing one another, clearly you are both very attached, but I do think that you should encourage Biddy to go dancing, meet other young men. And then, in a year's time . . .'

'I'd not dream of asking her to stay away from dances and fun, but she don't seem to want such things, not any more,' Dai said rather hopelessly. 'She used to go to the Acacia Dance Hall every Saturday night with her friend Ellen and meet young men and dance with them, but since she's come here she's lost interest, or so she says.'

'Oh! I didn't realise she used to go there.' Stuart, who had been standing with his back to the fire, sighed and sat down in one of the fireside chairs, motioning Dai to follow suit. 'Look, old man, I don't mean to interfere, but we're all only human. If you and Biddy keep meeting clandestinely, particularly when Biddy's only wearing a nightgown, what do you think is going to happen? I know you'll tell me you're a man of honour, but I know what would happen if I were in your shoes! And that would be very unfair on Biddy, very unfair indeed, with you out in the Arctic somewhere and her facing the music alone.'

'Oh!' Dai said. He had immediately seen the truth of Stuart's words because he knew that, had no one walked into the room, he would almost certainly have gone a good deal further than was right. But dammit, he loved her . . . if they married . . . . He put the point to Stuart who did not seem impressed.

'Yes, but you can't marry; not yet,' Stuart had pointed out briskly. 'You're still saving up, right? And Biddy is too. She'll want a wedding dress, a trousseau, all the usual things young girls want. She saves most of her wages and in a year she'll be in a comfortable position. So will you give her room to grow in that year? For Biddy's sake, Dai?'

What choice had he got, after that? And he knew it was true that if they kept meeting on the sly then sooner or later they would make love and Biddy could easily find herself pregnant. He had been with other girls, of course he had, but not young innocents like her. The sort of girl who roams the Grimsby docks knows how to take care of herself and is paid well for taking all the responsibility. Biddy was too good for him anyway, she certainly didn't deserve to be treated as if she was just another dockyard floozie.

'Right, Stuart,' Dai had said therefore, briskly but with a good grace. 'You have a point and I'll abide by it. No more cuddling in the kitchen after dark, just loving friends we will be. And in a year we'll marry and I'll steal her from you.'

Stuart had laughed and clapped him on the shoulder. 'It's a bargain! Your trouble, old man, was that you fooled us all. I never realised you and Biddy were more than acquaintances . . . . Do all the letters come from you, then?'

'Well, I hope so,' Dai said, grinning. 'Keep a postman occupied full-time we do, with the letters rushing across the country. I'll go to bed now . . . but it'll be good to know you're keeping an eye on her for me.'

Next day he gave Biddy a slightly watered-down version of their talk and Biddy had nodded thoughtfully.

'I'm not going dancing or anything like that, but I'll work hard and save up and in a year . . . in a year we'll talk about it again.'

That conversation, however, had taken place in the spring and now it was August and Dai's resolve was beginning to pall. Oh, not his resolve that he would never take advantage of Biddy, he was determined that they would not fall into that particular trap, but his resolve to wait a year before marriage. Better to marry than to burn, the Good Book said, and there were times when Dai burned for Biddy. Besides, it was over six months since they had met and fallen in love, he didn't see why they shouldn't at least get engaged. He was planning to spend his bonus this trip on a small ring, and if Biddy agreed they could at least name the day.

'All right you lot, grub up! Come on, get it in you whiles you got the chanst!' Bandy's round red face appeared through the hatch. 'Come on, the old man's swiggin' brandy an' stuffin' hisself wi' me beef an' kidney puddin'; you'd best look lively or he'll be bawlin' you all up on deck afore you've et!'

Elizabeth was growing up, and growing beautiful, what was more. She and Biddy often had their heads together over various matters, and Nellie had noticed that sometimes Elizabeth would accede to a suggestion which came from Biddy, whereas if she, Nellie, made that same suggestion, her daughter would unhesitatingly turn it down.

But Nellie knew it was all part of growing up so she just smiled and found a way of phrasing her suggestions so that they scarcely seemed to be suggestions at all, just ideas thrown out at random. That way, Elizabeth could believe herself totally independant of her parents, but Nellie could still keep her finger on the pulse of her daughter's activities.

Recently, Stuart had come home looking thoughtful, and had told Nellie, when they were alone, that he had been offered the chance to go up to Scotland and help to launch a new glossy magazine being started in Edinburgh.

'It's an opportunity, but I know how happy you are here, so I'll tell them I'm not interested,' he had said. 'No point in uprooting ourselves, though in a year or two it will be Elizabeth who will want to uproot, when she goes to university.'

'If she goes to university,' Nellie corrected, a slight frown marring her brow. 'You know our girl . . . she blows hot and cold, one minute she wants one thing, the next minute, another. Besides, things are so unsettled, Stu! The world situation, I mean. You believe there's going to be a war, don't you? There was the trouble over the poor Austrian Jews, then Hitler put the Austrian leaders into that Dachau place and no one tried to stop him . . . and the Air Force are running a huge recruitment campaign, you see the posters everywhere. I'm worried that war will come before poor Lizzie even leaves school, and if it does she won't want to go to university, she'll want to join one of the forces, I expect.'

'She's just at that stage in her development when the grass on the other side is always greener,' Stuart agreed. 'And you're right, sweetheart, I do think there'll be a war in the not-too-distant future. Even so, though, Lizzie may agree to further education, if that's still on the cards of course. She's a determined young lady, so she may easily stick to her guns over this.'

And then Dai turned up.

Nellie was alone in the house because Stuart had gone off to a meeting in Edinburgh – he might have decided not to take the job in Scotland but he was extremely interested in the magazine's birth-pangs – and Elizabeth and Biddy had gone into the city, to the Central Libraries on William Brown Street, where they would visit the Picton Reading Room and then go into the Lending Library where Elizabeth hoped to borrow books to help her with one of her subjects.

Biddy had gone along partly to borrow some books on her own account, though she also intended to visit her friend Ellen. Since it was her half-day it seemed a good opportunity to see Ellen since she would be in the city anyway, and could come home later, at her own pace.

'I'll go with Elizabeth to the library, then put her on the tram for home and catch another to Ellen's place,' she had said to Mrs Gallagher earlier in the day. 'We're going to have a snack at lunchtime – the Queensway Café, on London Road, is awfully good – and I'll have my tea with Ellen. I'll be home before the last tram, but I do love an afternoon with Ellen and little Bobby.'

So here was Nellie, standing in the kitchen making her Christmas cakes, although it was only September, and singing, rather appropriately, the song which came continually over the wireless these days, 'September in the Rain.' Some people might consider it too early to start Christmas cooking, but Nellie always made a great many rich fruit-cakes for her various charitable organisations and liked to do them in good time so that they could mature. So she was working away and singing lustily when someone knocked on the front door.

Nellie rinsed her hands hastily and ran across the kitchen and into the hall. The front door had a stained glass panel, all rich reds, glowing golds, jewel-like greens, and through it Nellie could see the outline of someone standing on the step. It looked like a young man, which meant one of Elizabeth's friends, Nellie thought rather despairingly, crossing the hallway at a trot. She remembered how shy she had been with young men when she was sixteen, but her daughter was completely at ease in any company and seemed to enjoy flirting with a number of rather nice young men. And she was so pretty, with that rich, golden-brown hair arranged at the moment in the popular Juliet pageboy, the clear blue eyes, the frank and easy manner which, Nellie privately thought, was the most attractive thing about her child. So undoubtedly it would be a young man wanting Lizzie, and Lizzie was far away and the onus of entertainment would be on Nellie, who wanted to continue to cook her Christmas cakes, sing her favourite songs and dream into the fire.

She opened the front door, however, with a rather guarded welcoming smile on her lips . . . which changed to delight when she saw who stood on the step.

'Dai! Oh my dear boy, how absolutely wonderful to see you! It's been such a long time . . . come in, come in!

I'm cooking in the kitchen since everyone else is out so you can come and watch me weighing tons of dried fruit, sugar, syrup, flour . . . and all the other good things which go into Christmas cakes.' She ushered him through into the kitchen, seized his ditty bag from him and slung it over the hook on the back of the door. 'Sit down, I'll make you a cup of tea . . . shan't be a moment.'

She filled the kettle, carried it over to the sink, took it back and put it on top of the stove. Then she turned to Dai. 'Well, your room's always ready for you, so that's no problem. How long can you stay, my dear boy?'

Dai smiled. He had taken off his navy jacket and now he sat there in his shirtsleeves looking calmly and contentedly about him, and when the kettle began to sing he told Nellie to get on with her cooking, he was a prince amongst tea-makers and would make her a cup in a trice.

'Well, I would like to get on,' Nellie admitted, cracking a dozen eggs into a jug, whisking them with a fork and then pouring them into her great yellow cooking bowl. 'And what brings you rushing over to see us, dear Dai, when I thought you wouldn't be back again until Christmas?'

Dai was making the tea, pouring water from the kettle onto the leaves he had just spooned into the big brown pot. Without looking round he said, in a slow, measured tone, 'Dear Nellie, I'm sure you must have guessed that I'm deeply in love with your girl. . . . I've brought her a ring and I'm going to ask her to be my wife. I know you'll say it's too soon, she's too young, but an uncertain world it is these days, with so many bad things happening. Felt I had to speak, see?'

Nellie dropped her spoon. A terrible, desolate unhappiness filled her and a deep sense of dread. This? She had dreaded that something bad would come of her behaviour with Dai's father all those years ago, but this went beyond her wildest nightmares! But she forced herself to think, to act calmly.

'Dai, my dear . . . she's too young! You both are, you've your lives before you . . . you mustn't jump into things, you must consider!'

Her adored daughter, her beautiful Elizabeth, she could not blame the boy for falling in love with her, she had noticed a certain fondness creeping into their relationship, but this!

'I know she's young, Nellie, and I'm prepared to wait, believe me. But I've saved up and bought this pretty little ring . . .' he was holding it out, smiling down at it, '. . . and I thought she could wear it on a chain round her neck if you feel she's too young for a formal engagement. It – it would give me such pleasure to know she wore my ring.'

A part of Nellie's mind acknowledged that Dai's logic was the sensible logic of a nice young man deeply in love, but another part could only scream a silent protest – she's too young, she's my baby, my little girl . . . and you were my baby once, my little boy – Dai, darling, you and Elizabeth are brother and sister!

But she could not say it. Instead, she took a deep breath and prepared to prevaricate. 'I see. I'm trying very hard to understand and sympathise, Dai, but it's been such a shock to me.'

'A shock?' He brought two cups of tea over to the table and sat down opposite her, pushing one of the cups across. 'I made sure Stuart would have told you – what a great gun he is, Nellie, to keep it to himself! The truth is, he caught us kissing one evening and guessed how it was with us and advised me to wait. Which I have done . . . only I long to give her a sign, I do . . . very dear to me she is.'

Stuart knew, and had not told her! But of course he

must have thought it was just puppy love and would be outgrown by both parties. And if it turned out to be true love, then why should Stuart object? Elizabeth was far too young, even Dai acknowledged that, but he did not mean to marry her for some time, he had made that clear. And if it had not been for the fact that they were brother and sister, Nellie realised, nothing would have given her greater pleasure than to welcome Dai officially into her family.

Oh, but she must stop it now, before it grew truly serious! She must put her foot down, tell him it was impossible – but she could not tell him why it was impossible, that was the rub!

'Dai darling, will you listen to me? Will you promise me not to take it any further until Christmas? Only till then . . . it's not much to ask. I'm sure you won't regret it. Stu thinks there'll be war . . . I'm in such a worry . . . if you'll just leave it lie for now . . .'

'We-ell . . . Nellie, is there someone else? Is that what you're trying to tell me? I'd rather have the truth, know where I stood.'

His face was pale, his dark eyes anxious. Nellie frowned across at him, biting the tip of her index finger. This would need careful handling; if he stayed and saw Elizabeth he would realise at once that she was still fancy free. Elizabeth was transparent, now that she thought about it she should have guessed – the way she looked at Dai, hung on his arm, begged him to take her to the park, skating in winter, playing tennis in summer. But Dai was still looking at her with that lost, vulnerable look . . . oh, how could she bear it? On the other hand if she lied to him, told him that Elizabeth had met someone else . . . but if it meant she would not have to break it to him that he and the girl he loved were brother and sister . . .

Nellie took a deep breath. 'Dai, there might be. She's

very young, but there's someone whom I begin to believe she really does like . . . a little more than she realises herself as yet, perhaps. Just wait until Christmas, and then . . . Dai! Wait! What on earth are you doing?'

But he had gone. He had snatched his coat from the peg, his ditty bag from the floor, and left. Without a word of goodbye, without a smile. She ran to the kitchen door; the garden was narrow but long, he could not have reached the end of it yet . . .

The garden ended in a high wall in which was set a small green door. The door was still swinging, but although she ran down the garden and into the jigger at the back there was no sign of him. Dai Evans had completely disappeared.

Nellie returned to the kitchen and began listlessly pouring ingredients into the scale pan and from there to her yellow mixing bowl, but her heart was no longer in it and her song had died on her lips. She had hurt him so! But she had had no choice, she could not let him continue to love Elizabeth, to break all their hearts.

If only he had not gone so abruptly; if only he had waited until Stuart . . . no, that would not have done, Stuart, in this instance at least, could not be relied upon to help her.

But the danger was over, at least for the time being. She had done a terrible thing, had hurt Dai to the heart. She acknowledged, now, that his affection for her daughter had been deeper and more profound than she could have possibly guessed. What else could I have done, though, she pondered, moving miserably round the kitchen, tossing ingredients into the bowl almost at random. How else could I have behaved? I had no choice, I had to drive him away, say something which would ensure that he never came back.

When she was putting the first cake into the oven, however, it occurred to her that she had not done it, not altogether. Dai would come back, any young man would. He would go now, bitterly hurt, and nurse his wounds for a bit, and then he would begin to think. He had not seen his love, nor heard from her own lips that she preferred another. He would be back, and next time he would not be so easily put off. Next time he would sit himself down at the kitchen table, smile at her coolly and a little grimly, and wait until he could see Elizabeth for himself. That tiny gold engagement ring with the little chip of a gemstone at its heart . . . her own heart ached at the thought of it. He really did love Elizabeth, he would have to see her if only once!

Nellie sat down with a thump at the kitchen table and put her head in her hands and prayed. There must be a way out, dear Lord, there must be some way of keeping them apart until they were older and had forgotten this first, early, attachment. He's a good young man, Dear Lord, and I love him, but their marriage would be an affront to Your church, it would be against nature! Please Mary, Holy Mother, look down on me in my fear and confusion and show me a way out, she prayed, squeezing her lids so tightly shut that whirling patterns formed in her head. Please, dear God, help me to help them!

And presently, as though the Holy Mother had pitied the little earthly mother so desperate not to hurt either of her children, Nellie saw the way.

When Stuart got back from his meeting very late that night he was met by a pale but determined wife who pounced on him the moment she heard his key in the door. 'Stuart, darling, I've been thinking. I want to go to Edinburgh; I think you should take the job they offered you. It's safer than Liverpool . . . but it's not just that, I think it would be best.'

She would say very little more, but was pale and distraught, making him a late-night snack, heating milk, adding a tot of rum so generous that he accused her, laughing, of trying to get him plastered.

'No indeed, you must have a clear head, but Stu, darling, you would like to take the job, wouldn't you?'

'Ye-es, but I'd quite made up my mind that it wasn't fair on you and Lizzie, I thought we'd agreed that . . .'

'Well, I've changed my mind. It would be very good for us, nothing could be better. We need a change, we've been here too long, I'm getting set in my ways. . . . Besides, we could see Lilac and the children quite as easily in Edinburgh as here and a change would be good for us. And dear Lizzie will talk with a Liverpool accent and I'd like to break her of the habit before she starts university, if she really means to start, that is. And . . . and if war does come, perhaps we would all be safer up in Edinburgh, further from bombs and dangers?'

'Have you asked Liz what she thinks? Darling, she won't want to go, all her friends are here, and I respect her feelings. But of course the job is rather important so your surprising offer is tempting, very tempting. It's not as if it's for ever, either, we needn't even sell this house, we could let it, because it would be a two-year spell in Edinburgh, that's all, just to set the thing up, get it running. . . . As for war, it'll come, but there's no point in worrying about it until it happens. Chamberlain's suing for peace; who knows? He may succeed in defusing the situation.'

'Then you'll do it? Take the job, move away? Oh Stu, darling, thank you so much! There is a reason why I think it will be best to go but I can't explain, not just yet. It's nothing awful, truly, but it's better that we go. When can we leave?'

Stuart looked down at her. She was pink-cheeked now, her eyes sparkling. Good thing I trust her, he thought wryly, giving her a hug. Because if I didn't I'd suspect that she was trying to get me out of the way and hiding some dark secret from me – a lover or something. But since I do trust her I guess it's some tiny little thing . . . probably one of the boys Elizabeth keeps turning up with has looked too long and lovingly at her darling, that would be enough to make her take fright. But it will probably come tumbling out presently, and prove to be some tiny, unimportant thing. Darling Nell!

Presently they went up to bed, but even in his arms she would only say, drowsily, that it was not important and that she was sure they would all be very happy living in Scotland.

'What about Lizzie's schooling, though?' Stuart said equally drowsily at one point.

'She'll find her level,' Nellie mumbled. 'It's for the best, truly, Stu. G'night, darling.'

Biddy was appalled by the news that the family were moving to Scotland, lock, stock and barrel, and within a month, too. She loved the family, trusted them totally, and was completely happy both in her work and her personal life. But going with them, tempting though it was, had to be out of the question, because of Dai.

'But we want you to come with us, of course, dear Biddy,' Mrs Gallagher said, smiling fondly at her. 'You'll be just as happy there as you are here, my dear, and you'll soon make new friends.'

'We shan't be gone long, either,' Elizabeth said threateningly. She had done her utmost to persuade her parents to change their minds, without one iota of success. Stuart merely said that the job was an important one and her mother knew best; Nellie tended to burst into tears, hug Elizabeth to her bosom and assure her that she would be grateful to her mother one of these days.

'I shan't be grateful at all,' Elizabeth had stormed when she saw there was no moving either parent. 'All my friends are here, how shall I *live* without Annie, Sheila and little Mimms? And there are others . . . what about Freddy Long? And Arthur? And nice, handsome Sullivan?'

'They'll all be here in a year or so, when we come back,' Nellie said soothingly. 'It will do you good, Elizabeth, not to have your own way for once in your life. Just settle down, there's a dear, and help me to pack. Your father has taken a beautiful fully-furnished house – it's a castle, really, out in the country with ponies and dogs and all sorts – but we'll need to take linen and all our clothes and personal possessions.'

A castle! Ponies, dogs and other animals! They had taken it for granted that Biddy would go too, but she spoke to Mr Gallagher quietly one day, as he was trying to pack in his study, and explained that though she would miss them horribly and be unhappy without them, she could not bring herself to leave Liverpool.

'I've felt like a member of the family, sir, but Mrs Gallagher doesn't know about Dai, and I don't think Lizzie knows, either,' she said shyly. 'It's only you that does know, Mr Gallagher. You see, Dai's coming back here at Christmas and – and we are to get engaged. I wouldn't like to go off to Scotland so that I wasn't here when he came home and I can't let him know because I had a letter only a day or so ago . . . he was just about to sail again. It might be four or five weeks before he docks.'

She did not tell Mr Gallagher, but the letter had been

rather a strange one, quite upsetting in fact. Dai said he understood that she needed to meet other people, he wanted her to do so, was all in favour of it. But then he went off at a tangent and said there was no one else in the world for him but if things had panned out differently for her then he could only wish her every happiness and do the decent thing.

The decent thing? What on earth did that mean, Biddy asked herself, reading the letter for the twentieth time. But even after all the re-reading she still could make nothing of it.

And after his fine remark about doing the decent thing the letter just rambled. There were bits in which he said he was ashamed of the way he had behaved towards Mrs Gallagher, another bit in which he complained that the journey back had been a hell on earth, with his mind going round and round what had been said – what *had* been said, Biddy wondered, thoroughly bemused – and that he had gone straight back on board the *Bess* to write to her before she sailed, despite what he now knew.

But I want to hear it from your own lips, the letter ended. *So I'm holding onto the ring until Christmas, when we shall meet again. All my love, darling, Dai.*

But fortunately Mr Gallagher did not want to see the letter; indeed, he seemed to understand perfectly why she felt she could not go to Edinburgh with them.

'We're letting the house to a gentleman from London and his family; he's the gentleman who will be doing my present job whilst I'm away,' Mr Gallagher explained. 'The family are called the Maitlands and they will be delighted to keep you on, Biddy. Same wages and conditions of service, of course. How would that suit you? I believe it will only be for a year at the most with the way the world situation is going, but if you and Dai intend to marry next spring, for instance, then you are quite right, your place is here, where you and Dai can be together.'

'I'll miss you all terribly, sir, but I shall have to stay,' Biddy said, feeling tears come to her eyes at the thought of losing the Gallagher family, who had been so good to her. 'But a year isn't so very long and I'll write often. Elizabeth will write to me, she's already promised.'

She did not add that Elizabeth had stormed at her and pleaded with her not to 'rat on us', as she elegantly put it, but to go up to Edinburgh as well, and Mrs Gallagher had wept and said that if Biddy should ever change her mind . . .

Biddy smiled and said again how she would miss everyone, but she was as firm, in her way, as Mrs Gallagher. She dreaded their going, knew she would miss them badly, but she could not let Dai down. She would not change her mind and go to Edinburgh, she would stay in Liverpool.

'I don't understand you. No, don't glare, Taffy, I ain't never knowed you sullen afore, but you're sullen now. Whass up, eh? You ain't been yourself not since you come back from the 'Pool afore this trip. C'mon, give!'

'There's nothing to tell, mun,' Dai said gruffly, trying not to look directly at Greasy's concerned face. 'I didn't see Biddy, I told you that – disappointed, I was.'

'Yeah, you told me, but I din't believe you,' Greasy said frankly. 'To go 'alf crost the country an' norra word or a look between you – well, that ain't like you, Taff. Any fool can see you're mad for that lickle judy.'

'Only a kid she is, that's the trouble,' Dai admitted. They were four days out of port and sitting on the mess deck eating ham sandwiches and playing cards whilst they waited for their watch.'Everyone said so, Nellie, Stuart . . . everyone.'

'On'y a kid? C'mon, wack, where's your common sense? She's seventeen, ain't she? Me Mam 'ad two kids at that age . . . an' she were married, an' all. Your Biddy's a woman, norra kid, an' it's time they all come to terms wi' the fac's of life . . . Biddy, too. She oughter be glad there's a feller pantin' to get 'er. . . .You go 'ome, Chrismuss, an' grab 'er by the 'air an' do your caveman act! Drag 'er to your lair, Taff – she'll love it, they all does.'

Dai grinned, he couldn't help it. He'd felt downright suicidal when he had stormed out of the Gallagher house and all the way back to Grimsby the black dog of depression had sat on his shoulder. She didn't love him, he should have known she wouldn't, what woman would love a feller like him? Nellie was right, he should make himself scarce, keep out of her way, let her fall in love with some landlubber, not a seaman who would worry her sick by his absences and perhaps, one day, not come home at all.

He had signed on again and told himself that he must forget her – but he could not! Biddy, Biddy! She had been the centre of his life and thoughts for almost a year, which was little enough time, but now he could not imagine continuing without her. Going home, not with her small hand tucked in his, but alone. Talking to his father, but not about what mattered, just about . . . the house, Menna, the boat. Seeing Siân and her Gareth, congratulating her on the birth of her baby son, dandling the child on his knee, trying not to think that, had things been different, Biddy and he might . . .

But as the familiar work on board the trawler began to take up more and more of his time he became, insensibly, more optimistic. Nellie had said there was someone else, but not that Biddy was in love with the fellow. She had said that, given time, Biddy might be in love with him, but now that he thought about it, he knew his Biddy better. She was in love with him, she was probably just being polite to the other bloke. He would not give up, no matter that Nellie clearly thought he ought. I'll go back at Christmas, give her the ring, and tell here we're getting married at Easter, take it or leave it, he decided, and gave Greasy a real smile, a great big one, and felt a lot better.

'There, you see? Course she'll come runnin', soon's she sees you mean business. The pair of you'll be billin' an' cooin' in no time, once you mek 'er see reason. Wanna take an 'and o' cards? Gin rummy? No, I suppose you'll be wantin' to write one o' them great fat letters what tek you a whole trip to git down on paper.' Greasy sighed gustily. 'Oh well, on me own 'ead be it! I'd rather 'ave you cheerful an' writin' letters than downright bloody miserable an' playing gin. Chuck us the pack, Taff, an' I'll play a bit o' Patience.'

The new people moved in on the Saturday. The Maitlands were a couple in their early forties with four children, two boys and two girls. Mrs Maitland made up heavily and had a stiff, rather unnatural-looking permanent wave. She wore fashionable Russian boots, skirts which brushed her boot-tops, slashed sleeves and low necks in the modern imitation of Shakespearian fashion. Closer scrutiny showed her to be sharp-featured, but she seemed pleasant enough. Indeed the whole family would probably prove all right, though nowhere near as nice as the Gallaghers, but Biddy was determined to fit in and do a good job for them and worked like a young Trojan to get them settled.

On the Sunday, which should have been her day off,

she cooked them a roast luncheon, took the children to a rather smart Proddy church and then went on to Mass at the far humbler place of worship she herself favoured. Then she came back and served the luncheon, cleared and put away, got a very fancy afternoon tea (cucumber sandwiches, sponge cakes no bigger than your thumb and some stuff called Gentleman's Relish spread on tiny squares of hot toast) for the adults and something more substantial for the children, and then prepared a cold supper.

She went to bed that night and slept soundly, though she was disturbed by dreams in which the Maitlands decided to buy a dog-cart and also decided that they could not afford a pony so Biddy must pull it. She awoke from a furious confrontation with Mr Maitland over what sort of harness was best for her and whether she should be shod, to find the alarm bouncing on the bedside table and another day's work waiting.

Although the family was bigger and more demanding, Biddy would still have coped, and coped well, what was more. She stated calmly on Monday morning that she usually took Sundays off and would do so in future, and Mrs Maitland was very nice about it.

'Of course, dear. I'm so sorry, what with moving in on the Saturday we were in such a state I never thought . . . and you have Thursday afternoons off as a rule, don't you? Well, this week take all day Thursday, and we'll sort Sundays out on our own.'

Biddy said that this would be fine and continued to work hard for the Maitlands. Until Wednesday.

Wednesday was Mrs Maitland's bridge evening. She was, it transpired, a fanatical bridge player and as soon as she arrived in Liverpool she had made herself known to other players. On both Monday and Tuesday afternoons Mrs Maitland rang for a taxi and disappeared for several hours, and on Wednesday evening, dressed up to the nines and with her handbag full of change, she set off again.

'I make all my pin-money playing bridge,' she told Biddy chummily as she stood in the kitchen giving her last-minute instructions about the dinner she was to serve Mr Maitland and the hour at which the young Maitlands were to go to bed. 'I daresay I shall come home with some fairly substantial winnings tonight – we from the metropolis do have our standards and people from the provinces aren't perhaps *quite* as up to the minute as ourselves.'

'I thought you came from London,' Biddy said before she had thought, and saw Mrs Maitland give a knowing smirk. Biddy continued to make the apple pie she intended for Mr Maitland's dinner, but she found herself hoping, with quite uncharacteristic spite, that Mrs Maitland might be taken to the cleaners by the good bridge players of Liverpool, which would show her who was a provincial and who was not.

The evening proceeded smoothly after Mrs Maitland had left. The children, whose ages ranged from a snooty, self-satisfied ten year old to a delightful little moppet of three, had their high tea, played some quiet games and then went to bed. Biddy oversaw this, making a game of it, and thought, as she tucked the two youngest into bed, that they weren't bad kids and would be quite good company in time. The eldest, Master Samuel, could do with taking down a peg, but the others were nice enough and would improve once their new schools had knocked the conceit out of them and some sense in.

Back in the kitchen she served soup, roast pork and the apple pie with some rich yellow cream to Mr Maitland, who ate everything, scarcely exchanged a word with her, and then got up from the table, carrying the bottle of port, and shut himself in the study. How different from Mr Gallagher, Biddy thought wistfully, whizzing through the washing up whilst she listened to Mr Chamberlain, promising 'Peace in our Time', on the wireless. When the News was over she switched to a light music channel, beginning to tap her foot to the catchy rhythm of a jazz band. She wondered whether she ought to go through and offer Mr Maitland coffee, but decided against it for the time being. He seemed a very odd sort of man, but the rest of the family would probably be all right, once they settled in and grew accustomed.

Having only fed one man and herself there wasn't a lot of washing up, so Biddy got through it in no time. Having cleared up she went to the study to ask Mr Maitland if there was anything else he wanted, and when he had said no, he was quite all right thank you, she told him that she was off to bed but would leave the hall light burning for Mrs Maitland.

'Oh . . . yes, thank you, Biddy,' Mr Maitland said. 'She is usually very late; you need not wait up.'

Oh, aren't I relieved, Biddy said sarcastically to herself as she headed for the stairs. Because the last thing I intend to do is wait up for silly old biddies who go out gambling and don't come home till the early hours. I can just see Mrs Gallagher's face if I said I'd wait up for Mr Gallagher when he was out late putting the paper to bed. The idea!

She was in bed by ten and so she wrote a bit more of her current letter to Dai, telling him all the silly, funny things about the Maitlands and adding that she hardly knew how she would wait until Christmas, and then she blew out her candle, said her prayers, including rather a lot of fervent ones concerning the safety and well-being of Dai, his craft, and the Gallagher family, and pulled the blankets up over her shoulders. Dolly was heaved out from under the pillow, where she was unaccountably lurking, Biddy's hand delved into the feathers, found and extracted the amber egg, and she fell happily asleep.

She came abruptly awake for no reason that she knew, to find herself staring into the darkness, convinced that she was not alone. She could see nothing, scarcely even the lighter patch which was the curtained window, yet she was almost certain . . . yes! She could hear someone breathing!

Biddy sat up and reached for the candle and the matches. She fumbled the box open and as she did so someone bumped into her bedside table and muttered a curse. Immediately she felt much better and her heart, which had been hammering fit to bust, slowed to a more normal rate. It would be one of the Maitland children, of course, in a strange house and losing their way in the dark . . . or perhaps seeking her out for comfort and reassurance.

'Hold on,' she said, therefore. 'I'll just light the candle and . . .'

She struck a match and in its quick flare she saw Mr Maitland standing by the door looking at once owlish and extremely foolish. He was wearing a nightshirt, a striped affair in grey and white, and beneath it his hairy, knobbly legs looked horribly bare and pathetic.

'Mr Maitland, this is my room, you know,' Biddy said in what she hoped was a motherly tone. 'Have you got lost? Your rooms are on the floor below.'

He laughed, rather uneasily she thought. 'Ah . . . yes, my dear, very understandable; yes, no doubt I am lost and need to be d'rected to the place I sh-seek. Perhaps we should have a li'l chat about it, eh?'

And to Biddy's alarm he came across the room, sat on the edge of her bed, seized her by the shoulders and gave her first a little shake and then a squeeze.

Biddy stared at him, aghast. This plump, balding, middle-aged man with the hairy legs and the squashy pink lips couldn't possibly be under the impression that she liked him, could he? Just in case, she brought her knees up under the covers and began to try to position her feet so that a good kick would send him flying off the bed. He seemed unaware of this strategy, but leaned forward and tried to kiss her. He missed her face altogether but got her on the ear, the kiss making a moist explosion which nearly deafened her.

'Hey! Stop that!' Biddy said crossly. 'Gerroff me bed!'

'Ah, you'd rather I got *in* your bed I daresay,' the horrid old man said cheerfully, leering at her. 'Anything to 'blige a lady, my dear.'

He heaved at the blankets and despite Biddy's valiant efforts they slid down to her middle. 'Move over,' Mr Maitland ordered, his joviality slipping a little as Biddy made no effort to help him. He let go of her shoulders and stood up, in order to stick a hairy foot into her bed. 'Come on, don' hog the whole m-mattresh, my dear, or we'll never have our li'l bit of fun before my goo' lady comes back from her bridge; eh? Eh?'

'If you don't get out of me room this minute I'll scream the place down and Master Samuel will doubtless come tearin' up the stairs,' Biddy said desperately. She doubted that a ten-year-old child would be able to do much against this horrible person, but it was a good threat. 'And then I'll tell Mrs Maitland of you, sir.'

Mr Maitland took his foot out of the bed and tugged peevishly at the covers again and, because Biddy was not expecting it, they descended much further. He gave a crow of triumph and sat down on the bed, then tried to swing his legs in so that he could lie down. And then he turned with surprising swiftness for one so fat and unfit, and clasped Biddy to his paunch.

'Pretty li'l crittur,' he mumbled. He kissed her neck, his arms imprisoning her. 'Ooh, pretty li'l Biddy's going to have such a wonnerful time wi' her dear old mate Maitie in a moment! Oh, old Maitie givesh all the girls a wonderful time, you don't know how lucky you are . . . experienshed man of the world . . . no time for these jumped-up youngsters, you wanna nolder man . . .'

Biddy managed to heave one hand free. It happened to be the hand which grasped the amber egg. She said, 'Mr Maitland, I'm warning you, either you get out of my bed right this minute or . . .'

'Never! Nevernever . . .' Mr Maitland declared, trying to get his pudgy hand inside Biddy's nightgown. 'Oh, you'll be coming down to fetch me up on a Wenn . . . Wess . . . Wednesday eve . . . evening, once you've met my famoush . . . famous . . .'

Biddy brought the amber egg down on Mr Maitland's head. It was an awkward angle but she did her best, though she did not hit hard enough, since he did not lose consciousness but merely shouted 'Ouch!' and then added, 'What wazzat?' before slowly slithering out of her bed and onto the floor.

'I do hope you're dead,' Biddy said, climbing out of bed and leaning over him. 'Are you dead, you old monster?'

'Dead, but not forgotten,' Mr Maitland said in a sepulchral voice. 'Jus' a teeny bit dead, thash all.'

'You're drunk,' Biddy said, with the air of one making a surprising discovery. 'You're a dirty old toss-pot and I'm not staying in this room another minute.'

This statement galvanised Mr Maitland into action, of a sort. He turned his head so that he could squint up at her and said heavily, 'Goin', sho shoon? But we haven't had our fun an' gamesh yet, little lady.'

'Oh yes we have,' Biddy said grimly, packing her belongings with great rapidity into her trusty carpet bag. 'And you owe me some wages, but I shan't be stopping to claim 'em. You can find yourself another maidservant just as soon as you like, Monster. I'm off!'

She was crossing the front hall when a key grated in the lock and Mrs Maitland came in, unbuttoning her astrakan coat as she came. She looked puzzled when she saw Biddy fully dressed and obviously about to leave.

'Biddy? What's wrong?'

'Everything,' Biddy said, not mincing matters. 'Your husband is lying on my bedroom floor; he's drunk. He's got some funny ideas, has Mr Maitland. I'll come back in a day or so to pick up my wages and the rest of my things, but I can't stay.'

'You're not leaving? Biddy, you can't leave, not just because my husband is a – a little the worse for wear! Look, you sleep in one of the spare rooms tonight and we'll sort things out in the morning.'

'No. I'm going. In fact, if you'll just give me some of my money now, I'll run after your taxi and go in that. The last tram must have left hours ago.'

Mrs Maitland looked shifty. 'I don't actually have any money. . . . I'm afraid I lost rather heavily, in fact I had to ask several ladies if they would accept my IOUs. Biddy, why are you laughing?'

'It's worth having to walk to hear you say that,' Biddy spluttered, opening the front door and stepping out into the balmy night air. 'Goodbye, Mrs Maitland,

I'm sorry things have turned out this way, but we in the provinces do have our standards.'

And with that Biddy walked rapidly away down the path, leaving her erstwhile employer staring after her.

Chapter Eleven

It was one thing to walk out of the house in the middle of the night, laughing like a drain and talking airily about taxi cabs, but it was quite another thing to find one. Biddy had enough money, since she had been saving up for some time, and though the bulk of her cash, at Mrs Gallagher's advice, had been lodged in the Liverpool Savings Bank on Smithdown Place, she still had several shillings wedged into her pillow. But there are times when money alone is not sufficient. In a quiet, suburban area of a large city there is little call for taxi cabs at one in the morning, so Biddy walked and walked and walked and began to realise that she might as well continue to walk; she would not find a cab until she reached the city centre, by which time she would have little need of one.

But she was very tired and not a little despondent by the time she arrived on Paul Street. She felt that the Bradley family would begin to believe that she was dogged by ill-fortune since she had already turned up on their doorstep, almost destitute, on a previous occasion.

The Gallaghers had been gone a week and she had worked for the Maitlands for only five days, that was the worst of it. What would Mrs Gallagher say when she found that Biddy had walked out after less than a week? For that matter, what would the Bradleys say when she confessed that she had not stuck with the Maitlands? Would they think she should have stayed, tried again? Or would they look back to her previous arrival on their doorstep and decide that she had no backbone and was always giving up?

Still. The last time she had cast herself on the Bradleys' mercy had been a year ago and since then she had done quite well for herself, and had given as much as she could afford to Ellen and the baby. And the Bradleys were such a jolly crowd that they would probably simply welcome her in and tell her to put her bed-roll down on the floor by Ellen's and not give a thought to her reason for coming.

Paul Street, when she reached it, was quiet and dark, save for a tabby cat which came out of a warehouse like a shot from a gun when it saw Biddy and curled itself fondly round her legs, purring like a sewing machine.

'Hello, puss – been shut out?' Biddy asked, bending to stroke it, though this meant temporarily standing her pile of possessions down on the pavement for a moment. 'Well, you can walk with me if you like, but I'm afraid that's no guarantee that either of us will have a roof over our heads tonight.'

Biddy turned into Samson Court, and the cat followed her. There was only one gaslight in the court and it was at the far end; it barely illuminated No. 7, where the Bradleys lived, but Biddy stumbled up the steps and raised a hand to knock . . . then hesitated.

It really was not fair to wake the entire household and it was a mild enough night. She would sleep on the doorstep, close up against the front door, then if by some unlucky chance a scuffer came by she would explain that she lived here but had been accidently locked out. Or if anyone tried any funny business she would screech and bang on the door.

Having made up her mind Biddy unfastened her carpet bag, withdrew her pillow, and placed it on the top step, resting it against the door. It looked really comfortable, she thought, and pulling out her blanket, carefully spread that out below the pillow. The cat, inquisitive as all cats are, climbed up the steps and examined both pillow and blanket carefully, and then, apparently deciding that Biddy had unpacked her possessions especially for its benefit, it gave a prolonged purr of approval and settled down on the pillow, curling into a neat ball.

'You cheeky devil,' Biddy said, but rather appreciatively than otherwise. 'Oh well, two's company, cat.'

She lay down on the blanket with her head on the pillow. The cat opened a yellow eye and stared at her, then closed it decisively. Now's the time for sleeping, it seemed to say. Don't watch me or I'll never drop off.

'Nor me,' Biddy muttered. 'G'night, cat.'

The cat did not again open an eye, though it continued to purr – or was it snoring? Biddy was still trying to work it out when she fell asleep.

Biddy woke when someone screamed right in her ear. She sat up groggily, her heart racing uncomfortably fast, and as soon as she did so she remembered where she was and why. She was on the Bradleys' doorstep because Mr Maitland had tried to get into her bed, and she had doubtless just given someone the fright of their life.

She looked up; Ellen, in a pink party-dress with her coat buttoned up wrong and no hat, was staring down at her. Biddy saw that her friend's face was greyish and unhealthy-looking, that her once-lovely blonde hair was lack-lustre and hung straight as string, and then, as sleep retreated, she realised that the front door was still firmly closed and it was still not morning. The sky was grey with dawn, but she doubted whether anyone in any of the houses was yet stirring themselves. It stood to reason, therefore, that Ellen had not just emerged from the house behind Biddy. She was returning to it after what, judging from her appearance, had been a rather wild night out.

'Good God, Biddy, you give me the most awful skeer! I th-thought you was a feller with a 'uman body an' a cat's 'ead! What in Gawd's name are you a-doin', lying on our doorstep?'

'I *was* minding my own business and sleeping soundly,' Biddy said in an aggrieved voice. 'Did you have to shriek like that, Ellen? And come to that, where have you been until this hour?'

Ellen looked a little self-conscious. She put a hand defensively to her mouth and Biddy realised that it looked sore and swollen.

'There were a dance . . . only when it ended I'd gorra friend, an' 'e asked me 'ome to 'is place . . .'

'Oh come on, Ellen pull the other one! What really happened?'

'Don't talk so loud,' hissed Ellen, looking agonised. 'You know what me Mam's like, she'd tell the Father soon as look at 'im, an' 'e'd start goin' on about mortal sin an' duty an' what'll become o' me an' I just can't abide lecturin'. Come inside, I've gorra key 'ere somewheres.'

Biddy rolled up her bedding, stuffed everything back into her carpet bag, and watched with some amusement as Ellen went through her clothing until she ran the key to earth. She had hidden it so well that it took her several moments, but she found it at last.

'Gorrit!' she hissed triumphantly. 'Now don't mek a sound, Biddy, or we'll both gerrit in the neck.'

Biddy followed her friend as silently as she could and they gained the tiny back bedroom where all the girls slept, without rousing anyone. In the bedroom five girls were all packed into one not very big bed, three in the bottom, two in the top, and Ellen's bedding lay against the wall with Bobby in a cardboard box beside her.

''E's too big for that bleedin' box,' Ellen hissed, pulling off her coat and pink dress and kicking off her shoes. 'I'm gonna gerra cot nex' week. I seen a lovely one in Paddy's Market, goin' cheap.' She pointed at a spare bit of floor. 'Kip down there, Bid. We'll talk in the mornin'.'

Biddy was as quiet as she could be, but even so Bobby began to mutter.

'I'm awfully sorry, I think I woke him,' Biddy was beginning, but Ellen shook her head tiredly and leaned out of bed to take the child in her arms.

'No, it ain't that. 'E likes to sleep wit' 'is mam, so's 'e can 'ave to suck when 'e fancies it. Come on then, Bobby, Mam's 'ere.'

She was wearing a soiled underslip and now she slipped one shoulder strap down and put the baby to her breast. Leaning against the pillow, her eyelids heavy with sleep, she smiled across at Biddy. 'Eh, 'oo'd be a mam, Bid? But 'e'll sleep like a top once he's et, then I can sleep an' all.'

And since Biddy was extremely tired herself and Bobby not all that hungry, in a remarkably short space of time everyone in the small back bedroom was fast asleep.

Explanations had to wait until morning, but then Ellen and Biddy went downstairs early and got tea for the rest of the Bradley clan, save for Eric and Tom, who worked in the docks and had left much earlier.

'Now then,' Ellen said when they had made and poured the tea. 'I'll take a cup up to me Mam in a mo, but I wanna know what you're doin' here when you should be in bed at Ducie Street.'

'I've run away,' Biddy said uneasily. 'I know you'll say that I didn't give it a fair try, but that horrible old man, Mr Maitland, tried to get into my bed. He were drunk as a lord, Ell, but I wasn't having any. I hit him over the head with me amber egg and legged it here as fast as I could. So I don't have a job right now. And what were you doing out at two in the morning, you bad girl?'

'I told you, I went to a dance an' met this feller, an' 'e axed me back to 'is place an' – an' we talked an' that, so I din't notice 'ow the time were goin'...'

'How much did he give you?' Biddy cut in.

'Two bob,' Ellen said promptly, then clapped a hand to her mouth. 'Oh Biddy, don't you go sayin' things like that, what sort of girl d'you think I am?'

'Daft and desperate,' Biddy said gently. 'Before I dropped off last night I couldn't help thinking about our flat on Shaw's Alley and how happy we were. Your Mam's awful kind, Ell, but this isn't a good place to bring young Bobby up, there's too many of you.'

Ellen looked at her for a moment and then burst into tears. She sat down on a broken chair and rested her elbows on the rickety table and simply howled. Tears channelled down her dirty face and Biddy, rather at a loss, patted her shoulder and murmured comfort and after a few moments Ellen dried her eyes, hiccuped, and turned to her friend.

'Biddy, I know it, but no one else does! I can't gerra job because Bobby's too young to leave an' me Mam's a lovely woman but – but she's got worries of 'er own, she can't add my lad to 'em. That cot we need – I've gorra find money for it from somewhere, 'cos I don't 'ave no money any more, all what I 'ad I spent when Bobby were new. So – so what's a girl to do? I wait till Bobby's asleep, then I put on one of me good dresses an' go down to the docks. I – I can earn a bit that way, an' workin' at night, like, means if Bobby did wake there'd be Minnie or Alice or Sal to see to 'im. But I know it's no use...I'm trapped, Biddy, the way I always said I'd never be!'

'There must be a way out, and I'll think of it,' Biddy vowed, taking Ellen's hands in hers and squeezing them gently. 'But until I do, don't go walking the docks again, there's a dear. I don't want to sound like your Mam, but . . . it really isn't right, is it, Ellie, love?'

Ellen grinned, a quick, bright grin, so that Biddy suddenly saw, behind the exhausted grey face and the dirty, stringy hair, the bright and perky little blonde whom Mr Bowker had loved.

'It ain't right, but it's a bit o' fun, Bid, a bit o' life! An' some of the fellers is good to me, in their way. Just stuck 'ere, day after day, that ain't life, Bid, it ain't even existin'. It's what makes young girls go after fellers for a few bob . . . or float away on Mersey-tide, when things go wrong.'

Her voice was light but Biddy could hear the desperation behind the words.

'Ellen, don't! Think of Bobby, think of what would happen to him if you weren't here to take care of him! And I'll find a way out, I swear it. Look, I've got savings and you and your family have done me many a good turn when I was desperate. I'll give you some money now, and when I've got a job I'll come back and we'll work something out for you. Only you'll have to get yourself cleaned up – wash your hair, have a good scrub down, – otherwise I don't suppose anyone will take you on.'

'I'll clean up . . . only when you walk the docks it puts 'em off if you're too clean an' fresh lookin',' Ellen said frankly. 'They like to know you're on the game just by lookin' at you, especially the younger ones.'

'No doubt,' Biddy said faintly. 'Look, take your Mam her cuppa. I'll be off soon, before I lose my courage. See you later, Ell – I'll leave my carpet bag and my bedroll here if you don't mind. I don't want everyone to think I was kicked out of my last place.'

'Right, Bid, I'll keep an eye on your traps. An' now I'll start in to get meself smartened up.'

Ellen went over to the sink and picked up the enamel

bucket which she had filled earlier from the communal yard tap. She tipped some water into a basin and began to wash her face. When it was clean she dunked her head under the water and rubbed vigorously with the bar of red soap, rinsed her hair in the water remaining in the bucket, then groped for a towel. Biddy put it into her outstretched hands.

'There you are, you've got your nice fresh complexion back,' she said as Biddy rubbed. 'When your hair's clean and dry you'll be pretty little Ellen again. See you tonight, Ell.'

It seemed only sensible to go back to the same Employment Register on Bold Street and Biddy had every intention of doing just that. But she had not stayed with Ellen to have breakfast because she guessed that there was very little food in the house, so having given her friend the last of her money she had set off to walk to the centre of the city.

And whilst she was still some way from Bold Street, hunger had suddenly made itself felt. My stomach's rumbling so loud that if I go and see Mrs Aspinall she won't be able to hear me above the din, she thought. I'd best get myself some breakfast first.

She went through her coat pockets and found four pennies which would buy her something to eat. I'm miles from the savings bank on Smithdown Place, so I can't get at my money yet, Biddy reminded herself, but I'd kill for a hot drink and a mouthful . . . where can I get a fill-up for fourpence? She did not regret giving the money to Ellen, but she rather wished she had thought to hang onto enough for a proper meal.

Still. Employment Registers did not open early, she knew that, so there would be no harm in walking up the Scotland Road to Paddy's Market. There was a busy café there which opened early to serve the porters from the market – Thorn's cannie house the local's called it, though over the door it said *Miss Elizabeth and Miss Agnes Thorn – Dining Rooms*. Their food was excellent, Biddy knew, and their prices reasonable.

It was not far from Kettle's Confectionery, either, but Biddy no longer worried that she might walk into Luke, Kenny or Jack. She was a part of their past, they might not even recognise her. And her guilt feelings over Ma Kettle's death had long since ceased to worry her.

So she did not turn right when she came out at the end of Paul Street, she turned left, anticipation making her mouth water, her fingers clutching the four pennies in her pocket. Along Bevington Bush she went, walking briskly in the pale September sunshine, for it was another nice day. She turned right when she reached Wellington Street, then left into the Scottie. Thorn's cannie house was not far and she could smell it even before she could see it; I'll have a big mug of hot tea and one of their roast beef sandwiches, Biddy decided. Or shall I have a bacon sandwich? Or I could have a bowl of that thick lentil and vegetable soup with a hunk of bread on the side.

She reached Paddy's Market and stood on the edge of the pavement, waiting to cross. It was still very early but there was already a good deal of traffic, mostly horse-drawn since they were mainly farmers and wholesalers delivering to the shops and markets. She heard someone shout her name as she reached the centre of the road but took no notice; there were a lot of Irish living and working on the Scottie and Bridget was a popular name amongst them, Biddy a popular shortened form. The shouter could have meant anyone . . .

She gained the further pavement and was able to see, through the doorway of Thorn's, that Miss Aggie was doling out a plateful of hot peas and bacon chops to a burly market porter. The scent of the food wafted out – it did smell wonderful, would that, perhaps, be even nicer than soup or sandwiches?

She was still wondering when a hand seized her arm. She looked down at it. A small, fat hand, with dirty nails. A strangely familiar hand. With a very odd feeling indeed curdling her stomach, Biddy looked up the arm, over the shoulder, and straight into the face not a foot from her own.

A large, round face, with shrewd little grey eyes and a rat-trap mouth. A blob of a nose and hair tugged up into a tight little bun on top. A small, determined chin resting on three more chins, all much fatter and softer than the first. A scruffy black dress, the collar grey rather than white. A shawl around the shoulders, and a big white apron slung low round ample hips.

It was, without a shadow of a doubt, Ma Kettle.

'Biddy, oh Biddy, I'm that pleased to 'ave found you!' Ma Kettle's small eyes brimmed with tears of sincerity – or something. Biddy was still too shocked to find her erstwhile employer apparently risen from the dead to query Ma Kettle's motives. 'Ow I reproached meself when you run off . . . you disappeared, chuck, disappeared off the face o' the earth. I t'ought you was dead, I t'ought dreadful things!'

Biddy could only stare for a moment, then she found her tongue. 'They told me *you* were dead – I saw the wreaths and Mrs Hackett, her next door, she said what a loss it was,' Biddy said at last. 'It wasn't long after I left . . . I *saw* the flowers, honest I did. Glory, Ma, I even saw the funeral and someone standing near me said you was well-liked.'

'And isn't that no more'n the trut', now?' Ma Kettle said complacently. 'Poor but honest, us Kettles . . . ask

339

anyone. But that weren't me in the coffin, chuck. That were my poor sister, Mrs Olliphant. You remember her don't you?'

'Yes, though I never met her – but she didn't live with you, Mrs Kettle, she lived out Crosby way.'

'Oh aye. But she moved in to 'elp out when you went, chuck, an' not bein' used to city life, she stepped out from be'ind a tram and . . . well, that ain't a mistake you can make twice, if you understand me.'

'How – sad,' Biddy said. Ma Kettle sounded so matter of fact about the whole thing that it was difficult to sympathise. 'But the day I did leave you'd gone to Crosby for tea – that was to Mrs Olliphant's, I assume?'

For the first time, Ma Kettle looked a little uneasy. 'Oh, aye . . . that. Well, my poor widdered sister were findin' things difficult, so she'd sold up . . . I t'ought if she moved in wi' us, took an 'and on the counter or in the boilin' kitchen . . . Luke was gerrin' wed as you'll recall, so 'is room would 'ave been goin' beggin' . . .'

'And you made the arrangements the day before I went? Why did you do that, Mrs Kettle?'

'It were Kenny, mainly,' Mrs Kettle said. 'What say we 'ave a bite o' grub at the cannie 'ouse, queen? We can talk in there.'

'All right,' Biddy said readily. She thought it would be a rare treat to be bought a meal by Ma Kettle, who so hated parting with her cash! 'I'm awful hungry though; I've not eaten since teatime yesterday.'

Ma Kettle sighed but waddled beside her into Thorn's and nodded glumly as Biddy ordered thick soup, roast beef sandwiches and plum duff.

'A nice cuppa tea will do me . . . an' mebbe a wet nellie,' she told the woman who came for their order. 'Still, the young 'ave to be fed.'

'Good thing they's 'ungry, Ma Kettle, or you wouldn't

sell so many of them sweets you make,' the woman observed. She went over to the food hatch and bawled their order down it, then turned back to them. 'Shall I make that two teas? Eatin' without a bevvy's thirsty work.'

Biddy said tea would be fine for her, too, and then turned expectantly back to Ma Kettle. 'Well, Mrs Kettle? So you left me to do all the work and went over to Crosby to your sister's place. Why was that?'

'Kenny said either I give you time off an' – an' pay you a trifle every week or 'e'd tell the Father, *an'* the nuns, *an'* me brother Perce what moved to Australy ten year agone, that I weren't good to you,' Ma Kettle said defensively. 'Blackmail, that was – from me own son! But I'd got used to you, Biddy, an' I couldn't see as 'ow I could manage, unless me sister Olliphant would come an' give an 'and. See, I'd been sendin' 'er the odd bob or two ever since Mr Olliphant fell off 'is perch, an' it wouldn't 'ave cost me nothin' to 'ave 'er to live. So back we comes from Crosby, wi' Mrs Olliphant an' 'er traps, all smiles, to tell you t'ings was goin' to be easier in future ... an' we found your note. Oh, our Kenny were mad wi' me! 'E rang a chime round my lugs, 'e said it were no more'n I deserved ... an' 'e moved out! Never come near nor by 'e din't, not till me sister Olliphant's funeral. An' even then 'e wouldn't come back to live, 'cos 'e ain't never forgive me for you runnin' off. Said I'd ruined 'is life, I seems to 'member,' she finished, miserably.

'I think I know what Kenny meant, but it wasn't true, I promise you,' Biddy said, unexpectedly touched by the expression on the older woman's face. It occurred to her that Ma Kettle really had aged considerably in the time they had been apart and she really did love Kenny; it must have cut her to the quick to find she had lost him. And Luke, being married now, would be as good as lost too, which only left Jack, who was at sea eleven months out of the twelve.

'No, I dessay it weren't,' Ma Kettle said, just as their food arrived. There was a pause whilst the woman slapped the dishes down on the rough wooden table, then Ma Kettle gave a cavernous sigh, picked up her tea, took a swig and eyed Biddy hopefully. 'But if you was to come 'ome, Bid, so's our Kenny could see for 'imself I 'adn't ruined 'is life? I'd be rare obliged. . . . I'd pay a fair wage, I'd keep young Penny what does me 'ousework, you could 'ave two days a week off. . . . No one's got a way wi' fudge like you, queen. You took the worry out of the work some'ow, an' I trusted you, never doubted you'd do your best. Well, what d'you say?'

'Well, my present job pays ten shillings a week all found . . .' Biddy began, thinking that this was the kindest way to close the conversation. But Ma Kettle, though she heaved a sigh, came back at once.

'Shall we say 'leven? An' all day Sunday an' Thursday afternoons off? Would that suit?'

Biddy was casting round for an excuse when she realised that Ma Kettle was doing her best, not only to make things up with Biddy, but to get her son back. And the job would not be for ever, but for a period limited, this time, by Biddy's own desire to stay with the Kettles and by the return of the Gallaghers to Liverpool. Besides, Ma Kettle's an old lady and I, Biddy reminded herself, have all my life before me.

'Well, I suppose . . .' she began, to be instantly seized and hugged against Ma Kettle's large and surprisingly soft bosom.

'Biddy, luv, you won't regret it, I promise you! Oh, you always was one o' the fambly . . . only I treated you bad, I admit it – there! But now . . . now t'ings will be so different you won't know us, chuck. Oh, you'll never regret this day! And aren't I a lucky old woman to 'ave found you agin?'

'Iceberg on the port bow!'

The Bosun's stentorian voice was laced with panic. They had entered pack ice hours before, in the early evening, but now, at midnight, they had just hauled the trawl, a trawl loaded with more than sixty baskets of cod. Not until the trawl was safe inboard did they alter course and manoeuvre themselves into clear water once more.

And now every man on board who could be spared was down in the fishpounds, gutting, but the Skipper had ordered that the trawl be shot again immediately. They had found fish and could not afford to steam into safer waters, not whilst every haul brought such rich rewards. So the crew had seen the trawl crash down into the blackness of the ice-scummed sea and then returned to the gutting, talking of their next meal, of the sleep which their bodies needed, of a game of cards and a hot drink.

And now the iceberg. It was enormous, but because the visibility in an icefield is always reduced by the black frost which rises from the pack, icebergs round here were far more dangerous than one encountered in open water and good visibility, and though the ship had a searchlight on her bows it scarcely penetrated the black frost.

They could all see the 'berg now, catching a million colours from the ship's searchlight and multiplying them within its crystal castles. It came on slowly, almost gracefully, surrounded by the debris of collisions with other 'bergs.

'She's not fifty yards off our port bow . . . by God, she's a big 'un!'

As the Bosun's voice rang out the Skipper opened the bridge window and leaned out. 'This one's keeping her distance but there'll be others. I want two hands on watch . . . Taff, Greasy, you'll do. Don't budge from the bows until I give you the word and shout at once if you even think you've got a sighting. At once . . . right?'

'Right,' Dai and Greasy said in chorus, taking up their position in the bows of the ship. It was the only chance you had of an early sighting . . . but it was cold work out here, with the sea freezing in the scuppers when a wave came inboard before it had a chance to run out again.

'How does the ole man know there's others?' Greasy said, straining his eyes into the darkness ahead. 'As 'e gorra crystal ball in there or somethin'?'

The Mate was standing by the winch drum, staring ahead. He half-turned towards them as Greasy spoke.

'He can tell by the growlers round her, for one thing. She's met other 'bergs, smashed into 'em, moved on. And you get a feel for 'em, in the end. Good thing, or . . .'

He turned just as a huge wave came racing out of the darkness, straight at the ship. It crashed down on the deck, causing the whole ship to shudder, and bowled Greasy and Dai over, then smashed them against the whaleback. The Mate was still clinging onto the winch drum but now he was turning to make a funnel of his hands, warning the bridge.

'DEAD AHEAD! DEAD AHEAD! DEAD AHEAD!'

'It's another bleedin' iceberg,' Greasy said, staggering to his feet. 'That must 'ave been its bow wave.'

And just as Dai was preparing for the impact there was a tremendous explosion, so loud that he was temporarily deafened by it. He stared into the darkness and saw, as the ship veered and bucked, great chunks of ice which had obviously been hurled sky-high by the force of the explosion, hurtling down again into the ragged sea.

All around them was pandemonium. The Skipper

roared to the man at the wheel to starboard his helm, then shot open the bridge window.

'Where away? Taff, where away?'

Dai and Greasy, still half-deafened, got the message. They hurled themselves at the bows. If the wild and natural evasive action of the *Bess* had chanced to turn them in the wrong direction then the danger was still imminent, death still hovered out there in the black frost and the dark.

And then, suddenly, the blackness began to ease; above their heads the sky showed pale and the water came into view – clear water, the wave-crests restless still, but unencumbered by either pack ice or 'bergs.

'All clear ahead,' Dai shouted. 'All clear ahead! All clear ahead!'

He looked across at Greasy; his friend was grinning and Dai knew that an equally idiotic grin stretched his own lips.

'What 'appened?' Greasy asked, but Dai did not know, he could only turn to the Mate, drooping now by the winch drum.

'She exploded; icebergs do, sometimes. Something to do with the water and air temperature,' Harry said. 'Wonder what happened to the trawl? We're still towing ... if it hasn't been crushed by the ice or had the cod-end torn to shreds.'

'When'll we know?' Dai asked. He was suddenly aware that he ached in every limb, that his mouth was dry and that he needed hot, sweet tea and a long sleep. But they would still be gutting down in the pounds and he – and everyone else – was still on watch.

The Mate consulted his watch. 'We'll haul in around three hours,' he said. 'Best go below now, Taff, in fours. Tell the hands, and say gutting will have to wait. Weary men can't haul.'

There was no argument. Dai went to the fish pounds to pass on the message; Greasy dashed onto the mess deck and grabbed a sandwich and a hot drink. He carried a slopping mug of tea for Dai too, and thrust it into his hand as the other man struggled out of his deck gear.

'Ere, get that down you,' he commanded. 'I could sleep for a week, but we'll be lucky to get two hours.'

'Aye,' Dai said, drinking the tea down straight off and getting wearily into his bunk. Harry and the Skipper would still be up there, working out a course which would take them clear of the pack ice but not of the feeding grounds. They would discuss what to do if the trawl was irreparably damaged, how long it would take to fit the spare – they always carried a spare – how many men could shoot the trawl once it had been hauled, how many might then go off watch.

Could he do it, if he was lucky enough to get promotion, become an officer? Could he be that dedicated, that selfless? But it had been a long and worrying night; before he had made up his mind, he was asleep.

It was strange being back in the Kettle household; strange and not too pleasant. Every time Biddy looked round the living-room she remembered how unhappy she had been here, but then she scolded herself. Everything was to be different now, Ma Kettle had promised and she would, Biddy was sure, keep her word. She had given Biddy Luke's room just for a start, no more talk of sharing, and had even gone out and bought a plant to put on the window-sill.

'Makes it more 'omely,' she had said proudly, centring the small and stringy aspidistra in the middle of the window-sill. 'Them's me summer curtings; I'll change 'em for me winter ones in a month or two. You'll like me winter ones; they're a nice warm brown.'

'These are fine,' Biddy had assured her. She did not like to say that it was possible she would not be here at winter-curtain time. 'The room will suit me very well, Mrs Kettle.'

But now, down in the boiling kitchen, she was preparing a big bowl of fudge whilst Ma Kettle sat in the shop and, she assumed, treated – and cheated – the customers as usual. Biddy had greased her tins, boiled her sugar, butter and conny onny and was about to test it for setting when the door opened softly and a skinny young girl entered. She had hair so red that you could have warmed your hands at it, a great many freckles, green eyes fringed with light lashes, and a beaming smile. She was wearing a garment which might have been brown or dark blue once, over which had been draped a very large and rather dirty apron which hid all of her person except for her cracked and patched boots.

'Ello, Miss. I'm Penny Ellis; I live wi' me aunt an' uncle in 'Ighsmith Court an' I'm fourteen come next March. I does me best to keep the 'ouse tidy an' I'm that glad you've come! Miz Kettle do get lonely . . . an' I likes to be 'ome in time for me supper.'

'I'm Bridget O'Shaughnessy, my friends call me Biddy, and I'm past seventeen,' Biddy said gravely. 'How do you do, Penny? I hope we shall be friends and I hope you'll get home in time for your supper now I'm here to help out.'

'Oh, you isn't to be axed to 'elp,' the child said anxiously, with a quick glance towards the shop, though it was unlikely that Ma Kettle could have heard a word they said. She was dealing, rather raucously, with a line of small children, mostly clutching ha'pennies or farthings. 'You're the best worker Miz Kettle ever 'ad, and she don't want you bein' driv into goin' off, she told me an' Gertie we'd gorra mind our manners wi' you.'

'Who's Gertie?' Biddy asked, dipping a spoon into her bubbling fudge and dripping it into the jamjar full of water standing by. 'I don't recall Mrs Kettle mentioning a Gertie.'

'Gertie's 'er gofor,' Penny explained. 'She's only eight but she comes in after school an' runs errands an' that. Gertie Parr, 'er name is. She's one o' them raggety kids.'

Biddy was about to remark, rather hotly, that Penny was no fashion-plate, when the door creaked open once more and a very tiny child burst in.

'Gorrany erran's, Miss?' the girl asked. She was thin as a pipe-cleaner, with fluffy hair that looked as though it had been cut with nail scissors and huge, round eyes which dominated her pale, thin little face.

'Not for me thanks, Gertie – you are Gertie? But you'd best ask Mrs Kettle,' Biddy said, feeling as though she had strayed into the workhouse, for the child Gertie was indeed raggety. She wore a very dirty man's shirt with a shawl tied round her waist and she was barefoot.

'Oh. Right.' Gertie padded purposefully across the kitchen and into the shop. They heard her shrill voice demanding, 'Gorrany erran's, Miz Keckle?' and then Penny jerked her head conspiratorially towards the shop.

'You thought I were bein' nasty when I said she were a raggety, but I weren't, were I, Biddy? An' she's a great gun, Gertie. Skeered o' nothin', not even o' Ma Kettle. She'll put 'er in 'er place right sharp, if the missus tries to bully 'er.'

'Well, that's good to hear,' Biddy said, taking her fudge off the stove and beginning to beat it with a big wooden spoon. 'Because I'm the same, and I hope you will be too Penny.'

'Jobs is scarce,' Penny said, sighing. 'I gets two bob a week – imagine that, Biddy, two bob! It keeps me uncle from thumpin' me, which is worth a bully or two.'

'Two bob,' Biddy said wonderingly. Leopards did not change their spots then, not underneath. Ma Kettle was still an old skinflint and would be until she died, but at least she was making an effort where Biddy was concerned.

'Aye, an' she on'y takes a few pence off if I'm slow, or eat too much, dinnertimes,' Penny said, plainly misunderstanding Biddy's wondering tone. 'So I don't wanna lose the job, like.'

'I'll tell you what, we'll stick up for each other,' Biddy said, visited by inspiration. That way, she could do her best to see that Penny got a fair deal without terrifying the poor kid. 'I reckon this is thick enough, don't you? Have a taste, tell me if it's smooth.'

Greatly daring, Penny peeled a small ball of fudge off the proffered spoon and sucked blissfully. 'It's jest right,' she declared as soon as it was swallowed. 'I'll get you the tins, Miss . . . I mean Biddy!'

When the sweetshop closed down for the day and Biddy and Ma Kettle had shared a meal of boiled ham, boiled onions and boiled potatoes – Penny was not an inventive cook – they sat one on either side of the living-room fire and talked for a bit.

'I'm axin' our Kenny round to tea, Sunday, when we're closed,' Ma Kettle said, eyeing Biddy anxiously. 'I ain't askin' you to tell no lies, Bid – poor but honest, that's us Kettles – but if you could 'splain to Kenny that you'd 'ave gone anyway, even if I 'adn't left you all that work, I'm 'opin' 'e'll see reason an' come back to us.'

'I'll explain, and I won't need to tell any lies, because I would have gone, anyway,' Biddy said. She could scarcely hurt everyone by telling Ma Kettle that Kenny's heavy-handed pounces would have driven her away regardless, but at least she could make it clear to Kenny that his mother was not entirely to blame. 'Does Kenny have a ladyfriend now? Or someone he likes more than he likes the others?'

'Our Kenny's been sweet on you ever since you walked t'rough that door,' Ma Kettle said impressively. 'Never looked at another girl, never mentioned one, neither. Why, if a lad casts aside 'is own Mam because 'e sez she ain't good to a gel . . . well, that tells you, Bid.'

'It was just because he didn't know many girls, I'm sure that was the reason,' Biddy said hastily. 'I do have a boyfriend, Mrs Kettle. He and I plan to wed next Easter at the latest.'

'Well, don't you go tellin' Kenny,' Ma Kettle said anxiously. 'We've 'ad one lorra bother, let's not 'ave another. Face Easter when we come to it, eh?'

'All right, but I do hate deceiving him,' Biddy said uneasily. 'Still, he'll have to come to terms with it sooner or later. And right now, Mrs Kettle, if it's all right by you, I'm going up to bed.'

'Certainly, certainly! Will I bring you tea in the mornin', dearie?' Ma Kettle asked, rubbing her plump palms anxiously against her skirt. 'Only young Penny don't get 'ere till eight.'

'I'll bring you a cup,' Biddy said magnanimously. A wage of eleven bob, she felt, entitled Ma Kettle to an early morning cuppa at the very least! 'Would half past seven suit you?'

''Alf past seven 'ud be prime,' Ma Kettle said, beaming so widely that her eyes all but disappeared behind the shelves of her cheeks.'Eh, you allus was a good girl, our Bid!'

The first thing Biddy did on gaining her room was to heave a huge sigh and sit down on the bed.

Why was life so complicated, she thought crossly? There she was, contented with her lot, just waiting for Dai to pop the question so that she might live happily ever after, and what happened? First, Stuart Gallagher got a job in Edinburgh, then 'Matey Maitland' tried it on with her so that she had no option but to leave his employ, and then having agreed to return to Kettle's Confectionery (upon certain terms, naturally) she had realised that Ma Kettle was hopeful not only that she would bring Kenny back to the Kettle fold, but that she might marry him into the bargain.

A nice little daughter-in-law who would make sweets, sell 'em, keep Ma Kettle comfortable in her old age . . . oh yes, that would be a complication all right!

But she had made it clear that Dai and she were to get married, and Ma Kettle – and Kenny – would just have to accept it.

Biddy sighed. There was no easy chair, no little gas fire in this room, but she had been really spoiled by the Gallaghers. Ma Kettle would suppose that Biddy would spend most of her time down in the living-room because that would be a natural, family-like thing to do and providing Ma Kettle with someone to talk to of an evening was what she was being paid for, amongst other things. So if she came up here once the cold weather started she would have to wrap her blanket round her and wear her winter socks over her cotton stockings. But right now she was warm enough, so she sat down on the bed and got out her pad and pencil. She was writing a nice, long letter to Dai and now she really did have something to tell him! There was Mr Maitland's strange behaviour for a start; she would have to tell Dai all about that, otherwise he would not understand why she had once again changed her address.

Then there was this odd business with Ma Kettle . . . oh, and she must tell him that the funeral had been that of Mrs Olliphant and not Ma Kettle at all, otherwise he would think she had run mad for she had told him all about her guilt over Ma Kettle's supposed demise and he had assured her that the old slave-driver had had it coming to her, that it had been nothing whatsoever to do with Biddy's defection.

And there were the little girls, Penny and Gertie. Where on earth did Ma Kettle find them? And how could she get away with paying Penny two bob a week – and docking her money when she was slow – to do all the housework and cooking and to start work at eight in the morning and finish twelve hours later?

Kids like that need someone to look after 'em, Biddy thought as she scribbled on and on, putting her darling Dai in the picture. There should be a society or something for 'em – a trade union, like. She wrote that down, then suggested that it might be something for Mrs Gallagher to look into, when she came back from Edinburgh.

'She's always so busy with her good works so I'm sure she'd take on keeping an eye on kids' she wrote. 'I wish they hadn't gone, but there's good in all things. Hopefully, Ma Kettle and Kenny will get back together again, and I'm here to do the best I can for young Penny. Gertie, it seems, can look after herself! She gets sixpence a week out of the Kettle for running errands, plus some toffees now and then, and thinks herself mortal lucky.'

She sat and sucked the end of her pencil for a bit, then said that she was about to go to bed where, with a bit of luck, she would dream about her dear Dai, but in any event she would not close her letter for another week or two seeing as how she knew he had only sailed quite recently so would not be back for a bit.

Then Biddy undressed, got into bed, and slept soundly till morning.

Nellie missed Biddy terribly, and so did Elizabeth.

'What's the good of a castle and dogs and cats if they

aren't yours and you've no one to share 'em with any-way?' Elizabeth said crossly when her mother told her to count her blessings. 'I don't like me new school all that much and I miss me pals and you keep sighing all the while and me Da's never home . . . I wish we were back in Liverpool!'

'Yes, well,' Nellie said guardedly. She was not particularly happy herself and sometimes, when Lizzie was grumbling at full throttle, it was really hard not to say, *If it hadn't been for you and your secret love affair, madam, we could all be in Liverpool still.*

But that would have been madness, of course. It had soon been borne in upon Nellie that the infatuation, love, call it what you will, between Elizabeth and Dai was completely one-sided. Elizabeth scarcely mentioned him, took it for granted that he would come up to Edinburgh to see them but was no more and no less enthusiastic over the visit than over Biddy's, which she was sure could not be long delayed, not when Biddy heard how unhappy she was.

Nellie had been shocked when Biddy had written to tell the Gallaghers of Mr Maitland's midnight visit to her room, though Stuart had laughed and said, 'The dirty old dog!' in a way which made Nellie suspect that her husband was not as surprised as he might have been.

'Stu, did you know Mr Maitland had . . . had *tendencies*?' she asked suspiciously after Stuart had had Biddy's letter read aloud to him. 'Because if so, it was wrong of you not to tell me. I would never have let Biddy stay with them had I suspected any such thing!'

'I didn't know he was going to cradle-snatch in his own home, but I did know he'd an eye for a pretty girl,' Stuart admitted. 'What a crass, insensitive fool the man must be, to get drunk and try it on with his wife's own maid!'

'But if she hadn't been his wife's maid, and if he'd carried on away from home, you'd have thought it acceptable behaviour?' Nellie said in a tone of sweet reasonableness. 'Is that what you're trying to say, Stu?'

'No, no indeed,' Stuart said hurriedly, seeing the trap his beloved was digging for him. 'What a swine you must think me, sweetheart.'

'You aren't a swine; just thoughtless,' Nellie said. 'Oh, Stu, I wish we'd never come, that I do! Poor little Biddy!'

'Judging by her letter, Biddy took very good care of herself,' Stuart said, chuckling. 'She hit him over the head and tipped him out of bed, then walked out on him. That isn't exactly the action of a milksop.'

'No, I suppose not. But I still feel we let Biddy down.'

'You don't like it here after all, do you?' Stuart said shrewdly. 'I didn't think you would, but you seemed so sure!'

'It's all right, it's just a bit strange, a bit different. And we've only been here a month, after all,' Nellie said with assumed brightness. 'I've written back to Biddy, telling her how sorry I am, and saying I hope she'll be happy with Ma Kettle this time round. And now I'm going shopping in the city with Elizabeth. She wants a new hockey stick.'

The *Bess* continued to steam on in appalling weather. They had hauled the trawl, or what was left of it, and chopped it free because it was no use to anyone in its torn and splintered state, and had replaced it with the spare, though that had taken time because of the conditions and the icing up on deck.

They were in uncharted waters now, in the darkness at the top of the world, and there was muttering from some of the old hands that not even the sort of catches they were taking would be worth the risk. But still they shot the trawl, hauled, filled the fish baskets, shot the trawl again. They had to pay for a new trawl now, on top of everything else, so they needed full fish pounds and the coal would have to be made to last.

Dai was at the wheel when they struck the iceberg, but it was no one's fault. The look-outs shouted their warning, but the *Bess* was steaming at speed, the collision could not be avoided. Dai kept the wheel hard over at the Skipper's instruction but it was as though the 'berg was pursuing them. The ship heeled over, came round . . . and the 'berg followed, so that the *Bess* seemed to slide almost willingly into that icy embrace.

It was the hidden ice which caught them, not the great cliff of blue, amethyst and rose which towered above them. Dai saw that they had turned in time to miss the eighth of it which surged and curtsied above water and began a quiet prayer of thanksgiving. Then, looking down from his perch he saw, through the pale green of the water, the spires and turrets of the ice-palace, pointing up, like the pale fingers of sirens, beckoning the *Bess* to her doom.

She crunched home with a terrible crashing, squealing roar, then she backed off as the Skipper's frantic orders brought her full speed astern, but it was too late for the port bow, with the teeth of the ice already imbedded in it. The Bosun shouted that they were holed and swung himself below to assess the damage, and Dai kept his eyes ahead and obeyed instructions though his back ached with tension and his eyes stung where the sweat ran down.

Presently Harry came and took the wheel from Dai's hands. 'You done all right; now it'll be all hands to clear up the mess below,' he said calmly. 'First time you've struck, eh? Well, it won't be the last, and you'll still go for your certificates if you've the mind.' He clapped Dai's shoulder. 'We'll seal the damage with canvas, cement, anything that'll keep the sea out. The donkey-engine will pump out any water left. We've coal to get us home, full fish pounds, and the engine's still working. We've done well, Taff.'

Dai relinquished the wheel and rubbed his arms, walking off the bridge. As he went below, the Bosun was rounding up any crew not already working.

'Taff . . . icebreaking on deck. Mal, you're for the forward hold with the working party already down there. Bandy, you won't be needed here for a bit so you can clear ice with the rest. Where's the galley boy? Ah, make a big pot o' tea, lad, an' see all hands get a dram o' rum in each mug.'

It was so down-to-earth, so sensible! Dai went and got his foul weather gear, stopped off at the mess deck for his tea with rum, felt it coursing hot through him, and went up on deck.

Dai could see, now, that the *Bess* was heeling to port, partly from the strike and the resultant flooding, partly because of the weight of ice. He joined the other men, axes already beginning to bite. They could not afford to let her list too far or she'd turn turtle, leaks or no leaks.

Dai raised his axe shoulder-high and brought it down on the great mound of ice he knew to be the whale back. Beside him, the galley boy used a marlin spike to good effect, beyond him, Greasy worked like a maniac, ice chips diamonding the front of his smock.

A man's world. But probably every man on board, at the moment of impact, had thought of his woman. If I live through this, Biddy O'Shaughnessy, you're mine, Dai had told himself. I love you, I'll fight for you – and anyway, you're mine as I'm yours. No more shilly-shallying, no more trying to be fair. Biddy and me are two halves which together make up the whole. When – if – I get home I'm going to tell her so.

The thought comforted him through the trials and dangers of the rest of that long and dangerous voyage.

'Biddy! Eh, you look fine – well, well, well! Mam said a surprise, but I never thought it 'ud be our Biddy, back wi' the Kettles again!'

Kenny looked fine too, Biddy thought. He had grown up since she had seen him last, he was finer-drawn somehow, his face less complacent, less pudgy altogether.

Ma Kettle had brought Kenny through into the living-room and sat him down on the couch beside Biddy and gone out, ostensibly to see to the tea but really, Biddy realised, so that she and Kenny would have a chance to discuss the circumstances under which she had fled from the household. Well, she told herself, I shall do my best to see that Ma doesn't get all the blame; poor old soul, she's done her best, now, to put things right. And she does love Kenny so, he ought to come back.

'Hello, Kenny, it's nice to see you,' she said now, smiling up at him. He was wearing a dark suit and a blue necktie, and the spots which had marred his neck and jawline had disappeared, leaving his skin as smooth as anyone else's. Whilst he lived at home Ma Kettle had cut his hair once every six weeks or so but now Biddy supposed a barber must be doing it, and making a very much neater job of it too. Kenny had a nice-shaped head and his neck was clean and fluff free – a considerable improvement on the old Kenny. 'I expect you're awful busy, because I've been back wi' your Mam for over a month and not seen you earlier. How are the exams coming along?'

'Yes, I've kept pretty busy; and thanks to your 'elp I passed the first lot of exams last summer,' he said at once. 'I did awright – the boss was pleased wi' me. Though I shan't be takin' exams much longer if there's a war. Me sight's not up to much, but the Army will take me on, I reckon. And what about you, Biddy? How've you been? Where did you go when you . . . when you left? Did me Mam tell you what a tizz we was in – me specially? I worried about you, our Biddy, I really did.'

'That was kind, but I went and shared an old schoolfriend's flat, we stayed together for a long time,' Biddy explained. 'We'd always got on well, me and Ellen, and I worked in the city doing deliveries for a gown shop and lived with Ellen until she . . . well, until she decided to go home.'

'Oh ah. And then?'

'Oh, then I took a job in service. I liked it, they were such good people, so kind to me. But Mr Gallagher was moved to Edinburgh, just for a year or so to start up a new magazine, and I – I didn't like the new people so I moved out and I was staying with Ellen's Mam in Paul Street when I met Mrs Kettle again and she offered me my old job back. Only on – well, on better terms. And I took it.'

'Bet she begged, acos she's always said it weren't just her what made you run away from us. Is that true, Bid? Were there – other things?'

Biddy looked up at him. 'Yes, Kenny,' she said frankly. 'I wasn't old enough to know how to tell you I didn't want you as anything but a friend. I'm sorry, but it frightened me rather. I felt trapped.'

Echoes of Ellen, Biddy thought as the words left her mouth, but she knew they were true. Kenny had made her feel trapped, as though she had no right to spurn his advances whilst living under his mother's roof. But Kenny was nodding understandingly.

'Aye, I know what you mean. And I know because I did 'ave the feeling meself that you'd no right to refuse me. Awful young beggar, weren't I? But I know a bit better now, Bid. You won't catch me carryin' on like that again, I promise.'

'Then you will come back? You'll live with your Mam again? I think you should, Kenny, because I shan't be here for always and she does get so lonely. The young girl who does the housework whilst your Mam runs the shop is a nice little thing, but she lives out and she's a bit in awe of Mrs Kettle. It doesn't make chatting or having a laugh any too easy – well, it was the same for me last time I worked for your Mam.'

'My Mam's all right if you know how to handle her,' Kenny said knowingly. 'Yes, I'm movin' back, for the time bein', anyroad. There's nowhere like your own place an' all I've had since I left has been a room in someone else's house.'

'But it's done you good, Kenny,' Biddy said thoughtfully. 'You were a boy before, but now you're a man. And that doesn't happen when you're dependent on your Mam for everything you know, it happens when you take on responsibility for yourself.'

'Aye, I reckon you're right,' Kenny said. 'When you left here, Bid, you was a frightened little thing, you scarce said boo to a goose. But now you're a young woman with a mind of your own – I guess my Mam realised it, or she'd never have offered you a decent wage. It ain't that she doesn't want you real bad,' he added hastily, 'it's just her business sense. It steps in whenever she'd rather give a bit, act generous, and stops her smartish. Awful to be like that. Folk say she's mean, you know.'

'Well, she is a bit tight with her cash,' Biddy said mildly. 'Not to her boys, but to everyone else. She gives her little errand girl sixpence a week and the kid walks or runs miles to get the ingredients your Mam needs, to say nothing of shopping around Great Homer when she ought to be in bed.'

'That's business to Mam,' Kenny said a little too complacently, Biddy thought. 'But you'll keep her on the straight and narrer, see she treats folk fair, won't you, Bid? She means well, but . . .'

'I will whilst I'm here. But when I leave you'll have to do it yourself, Kenny,' Biddy told him. 'One day she'll not be able to manage the shop alone, either. Why don't you marry some nice young girl who would gladly help out for a decent wage? Then you could concentrate on moving up at work, knowing your Mam was well looked after.'

'When I marry it won't be to gerra minder for me Mam,' Kenny said a trifle reproachfully. 'Talkin' of marriage, Bid . . .'

'Yes, I am talking of it, with my young man,' Biddy said quickly. She simply could not allow Kenny to say something he would later regret, even if it did hurt a little right now. 'We're planning an Easter wedding.'

He nodded gloomily, looking down at his feet. 'Aye. I always knew it 'ud happen once you got clear of us. You're far too pretty, chuck, to be hangin' around waitin' for a feller like me. So; do I know the bloke?'

'I don't think so, in fact I'm sure you don't know him, because he isn't from Liverpool at all, he's from the Isle of Anglesey. He's a seaman, he was on a coaster but he's distant-water trawling right now.'

'Oh ah? Good money in it, is there?'

'Enough,' Biddy said briefly. 'Ah, here comes the tea-trolley, I can hear it crashing along the hallway. Have you told your Mam yet that you'll be moving back in?'

Kenny grinned. He looked really nice when he grinned, Biddy thought. 'No, not yet. I'll surprise her when she comes in wi' the tea. And . . thanks Biddy.'

'Thanks? What for?'

'For comin' back after all the pain we must ha' caused

you. And for bein' so nice to me Mam. I'm fond of the old girl, in spite of everything.'

'Oddly enough, so am I,' Biddy said as the living-room door shuddered under the impact of a carelessly pushed trolley. 'Yes, against all the odds, I rather like your Mam!'

Chapter Twelve

It had been a beast of a voyage, they were all agreed on that. But somehow, with the ship's bows turned for home and their fish pounds groaning under the weight of fish, with everyone aboard secretly counting up the bonus he would have earned, and with just enough coal to get them right back into the mouth of the Humber, no one was inclined to quibble about the Skipper who had taken them into uncharted waters, rammed an iceberg – and got them out alive.

Dai worked like a Trojan because he felt that, by doing so, he was personally helping to get the ship back to Grimsby and that meant nearer to Biddy. The trip had taken much longer than usual, the Mate reckoned it would be seven full weeks before they docked, and he knew there would be worried faces at home whenever the ship's name was mentioned. But the *Bess*, which had borne up wonderfully under everything which had happened to her, was creaking home, unable to increase speed, eking out her coal, the donkey engine working day and night just to stop the forward hold from flooding, the radio useless, crushed into fragments by that collision with the 'berg.

The men, who had strained every nerve and sinew as the ship had made her way uncertainly through the dark, uncharted waters at the top of the world, could not rest even now. There was always work to be done. Ice had to be cleared every day, the gear kept oiled and in readiness, the leaks checked and plugged. Meals were a worry but the men thanked their stars for Bandy, who would some-how stretch the four weeks' rations to seven so that they didn't starve.

'Fish for breakfast, fish for dinner, fish for tea,' some-one grumbled, but they all understood that it was sheer necessity which sent Bandy down to the fish pounds for provisions. The flour and margarine were holding out, he reported, but they had eaten the last of the fresh vegetables a week ago and nearly all the tins were gone.

'Thank your lucky stars it ain't raw fish,' Greasy said quite sharply. 'Bandy's burnin' old socks in the galley to save coal for the engine room.'

Harry laughed. 'So long as they ain't my old socks. . . . Reckon I'll lose a toe this time, half my left foot's gone black. Did you see that gannet?'

They had all seen it, frozen to the rail, dead as a dodo before anyone realised that the black frost was rising again.

'Unlucky, that,' Mal grumbled. 'Someone should've noticed; as bad as having an albatross dead is a gannet.'

'It's only bad luck if you kill it, not if it dies,' the Mate said patiently. 'All birds have to die in the fullness of time.'

'Not on the rail, fruzz to it, its wings half out,' another man said. 'Still, I reckon that's not goin' to bring bad luck.'

'Except to the gannet,' Dai put in, and got a reluctant laugh.

'That's it, Taff, you cut us down to size – what's a Welshman think is unlucky, then?'

'A woman aboard? A seal swimmin' alongside? I dunno that I believe in that sort o' bad luck, do you, Grease? Mebbe we're more practical on the West side o' the country than you Easteners.'

Greasy shook his head. 'Nah, I don't believe in that

sort o' bad luck. You makes your own, I reckon. Bad management, bad decisions, but I've norra lorra faith in a bird makin' the difference between good an' bad, life an' death.'

They were still arguing good-naturedly about the differences between luck, chance, and human failure, when the Bosun's head appeared round the mess-deck door. 'Ice-breakers wanted; this lot's comin' below for a fag an' a cuppa. Come on fellers, let's be havin' you!'

'A quarter of bull's-eyes? Certainly, madam. In two separate bags? Of course. And two ounces of peppermint fondant? Here we are, then.'

Biddy was working in the shop, enjoying the chance to meet customers and mingle with people instead of always slogging away by herself in the boiling kitchen. She had been allowed to take over in the shop for two reasons. One was that Ma wanted to do some Christmas shopping and the other was that Ma thought it would do Biddy good.

'You're lookin' that long-faced an' mis'rable, it's time you 'ad a change,' she had declared earlier in the day. 'Makin' yourself ill over some worthless young feller what don't know you're born . . . jest acos he's not writ for weeks . . . fellers are all the same, no doubt 'e's wettin' 'is whistle in some waterfront pub an' never givin little Biddy O'Shaughnessy a thought.'

'I rang the port authorities,' Biddy said, white-faced. 'They said the *Greenland Bess* was more than two weeks overdue. There's been no word from her for weeks, not even a radio message to another trawler. They can talk amongst themselves at sea the trawlers can, but they've not heard a word from her since she reached the fishing grounds three weeks or so back.'

'Likely the Lord'll look out for 'em,' Ma Kettle said

with all the comfortable blandness of one not personally concerned. 'Now gerrin there, queen, an' don't forget – no weighin' your thumbs!'

She gave Biddy a roguish wink, slung an extra shawl around the multitude of garments already disposed about her person, and rolled out of the doorway and into the busy street.

The customer, satisfied, left the shop and Biddy's mind turned in on itself once again. There was nothing she could do, that was the trouble. She made time during each day to ring for news of the *Bess* and always the voice answered, with compassion, that she was overdue by so many days and that there had been no word of her.

If we were married then at least I'd be able to go and watch for him; if we were married I could talk to other wives and girlfriends, Biddy thought, automatically turning to clean down a shelf and give the big glass bottles a rub whilst there was no one but herself in the shop. Oh if only Mrs Gallagher and Elizabeth were still in Liverpool, they would understand how desperately, horribly worried I am.

She could ring them! The thought, which crossed her mind just as a small, fat woman walked in with three even smaller and fatter children in tow, brought the first natural smile to Biddy's face for days. Mr Gallagher was in newspapers, he had to be on the telephone at home, she had the number in her room upstairs . . . she would ring as soon as Penny had a moment and could take over in here!

'Good morning, madam! Can I help you?'

The little, round woman looked gratified. She was a regular customer, more used to Ma Kettle's approach, which was to lean over the counter and clack the head of any child attempting to molest the trays of farthing dips.

'Mornin', chuck. Them's me grandchilder, they'd like

a penn'orth o' Kettle toffee an' I'll 'ave an ounce o'
peppermints.'

'A penn'orth *each*,' the smallest child squeaked, hanging
onto her grandmother's coat. 'Can I 'ave a sherbet dip?'

'If you're good for your Nan till your Mam comes
'ome,' the doting grandparent replied, smiling fondly
down at the three children. She turned to Biddy. 'Gorrany
kids, Missus? Eh, I wou'n't be wi'out 'em!'

Nellie was wending her way down Princes Street, trying
to buy Christmas presents, but despite the enticing displays in the shops, she had not enjoyed the orgy of buying
which she had indulged in over the last few days.

The truth was that Nellie was still, after more than two
months, terribly homesick. She could not forget that the
move to Edinburgh was all her doing, and she would
have begged Stuart to let them go home had her conscience allowed her to do so. But she had leapt to
conclusions about Lizzie and Dai, acted fast to prevent
what she was sure would have been a catastrophe, and
now she was stuck with the consequences.

So her Christmas presents this year would reflect the
state of her conscience rather than her love, she thought,
because she would buy Lizzie a wriggling, squiggling
puppy from the pet shop, since it was her fault that her
child was unhappy, and she would send Dai an expan-
sive fisherman's guernsey she had seen for sale in a
side-street, made of the thick, oily, island wool which
would keep him warm as toast under his foul-weather
smock. He was unhappy too, that stood to reason, but
first love would pass, given time, and one day he would
thank her for preventing him from declaring himself to
the uncaring Lizzie.

Nellie had always fought against having a dog, feeling
that one should spend any spare money on one's fellow

human beings and not indulge an animal, but that was before she had lived in a cold, rambling Scottish country house and got to know the previous owner's dogs – Mattie, Angus, Willy and Bosh.

The dogs were looked after, fed, exercised and generally seen to by the gardener, old Jamie, but they soon realised that they had found a soft touch in the Gallaghers and insinuated themselves into the kitchen on every possible occasion.

'They're cold, they need to dry out and get comfy,' Elizabeth would plead, letting the four very large and shaggy retrievers into the kitchen, where they took up far more than their fair share of the hearth. 'Oh, they're the only things I'll miss about this place when we go home!'

Well, with a puppy of her own, at least she would not be able to reproach Nellie over having introduced her to the joys of dog-owning and then taking her away from dogs when Stuart's job came to an end . . . and it couldn't end soon enough for Nellie. As soon as she was certain Elizabeth did not share Dai's feelings she allowed her homesickness full rein and simply concentrated on longing for home. It was all very well to tell herself that Dai would thank her one day, but first, she knew, he would suffer dreadfully when he discovered that Lizzie really did not love him. His pain would hurt Nellie, but she could do nothing about it because discover he would; Elizabeth, sensible girl that she was, would never pretend an affection she did not feel.

And she had let Biddy down too, practically thrown her into the arms of that terrible old lecher, because she hadn't thought of a complication like that when she'd rushed into moving to Scotland the way she had. So to salve Nellie's conscience anew, Biddy would have one of those wonderful pleated skirts in the Black Watch tartan, and one of the very fine dark green wool jumpers to go with it. Unless I buy her a honey-coloured jumper, with a chocolate-coloured skirt, and forget the tartan, Nellie thought now, gazing into another window. Or there's always blue . . .

Fancy Biddy going back to Ma Kettle, though. Her first letter from Kettle's Confectionery had been so funny and sweet, the whole family had read it and laughed and agreed with Lizzie, who had announced that she was desperately homesick for Biddy, and couldn't they ask her up for Christmas, please?

'We'll ask,' Nellie had said doubtfully. 'But judging from what Biddy says, Ma Kettle will want her there for the holiday.'

'Oh, let the old horror want, for once,' Elizabeth said impatiently 'Bribe her, Mum – tell her Dai might come to Scotland for Christmas. She likes our Dai.'

Oh, wouldn't it be nice, Nellie thought now, staring into a window full of scarlet and green, wouldn't it be nice if Dai liked Biddy instead of my dear little daughter, and could be persuaded that it was Biddy he wanted to marry? All I want is their happiness, both of them – all three of them – she told anyone up above who happened to be listening. If only people fell in love sensibly, then there would be no such thing as the terrible ache that was unrequited love. She could scarcely forbid Elizabeth to ask Dai up for Christmas, but she did so hope something would come along to prevent his arrival – a more pressing invitation, anything!

But after a moment she shook herself and walked on. It was no use wishing, she would circumvent Elizabeth's invitation if she possibly could; she would even write to Dai privately and tell him the truth – that Liz was no longer interested in him in that sort of way. But it was no use meeting trouble half-way, she had watched the post carefully ever since arriving here and Dai was playing fair; he had not written to Elizabeth once. It will all work out, she decided, moving along to look in the next window. She always worried far too much and usually for no reason that anyone else could understand.

Nellie peered through the glass and tried to show an interest in a window full of snow-boots. She had not yet decided what to buy her dear Stuart; she had best look at a few more shops before turning her footsteps home-wards once more.

Elizabeth was in the kitchen with the dogs when the telephone rang. She was tempted not to answer it because it was always for her father, but conscience was stronger than an urge to go on sitting before the fire, stroking Mattie's tangled fur and sipping at a cup of hot cocoa which the maid, Flora, had given her before going upstairs to tackle the bedrooms.

Flora hated the telephone, which she seemed to regard as an instrument of the devil, so Elizabeth got to her feet on the third ring, loped across the kitchen and into the hall. She sank down on the edge of the square hall table and snatched the receiver from its rest.

'Hello – Elizabeth Gallagher speaking.'

Faint and far off, she heard pennies clattering and someone pushed Button A. Someone was ringing from a call-box, then. Elizabeth brightened. It might even be a friend of hers for a change.

'Hello . . . you're through, caller.'

Another slight clatter, and then a voice spoke, faint but clear. Elizabeth's heart gave a great, happy bound. She would have known that voice anywhere!

'Biddy, it is you, isn't it? Oh, it's grand to hear your voice, absolutely grand! Are you comin' up for Christmas? Do, do come for Christmas. We'll have such fun . . . Dai might come too, if he's back home and has long

369

enough between voyages. You'd like that, you two get on rather well, I've always thought. Biddy?'

The voice sounded fainter now, further off. But even so, Elizabeth could hear the desolation in it.

'Dai's ship is posted as missing, Liz. It's almost two weeks overdue. So he – he may not come home for Christmas at all.'

All Elizabeth's happiness drained away; Dai's ship was missing? This was terrible, a dreadful tragedy, surely Biddy must be mistaken? She said as much, her own voice small and frightened now, but Biddy's voice strengthened a little.

'No, I'm not mistaken, I ring the Port Authority every day and there's been no word for weeks,' she said. 'I – I don't know what to do, Liz. I'm very fond of Dai.'

'We all are,' Elizabeth muttered. 'Oh Biddy, I'll tell Mam an' Dad, see if they can think of anything. Ring me again tomorrow, whatever happens, won't you?'

'I'll try . . . no more time now, Liz, me money's running out . . .'

There was a very final sort of click and then the operator's voice came across the line saying that the caller had disconnected. Elizabeth hung her own receiver back and turned blindly away from the telephone. Tears had filled her eyes and now she let them run down her cheeks, made no effort to stop their flow.

Poor Dai, out in all that terrible cold! And poor Biddy, who was so fond of him – she must have been fonder than we ever realised, Elizabeth thought, to ring the Port Authority every day like that. But what can we do to help, what can anyone do? All we can do is wait, and pray, and comfort each other as best we can.

Nellie came into the house quickly, letting herself in through the front door and slinging her soaking coat at the hat-stand without even waiting to adjust it properly. She kicked off her short boots, massaged her icy toes with one hand for a moment, then pulled off the extra socks she had put on that morning; they were soggy, which meant she could do with some new boots. It was snowing outside and although she could have hailed a cab she had got the omnibus from the village and then walked, and now she wished she had had more sense.

I've probably caught my death, she was thinking as she went into the kitchen, positively wringing out her hair with one hand and watching a stream of water run out of it. I'm sure Scottish snow is colder than the Liverpool sort – certainly this house is colder than the one in Ducie Street, but it's scarcely worth doing anything about it, because we won't be here next winter, I'm sure of it.

Elizabeth was sitting by the fire, surrounded by dogs. She jumped to her feet as soon as her mother came into the room.

'Oh Mam . . . the most awful thing! You know Dai's ship, the *Greenland Bess*? It's two weeks overdue and posted as missing!'

Nellie stood stock still for a moment, feeling all the colour draining out of her face, leaving it cold as the snow which was falling outside. Then she sat down heavily on the nearest chair. One of the dogs, she could not tell which one, came and nuzzled her, pushing its wet nose into the palm of her hand, rubbing its head on her knees.

'Oh, dear God! Missing, you say?'

It was like some terrible nightmare, the sort where you ran in quicksand, unable to take a step, where the monster's hot breath is on your neck, his teeth a hair's breadth from your throat. Dai was missing, and she had been hoping, praying almost, that he would not be able to come up to Scotland and spend Christmas with them! She had brought this about herself, with her own selfishness, and now that her secret was safe she could see too clearly what a mean, pathetic little secret it was, how shallow and pitiful had been her attempts to keep the truth to herself.

'Mam, you look terrible! I'm sorry, I know you were fond of him, but we didn't know him all that well. . . . Mam, sit still, I'm going to telephone the office and get my father to come home.'

'Don't be silly, love.' The words should have come out strong and steady, but they emerged as a tiny whisper. 'I'll be all right, leave your Da out of this.'

'But – but Mam, I was going to ring Dad anyway, to ask him if there was anything we could do – anything the newspaper could do, really. Surely they could do something? Send out a – a rescue ship or something?'

Nellie suddenly ducked her head down into her lap. The room was starting to swim – she mustn't faint, she must be strong and sensible! If Stuart came home and saw her like this . . . no point in telling anyone that Dai was her son now, because . . . because . . .

A hand, warm, on the back of her neck. A face, young and soft, against hers. Elizabeth, as worried, now, over her mother as she had been worried just now over Dai. 'Mam? It's all right, I'm sure he'll be all right, ships do get lost at sea, don't they, and then the crew turn up? I remember you telling me once . . .'

Her voice went on, telling a comforting story, but it had reminded Nellie. Davy had been posted as missing and mourned for dead during the war, but he had been safe. Picked up by an enemy ship, put into a prison camp . . . there was no war on now, but it could still happen, couldn't it? Men were sometimes saved at sea . . . she tried to put out of her head all that Dai had told them about fishing the Arctic, about the conditions which meant that a man overboard was dead before his body touched the water. No use to bring the bad things to mind, think positively, she urged herself. And pray, Nellie Gallagher, pray for your boy!

After Biddy had made her phone call she felt much better, as though having told Elizabeth meant, at least, that there were two of them going to be thinking and praying for Dai and the *Bess*.

She returned to the shop and sold sweets until Ma Kettle returned, a fat and chuckling Santa Claus, from her shopping trip.

'I done us proud,' Ma Kettle crowed, rooting through her brown paper bags with much mystery in the boiling kitchen. 'I've got more peppermint oil an' more almond essence, but the rest of the stuff's for upstairs. Wait on, chuck, I'll be t'rough there any moment, then you can put another boilin' o' toffee on. You've done well this mornin', but it's near enough to the 'oliday for sales to keep up an' it don't do to run out o' toffees.'

'All right,' Biddy said, but she was beginning to be aware, within herself, of a strange restlessness, a feeling that if she did not *do* something she would burst. What she was supposed to do she did not know, but there was something... should she go back to the Maitlands' house and see if there was a message? Should she ring the Port Authority again? But she had been round to Ducie Street earlier in the week and she had rung the Port Authority before getting in touch with Elizabeth.

She finished boiling the toffee mixture soon after noon and as soon as it was in its trays she found her hands going round to the back of her to untie her apron strings.

What's got into you, Biddy O'Shaughnessy, she scolded herself, with the apron in her hands instead of round her person. You've finished the toffee but there's no end still to do, you can't go yet!

Oh can't I, you try to stop me, a little inner voice replied defiantly. Just you tell old Kettle you're off and you'll be back as soon as you can and let her do some toffee-boiling for once. 'Twon't hurt her.

Biddy went upstairs and packed a few necessities into her carpet bag. Then she got her money out of her pillow and hurried downstairs again. She went through to the boiling kitchen and checked that everything was clean and as it should be, then she gave Penny a shout but before the younger girl had arrived she was going into the shop.

Biddy entered the shop quietly and closed the door behind her. Ma Kettle was weighing an ounce of aniseed balls for a waiting child and including quite a bit of thumb on the scales. Normally Biddy would have dug her in the back and Ma Kettle would have taken her hand away from the pan sharpish, but today Biddy didn't bother. She had her own affairs to attend to. 'I'm going out, Ma,' she said. 'I'll be back in an hour, but then I'll be off again maybe for a day or two. I'm off now, to fetch help.'

'Help? Back in a *day or two*? Biddy, I pays you good money . . .' Ma Kettle began, but Biddy swept round the end of the counter and headed for the shop door.

'You've already had most of this week free, because I won't charge you,' Biddy said recklessly over her shoulder. 'I've got to go, Ma, I really have. Penny's a good girl, she'll stand by you, and Kenny can give a hand in here Saturday afternoon, when he's not working. I won't be any longer than I have to be.'

'But you don't 'ave to go, no one 'asn't come after you,' Ma Kettle called plaintively after her retreating back. 'Think o' me, Biddy . . . think o' our livelihood . . . Christmas is our busiest time, if I got the toffees I can make a mint, Christmas, but without you to boil 'em . . .'

374

'Can't stop. You'll be all right Ma, honest you will. Would I leave you in the lurch at this time o' year? 'Course I wouldn't. But I can't stop now, I've got a goodish distance to walk.'

And Biddy was on her way, hurrying down the Scotland Road towards her destination.

She reached Paul Street and hurried along it, then turned into Samson Court. Despite the cold, half a dozen small children were playing out on the paving before the Bradley house.

''Ello, Biddy,' a small urchin squeaked cheerfully. 'Our Ellen's indoors. She's been cryin'.'

'She won't cry soon,' Biddy said recklessly, giving the door a bang and then opening it and entering the house. 'Ellen? Where are you?'

Ellen came down the stairs. Her eyes were pink-rimmed, but she smiled as soon as she set eyes on her friend. 'Oh Biddy, it's good to see you! I were that down ... I went along to the market this mornin', bought Bobby a nice little coat 'cos it's gerrin' cold out, an' it's too bleedin' small, it catches 'im under the arms! Oh, I were fit to be tied!'

'Never mind that now,' Biddy said. 'Ellen, d'you remember in the flat, when you and I made sweets to sell, Christmas and Easter?'

''Course I do – we 'ad some fun in them days,' Ellen said wistfully, looking as though she was about to burst into tears again. 'Oh, poor Ted, if only . . .'

'Could you do it again?'

'Again? Do what again? If you mean live wi' a feller, there ain't no question . . .'

'Ellen, I could shake you!' Biddy said roundly. 'I'm in a tearing hurry . . . just listen to me! Could you make sweets still or have you forgotten how?'

375

'Course I could, even wi'out the recipes, what I've still got, anyroad,' Ellen said quite sharply. 'Small chance 'ere, though. No sugar, no butter, no . . .'

'And would you like a room of your own, decent wages, a kind o' uniform so's your own clothes didn't get mucky?'

'Would I! Bit it ain't no use, Bid . . . it's Bobby, I can't leave 'im 'ere wi' me Mam and no one wouldn't want me an' the kid 'cos 'e's too young to leave whiles I work.'

'I know all those things. Look, Ellen, sit down whilst I explain. The thing is that I've – I've got to go away for a day or so, perhaps longer. And Christmas is coming and old Ma Kettle is making masses o' sweets. She needs help, but I'm off, so I said I'd find someone. And Ell, dear, that someone can be you, if you'd like it and could cope.'

'Like it? Gawd, it 'ud be a real life-saver,' Ellen said fervently. 'But I couldn't boil toffee wi' Bobby on me 'ip, and I can't leave 'im . . .'

'You could leave him with Penny, the girl who does for Ma Kettle,' Biddy said slowly and clearly. 'Penny could keep an eye on him whilst you worked in the shop and the boiling kitchen. She's a good little girl, sensible and hard-working. And Bobby's no trouble, he'd be happy enough playing wi' bits and bobs whiles you were workin'. Right?'

'Yeah, absolutely right,' Ellen agreed. She was beginning to look hopeful. 'The trouble is, Biddy, that folk don't believe you can work wi' a baby around. There's always someone wi'out a kid who'll tek the job from under your nose. Believe me, I been for 'undreds o' jobs an' norra sniff 'ave I got.'

'No, but you can make sweets, which not many girls can, an' Ma Kettle's desperate. An' I'll vouch for your honesty, because I've never known you take what isn't yours, chuck, so the old girl won't have to worry about you prigging her toffees or her cash. So what about it? Will you come back wi' me now, leave a note for your Mam, an' give it a go?'

'Oh, Bid,' Ellen breathed. 'Oh, Bid, if it worked! If she liked me, wanted to keep me on! Oh, I'd work real 'ard, you know I would! Just to 'ave a place o' me own to lay me 'ead, just to 'ave Bobby looked after by someone who wasn't me, once in a while . . . oh, Bid!'

'I'll write the note, you sign it,' Biddy was beginning, when Mrs Bradley came into the kitchen backwards, towing a large sack of potatoes. She straightened up and grinned at the girls through the sweat running down her face.

'Gorrem cheap,' she said triumphantly. 'Spuds for a fortnight there, I reckon. 'Ello, Biddy, what's up wi' you, then?'

Breathlessly, Biddy explained about the job whilst Ellen flew upstairs to pack a few bits as she put it. And she was down almost before Biddy had finished her explanation, with a bulging bag and Bobby under one arm.

'Is it awright, Mam?' she said a trifle anxiously, standing her bag down for a moment. 'Only it ain't as if I get many chances.'

'You go an' grab it wi' both 'ands, flower,' Mrs Bradley said. 'You'd be best out o' here . . . too many of us.'

'Thanks Mam,' Ellen said. She picked up her bag and headed for the door. 'Come on, Bid, in case someone else gets there first – it 'ud be just my luck!'

It would not be true to say that Ma Kettle welcomed Ellen with open arms, because she viewed both girls with deep suspicion, but she was very taken with little Bobby.

''Oo's a fine feller, then?' she cooed, dangling a sugar mouse before his rounding eyes. 'Are you comin' to sit wi' Auntie Kettle for a moment then, whiles your Mam teks 'er bag upstairs?'

And seconds later Ma Kettle and Bobby were conversing in coos and gurgles and Ma was holding the child to the manner born, calling out to customers that she wouldn't be a mo, but she'd a young gennelman caller what was tekin' a deal of attention, right now.

'Be firm with her,' Biddy begged Ellen as they descended the stairs together. 'Remember if you walk out she'll be in a fair old pickle wi' Christmas so close and all. Oh, thanks, Ell, for coming over, and the best of luck.'

'But where are you off to?' Ellen said suddenly, realising that Biddy was actually about to leave. 'When'll you be back?'

'I'm – I'm going to Grimsby. I have to go and I dunno when I'll be back but it probably won't be more than four or five days. Thanks, Ell . . . bye, Mrs Kettle!'

'I only 'opes you're right about this young man's Mam,' an injured voice called through from the shop. 'She can start off by doin' me a boilin' o' the best Kettle toffee . . . . Don't you dare leave me for long, Biddy O'Shaughnessy, or . . . or . . .'

'Be good, both,' Biddy shouted out, then banged the door and fled along the icy pavement. Glancing back, she saw the first flakes of winter begin to meander down out of the grey and lowering sky. If it really began to snow that might make her journey a difficult one, but there was no point in worrying. Get to the port, Biddy, she ordered herself. Worry then if you must, but get there!

She was snug aboard the tram when the snow really started in earnest. I hope to God the trains don't get held up seriously by the snow, she prayed to herself, rubbing the steam off the window nearest her so she could look out. I need to get to Grimsby, I must get to Grimsby, I'll get there if I have to walk!

The pavements were wet so the snow was not yet lying, but the shoulders of passers-by were soon speckled with white and as the tram came to a halt on St George's Plain Biddy could barely see the big hotels which lined the other side of the road. This was not going to make her journey any easier, but she hopped down and hurried across the road, feeling ridiculously light-hearted. It was because she was doing something, not just waiting for whatever news was to come.

She reached Lime Street Station and glanced up at the clock; it was nearly three o'clock – what an hour to start a long, cross-country journey! But she went straight to the ticket office and put her problem to the expert, who was a rather tired-looking young clerk behind the little window. He was sipping a cup of tea, chewing a bun and reading what looked like a timetable, all at the same time; but he put everything down when Biddy tapped and shot up his little hatch.

'Sorry, queen, 'avin' me snap,' he said rather thickly. 'First quiet moment I've 'ad all day. Can I 'elp you?'

'I want to get to Grimsby, by tonight if possible,' Biddy said promptly. 'Can you work me out a route, please?'

Dai always moaned about the changes necessary on a cross-country route, but she was prepared for anything so long as she ended up in the port.

'You couldn't 'ave come to a better person,' the clerk said, picking up the big book he had been reading and flourishing it at her. 'New timetable, see? Just been familiarisin' meself with it, so to speak. Now Grimsby, you said, queen . . . hmm . . .'

Ten minutes later, with directions scribbled in the clerk's neat writing on a piece of L & NWR paper, Biddy set off again. She had half an hour before her train left, so she could go into Lime Street and buy herself a magazine and something to eat on the journey. The clerk was sure she would find herself waiting on various platforms and said she could probably nip out and buy herself something to eat then, but Biddy was taking no chances. Homelessness had taught her the importance of being prepared for anything, and she had no desire to spend a hungry, cold night on some lonely station in the middle of the country.

She found a café and bought sandwiches and some buns, then added a bottle of lemonade. It was rather heavy, but the horrors of thirst on a long journey could be imagined all too clearly. A nice new edition of *Woman* magazine came next, then Biddy returned to the station, brushing snow off her shoulders as she went.

She was in good time and easily secured a seat in the third-class section of the train.

'It ain't near enough to Christmas for the rush to 'ave started, and since folk don't travel much when it's wintry, wi' Christmas preparations to make, you won't find the trains overcrowded,' the clerk had explained as he sold Biddy her ticket. 'Good luck Miss, an' a pleasant journey.'

I don't think it will be all that pleasant, Biddy thought as she settled into a corner seat. It was already dusky outside but the train was not yet lit up and suddenly the adventure seemed more like a vain hope. Why am I going to Grimsby, when the ship isn't back and I'm a stranger there? Biddy asked herself helplessly as the train chugged out of Lime Street and into the whirling snow. I must be mad!

But in her heart she knew she was not mad at all. She had simply obeyed a feeling that Grimsby was the place to be and she intended to go on obeying that feeling until she felt the docks beneath her feet.

Presently she got her directions out and went over them again so that she would know when to get off the train and which connection she needed next. And having read it until the words were engraved on her memory she pushed the paper into her pocket, leaned her head back on the prickly upholstery, and allowed herself to doze.

'Thank you love, that was a kind thought. Now you go and – and do whatever you want and leave me quietly here. I need to think.'

Elizabeth smiled at her mother, then slipped out of the bedroom and closed the door gently behind her. On the opposite side of the galleried upper landing, Flora hovered. They had only been in Scotland a short while, Elizabeth reflected, but already Flora was extremely fond of her mistress and that fondness was reflected now in the worry on her small, bony face.

'Is she all right? No' ill, is she?'

Elizabeth shushed the maid with a finger to her lips and then walked round the gallery to where Flora stood.

'Hush, Flora, I gave her a couple of aspirin tablets and a hot drink; now I'm hoping she'll sleep. We – we had some sad news this morning.'

'Oh aye? Was it that telephone call?' Flora's small face reflected her distrust of the machine. 'I might ha' known it boded no good; that thing is an instrument o' the devil, have I no' telled ye so often and often?'

'Yes, you have,' Elizabeth admitted. 'But it wasn't the fault of the telephone, Flora. A friend called me to tell me that someone called Dai Evans, who is my Mam's friend's son, is lost at sea. Mam is fond of him, and I think since his own mother's death he looks on my Mam as her deputy. We – we were hoping he'd spend Christmas with us. It's been a sad blow.'

'Aye, aye,' Flora muttered. 'You'll get in touch with

your father, nae doubt, tell him your mother is unwell?'

'I was going to, but Mam doesn't want me to worry him; she says there's nothing anyone can do, not even my Da, but I thought perhaps the newspaper could help in some way.'

'Och no, men are lost at sea all the time,' Flora said. 'I'm frae a trawlin' family. Terrible sad it is, but all ye can do is pray, Miss Liz.'

'Yes. And now I'm going downstairs to make my mother a rather late luncheon. What do you recommend, Flora? I thought hot soup, because it's still snowing, and perhaps an egg on toast?'

'Aye, she's gae fond of an egg,' Flora said. 'I'll gi' you a hand, we've already got some fine leeks an' a ham bone in the larder an' Jamie will fetch in onions frae the shed if we need 'em.'

The two of them descended the stairs and presently began working companionably in the kitchen. Elizabeth, cleaning leeks, said that they might as well make sufficient soup for tonight since the snow, which had whirled ever since breakfast, showed no sign of letting up and it would be pleasant to have leek-and-ham soup at dinner.

By one o'clock the tray was laid, the meal ready. Flora went ahead to open doors, Elizabeth carried the tray with the soup steaming gently and the egg on toast under a silver cover.

They reached the bedroom and Flora threw open the door. Elizabeth sailed through with a big smile . . . then stopped suddenly. The soup, unwarned, slid across the tray, teetered frantically on the edge for a moment and then plummeted to the floor.

'Mam? Oh, she must have popped out for a minute to . . . hang on, what's that on the pillow? Oh Flora, I wish I'd not listened to her, I wish I'd telephoned my Da! There's an envelope addressed to my father and a tiny note for me, telling me not to worry, she's had to go out. Oh dear, I *knew* she was ill, I'll have to find her!'

'She won't be far, no' in this weather,' Flora said, having thought about it for a second. 'We'd best tell the men . . . we'll soon find someone who's seen her.'

And Jamie, the gardener, knew at once what had happened to his mistress.

'Went off on the bus into Edinburgh,' he said in his soft, elderly voice. 'Right as rain, she was, gave me a big smile an' said it was the Christmas shopping she was tackling today.'

'There, we're worrying for nae reason,' Flora said comfortingly. 'But telephone your father, Miss Liz, because of the letter.'

Elizabeth was on the phone almost before the maid had spoken, but she presently put it down again, disappointed. 'He's out on business, not expected back until five,' she said. 'Oh Flora, I am worried! Whatever ought I to do?'

Nellie boarded the first of her trains in mid-afternoon, and sat in a corner of the carriage wishing her feet would warm up and wondering whether she was doing the right thing. Not that she had had any choice. Once she had got over the initial shock of Elizabeth's news she had simply longed, with the whole of her heart, to be near Dai. I should have told him, she mourned, sitting icy in the carriage. I should have told him, quietly, that he was my boy. That way at least we could have exchanged letters, he could have confided in me. If only I'd not been so secretive . . .

But she had not wanted – still did not want – to hurt Stuart. The fact that she had run away to see whether there was anything she could do about the missing trawler should not worry or hurt him, she told herself, because he would simply think she was concerned for her friend's lad. But she could not sit at home and wait in idleness, this was the least she could do.

When the train stopped she got out and went into the small station buffet. She drank hot tea and ate a ham sandwich and wondered whether to telephone home from the booth just outside the station, but it would only lead to a lot of questions she did not feel capable of answering. So she climbed aboard the next train and settled herself for a long and very cold journey.

Dai was on deck when they first sighted the Spurn light, but the gulls were already aboard by then and circling overhead so everyone knew a landfall was imminent. The *Bess* was still proceeding cautiously, like an old lady with a gammy leg, low in the water and lopsided, too, but at least the coal would last out – just. And though the meals now consisted of fish with fish, followed by fish, with chunks of Bandy's soda bread the only relief, at least meals were still being provided – just. And no one was badly hurt; Dai himself nursed a sprained wrist from ice-breaking, Greasy had pulled a tendon in his leg and limped, the Mate was still in pain from the blackened toe. But there had been no loss of life though it had been a near-run thing.

They broke out the bonded rum in the Humber estuary and several of the men got drunk, but Dai was too excited to take more than a token sip. The *Bess* would be in dry dock for six weeks, possibly longer. The iceberg's toothmarks were deep and the damage done in the collision would take a deal of work to put right. The little donkey engine toiled ceaselessly, pumping her out, and whenever you looked in the forward hold you had to wonder at the little ship's stubborn ability to remain afloat with so much water sloshing around below.

Next stop Liverpool, next stop Biddy, Dai kept repeating to himself. Oh, he'd stay in Grimsby long enough to collect his pay, to telephone the Gallaghers . . . oh no, he couldn't do that, Biddy wasn't with the Gallaghers any more but the Maitlands would still be on the telephone. Or he might get straight on a train; the surprise would be all the better when he turned up and swept her into his arms, told her no more silliness, they would get wed before he returned to sea and find themselves lodgings in Grimsby. He realised he had been mad to listen to Nellie because the only thing one should listen to regarding a loved one is your own heart. She can't love anyone else, she just can't, he told himself over and over, to still the niggling little doubt that sometimes came in the night and made him sweat with fear in case Nellie had been right. My Biddy's a girl in a thousand . . . wonder if there'll be a letter? If there isn't a letter . . .

The ship nosed slowly out of the fierceness of the North Sea, butting through the snow which was falling, heading up-river like an old hound who smells its home and its warm bed on the wind. Objects which had clattered ceaselessly to the wave's rhythm for six weeks fell silent and men looked around, puzzled by the stillness. You could play cards without having to grab the loose pack, you could stand a drink down and find it there when you turned to it once more, you could sleep without hanging grimly onto the side of your bunk, unable to relax because if you did you'd wake up half-way across the cabin.

You could smell the docks, despite having been amongst fish for six weeks. A strong, salty odour which was mixed with the smell of the land, an indefinable scent which Dai could not describe, but could only enjoy.

And as they made their slow way into the fish docks they saw other trawlers with men aboard who could understand what the marks on the bow meant, the reason for the lopsidedness, the constant discharge of water from the donkey engine. Men waved and shouted to them, asked questions, told them they'd been posted missing. . . . The crew called back, exchanged badinage, made light of *Bess's* wounds, her beast of a voyage.

'It'll all be the same in a hundred years; and we'll be having Christmas at home,' the Mate said as he stood beside Dai, watching the Skipper bring the *Bess* so neatly and quietly alongside that you never would have guessed all was not right with her. 'Hope you've been putting money away, lad. Six hungry weeks ahead, unless you sign on with another trawler, of course.'

'I'll go to Liverpool first, to see my girl, arrange our wedding,' Dai said matter-of-factly. It made it more real, somehow, putting it into words. 'Then . . . I'll go home, to Anglesey. Been meaning to go, meaning to talk to my Da these twelve months but never got round to it somehow. Now I'll go, sort things out. Take my girl so they can meet her.'

'Aye,' the Mate nodded thoughtfully. 'Never leave things till tomorrow, Taff, not if you're distant-water trawling. For too many there isn't a tomorrow. Riskiest business in the world bar none, ours. Not for everyone, not by a long chalk.'

'Not sure, after this little lot, if it's for me,' Dai admitted ruefully. He thought he would see the prow of the iceberg bearing down on their little ship in nightmares for the rest of his life. 'But I'll sign on again, just to see.'

The Mate grinned. 'That sounds like me, twenty year ago. Well, whichever way it goes, good luck, Taff. And see you in six weeks.'

The fenders were out, kissing the quayside, the gangplank was lowered, the crew were lining up to leave.

There were shouts, rude jostlings, remarks about other people's wives and mothers which could only have been exchanged amongst men who knew each other very well indeed.

'Comin' to collect your wages, Taff?' Greasy said as they shuffled in line towards the shore. 'The fish'll fetch a good price, they say, 'cos we're one of the last boats in afore Christmas. Eh, look down there – someone's sweet'earts can't wait to see 'em!'

Down on the quayside two women stood, an older and a younger. They ignored the howling gale, the snow swirling past. They were both waving, but there was something in the way they stood which told Dai that tears were being held at bay, that the joyful smiles which he could just about make out through the snow were relief as much as pleasure. Of course, we were posted missing, he was telling himself, I hope Biddy didn't know, I hope she wasn't too worried . . . and all in a moment he recognised her.

Biddy! Soaked hair hanging in rats' tails down onto her shoulders, her coat almost black with wet, but the pink in her cheeks showing even through the snow, and the sparkle in those blue, blue eyes!

Dai had been at the back of the queue. Now he gave a hoarse, strangled shout and simply flew down the gangplank, knocking men twice his size and with double his seniority aside without a thought. He covered the snow-wet, fish-slippery quay in half a dozen strides and she was in his arms, cuddling close, weeping, laughing, trying to talk whilst he tried to silence her with his mouth, kissing her eyelids, her cheeks, her ice-cold nose and then those tender, opening lips!

'I thought . . . I thought . . . you were posted missing. I'd – I'd been ringing every day . . .'

'There, there, sweetheart, and here I am, safe and

sound,' Dai crooned against her wet hair. 'Oh, Biddy, thought you'd met someone else, I did, then I told myself it just wasn't possible, but . . .'

It was her turn to croon now, her turn to comfort. 'Oh darling, as if I could ever think about anyone else, when I love you so very much! And we'll get married soon, won't we? Before you go back to sea again – as soon as we can arrange it?'

He stood back from her, the snowflakes floating between them kissing cheek and brow unnoticed. It could have been forty degrees below or baking hot for all they knew – or cared. The crew from the *Bess* streamed past them, ribald remarks were uttered, they were jostled and chuckled over, but neither one of them noticed.

'We'll get married in Moelfre, when we go back to see my people,' Dai said. 'I wish Mam could have known you, but . . . oh Biddy, I'm so happy!'

But Biddy had remembered her manners. She turned to the woman standing back, watching them with a gentle smile curving her lips. 'I'm so sorry . . . I quite forgot. Mrs Gallagher's come to welcome you home too, Dai. She – she's got something to tell you, my love.'

'Nellie!' Dai exclaimed. He turned and took both Nellie's cold little hands in his. 'Oh Nell, I'm sorry, I didn't see you standing there.'

'You two saw nothing but each other,' Nellie said, smiling up at him. 'Let's go and get a cup of tea and a bun; perhaps we should talk.'

'Sure,' Dai said. He put his arm round Biddy, holding her close, and then had to go on board the *Bess* again, to rescue his ditty bag, cast down at the moment of seeing Biddy. Returning to their side, he looked rather suspiciously at Nellie. 'Nellie, it was you who said . . .'

'I'll explain in a moment, dear,' Nellie said. 'Come along, we arrived here very late last night – we met on a station somewhere in the heart of Yorkshire and came the rest of the way together – and we've got a room on East Marsh Street, so when we came down to the docks we had to find somewhere to go and eat, dry out a bit. . . . There's a nice little place on Church Lane . . .'

'You arrived last night? But no one knew we were coming in, our transmitter was a casualty of the first iceberg. What made you decide to come to Grimsby?'

Nellie shrugged and beside him, Dai felt Biddy's shoulders rise and fall in an identical gesture.

'I don't know, Dai dear.' Nellie said quietly. 'I just felt I had to be here, and Biddy was the same. We've been on the dock since before dawn though, because the lighthouse saw you and reported that the *Bess* was heading for home. Now come along, we can talk in the cafe.'

The café was steamy, crowded, noisy. They managed to find a table in the window and all the while they were there the snow blew against the glass in little gusts as if to remind them that, outside, other men on other ships still risked their lives on the cruel and turbulent ocean.

They ordered a large pot of coffee, some hot buttered toast and a quantity of the small currant buns the proprietress was famed for, and started to eat and drink at once, at first almost without a word. But then Nellie put down her cup and spoke. 'Dai, when you came to me you told me you wanted to marry my girl . . . . Remember?'

'That's right. And you said . . .'

'Wait a moment, dear. Who did you mean when you say *my girl*?'

'Why, Biddy, of course. Whoever . . .'

'Ah, but when someone says *my girl* to me, I don't think of Biddy, I think of Elizabeth.'

Dai goggled; there was no other way of putting it. His eyes rounded and his mouth dropped open, but he could say nothing. Biddy could tell he was working it out, taking it in. Finally, he heaved a great sigh and grinned, a flash of amazingly white teeth in a face which had been weathered to a deep tan by wind and snow, never by the sun.

'Lizzie! You thought I was in love with little Lizzie! And she's got a boyfriend, eh?'

Biddy wondered whether Nellie would seize the offer of a get-out or tell the truth, but Nellie simply shook her head.

'No, not really, dear,' she said steadily. 'But there's something I've never told you – never told anyone but Biddy here, when we were stuck in that icy cold train, coming across country with infinite slowness. Dai, when I was very young I – I had a baby boy. I wasn't married, but the – the father of my baby was. He was a sailor on a coaster and his – his name was Davy Evans. When I found I was expecting his baby I went to Moelfre, and Bethan, your mother, befriended me. She was so good! But she had no child, she believed that her husband was dead, lost at sea, and there was I, about to give birth to Davy's baby, with no hope of giving the child a proper home, a real place in society. So when she said she would give you a home, and all the love at her command, I – I was glad to accept.'

Dai was staring at Nellie as though he doubted his hearing. Was this giving him pain, Biddy wondered compassionately? Did he hate the thought that his beloved Mam had not actually given birth to him, that he was the offspring of his father and his father's mistress?

'Nellie, what are you saying, woman? That I am not my mother's child? That I'm . . . I'm . . .'

'You're my son. Which is why, dear Dai, I panicked and lied desperately when I thought you were in love with Lizzie. She's – she's your sister, you see.'

Biddy had never taken her eyes off his face and now she saw the slow smile dawning in the dark eyes she loved so much, reaching his mouth so that suddenly he was smiling, then laughing. He leaned across the table and put his hands round Nellie's face, then kissed her forehead, suddenly sobering.

'When my Mam was dying she told me to turn to you if I wanted mothering,' he said slowly. 'Perhaps I should've known, guessed . . . but I didn't. Oh Nellie, fach, only one Mam there could ever be for me, and that one Bethan, but I can love you like a Mam, and I do.'

'That's more than I deserve,' Nellie said, tears trembling in her eyes, then spilling over. Dai leaned across and wiped them away with his fingers and Nellie laughed shakily. 'Oh Dai, what a sad mess I nearly made of your life, when all I wanted was to see you happy! And when I met our Bid in the station, with a face like a ghost and great, dark eyes; when she told me she was going to Grimsby . . . then I knew. It all came tumbling out, all the stupid things I'd done, and she said it didn't matter, because she was certain-sure that you weren't drowned, certain that we wouldn't both have been drawn to Grimsby without a purpose.'

Biddy smiled at Nellie and rubbed her face against Dai's sleeve.

'And when we reached the port they were talking about the *Bess* down on the docks, saying what a blessing it was that you'd not all been killed, talking about your catch, your Skipper . . . and we just hugged one another and grinned like loonies, didn't we, Mrs Gallagher?' Biddy said, smiling across at Nellie. 'So we're going to get married, eh, Dai? I'd best write a nice letter to Ma Kettle, telling her what's been happening, though I'll have to go back there, collect my things and so on, but I'd rather a letter reached her first, somehow. And you'll tell

Lizzie, Mrs Gallagher? She's been a good friend to me, I'd like her at my wedding, even if you and Mr Gallagher don't feel you could rightly turn up.'

'Of course I will, and you must call me Nellie since you're to be my daughter-in-law,' Nellie said gaily. 'In fact I'm going to tell Stu and Elizabeth the truth if you don't mind, Dai. There's a deal of harm done by lying, even if you lie for what you think are the right reasons.'

'Tell 'em all,' Dai said generously. 'But I won't spread it around at home, not in Moelfre. My Da doesn't know, I take it?'

Nellie smiled. 'No. Bethan would never have told him. My recollection of Davy is that one didn't tell him secrets.'

'Right. So that's settled. Now are you two lovely ladies coming down to the office with me, so's I can get paid off until the next trip? Or do you want to go back to your lodgings and try to dry out a bit? Because Biddy and me ought to catch the next train for Liverpool – we've a lot to do!'

'I'd best go straight home, I think,' Nellie said rather regretfully. 'You know we're living in Edinburgh now, Dai? I – I suppose you wouldn't both like to come back with me, just to get some of the explaining over? It wouldn't take long, then you could go to Moelfre for Christmas. Say you will, just for a few days! I'll pay your fares, of course.'

'I think perhaps we ought,' Biddy said slowly. 'Poor Nellie, you're going to have quite a lot of explaining to do, and if it would make it easier for you . . . I mean, you are Dai's Mam when all's said and done, and Mr Gallagher – Stuart, I mean – does deserve an explanation, all things considered. And I'd desperately like you Gallaghers at me wedding because I've no relatives of my own I can ask. Only it's up to Dai, really. What do you think, my love?'

'So long as no one starts brooding over what's long

past,' Dai said slowly. 'Yes, we'll come. Only he's a good feller is Stuart, not the sort to cast blame. I think you'll hear few reproaches, my little Mam.'

And he squeezed Nellie's hand and looked away as the tears ran down her cheeks.

They arrived in Edinburgh very late at night, and left the station to find themselves in the middle of a blinding snowstorm. The wind dashed snowflakes against the windows of their cab and caused the driver to slow to a crawl and to use some extremely Scottish words beneath his breath.

'I wonder if Lizzie's still up?' Biddy said as Nellie opened the big front door. 'She knows you're bringing us back, doesn't she, Mrs Ga . . . I mean Nellie?'

'Yes; I rang her earlier though and said we would be late,' Nellie said, ushering them inside. Dai, who had stayed to pay the cab-driver, joined them in the hall, beginning to take off his coat, already damp across the shoulders even in the short dash from the car to the house. Nellie unbuttoned her own coat, then glanced up the stairs, beginning to smile. 'Ah, here she comes, tearing about, as usual! Lizzie darling, we're back! Take Biddy and Dai into the kitchen and make them a hot drink, will you? I just want a word with your father. He's in the study, I take it?'

Lizzie, bouncing down the stairs, kissed her mother and Biddy, then stood on tiptoe to kiss Dai's cheek before turning back to her mother. 'Oh Mam, I'm glad you're back, things have been a bit difficult here . . . yes, me Da's in the study, go and have a word. I'll make a tray of tea for everyone and get out the biscuits. . . . I can make some sandwiches if you're really hungry, or I can heat up some soup.' She turned to examine Biddy and Dai as she led the way across the hall to the kitchen. 'You two look very happy – but you can tell me what's been happening whilst Mam explains to me Da why she ran off like that. Come on.'

She bustled them into the kitchen and Biddy, looking over her shoulder, saw Nellie hesitate outside the study for a moment, as though she dreaded what was to come. Poor thing, Biddy thought, fancy having to tell Mr Gallagher what had happened all those years ago! Nellie was still wearing her damp and travel-stained coat, too. . . . Biddy would have advised her to take it off, but suddenly Nellie straightened her shoulders, tapped on the door and opened it, then went through and closed it softly behind her.

'Come on, Bid. You can give me a hand with the soup,' Lizzie said gaily, as they entered the kitchen. It was a large room with a flagstoned floor and a bright fire, before which three or four dogs lounged at their ease. Biddy entered the room rather carefully – she knew almost nothing about dogs – and looked around her whilst Lizzie went through a narrow doorway into what Biddy now saw was a very commodious pantry. 'It's leek and potato, made with cream – do you like that?'

Assuring Lizzie that she loved leek-and-potato soup, Biddy shot a quick and anxious glance at Dai, now standing beside her. 'Will she be all right? Nellie, I mean,' she hissed. 'Oh, poor Mrs Gallagher, Dai.'

'She'll be fine,' Dai whispered back. 'A grand feller, is Stuart. I've no worries there.'

'Oh, good,' Biddy said, turning back to the kitchen and trying not to imagine the scene in the study. Dai said it would be all right and he was older and wiser than she, he probably knew best.

But privately, Biddy had her doubts.

Nellie slipped inside the study and closed the door behind her. Stuart was sitting behind the desk, writing something on a pad of paper. He glanced up and stared expressionlessly across at her for a moment, then he bent his head over his work once more. He continued to write, finished his sentence, blotted the page, then put down his pen and leaned back in his chair. For the first time in their lives together, the glance that he sent her across the desk was cold and antagonistic.

'Ah, Nellie. So you did decide to come home.'

It was like a slap in the face, but though Nellie swallowed nervously she did not flinch. This was the reaction of a man who had been terribly worried and deeply hurt and she could scarcely blame him. She had not expected to be welcomed back with open arms – had she?

'Did you doubt it, Stuart?' she said, her voice trembling a little. 'I rang Lizzie and explained I'd gone to meet Dai's ship, I rang later and said I was bringing him and Biddy home here for a day or so. . . . Did you think I'd do that if I didn't mean to return?'

'Lizzie said you'd rung,' Stuart said heavily. He spoke without raising his eyes from the page before him. 'But your note gave no explanation for leaving the way you did. Lizzie told me you fainted when she gave you Biddy's message about Dai's ship being overdue. That doesn't seem a normal thing to do. Not for a friend's boy, anyway.'

'No. But . . . Dai's my boy, Stuart.'

That jerked his gaze up to meet hers, his eyes wide, darkening with shock, an expression of incredulity replacing the censure for a moment. '*Your* boy? Dai Evans is . . . I don't understand.'

'No. You couldn't possibly understand, but I'm here to explain, Stuart.' She took a step nearer the desk, trying to control the trembling which was racking her. 'Will you listen to me? It's – it's rather a long story and it starts rather a long time ago.'

'Will this *explanation* include the name of your lover, the name of the man who was so important to you that you insisted we move to Edinburgh? Will it include what you've been doing these past two days?' Nellie began to speak, feeling her face grow hot, but he overrode her, his voice rising to something perilously close to a shout. 'No, no, don't pretend indignation, I'm not a fool! There's always been something, something you wouldn't tell me, and I'm well aware that you had no message about Dai's ship, no telephone call to this house telling you he was safe. You went off somewhere else, then heard about Dai and used the information as an excuse for your sudden flight. . . . Nellie, I'm not a fool!'

Nellie put both hands to her hot cheeks and felt all her resolve, all her determination, draining away. How could she tell him, when he was so angry with her, so eager to believe her unfaithful, wicked? Yet if she did not tell him, did not make him listen, their relationship would founder, their marriage would become a mockery.

'Don't judge me, Stuart,' she said tremulously, trying not to glance at his hands, curled now into fists. She had never known him so angry and unyielding, not in all the years they had known each other. 'Not until you've heard the facts. As I said, it's a long story. May – may I sit down?'

He tightened his lips, scowling at her, but he nodded ungraciously. 'Very well . . . but pull the chair round to face me, if you please.'

She did as he asked, then sat down, facing him. It was impossible not to feel like a prisoner in the dock, on trial for her life, but she took a deep, calming breath, then began to speak, though she lowered her eyes as she did so, unable to meet the scorn in his glance. 'Years ago, before we married, I – I went with a man and fell for a child. I was very young and ignorant, Stuart, and very frightened, but my child's father had promised to marry me so when he did not come back for me, I decided to go to his village on the Isle of Anglesey and find out once and for all what had happened.

'I went to Davy's house – his name was Davy Evans – and found he was married to a dear girl called Bethan. She told me that Davy's ship had been sunk and Davy was drowned, and when I explained my state she asked me to stay with her, and to let her adopt my baby when he was born. She had no child, you see, nothing to remind her of Davy, and she said, truly, that the child would have a good life with her, and an inheritance. All I could give him would have been the shame of illegitimacy.

'So I agreed and in due course I gave birth to a son. I called him David, after his father. Everyone believed that Bethan was his Mam – we had kept my secret well – and when the baby was old enough I went back to Liverpool without him.

'Later, Davy went home. He hadn't been drowned, he'd been picked up by another vessel and taken to America I think it was, and when he got back to Anglesey he found he had a son. Stuart, we neither of us loved each other, it was just – just a mistake for us both. Davy settled down happily with Bethan and their boy and quite soon after that they had a girl, a sister for – for Dai, as they called him.'

As Nellie finished speaking Stuart looked across at her once more. His eyes were still cold. 'And when did your lover turn up again? Quite soon after Dai did – is that it? Freed by his wife's death, wanting you all over again? Finding you married to another man was clearly no bar to what *he* had in mind. And you couldn't resist the chance to see him again . . . you'll tell me that was all, I suppose? That you just wanted to see him, nothing more?'

'Who, Davy? Stuart, of course he didn't turn up, I've never seen him from that day to this and besides, Dai says his father has remarried.' Nellie smiled slightly. 'A girl young enough to be his daughter . . . typical of Davy, I imagine. But can't you see, Stu, that I couldn't tell you before? You knew I'd had a baby, I told you that, but I could scarcely tell you that my friend Bethan had passed the child off as her own, even to her husband! It wasn't my secret to share, was it?'

'None of that matters; I accept that you had an affair with this Davy Evans and that Dai's your child. But what matters to me is where you went these past two days? Why did you run away?' Stuart leaned across the desk now, his expression almost pleading, his eyes full of pain. 'If Davy Evans isn't your lover, who in heaven's name is?'

'It's you, Stuart, it's always been you,' Nellie said. Tears ran down her hot cheeks and dripped off the end of her chin. 'There's never been anyone else but you for me, Stuart, and you must know it! I went to Grimsby as soon as I got Biddy's message because I felt I must *do* something, be as near as possible to my boy. That's absolutely all there was to it. Stu, I'll swear it on the bible if that's the only way to convince you . . . but why should it be? We've never lied to each other, why should you think I'd lie now?'

'And coming to Edinburgh? When you'd quite made up your mind to stay in Liverpool?'

'That was stupid, but I thought Dai wanted to marry Lizzie and – and they're brother and sister, or half-brother and sister, anyway. He came round to the house in Ducie Street and asked me whether I would object to his asking "my girl" to marry him. And Stu, when anyone says "your girl" to me, I think of Lizzie at once, because she is my girl. I just never thought of Biddy.'

She was watching his face and saw, for the first time, a glint of what might have been amusement lighten his dark eyes. 'You thought Dai wanted to marry our girl? Nellie Gallagher, you want your head examinin'! And that was why you insisted that we leave the 'Pool? *That* was the reason you left your beloved home?'

'I know; I've been every sort of fool,' Nellie said ruefully. 'Do you remember me telling you I thought it would do Lizzie good to move up here? Well, that was why. I was terrified that she and Dai might want to marry . . . oh Stu, it was a nightmare, and I couldn't tell you, couldn't say why I was afraid. And of course quite soon I realised I'd made an awful mistake, that Lizzie and Dai were just friends, but I couldn't go back on it, could I? We were here, and you were settled into the job . . . so I had to make the best of it.'

'And . . . and you honestly set off in this dreadful weather, just to try to meet Dai? Just to see your boy? There wasn't anything else? Anyone else? You've not met Davy since you and he were lovers all those years ago?'

His eyes were soft, the expression in them anxious, but lovingly so, now. Nellie jumped up from her chair and ran round the desk. She cast herself into Stuart's arms and kissed him violently, then collapsed onto his lap with a blissful sigh.

'Oh Stuart, darling, if only you knew how much it hurt me to see you looking at me as if I was a stranger! I swear on – on Lizzie's life that I went to meet Dai and nobody else, and that I wouldn't want to see Davy if he turned up on our doorstep tomorrow. The last time I saw him, in fact, was when I was nursing in Liverpool. He was one of the injured to come onto my ward and I was so totally out of love with him that I applied for the job in France so that I wouldn't even have to set eyes on him again.

And then you and I met, so in a way you could say that not loving Davy brought us together.'

Stuart's arms went round her in a tight hug and he pressed his face against her tear-wet cheek. 'Oh Nell, sweetheart, if only *you* knew! I love you and trust you, only a fool would do otherwise, yet there has always been a little ache in the back of my mind because you'd never explained properly about the child you'd born, the man you'd . . . been with. It wasn't jealousy exactly, it was because I couldn't understand why you wouldn't be frank with me. And it hurt.'

'Well, now you know,' Nellie said contentedly. 'Do you mind about Dai, darling? Only he needed me and perhaps in a way I needed him. And now we've found each other, I'd hate to have to send him away.'

'He's a grand lad; I can't think of anyone I'd sooner have as a stepson,' Stuart said. 'But I'd rather that Davy fellow never knew.'

'Dai and I feel the same,' Nellie said fervently. 'Dai couldn't think of me as his mother – Bethan was all the mother he had or needed – but I hope we'll always be close. Oh Stu, no one ever had a nicer husband than you.'

'That's the truest word you ever spoke,' Stuart said. He tipped her off his lap and stood up, putting an arm around her shoulders and turning her towards the door. 'I bet all that talking's made you thirsty; let's go and find ourselves a drink. . . . God, woman, your coat's wet! Take it off and we'll put it over the airer in the kitchen. It'll be dry by morning.'

They went across the room and into the hall, where Nellie took off her coat and kicked off her short boots. Stuart found her slippers and put them on her icy feet and was about to open the kitchen door when Nellie caught his hand.

'Stu, the children are in there. I'd rather not face them tonight. Shall we go straight to bed?'

Stuart squeezed her shoulders, his expression very tender. 'Well, I still think you should have a hot drink after that long journey, but if you feel you can't face . . .'

The kitchen door opening cut his sentence off short. Lizzie stood framed in the doorway, a tray in her hands. She smiled at them. 'Ah, I was just about to bring your drinks through! Biddy and Dai have gone up – Biddy's in my room, Mam, and Dai's in the room over the porch – but I thought you'd like a hot drink and some sandwiches.'

'Good girl,' Stuart said, taking the tray from her. 'You're not such a bad kid after all, our Lizzie. Oh, hang your Mam's coat on the airer, would you? And we'll see you in the morning.'

Biddy and Dai stayed in Edinburgh, in the end, for the best part of a week.

Biddy said nothing to Lizzie as to what had passed between her parents that stormy night, but next day Stuart and Nellie seemed to be as loving as ever, and when Biddy, highly daring, asked 'Is it all right?' Nellie had nodded and smiled so blissfully that Biddy realised whatever had happened in the study the previous evening had probably strengthened the already strong relationship between the Gallaghers.

Dai, in the woodshed next morning chopping wood and hoping that poor little Nellie had not had a hard time, told Biddy that Stuart had simply come up to him and clapped him on the shoulder. Stuart's eyes, he said, were full of tears. 'My dear Dai, there's no one I'd rather have for a stepson,' he had said, his voice full of emotion. 'My poor darling Nell – the lengths she went to, and just so that I wouldn't be hurt when I'm not hurt in the slightest! I knew she was keeping something from me, you see, and

I imagined . . . dreadful things. Now I know the truth I'm just delighted that you felt you could turn to us, even before you knew of your relationship with my dearest Nell.'

'Give each other a hug, we did,' Dai told Biddy that evening, when they had gone out into the snow to give the dogs a walk before bedtime. 'Stuart's not the feller to hold a grudge, so pleased he was that Nell's secret wasn't a bad one he would have forgive her anything. Loves her deeply, does Stu.'

And Elizabeth was, quite simply, ecstatic. 'A brother! Well, all right, then, a half-brother,' she said to Biddy as the two of them worked side by side in the kitchen. 'And you as good as a sister to me, Biddy! It's what I've always wanted, a brother or sister of me own, and now I've got both of you.'

'I'll be a sister-in-law, not a proper sister,' Biddy reminded her, but Elizabeth just laughed and nudged her in the ribs.

'Who cares about that? You don't know what it's like, Biddy, having a Mam and a Da but no real uncles or aunts, let alone no cousins near enough to visit. I'm so pleased . . . and Mam says we will come to your wedding, even if it is just as friends. She says Davy will just have to get used to seeing her because she's going to enjoy Dai's company whenever she can, to make up for all the years she lost.'

But Biddy and Dai could not stay for Christmas, despite all the Gallaghers' urging.

'I've written to my Da, told him we'll go back there for the holiday,' Dai said. 'And Biddy's on pins in case Ma Kettle turns Ellen off. . . . Best get back.'

So just over a week after Biddy had left the shop to go to Grimsby, the two of them walked back into it again.

Ma Kettle was behind the counter and to Biddy's

pleasure, greeted her like an old friend and demanded to be introduced to the young feller she'd heard so much about.

'So you're gerrin' wed, eh?' Ma Kettle said, nodding wisely. 'That's a good girl you got yourself, young man. You tek care of our Biddy or you'll 'ave the Kettles to deal with.'

'And . . . and how's Ellen going on?' Biddy asked rather nervously, but she need not have worried.

Ma Kettle beamed. 'She's a good girl,' she said in a surprised but self-congratulatory tone. 'Eh, the lad's a bright 'un – puts me in mind o' Kenny when my lad were small. An' you teached that Ellen to boil a good, flavoursome batch o' toffee, I'll say that for the pair o' ye . . . and them fancy fudges, wi' nuts an' cherries in, they're goin' down well wi' Christmas comin' on. Oh ah, we shan't let young Ellen an' Bobby leave in an 'urry.'

'And how does she cope in the shop?' Biddy asked. 'Because she was in a very posh department store before Bobby was born.'

'She's a natural wi' our customers, young an' old, an' the little lad's a joy to the kids an' the grans,' Ma Kettle said simply. 'What's more, Kenny's right taken wi' the pair of 'em. Never did like 'elpin' in the shop, our Kenny, but I've noticed 'e don't mind doin' a turn be'ind the counter when young Ellen's 'ere. Course, I'm real sorry you've gorra leave, chuck,' she added hastily. 'But we'll manage.'

Ellen didn't have much chance of a private conversation, but she and Biddy exchanged a few words when Biddy nipped into the boiling kitchen for a minute, to find her friend, swathed in one of the huge white aprons, beating vanilla fudge.

'It's prime 'ere, Biddy, I'm ever so 'appy. Ma Kettle's ever so nice to Bobby an' that Kenny – I wish you'd brung 'im round to the flat years ago, our Biddy, 'stead of tellin' me about 'im all wrong. 'E's quite nice lookin' when you get to know 'im.'

'You're two very nice people, you and Kenny, and I hope everything goes on well for all of you,' Biddy said sincerely. 'Ma Kettle's not a bad old thing, you just have to know how to handle her – and it seems to me you're doing pretty well.'

Ellen dimpled at her. She was clean as a new pin, her hair was its old bouncy self and she was neatly clad in a grey cotton dress under the toffee-smeared apron. 'You aren't doin' too bad yourself! I like that Dai.'

'You don't know him! Did you see him just now, as I slipped through from the shop?'

'Aye. An' I listened at the door. He's right for you, Bid, I wish you every 'appiness. After all what you've done for me an' Bobby, you deserve it.'

'Yes, Dai is . . . is special. We're going away now to spend a few days with his people on Anglesey, but I'll be in touch when we get back.'

'Have a good time; they'll love you, never fear,' Ellen said generously. 'I'll explain to Kenny.'

'Kenny's grown up; he likes me, but that's all,' Biddy said serenely. 'Goodbye for now, dear Ellen. Give Bobby a hug for me when he wakes.'

The train was too slow at first and Biddy fidgeted and bit her nails in an agony of mixed boredom and apprehension. Then it seemed they were nearly there and the train seemed suddenly much too fast.

'It's all right, they'll love you,' Dai kept assuring her, but Biddy wasn't so sure.

'Why should they? They don't even know me, and anyway, your Da was cross with you when you last met,' Biddy said uneasily. 'They'll probably think I've caught you, that I'm just after a husband.'

He grinned at her, then leaned across and nuzzled the side of her face. 'Silly Biddy! Besides, you are just after a husband, be honest. Any man would do so long as he kept you out of Ma Kettle's ' itchen.'

Biddy shook her head at him. 'Don't try and make me laugh, I'm too scared to laugh. Oh, oh, we've arrived! I wish I'd never come!'

'Arrived? We've miles to go yet. Come on, collect your traps and we'll get down and find ourselves a taxi.'

Biddy had stared in the train, but now, in the taxi, she got as close to Dai as she could and clutched his hand with feverish fingers. It was all so chilly and grey, so totally unpeopled! She was used to city streets, crowded housing, and people everywhere, this austere island with its grey stone cottages and slate-roofed houses frightened her.

'Are we nearly there?' she kept asking in a very small whisper. 'Is it far?'

They arrived. Down the hill they went and there was the sea on their right, a cold December sea but still more familiar to Biddy, reared by the Mersey, than was the gentle rolling Welsh countryside. The taxi was old and slow; it chugged over the grey stone bridge and Dai pointed out the foaming waterfall dashing down to the sea. They passed the beach, pale in the wintry twilight, and then turned left, away from the sea, the cottages and the pub, crowding close to the harbour, and began to climb a long hill.

'It's that house, the one with the ship's lantern outside the door,' Dai said. Biddy could tell from his tone that he was half-scared now, half so homesick for this place that even the memory of the quarrel between his father and himself could not make him hold back any longer. 'Put us down here . . . but don't go,' he told the taxi driver, 'we may need you presently to take us on.'

It was the first time he had acknowledged that he

might still have to back down, leave Moelfre and go to Sîan and her husband Gareth in the next village.

When it stopped they climbed a little stiffly out of the taxi and walked up the garden path. Dai waited in the porch a moment, then knocked on the door. There was a light in the room, softly burning, and someone came slowly across to the door and opened it.

A very young woman stood there, fair hair tied back from a pink-and-white country face, eyes fixed on them.

'Dai!' And then a gabble of Welsh which Biddy did not understand. It sounded threatening, but was probably nothing of the sort really, Biddy realised. Then the girl was ushering them in, calling something . . . and a man came in from the back, a large brown towel in his hand, his face still streaked with water. He must have been washing himself when they knocked, Biddy realised.

'Dai! Oh, Dai bach!'

The man was very like his son, so Biddy guessed that it was Davy and there seemed to be no ill-feeling here. The two embraced, then Dai turned and took her hand, pulling her forward.

'There's sorry I am to be so rude to you, cariad. Biddy, this is my Da, Davy Evans. And this is . . . is Menna, who is his wife now.'

'Aye married several months since,' Davy said. 'Wanted you to come to the wedding, we did. I wrote – did you not receive it, mun?'

'Not until long after the date – at sea we was, Da. But I'm here now.' Dai glanced across at Menna. 'Menna, Da, this is Bridget O'Shaughnessy; she and I . . .'

'Nice to meet you, Miss O'Shaughnessy,' Davy Evans said, giving Biddy a smile and offering a hand. Biddy shook his hand and smiled at Menna, then Davy turned back to his son. 'Dai, I wanted to see you at my wedding, but there was more beside. Menna's in the family way, truth to tell, and we was wantin' you home because Menna's Da isn't so well, see? A stroke he have had, very poorly he's been. So Mrs Owens wants us to take over the pub . . . only we could do no such thing whilst I had no one to take over here.'

'Take over?' Dai sounded dazed. 'What are you trying to say, Da?'

'If you'll come home, mun, an' take over here, look after the cows and sheep, go fishing, same's you used, then Menna and me can go back and run the pub in Amlwch. Good money there is in a pub, and easier, when a man's getting on in years, to stand behind a bar and smile and be mine host, rather than sweat in a boat and see to the sheep an' cows.'

'We'll have to think about it, Da,' Dai said. He sounded offhand, as though the thought of such a rural way of life was more amusing than practical. 'We're getting married, Biddy and me. We've not thought of coming back here, only to say hello to everyone, so you could meet Biddy and she could meet you.'

'It's a good old place,' Davy said. He smiled at Biddy and she saw he had a tooth missing in front which gave him a piratical air. 'Like living here you would, cariad . . . and fresh air and good food for the kiddies, when they come along. A good life and your man beside you, not off on a coaster eleven months out of the twelve.'

'I'm trawling now, Dad . . . distant water,' Dai said. 'I don't know, we'll have to talk it over, eh, Biddy? But we've not eaten since noon; do I go down to the Crown, book a room?'

'No indeed,' Menna said. She looked uncertainly from father to son. 'Spare rooms we do have, and a stew on the stove which can stretch like a piece of rubber for us all. I'll just peel a potato or two . . . a cup of tea, Biddy, while you wait for the meal?'

Biddy smiled at the other girl.

'I'll come and make it with you,' she volunteered. 'It'll give the men a chance to talk.'

Later, when they had eaten, Dai put his arm round Biddy and took her walking in the wintry night. There was no snow here – it rarely snowed on the island, Dai told her – but the stars overhead twinkled frostily and the wind off the sea lifted the hair from Biddy's head and tossed it behind her like blown spume.

'A quiet, rural life it is out here, Biddy, and I'm not so sure you'd take to it,' Dai shouted against the wind as they fought their way to the clifftop. 'There's folk in the village and sheep and cows in plenty – rabbits, too, and birds – but it's not what you're used to at all. If you'd rather, I can keep on with the trawling, or I can join another coaster . . . I don't want to make you unhappy.'

Biddy thought. She thought of the dreadful danger which he went into, jauntily, every time the *Bess* sailed. Could she stand it? The constant fear, the knowledge of his danger, the fact that a quarter of all those who sail the sea in search of the fish die of drowning? But he loved the excitement, the danger even, and the beauty of Arctic waters, she knew that.

If she asked him to do so he would join a coaster, which was far less dangerous, and she would see him between voyages. But his heart wasn't in a dirty little vessel nosing along inshore waters, he would lose all his pride in himself, all his gaiety and courage.

And what of me? she thought next. Biddy O'Shaughnessy, who has lived in the great city of Liverpool all her life and who loves it, understands it? What would I do out here, with the sea and the birds and cows which scare me and sheep about which I know nothing? There are people, but they speak a language I don't understand and live lives which are strange to me. Could I bear it?

But she knew she could, because she would have Dai beside her. He would go out in his fishing boat and she would worry, but he knew the waters, understood his small craft; she could come to terms with a worry like that. And he would be happy in a way she had probably never yet seen him, because he would be his own master in his own place, at last.

'Biddy?'

She leaned closer to him, so that she could feel the warmth of his body against her even through her coat. She kissed his chin, which needed a shave, and then her mouth found his lips. For a moment they simply kissed, then she drew back with a little sigh. 'Dai, wherever you are I shall be happiest. You're right that I don't know much and will be a burden to you, but if you please, let's live here, where you were born.'

He gave a shout of triumph and lifted her in his arms, squeezing her until she was breathless. Then he stood her down and took her hand. His delight and relief shone out of him – but he would have given it all up had she wished it, gone uncomplaining back to the trawling, or onto a coastal trader.

'Biddy, I do love you! Come on, let's run down the hill and tell my Da he's on – he and Menna can take over that old pub as soon as they like and we'll move in here. Oh, I've just thought of something!'

'What? Not something bad, I trust?'

'Well, cariad, it depends on your viewpoint. Only one spare bed we do have at Stryd Pen, and that's the big double in the back room. I'm afraid that they'll expect us to share it.'

Biddy squeezed his hand and started to run, tugging him behind her. 'So we'll get us a dear little baby, like

Ellen's Bobby,' she shouted, and the words were torn from her mouth by the wind of their going, but Dai heard every one. 'Come on, I'll race you!'

Hand in hand, they pelted down the hill and disappeared into the tall house in Stryd Pen. And presently the lamp was lit in the big back bedroom, and the soft golden light was like a beacon in the dark, leading weary mariners home.